Dana's Loves
Book One: Lind

By
Dana Samantha Lindsey

I0649337

Copyright

Published by Dana Samantha Lindsey

Published in the United States of America

ISBN (Print Book): 979-8-9996057-1-9

First Edition

For more information, visit:

www.DanaSamanthaLindsey.com[1]

Dedication

To the 6% who escaped the bars love was never meant to have,
the 16% still searching for that escape—
May you find love without limits, life without walls, and dreams
that come true.
And to members of The Las Vegas Bares, circa 2000—
thank you for showing me what it looks like to live openly,
laugh freely, and love without shame.

Author's Bio

I write about love in all its complexity—especially the kind that doesn't follow the rules. The stories are intimate, emotionally honest, and often explore the quiet ache between what we want and what we're allowed to have.
I believe in tenderness, difficult conversations, and the kind of heat that only grows when people dare to be fully seen.
I believe that the truest parts of ourselves show up not in what we say, but in what we choose. That's where these stories live.

This is not a work of fantasy.
It is fiction rooted in truth.
Truth rooted in choice.
And choice rooted in love.

Dana Samantha Lindsey

> *She should have stayed home*
> *I'll eat in the kitchen*
> *Her hand reached back*
> *I could use more soup*
> *What are you wearing*
> *Or maybe I was just being a man*

> *That's not part of the plan*
> *An invitation into her space*
> *I need to go to the bathroom*
> *Bare skin against bare skin*
> *Let her enjoy*
> *God, she tasted good*
> *I flicked. I stroked. I circled*
> *I pressed it between her legs*
> *That wasn't funny*

> *Shots of penis-cillin*
> *Fair's fair*
> *Yellow pajama bottoms*
> *Breakfast was ready*
> *This little ole button*
> *That smile*
> *Waited for her to decide*

She was in control now
And I couldn't resist
The way she melted
But I wasn't done
Oh God, Lind
We both froze

I do this for her
Yeah, that sealed it
I was missing her already

A job, not a passion
Lind's first day
You're a pretty good teacher
Cackling geese
Hazelnut. Vanilla. Hope

Cliché romance is the point
"Fine" isn't good enough
Casual sex once in a while
I went with a friend

What's the right question
You could let me do it

So, Sam is a woman
Where would I fit... if I let myself
This puzzle that is Lind
You mean, like... open

Honesty—real, uncomfortable honesty
Black-coffee-only cult
Breakfast king & Puzzle master

Pizza, beer, and latte of love
Records, rebounds, and red flags
Are you asking about my appliances
I like your personality
That wasn't so hard, was it

Ready for this hike
Yeah. He's definitely a man
Still being careful. Fine. Frustrating man

You were taking too long
This man is going to drive me crazy
Dana's not going to let me do slowly anymore
You're just scared of a little complexity
Like you even know what subtle means
Dinner at my place. You in
I'm fine, Dr. Lind
That's what you said yesterday

No, you're not fine

I come bearing sustenance for thy lady
I'll eat in the kitchen

None of my fantasies
What are you wearing

He's naked
Does this man know my fantasies
Was he waiting for me
First stroke of his tongue
And then I came... hard
I wanted to feel him

No one had ever done this for me
Penis-cillian
The morning after

Let's make breakfast
So, you're playing it cool now
What am I working with here
Maybe he did make a mean breakfast
Yes, that one

Still wanting, huh

Did I want him to
One orgasm wasn't enough
His hunger matching my own
This wasn't just sex
His touch was deliberate
Fire and electricity racing through me

It wasn't just practical—it was tender
I don't want you to leave
What is this man doing to me

You're really going to leave me
See you Friday

It's just Lind
First-night sleepover test
What's on your mind
Vasectomy? Wait, what
You mean STIs

Dana, you're still overthinking
I don't know what I'm doing

I'm trusting you
Zombie apocalypse
Normal? With you? Not a chance
Damn. I knew I should have brought my pack

Earth to Dana
Something you want to share, Dana
Oh, come on, Dana. I'm not blind

Demisexual
Survive is a strong word

Morning, sunshine
Brenda, don't start
You miss me already

It's only been a couple of hours
Pretty damned fast for slow
Maybe we could go someday

Wherever we decide there is
Every time with this man
Not my fault you're distracting
Now you owe me the details

What's that supposed to mean
God, I love this man
Lind... it's beautiful
Every moment, every thought

For as long as you let me
Those would look great on you
Then let's make it happen

My weekend with Sam is coming
He wasn't leaving her
What's really bothering you
Then let's plan something

You did good, woman
Guess we'll experience it together
A moment later, Lind stepped out
But this? This is ours
I have plans
Hungry? Starving

Just thinking about next weekend
He knew what weighed on her
Lind's warmth surrounded her
Glad you approve
Goodnight Lind
About you going away

You're spoiling me
She allowed herself to hope
Fridays, Saturdays and, Sundays
They should have stayed home
Though they never let go
Have you ever had a threesome
This has been the best night
That's the music festival

Ready for some wine and countryside
Sam would've loved this place
The purple Buddha out front
Are we ready for bed
Shower? Together? Absolutely
You just like taking care of me

One step at a time
There's nothing to measure
And suddenly she needed more
Not how I remember it
I'll miss you this weekend
Hey, where's Lind
Then she could breathe again

Want to grab brunch
You could use a mimosa
Just got home. I'll call you soon

He was trying. She knew that
Dana's Reflection

I'm driving this year
You're in cabin 6
The second I walk in here
Now get naked so we can get going
I'm very bendy, you know
This place is magic, isn't it
She means a lot to you

This time is for us
I keep coming back here with you
Always prepared
This was Sam's time
Consider this your preview
Look, it was almost gone

Karen! Steve!
This is the life
Fundamentally different
Dana's Worldview
Sam's Worldview
Lind's Realization
I'm just now really getting it
There you are
Would Dana ever fit here
Three naked bodies

You're a good man

But this? This is special
Sure you don't want anything
Let Me Take Care Of You
Even after all this time
Shower first, then food
Heading back later today

Pretending it's a normal Monday
You're not going to give her up
I'm not ready for that

Stop it! That's Ridiculous
No one does this kind of thing
I cannot say no to this man
More and more like beer time
Yes, she matters—but so do you
For all my doubts
Goodnight, beautiful

She didn't rush
She wanted the control

Mornings like this, I could do forever
I like seeing you like this

Playful glances
You're shameless
Just Lind being Lind
But she was here, with him

What am I doing wrong
I was right back where I started

Spending the whole weekend together
She wanted this. Wanted him

This is what I'll remember
Promise me you will
I'm just enjoying this

Oh, God, Lind
Who was this woman tonight
It was perfect
Mesmerized by her every movement
Goodnight, Lind. I love you

If you don't put some clothes on
It was certainly a night to remember
You know I love you, right
Picking up Sam after work
She wouldn't cry now

Something's wrong with Dana
I really had high hopes for you two
I'm a woman. I know things
They simply existed in the moment

Well, his other girlfriend
You two haven't met, have you
I love them both

But calm wasn't peace
Stop it. Just stop
She's not the problem
Hey, I'm back home

We need to talk
Subtle nods
I'm going to tell him
Am I really doing this
It's done
She's gone

It's about Dana and Lind

The Farmhouse
Dana – age 80 – family matriarch

Book 2: Zach

Part 1

24 Hours With Dana

The first twenty-four hours with Dana were magical—
  the kind of time you don't plan but end up remembering forever.
  It started something great between us.
  Then grew into the kind of love I didn't think I would find again.
  Until I lost her.

Chapter 1

She should have stayed home

Dana moved like she was wading through water—slow, heavy.

She squinted at the planogram, rubbing her forehead, her breath uneven. Her nose was red, her skin pale, her usual sharpness dulled by whatever had its grip on her.

It was Monday morning—she should have stayed home.

I caught her coughing into her elbow, the sound dry and rough, before she straightened and tried to act normal.

But she wasn't fooling anyone.

By mid-morning, Georgette sent her home.

Dana didn't argue. She clocked out, shoulders slumping, and walked out into the cold.

I watched her leave. I felt powerless.

Checking In

We've worked together for a while now. We'd made plans for Saturday, but she canceled—said she wasn't feeling well.

And today... watching her leave—I couldn't get her out of my mind.

When work finally wrapped up, I texted her.

How are you feeling?

She answered quickly.

Lying down, bundled up. Fever and chills. Can't breathe through my nose.

A few seconds later, another message.

Took some meds. Gonna try to get some sleep. Good night.

I stared at the screen for a minute, picturing her wrapped up in a blanket, stubborn as ever, trying to power through it on her own.

I want to help. I just hope she lets me.

Not COVID

Next morning, she called in sick.

I texted her again at 10:30 a.m.

But no reply. Not until after noon.

Dana: *Not COVID, but a bad upper respiratory infection. Urgent care gave me antibiotics, decongestant, told me to rest.*

Rest.

I knew Dana. Rest wasn't something she did well. She lived alone. A two-story condo. Getting up and down those stairs while sick wouldn't be easy.

Me: *Let me know if you need anything.*

Dana: *Thanks, I will.*

I doubted she would.

I hesitated, then asked if she had enough food to last a few days.

Dana: *Yeah. But I don't feel like cooking. Or moving. Or doing anything, really.*

That stuck with me.

I offered to bring her something, asked what comfort food she wanted.

She thanked me again but said she'd be fine.

I ignored that.

Me: *How about chicken noodle soup? Classic, easy, and literally the only food you need when you're sick.*

She replied with three emojis: *shiver, sick and snowflake*

I stared at them for a bit. Was she laughing? Shivering? Sarcastic? What the hell was she trying to say?

Didn't matter. I already had a plan.

***

The rest of the day, I couldn't stop thinking about her. By the time I punched out at 2:30, I'd made a decision. A risky one.

Just showing up at her door felt like a bit of a gamble. Would she think I was overstepping? Would she let me in?

I had no idea.

But I couldn't stand the thought of her alone, sick, exhausted.

So, here I am, at her door.

I knocked once and waited, nervous. Nothing. Then I knocked again, hoping.

Shuffling sounds came from inside. A pause. Then the click of the lock before the door creaked open a bit.

Dana stood there, blinking up at me.

She wore pajamas, her hair was tangled, her lips chapped, her expression caught somewhere between surprise and suspicion.

I held up the deli bag, with soup and a small sandwich, in one hand, my backpack half hidden behind me in the other.

"Hi," she croaked, voice hoarse, her breath shallow.

"Hi," I echoed. "I come bearing sustenance for thy lady."

That earned me *a look*.

The kind that said, *What do you think you're up to?*

She hesitated, an arm crossing over her chest like she was suddenly self-conscious.

Then, finally, she sighed and stepped aside.

"Come in."

I'll eat in the kitchen

I set the soup and sandwich down on the counter and glanced at her. "I can heat up some of this and bring it up to you."

"No." She said, shaking her head. "I'll eat in the kitchen."

She pulled a throw blanket off the couch, wrapped it around herself, and sat at the table.

I pulled the soup out of the bag and suddenly realized I didn't know where anything was in her place. With soup in hand I looked at her, she pointed toward a cupboard. I found the bowls. I glanced at the drawers before looking back at her, she pointed again. I found the silverware.

Did she want the sandwich now?

No, maybe later.

So half the soup and sandwich went in the fridge. The other half in the microwave.

I set a bowl in front of her and took the seat across from her with some of my own.

She looked miserable. Hair a mess. Red nose.

I caught her eye and asked, "Is it OK that I'm here?"

She lifted her spoon, blinking at me over it.

"Yeah," a tired smile played on her lips. "But only because you brought me soup."

"Oh? That's the way to your heart?" I asked, watching her across the table.

She gave a faint laugh. "One of them."

I smiled. "Really?"

She paused, tilted her head slightly, looking at me. She almost smiled.

With the exception of the occasional scrape of spoon against ceramic, we finished eating in easy silence.

After a while, she sat back with a sigh. "Thanks for this."

"You're welcome."

You know, to tuck you in

She had finished most of her soup and it looked like she was done.

I stood, picking up both bowls before she could argue.

"Leave them," she murmured, voice soft. "I'll get to them later."

I ignored her and rinsed them anyway. When I turned back, she looked ready for bed again.

"Could I take you upstairs?" I said, keeping my tone light. "You know... to tuck you in."

A smile tugged at my lips, waiting for her reaction.

Dana gave me that familiar, suspicious grin—the one that said she wasn't sure whether to take me seriously. Her narrowed eyes flicked over me, assessing, weighing.

For a second, I thought she'd brush me off.

But then, she stood, tossed the blanket back onto the couch, and turned toward the stairs.

"Come on," she said.

Smiling, I followed.

I paused, letting her decide

Dana climbed into bed, burrowing into the blankets. Even through the layers, I could see the fine tremor of her shivers.

I took off my shoes and stretched out beside her—on top of the covers, leaving a respectable distance. She turned onto her side, her back to me, like she was bracing against the chill.

Carefully, I moved closer, draping my arm lightly over her. A test, an offering.

She stiffened. I paused, letting her decide. After a bit she exhaled, her muscles loosening, and then she eased back into me.

I let out a slow breath, pressing my face into the back of her head, inhaling the familiar scent of her hair.

She didn't say anything, but the way she pressed against me, and let me hold her, felt like quiet trust.

***

An hour passed. Maybe more.

I was warm, and comfortable—except for one problem.

My left arm was completely numb. Pinned beneath me, it was tingling, and useless. I shifted slightly, trying not to disturb her too much.

"Do you need anything?" I whispered.

She murmured something, I wasn't sure, maybe...

"Water?" I asked.

A slow nod. "Yeah, water."

"Okay. Be right back."

I eased off the bed and headed downstairs, grabbing two bottles from the fridge—one for her, one for me. The cool air felt good on my skin, a relief after lying still for so long.

When I returned, she was exactly where I'd left her, cocooned in the blankets. As I stepped around to her side of the bed, she sat up slightly, reaching for the water. She took it from me, the plastic crinkling as she drank—slow, careful sips—before setting it on the nightstand.

She looked a little better now. A little less pale.

Back on my side of the bed, I set the water down, after taking a few sips myself.

Smiling as I thought, *my side*.

Funny how easily I could fit into this space.

"I'm gonna use your bathroom real quick," I said, keeping it casual as I headed toward the door.

The truth was, I wanted to splash some water on my face and stretch out my arm, now that the tingling stopped.

Her hand reached back

When I returned, Dana was still laying on her side, the blankets tucked snugly around her.

I hesitated at the edge of the bed.

Should I lie back on top of them or take the next step—under them, closer to her?

Taking a chance, I took off my socks, removed my belt, and emptied my pockets onto the nightstand. Then, I slipped under the blankets, easing up behind her, so I wouldn't jostle her.

I draped my arm over her waist. My hand resting on the bed.

Her arms were crossed over her chest. Was she shielding herself? Just trying to stay warm? Or maybe it was something else—an unconscious attempt to comfort herself.

I wasn't sure, maybe she wasn't either.

But her shivering had mostly stopped, she looked almost content beneath the layers.

I stayed still, waiting, watching, to see what she would do—go back to sleep, talk to me, look back...

Then, a small movement.

Her hand reached back, just barely touching my leg before retreating. A hesitation. A question.

A few seconds passed. Then, without a word, she shifted, pressing tight against me again, closing the space completely.

I could feel the soft rise and fall of her breath beneath my arm.

I could use more soup

Hours later, when I thought back on it, I realized that first touch wasn't what I thought it was.

She hadn't reached back to check if I was still there, or to see if I'd slipped under the covers instead of staying on top.

It wasn't even a silent thank you for being there with her.

No, I think she reached back to confirm I still had my clothes on.

Looking back on it now, the thought of it makes me smile.

But what really stayed with me was the way she slid back against me. That small move gave me confidence—not just in my plan, but in the possibilities.

Sometime in the early evening, drifting in and out of sleep, with the steady rhythm of our breathing filling the quiet between us, we slipped into small, easy conversation. Nothing heavy—just the kind of quiet talk that didn't require effort. Dana told me some more bits and pieces about her life, funny little quirks about her family that made me smile. I shared a little more about myself, too.

Then she shifted slightly and murmured, "I could use more soup."

I grinned against her shoulder. "Is that a very polite way of telling me to go get it."

Dana huffed a quiet laugh. "If I had the energy, I'd say it less politely."

I chuckled, shaking my head. "No, you wouldn't." I touched her hair as I asked, "do you want the sandwich or part of it?"

"Yeah, I think I could eat a little of it," she said quietly.

I stretched, got up, and headed downstairs. I reheated the rest of the soup, grabbed some crackers, and cut the sandwich into quarters, bringing it all back up. Most of it was for her, but I kept a small bowl and a quarter of the sandwich for myself.

When I returned, she was sitting up, propped against the headboard with pillows stacked behind her. I handed her the soup, placing the quartered sandwich, wrapped in a paper towel, on her nightstand.

I sat on the edge of the bed, facing her as we ate.

I tried to keep my eyes on her face. I really did. But the way her pajama top clung to her chest made it very hard to concentrate. She caught me looking once or twice but just smiled and kept eating.

Her hair was still a mess, her cheeks flushed, and yet, she looked incredible.

When we finished, I took the dishes downstairs, rinsing them off. As I grabbed my backpack, I heard the toilet flush upstairs.

By the time I made it back up, Dana had already climbed back into bed, the blankets tucked up under her chin, her eyes fluttering closed.

I set my backpack down just inside the bedroom doorway before lifting the covers a little and spooning in behind her.

For a minute, I just watched her. The quiet rise and fall of her breath. The faint smile on her lips. A matching one spread across mine.

She looked content. With me. With the food. With all of it.

I laid back down, draping an arm over her again. She let out a barely audible sigh.

Her hand reached back, settling lightly on my thigh, her thumb tracing over my pant leg every so often.

It felt good. It felt like... *acceptance*.

***

A couple of hours passed in warm, quiet comfort.

The bed had turned into a little furnace, the blankets trapping the shared heat we'd generated.

Dana shifted slightly, adjusting the covers around her. "I want to shower in a little while," she murmured, voice soft, like she was thinking aloud.

Then she pulled the blankets up to her chin. "But I think I'll sleep a bit more first."

I ran my hand lightly over her arm. "I'm going to the bathroom. I'll be right back." She made a faint noise of acknowledgment, already half-asleep again.

I grabbed my pajama bottoms and T-shirt from my backpack and took them into the bathroom with me. Stripping down, I splashed cold water over my face, neck, and a few other sweaty parts, letting the coolness refresh me before pulling on the pajamas.

Catching my reflection in the mirror, I studied myself for a moment—messy hair, tired eyes, but the smile was still there.

What are you wearing

Back in the bedroom, I slipped under the covers again, spooned in behind her.

She shifted closer almost instantly, her body fitting back against mine like it had been waiting for me.

This time, her hand reached back almost immediately, fingertips brushing lightly against my leg, her fingers doing a double take at the different texture.

"What are you wearing?" she asked softly.

I broke away just enough to prop myself up on one elbow. "Pajama bottoms," I said. "It was getting hot under the covers."

Her lips curved into a small smile, her eyes catching just enough of the fading light to sparkle. "You came prepared," she murmured. "How'd you know I'd let you stay?"

"I didn't," I admitted, grinning. "I thought, you know, just in case."

Her laugh was soft but genuine, the kind of sound that stuck with you. She crossed her arms over her chest, tucking her hands under her chin, then melted into me again—pressing closer, tighter than before.

Bare skin. The heat of her body—separated from mine by only the thinnest layers of fabric now.

The way she pressed against me, the way the fabric barely muted the sensation.

I felt it as she shifted slightly, adjusting herself against me.

A quiet hum escaped her lips... as if she felt it too.

I laid back down, wrapping one arm around her, positioning the other under her head. The room grew quiet except for the steady rhythm of our breathing.

By then, the sun was dipping below the horizon, and the world outside was fading into darkness.

Or maybe I was just being a man

We dozed off now and then, our bodies tangled in the warmth of the bed.

At some point, her fingers began tracing along my left arm—soft, deliberate touches. Then she reached for my right hand, holding it in hers for a while before shifting her touch lower, fingertips gliding lightly up and down my hip and thigh.

The slow, intentional movements sent a hum of awareness through me.

Was it an invitation? A thank you? Just an unconscious habit? Maybe all three.

Or maybe I was just being a man, overthinking something that didn't need to be complicated.

She wasn't in any condition for more than this—not right now. And I wasn't going to push for something she wasn't ready to give.

In the dark, we spoke occasionally, little fragments of conversation breaking the silence. Nothing deep, just easy, sleepy words that filled the space.

During one of those quiet moments, she took my right hand again—this time tucking it up close across her chest, just below her chin. She curled her fingers over mine, her breath slow and even.

She was so at ease in that moment.

And so was I.

Just the two of us, lying together, while the rest of the world faded away.

Chapter 2

That's not part of the plan

The soft amber glow from the nightlight stretched across the room, casting gentle shadows along the walls. It wasn't much—just enough to navigate without tripping over anything or waking her.

I slipped out of bed quietly. The warmth of her body still clung to my skin as I made my way into the bathroom.

In the mirror, I caught my reflection—face relaxed, eyes softer than I was used to seeing. I barely recognized myself.

I grabbed a washcloth from the neatly arranged shelves, ran it under cool water, and wiped myself down. The sensation was refreshing against my warm skin.

Dana ran warm—hot, even. For someone so slender, she radiated an impressive amount of heat, leaving me sticky in the best way.

When I finished, I reached for my pajama bottoms—but hesitated.

What am I doing? That's not part of the plan.

I exhaled, my heart beating a little faster. Then folded the pajamas and T-shirt neatly, placing them on top of my backpack.

And I slipped back into bed with her.

An invitation into her space

I moved carefully, not to disturb her. But the moment my body fit against hers, I felt it.

The difference.

The shift from simple comfort to something charged, something intimate.

The heat. The awareness. The unmistakable press of her warmth against me.

Dana stirred, just slightly, her body shifting—then pressing back.

This was intentional, an unspoken need or want, an invitation into her space.

I need to go to the bathroom

The quiet filled the room, except for the soft rasp of Dana's breathing, the occasional sound of her stuffy nose breaking the silence. I focused on the slow rise and fall of her shoulders, the way she fit so effortlessly against me.

Then, her hand moved.

Fingers, warm and light against my leg—bare skin against bare skin.

A small touch, soft and fleeting but it sent a sharp thrill through me.

But just as quickly as it happened, she pulled her hand back, tucking it under her chin, curling inward away from me just slightly.

I stayed still, my pulse thudding a little harder.

Before I could decide whether to say something, she stirred again, voice soft.

"I need to go to the bathroom."

She sat up, slipping out of bed, her silhouette a quiet shadow in the dim light as she moved across the room.

I watched her disappear into the bathroom, uncertainty twisting inside me—

Oh shit, had I crossed a line—or was I just standing on it?

Was she second guessing?

I stayed where I was, hoping I hadn't just screwed this up.

***

She was in the bathroom longer this time—or at least, it felt that way.

Then again, she probably thought the same about my earlier trip.

When the door finally opened, the light flicked off, leaving only the soft glow of the nightlight.

She moved to her side of the bed, but didn't climb in right away.

She paused, watching me—head tilted slightly, like she was considering something.

Then, without a word, her hands went for her pajama top.

She pulled it off, in one smooth motion, and let it fall to the floor.

Her bottoms followed as she pushed them down, pooling at her feet.

She stepped out of them and climbed back into bed, pressing her back against me.

The warmth of her bare skin against my chest sent a slow, deep shiver through me.

I exhaled, letting my palm drift over the curve of her hip as my right arm slipped around her waist.

The growing evidence of my excitement pressed gently against her.

She wasn't pulling away.

Bare skin against bare skin

The back of her head rested against my chin, her soft hair. tickling against my lips.

Every inch of her was pressed into every inch of me like we were melting into one.

Then, she moved.

A slow, unmistakable shift—her hips rocking, just slightly. Then again.

Bare skin against bare skin. A quiet exhale slipped from my lips.

I bent my left arm up—the one under her neck—and reached over her body, my fingers playing against the smoothness of her breast.

Her skin was warm, her nipple hard beneath my palm.

She reached for my right hand, guided it to her other breast, and held it there.

I kissed her shoulder softly, then let my lips trail along her neck unhurried, my breath tickling her hair.

She arched into me—Inviting.

Letting go of her breast, I traced my hand down the length of her body, around her waist to the dip of her stomach, the gentle slope that led between her legs.

Her skin was warm beneath my fingertips, the heat of her body pulling me in, as my fingers found her lips, she responded instantly—lifting her right leg and hooking it over mine in an unmistakable invitation.

No hesitation. No second-guessing. Just *yes*.

My fingers played in her wetness, careful strokes, savoring the way she reacted—how her breath caught, how her hips arched, how her slick heat reacted to my touch.

Then, she reached down, her hand covering mine. But she didn't guide me.

She simply held her hand on mine, as if she wanted to share in the connection, to feel every movement as deeply as I did.

That small gesture struck me as deeply as the intimacy itself.

Let her enjoy

Then, she let go of my hand and reached back, finding me in the dark.

At first, her fingertips explored me with slow, curious movements—tracing, mapping the shape of me, sending sharp pulses of need through me. The soft graze of her fingers along my length made me ache with anticipation.

Then, she held me a little tighter...

Guiding. Positioning.

She shifted again, pressing back into me, aligning our bodies in a way that left no room for doubt.

She was deliberate. Intentional. When she let go, I knew exactly what she wanted.

And God, I wanted it too.

I pressed forward, slowly, feeling her envelop me, wanting me, coaxing me, inch by inch.

Her breath hitched, her hips tilted, her body tightening around me sending pure pleasure rolling through me.

The way she took me in—held me inside her—made me ache for her.

Our rhythm started slow but gained momentum quickly, chasing the sensations we both wanted, that we both needed.

But then, I noticed it. Her breathing.

Even at this point, I could hear it—short, uneven exhales, each one requiring more effort.

We had barely started to move, and already, she was straining.

The sound pulled me out of the moment. I couldn't push her—not like this.

I wouldn't.

I slowed down, shifting my focus.

My fingers back between her legs—slow, deliberate strokes, a steady rhythm—up and down, back and forth, circling lightly.

She responded instantly. A tremor rolled through her body. Her legs tighten around me.

A soft whimper escaping her.

I kept my movements slow, unhurried, letting her feel everything without strain.

Kissing her shoulder, I traced my lips along to her neck—tasting the warmth of her skin, feeling her arch into me, pressing into every part of me.

I wanted to simply let her feel. Let her enjoy.

Still, her breathing grew more strained.

So, I shifted again.

As I pulled out of her, she made a sound—half protest, half plea—a quiet, aching noise like she was losing something she desperately wanted.

I didn't want to disappoint her—I wasn't going to.

I gently rolled her onto her back, positioning my knees on either side of her hips, her legs wrapped around me instantly, her ankles crossing at my lower back, pulling me in close, as if she were afraid to let me go.

Even in the dim light, I could see the way her eyes locked onto mine, the anticipation. A silent question. A plea.

I hesitated.

Her brow furrowed slightly, confusion flickering in her eyes as she realized I wasn't moving to enter her again.

Her eyes were questioning me.

So I answered her. I leaned down, my lips starting at her collarbone, trailing lower—lightly over her breast, tweaking her nipples as I kept inching down the center of her stomach.

Her hands traveled up my back, fingers pressing into my skin, holding me close, reluctant to let go.

I kissed my way lower, my mouth tracing the soft dips of her stomach.

She exhaled slowly.

Realizing where I was headed.

What was coming.

She loosened her legs from around my back but kept them close against my sides.

When I reached her bellybutton, I paused, using my tongue to tickle her.

She giggled, her fingers slipping into my hair, holding me there for a moment.

Then she shifted her hips a little, hands gently pushing my head lower—impatient. I kept going, my mouth gliding lower, my fingers exploring, memorizing the way her body responded.

As my mouth passed over the small patch of hair near my destination, I gave it a playful tug with my lips.

Another soft giggle, then a soft moan.

I smiled against her skin.

God, she tasted good

When my tongue finally found her clit, a shudder rippled through her thighs.

Her fingers tightened against my scalp, her breath catching in her throat.

I started slow, my tongue barely touching her—up and down, back and forth. Until the first real moan spilled from her lips.

Her body tensed beneath me, her head tilting back as pleasure spread through her.

She wanted more.

I wanted more *for* her.

Circling her clit, I took my time—trying slow patterns, learning the exact movements that made her thighs react.

Then I changed the pressure—stroking along the clitoral shaft, flicking lightly back and forth before returning to the tip.

I explored lower, my tongue exploring her entrance, slipping inside just enough to make her reach out and grab a handful of sheets.

God, she tasted good.

And the sounds she made—soft gasps, breathy moans—only made me want to give her more.

I pressed my tongue deeper, moving in slow circles, letting myself get lost in her reactions.

For a moment, I moved lower, ghosting the sensitive skin just beneath, watching the way her hips flexed under me, as if chasing my mouth.

Every touch, every flick of my tongue, every shift of my fingers pulled her deeper into this moment with me.

I stroked her with my tongue and nose, adding my thumb, gently over her clit.

Curious, I let my tongue trail lower still, making a slow pass over her butt, teasing, testing, waiting.

The sound she made—a quiet moan, a breathy exhale, the reaction of her hips—was exactly what I was hoping for.

I moved back up, slowing down.

Savoring every other part of her.

My lips closed around hers, sucking them lightly, one side, then the other. Not rushing, just learning.

The way she twitched—responded to every shift of my mouth made me want to explore every inch of her.

Then, my tongue singled out her inner lips, licking them with slow, lazy flicks, treating them the way I would her nipples—soft, focused, purposeful. Nibbling, pulling, sucking.

Returning to her entrance, my tongue traced the edges before slipping inside. Feeling her body tighten, then release, tightening again. Moving in perfect time with me.

Her moans deepened.

I adjusted my angle, pressing my tongue deeper.

I could feel it—the way her thighs tensed around my shoulders. The way her hands clutched at the sheets.

She was close.

And I wanted to take her there.

I flicked. I stroked. I circled

I worked my way back up to her clit, keeping my rhythm exactly where she needed it—steady, focused, my tongue stroking her with a mix of light flicks and deep, intentional pressure.

I loved this.

Loved the way her body responded—the sharp inhale when I slowed down, the desperate whimper when I didn't give her what she wanted right away.

I flicked. I stroked. I circled.

My thumb slipped inside her, keeping the sensation building.

Building.

Building.

Her breath hitched, the sounds slipping from her lips shifting into something higher, more urgent.

Her body tensed beneath me, thighs trembling, back arching, hips rolling in a slow, helpless rhythm against my mouth.

And then—

She came.

I stayed there, keeping my movements light, controlled.

Letting her ride it out.

Feeling every pulse, every ripple of her release.

The sounds she made—breathless, soft, completely undone—sent a wave of satisfaction through me.

Eventually, the sensitivity became too much.

Her fingers in my hair, gently pushing me away.

I pressed one last kiss against her inner thigh before releasing her.

She rolled onto her left side, exhaling a deep, shuddering breath.

Her body still trembling slightly.

The aftershocks rolling through her.

I stayed close, watching her recover.

Her chest rose and fell in uneven waves, her breathing—ragged and strained.

The look on her face—sated, soft, eyes half-closed, full of quiet satisfaction—

It was everything I wanted to see.

Dana rolled onto her back, her knees bent, legs parted.

Her body open.

Waiting for me.

And God, I wanted her.

But I could hear it—the way her chest rose and fell, too strained.

A couple of soft coughs slipped out.

She was trying to push through it.

But I couldn't ignore it.

Now wasn't the time for more sex.

Now was the time for something else—affection. Support. Winding down.

For her.

I reached out, gently pushing her legs aside, making space as I laid down beside her.

We lay on our backs, shoulders touching, her leg draping over mine. The warmth between us still humming.

Still pulsing. But quieter.

So close, I could hear every strained breath she took, each one a quiet reminder that she's sick.

Without thinking, I placed my hand on her stomach. My fingers caressed her lightly, feeling the faint tremors slowly fading in her muscles. My touch drifted lower, playing through that small patch of hair. Just familiar, affectionate.

She reached down in return, her hand soft, unhurried. Moving across my stomach, along my side. Down to my cock. Not searching for more. Just feeling.

As her breathing steadied, I slipped my arm under her head, coaxing her closer. Guiding her onto my chest. She came easily, her body resting on mine.

The other leg draping over me, her thigh resting against what remained of my erection. Her fingers drifted over my chest. Then higher. Up my neck. To my jaw.

I closed my eyes for a moment, letting her . Letting her take whatever she wanted...

I pressed it between her legs

After lying there for a while, I carefully slipped out from under her and made my way to the bathroom.

Once I relieved myself, I grabbed a washcloth from the shelf, running it under hot water. The warmth felt good.

I pressed the cloth to my skin, wiping my face first, then washing off my cock. I rinsed it out, ran it under the water again, and wringing it out.

When I stepped back into the bedroom, Dana was still lying on her side, exactly as I'd left her—bare, relaxed, utterly at ease.

I gently rolled her onto her back, easing her legs apart just enough to tend to her.

Folding the washcloth, I pressed it between her legs. A faint sound escaped her lips. I ran the warm cloth over her skin, cleaning her with care.

I took my time, mindful of how wet she'd been. The way her body had responded. But maybe it was something more. Or maybe that was just me.

When I was done, I reached for the hand towel, drying her carefully—every touch slow, relaxed.

That wasn't funny

The entire time she watched me, her expression was... unreadable—a mix of curiosity, excitement, and something else.

Wonder, maybe.

That's when it hit me. No one had ever done this for her before.

And that made me wonder...

I was smiling as I leaned back in to kiss her... Then—because I couldn't help myself—I nibbled lightly on her outer lips with my teeth. Grinning when her breath hitched in surprise.

Before she had a chance to react, I let my tongue flick over her clit—just once, quick and sharp. She jumped slightly, squeaking.

"Lind!" she exhaled—half-surprised, half-laughing.

I smirked, tilting my head innocently. "What?"

She swatted at me, a sleepy, amused protest, her hand landing against my shoulder.

"Just when I was beginning to like you," she muttered. The small, reluctant smile—and the look in her eye—told me that she did.

I pressed one last kiss to her inner thigh, then grabbed the washcloth and towel, headed back to the bathroom to rinse them out.

When I returned, the clock on her nightstand read just after 11:00 p.m.

I bent down, retrieving the covers from where we'd kicked them onto the floor, shaking them out before laying them back over her, tucking them gently around her.

She watched me—eyes soft, thoughtful.

Something unspoken in her gaze.

When I climbed into bed beside her, she smiled.

For a while, we lay face to face. The room quiet, except for the slow, even rhythm of our breathing.

We talked—nothing heavy. Just light conversation, the kind of easy back-and-forth that made it feel like we'd been doing this for... well, a long time.

Fingers drifted over arms, shoulders, faces. Casual touches not meant to lead anywhere—just meant to feel.

Between moments of quiet connection, we dozed. Eventually, Dana rolled over, and settled into our now-familiar spooning position.

I wrapped an arm around her, pulling her close, feeling her body fit against mine one more time before sleep took us both.

Chapter 3

Shots of penis-cillin

My alarm went off at 4:35 a.m., dragging both of us from sleep.

I groaned, reaching blindly for my phone on the nightstand, shutting it off before the sound could really wake us up.

Dana barely stirred—just a soft exhale, like she was only half-awake.

Still lying on my side, I sent off a quick text to Georgette, letting her know I wouldn't be coming in.

As I set my phone back down, Dana mumbled, her voice thick with sleep, "Are you going to work? Who are you texting?"

I smiled against the pillow. Still half out of it, but I couldn't resist.

"Texted Georgette," I murmured. "Letting her know I'm not coming in because I'm warm and comfortable in bed with Dana... taking care of her... and giving her shots of penis-cillin now and then."

She whipped around instantly, eyes wide, her expression somewhere between horror and suspicion.

"You did what?"

The look on her face was priceless—like she wasn't entirely sure whether to believe me.

I let the moment hang for just a second... before I grinned—couldn't help it.

"Kidding," I said, putting my hand up in surrender. "Told her I ate something from my fridge that I probably shouldn't have and wasn't feeling great."

Dana's expression shifted from horror/suspicion to mock-annoyance, her hand smacking lightly against my shoulder.

27

"That wasn't funny," she muttered. But the way her mouth twitched, fighting a smile, told me she thought otherwise.

She turned back over, getting comfortable again.

I grinned into my pillow.

I thought it was.

***

The next time we woke up, the room was filled with daylight.

Dana stirred first, slipping out of bed and heading for the bathroom.

Last night, I'd been straining to see her in the faint night light—the look in her eyes, the curves of her body.

Now, with morning light streaming through the window, there was no need to guess.

As she climbed out of bed, my eyes followed her automatically.

Her movements were slow, unhurried, a little groggy.

I only got a side and back view, but... *Oh, God.*

She walked around the bed and out of the bedroom, giving me the perfect opportunity to admire every inch of her backside.

And I did.

Lying there, I already found myself anticipating her return, hoping for an even better view when she came back.

Fair's fair

She reappeared a few minutes later—wrapped in a towel.

Oh, the disappointment.

After everything I'd imagined while waiting, this was not the view I'd been hoping for.

She walked around to her side of the bed, glancing at me.

"I'm hungry," she said. "We should make some breakfast."

Sounded like a solid plan.

As she bent down to pick up her pajamas, I took the opportunity to return the favor.

Sliding out of bed, I walked toward the bathroom—giving her the same back view she'd just given me.

Fair's fair.

I heard her huff a quiet laugh but didn't look back.

Victory.

My grin accompanied me all the way into the bathroom, along with my backpack.

Yellow pajama bottoms

When I stepped out of the bathroom, Dana was already gone.

I set my backpack down where it was and followed the sound of movement downstairs.

I found her in the living room, tidying up, moving with a little more energy than last night. She was starting to look like herself again.

"Want some coffee? Only got instant." she said, glancing up at me.

"Yes, please," I said, watching as she headed into the kitchen.

She filled two mugs with water, and popped them into the microwave.

She was still in her pajamas, her top loose, comfortable, moving with every gesture she made.

When she bent over to pick something up, the fabric fell open, giving me an unobstructed view all the way to her bellybutton.

And then, cruelly, she straightened back up.

Shame.

I could've watched that all day.

The microwave beeped.

Back into the kitchen, she pulled out the two mugs. Set them on the counter next to the jar of instant coffee and added 2 spoonfuls into each.

Dana handed me one, added a little something to hers, then took it to the small table.

I leaned against the counter sipping mine. That's when I caught her glancing at me.

At first, it was just once—a flicker of eye contact, then away.

Then she did it again.

This time, her gaze dipped a bit, then lifted, just long enough for me to register exactly where she was looking.

I glanced down at myself. Yellow pajama bottoms.

Not doing much to cover my varying stages of excitement.

Her eyes flicked back up to meet mine.

The corner of her mouth twitched. A quiet game. A silent tease.

I could feel it simmering between us—her looking, me knowing, the awareness stretching between us like an invisible thread.

I finally broke the moment, taking another sip of coffee.

"What do you have in mind for breakfast?"

The way she looked at me—I swear her eyes said—*You.*

Breakfast was ready

She looked at me with a grin I would come to know well.

Then her shoulders slumped. She sat back in her chair.

With her coffee in hand she started listing off eggs, frozen hash browns, and cheese.

"Perfect," I nodded, not hiding my grin worth a damn. "What about green, red, or yellow peppers? Any onion? Ham? Bacon? Sausage? Toast?"

I'd already spotted the toaster on the counter, my mind running through the possibilities.

"I'm not sure what's in there, been sick, remember?"

I started rummaging through the fridge and came back with a green pepper, some red onion, and part of a small ham steak.

Not much, but I could make it work.

I also found a handful of fresh mushrooms.

I got to work, dicing the vegetables and ham while she watched.

The sound of the knife hitting the cutting board filled the kitchen.

I heated some oil in a pan, tossed in the hash browns, and sprinkled in a little onion and pepper, letting the flavors mix into the potatoes.

The smell of frying vegetables filled the room as I cracked and scrambled a few eggs, mixing in the diced ingredients.

While everything cooked, I glanced over. "Bread?"

She got up and grabbed a loaf from the counter, and I pointed to the toaster.

As she popped in a couple of slices, I hunted down the butter.

I flipped the hash browns, ensuring they were golden and crisp, the way I like them.

The toaster popped up just as I finished cooking, and she buttered the toast while I split the hash browns between our plates.

The eggs followed—perfectly cooked, and flavorful - as usual.

Breakfast was ready.

And it smelled great. Apparently I was hungry too.

We sat down at her small table, plates in front of us, coffee within reach.

The first bite?

Everything was perfect—crispy hash browns, fluffy eggs, great flavor.

We ate, talking a little—nothing serious. Just light conversation between bites, easy and familiar.

Then, she looked up at me, grinning.

"Damn, you really do make a good breakfast."

Yeah. I knew.

This little ole button

A few moments passed in comfortable quiet before I broke it with a casual—

"Dana?"

She glanced over, her expression curious. "Yes?"

"Will you do me a favor?" I asked, pitching my voice a little softer, almost childlike.

Her eyes narrowed instantly, suspicion thick in her tone. "Probably not."

"Please?" I pressed, adding just a hint of pleading.

She crossed her arms, tilting her head slightly. "What is it?"

I pointed to the button on her pajama top—the one right between her breasts.

"Would you unbutton that one more button for me?"

Dana's lips parted slightly before curving into a flirty grin.

"This little ole button right here?" Her fingers toying with it in an exaggerated motion that made my heart kick up a beat.

"Yes, that one." My anticipation was very clear.

She paused, giving me a mock-thoughtful look before shaking her head.

"I don't think so."

Playful words.

But her expression? Smug enough to let me know she was enjoying this game as much as I was.

Then, just to drive the point home, she picked up her plate and jokingly threatened to throw the rest of her eggs at me.

I threw my hands up defensively, grinning crookedly.

She chuckled, shaking her head before turning toward the sink.

I didn't get the half-undressed view I'd been hoping for—but our little exchange wasn't a total loss.

Because now, her nipples were firmly pushing against the soft fabric of her pajama.

Mm hmm...Oh yay.

We moved easily into cleaning up the aftermath of breakfast.

Dana cleared the table, stacking plates and mugs on the counter while I started on the pans.

"I can help with the dishes," she offered, stepping toward the sink.

"Nah." I waved her off. "I've got it. You go upstairs, take your meds, and rest. Maybe jump into that hot shower you've been wanting?"

She hesitated for a second before nodding. "Good idea."

Grabbing her half-full coffee mug, she headed upstairs.

I took my time with the dishes, listening to the faint creaks upstairs.

She'd be a while.

I wasn't in any rush.

Once I finished, I headed upstairs too. The carpet was soft under my feet.

Outside the bathroom door, I paused.

The water was running.

Curiosity got the better of me.

I cracked the door open just enough to peek inside.

Not locked. *God bless her.*

But the sight I'd hoped for wasn't there.

A solid white shower curtain blocked everything.

I sighed.

Cruel.

Closing the door quietly, I made my way to the bed, lying down, staring at the ceiling, imagining what was just out of view.

It was just past 10:00 a.m.

That smile

When Dana emerged from the bathroom, her hair damp, wrapped in fresh pajamas, she looked at me and smiled.

That smile.

A little sweet, a little mischievous, as if she knew exactly what I'd been thinking about while she was gone.

"I'm going to jump in the shower, if that's okay," I said, sitting up.

"You better." Her tone was light, casual.

She crawled back into bed as I grabbed my backpack and headed into the bathroom.

I took a quick shower, the hot water waking me up... in more ways than one. My anticipation may have had something to do with that.

After brushing my teeth and putting on deodorant, I pulled on my pajama bottoms and T-shirt, feeling fresh, feeling good, ready for what was next... hoping.

When I stepped out of the bathroom, she was lying in bed... waiting.

I set my backpack down where it had been.

I laid down beside her, facing her.

Before I could say anything, her hand found my shoulder, fingers soft against my skin, drifting up to my hair, my face.

The simple touch made everything in my body tighten.

In return, I traced my fingers lightly over the fabric of her pajama top, gliding from her shoulder to her hip in a slow motion.

Her skin was warm beneath the fabric.

The way she looked at me? It was impossible not to push the moment further.

I reached under her pajama top, fingertips grazing the smooth skin of her stomach and her waist, then as far around her back as I could reach.

Her breath hitched. Then, she moved.

With a smooth, fluid motion, she rolled on top of me, her thighs straddling my hips, her weight pressing down on me.

Waited for her to decide

Her hands pressed against my chest, holding me down just enough to make me feel pinned, controlled—held exactly where she wanted me.

Her hips rocked slowly, grinding against me—the pressure just right, just enough to make my head spin.

She smiled down at me. Knowing exactly what she was doing.

Then, she leaned in, her lips finding mine—soft at first, before deepening into something more.

The feel of her, the weight of her body against mine—impossible not to get lost in it.

Her fingers moved over my skin, tracing my collarbone, slipping under the neckline of my T-shirt.

She kissed me again, pressing even closer, the heat between us building gradually.

I let my hands drift lower, gripping her hips, guiding her just enough to let her feel what she was doing to me.

She felt my excitement, shifting again, pressing down harder.

I exhaled, my fingers tightening their hold, my body aching to push this further.

But instead, I waited. Waited for her to decide how far we were going this time.

Chapter 4

She was in control now

Dana pulled her pajama top over her head, tossing it aside before leaning back down, her lips warm, eager, kissing me again.

My hands moved on instinct, tracing the soft lines of her waist, her back, her hips, exploring her.

Her breath hitched when I kissed below her ear, slow, deliberate nibbles against her skin before trailing my lips down her neck.

She shifted higher, moving against me, her thighs straddling my hips as I kissed my way lower, her skin soft and warm.

When I reached her chest, I took her nipple between my lips, sucking gently, tracing around it with my tongue.

Her fingers threaded into my hair, holding me there.

Her moans filled the space, each sound pulling me deeper into her.

I shoved my pajama bottoms down and kicked them off.

I reached for hers, slipping inside the waistband, gripping her ass.

I pulled her closer as I slid the fabric down, exposing her.

One hand moved down her thigh, moving between her legs, finding her lips, her clit—wet, wanting.

I explored her slowly, savoring the way her body reacted—the shift of her hips, the way her thighs tensed, the sharp hitch in her breath as my fingers entered her.

Her fingers found me as she reached down between us, wrapping around my cock, stroking... slow... firm.

She was in control now—enjoying the feel of me, the way I wanted her to.

I couldn't tell if she was driving me crazy for her own amusement or simply taking her time, lost in the moment like I was.

Maybe both.

And then—I couldn't take it anymore.

And I couldn't resist

I rolled her onto her back, pulling her pajama bottoms off, and tossing them aside.

She was naked, fully exposed—her body a perfect contrast of softness and strength.

I sat up, straddling her hips, her legs wrapping around me, pulling me closer.

Reaching over my head, I pulled my T-shirt off in one motion, the other hand already guiding myself between her lips, experiencing her in the sweetest way.

A sharp inhale as the head of my cock glided over her clit, dragging slowly through her slickness, up and down. I paused at her entrance, waiting.

Her eyes fluttered closed. Her mouth parted. Her back arched—every part of her asking for more.

And then, finally—

I pushed into her.

Slowly. Deliberately. Filling her, stretching her. Taking my time.

The pleasure radiated outward—joy, ecstasy, starting between my legs and spreading everywhere.

The heat of her, the way her body enveloped me, the raw pleasure of it.

Her eyes closed, her head tilted back. Her breasts lifting toward me with the arch in her back.

We were both feeling it—all of it at once.

She gasped, her fingers digging into my shoulders, her hips lifting, her legs tightening, taking me deeper.

A quiet, desperate moan came from her—the kind that made my pulse stutter, my chest tighten, my control nearly snap.

We moved together, our rhythm growing faster. Each thrust pushed us further into the moment, further into each other.

I let my gaze roam—her hips, her stomach, the rise and fall of her chest, the way her blonde hair fanned out across the pillow, her lips parted, her expression pure, unfiltered pleasure.

Then, her eyes opened, locking onto mine. Then she looked down to where our bodies met, watching, fascinated. The want and desire showing in her eyes was so... intoxicating.

A sharp, electric current passed between us—the thrill of knowing exactly what we were doing to each other.

And I couldn't resist.

Gently, I reached back and took her by the ankles, spreading her legs wider, opening her up completely.

Her head fell back against the pillow, her body fully exposed to me, fully surrendered.

Her breathing quickened, her moans growing louder, punctuated by the creak of the bed, the sheets twisting in her fists as she held on.

Her breasts bouncing with every movement, her body arching to meet me, taking me in, pulling me in.

The sight alone was almost enough to push me over the edge.

But then—

She coughed. Once. Then again.

The moment stalled. I let go of her legs—she immediately wrapped me up in them again.

I shifted my pace—something softer, something slower.

Her moan dipped—she wasn't ready for me to slow down.

Leaning forward, I propped myself up, keeping my weight off her chest, pressing my lips to her neck, staying there as her breathing evened out.

Then her fingers tangled in my hair—asking, pleading. I began working my way down from her neck—savoring every inch, feeling every tremor.

I paused at her breasts, circling her nipples with my tongue, pinching lightly with my lips, adding just the barest hint of teeth.

With each touch her grip on my hair tightened, pulling me closer, tilting her head back, making sounds that sent a pulse of warmth through me.

I stopped, holding myself deep inside her, motionless, just feeling her wrapped around me, my focus completely on her pleasure—on giving her something more than just the sex itself.

And then, I moved lower.

I withdrew from her slowly.

She whimpered, her legs and arms clenching around me, trying to keep me inside, keep me in place.

Wanting me to keep going. Wanting me to stay.

But I had other plans.

As I kissed my way down she knew where I was headed. But I think she had been close—so close—before we slowed. Before I slowed. That she didn't want to lose that.

But she had to. Her breathing had been too ragged to continue. So now, I was going to finish this another way.

I trailed kisses over her stomach, her hips, moving lower, until I was exactly where I wanted to be. Where she needed me to be.

She shifted beneath me, her legs let go and spread instinctively, anticipation filled every sound she was making.

I let my tongue play with her bellybutton, drawing out a soft, breathy giggle before moving lower—past the hair on her mons, down to the want burning between her thighs.

This time, I wanted to focus entirely on her.

I took her clit between my lips, sucking gently, letting my tongue toy with it the same way I had with her nipples.

Her moans were probably carried through the walls.

Then, I let go momentarily, parting her with my fingers, exposing her to me completely.

Her fingers tangling in my hair as my tongue moved over her, tasting her, experiencing her, feeling the way her hips moved in response to me.

I flattened my tongue, pressed it firmly against her, moving my head in small, rhythmic circles, stimulating everything at once.

Her hips began rolling with me, meeting every movement, her moans grew louder.

I gripped her hips, pulling her against my mouth, against my tongue. Encouraging her to grind against it.

Dana's body responded eagerly, her fingers pulling tighter in my hair, holding me there—firm, urgent, wordless, as her hips continued to move against me.

She was so close. And I wanted to take her there. But I knew her limits.

Her breathing was already quickening again, her body trembling beneath me.

If I pushed too hard, she'd start coughing again, pulling her out of the moment.

So, I slowed, keeping my movements precise and controlled.

Her fingers tightened in my hair again, not ready for me to stop, not wanting me to stop.

She was anchored to me, riding the edge of what she was chasing.

And I was going to keep her there, make her feel everything, hold her at the peak as long as she could stand it.

The way she melted

I slipped my two fingers back inside her, finding the spot that has always amazed me—a distinct area, small, but mighty.

Her body responded instantly. Her hips shifted again. Her inner muscles clenching around my fingers in rhythmic pulses.

The sounds she made—soft, breathy moans, punctuated by sharp inhales—told me exactly how much she was feeling it.

I curled my fingers, stroking in a slow rhythm. Applying just the right amount of pressure. Listening to her. Feeling her body communicate with me.

With my free hand, I drifted lower. Exploring the sensitive and delicate strip of skin between her pussy and her butt. Stroking the area with light strokes, slow pinches, and soft, circular touches.

Her sounds—encouraged me.

I let my fingers wander lower, ever so lightly over her ass—just a whisper of contact, a silent question.

A sharp inhale. A slight pause. But no objection.

So I stayed light, touching, exploratory, gauging the way her hips moved, the way her moans deepened, the way she melted beneath me.

This was just as much for me as it was for her—learning her body. Unraveling her reactions. Watching the way she came undone as I pleasured her.

And it was intoxicating.

But I wasn't done

When I finally withdrew my fingers, her soft whimper of protest sent a pulse of satisfaction through me.

I smiled, placing my damp fingers on her mons, letting my thumb take over, gently, rhythmically, stroking her clit.

I licked down—replacing my fingers with my tongue. Inside her, I explored the ridges, the textures, the heat.

I moved slowly, my tongue stroking deep. Just catching the edges of her G-spot.

As the sensations built, her moans turned into desperate gasps. Her hips rising to meet every flick, every stroke.

I pulled back just enough to watch—the way her body trembled, the way her fingers twisted into the sheets—the way she bit her lip as she fought for control.

God, she was beautiful like this.

But I wasn't done.

I shifted, letting my tongue glide back up, replacing my thumb on her clit.

Her breathing quickened. Her moans rising in pitch. Her thighs trembling against my shoulders.

And when she tipped over the edge, when her orgasm hit—I didn't stop.

I adjusted, shifting my focus just below her clit, where the sensation was still sharp but not overwhelming—drawing out her orgasm. Prolonging the waves of pleasure as long as she could take them.

Both hands found my head, gripping tightly at first, then gently pushing me away. Her body shaking, caught in the final tremors of her climax.

I pulled back slowly, watching as she closed her legs instinctively, as she rolled onto her side. Her breath uneven. Her expression blissful.

I stayed close, watching her as she rode out the last of the aftershocks.

It was a fucking gorgeous sight.

Oh God, Lind

As she lay there, her body still unsteady from release, I gently guided her onto her stomach, coaxing her toward the center of the bed.

With her legs together, I straddled them just below her hips. My weight pressing into her in all the right places.

My erection had softened some. But I wasn't ready for this to be over.

I moved against her, rubbing along the soft curve where her ass met her thighs. Feeling the slick heat of her against me.

I drew patterns across her back, my fingers gliding in circles, tracing her spine, the dip of her lower back.

At the same time, I stroked myself against her, sliding through the wetness between her cheeks.

Coaxing. Tempting.

The slow, steady return of my erection, the growing ache of need between us.

She shifted beneath me, her hips pressing into my movements, her small, breathy sounds of encouragement making my head spin.

She arched a little, pushing herself back toward me.

When I was ready again, I parted her thighs, and with one slow, fluid movement, I was back inside her.

The sensation was incredible—the slickness of her, the warmth, the way she clenched around me as if pulling me deeper. The raw pleasure returning, only deeper, more intense.

Her body reacting instantly, her hips lifting, pressing back against me, wanting more. The raw sounds of need—want—pleasure escaping from her.

I kept my movements slow at first with deep, steady strokes, my hands exploring the shape of her back, her waist, her hips.

The rhythm between us built naturally, her moans growing louder, my grip on her tighter, anchoring us.

And then—

"Oh God, Lind," she moaned, her voice ragged with intensity. "Cum in me, Lind, cum in me!"

Those words ripped through me like lightning.

Her plea shattered my control.

I thrust deep, calling her name as the orgasm ripped through me, shuddering, emptying into her, lost in the intensity of it.

I felt the subtle tremors of her 2nd orgasm echoing mine. The way she tightened, clenched, and pulsed with me.

And this time, I didn't miss it.

She was right there with me, wrapped up in the moment we created together.

We both froze

As my orgasm faded, I leaned forward, pressing soft kisses along her back. My weight hovering just above her, careful not to crush her.

Her breathing was still uneven. The contented sighs she let out made me smile.

I wanted to hold her, to anchor us in this moment. I wrapped one arm around her waist and gently rolled us onto our sides. My body fit perfectly against hers in our familiar spooning position.

My softening cock still inside her. It felt like the most natural place to be. For a long moment, we just lay there, basking in the afterglow, the heat, the rawness of it all.

And then—

A deep, sudden cough that shook her entire body. And just like that—

I was out!

We both froze. Then, the absurdity of it hit us at the same time.

Dana burst out laughing, and I followed, the sound bubbling up until we were both shaking, crying, laughing so hard neither of us could breathe.

The sound filled the room, unguarded, ridiculous, playful, genuine... the connection, the desire, the want—it all felt natural between us.

Chapter 5

I do this for her

After a while I got up, I set my hand briefly on Dana's hip, a reassurance that I'd be right back.

In the bathroom, I grabbed a washcloth and ran it under hot water. I cleaned myself off—face too. The sound of the running water reminded me of another need, so I took care of that.

Rinsing the washcloth out, I soaked it again with fresh, hot water, then grabbed a soft hand towel before heading back to the bedroom.

Dana was already watching me, her expression laced with a knowing amusement, her body a little tense, waiting.

As I approached, she rolled onto her back, her legs parting a little, an unspoken invitation.

I placed the warm washcloth between her legs, letting it rest for a moment over her sensitive skin. She let out a soft, contented sigh, the tension seemed to melt away.

Slowly, I began to clean her, starting with gentle strokes over her clit, then working downward, over her entrance, lower still, making sure to be thorough but delicate.

I passed over her clit once more and couldn't resist.

Leaning down, I pressed a few quick licks over the sensitive nub.

Dana jerked her thighs closed, her voice a mix of over sensitivity and exasperation as she reached down to swat at me.

"Lind!"

I chuckled at her, as I opened her legs a little to lean back in and kiss her inner thigh before pulling back.

A playful moment I would repeat often.

I pressed the washcloth into her palm.

"You can finish up if I missed anything."

She shot me a knowing look, but took it without protest.

When she was done, I dried her off gently, then took everything back to the bathroom, rinsing and hanging the washcloth alongside the towel.

A thought flickered through my mind as I stood there.

I do this for her because I want to. Because it means something to *me*.

And knowing she trusts me—lets me in—makes it mean even more.

When I returned, Dana had already pulled the covers over herself.

I slid back into our familiar spooning position, and without a word, she took my right hand and placed it on her breast, holding it there as she pressed against me.

With the warmth of her body, and her steady breathing—

It didn't take long before sleep found both of us.

And as I drifted off, I thought—

This—whatever this was—felt easy.

It felt right.

The last 24 hours had been... unexpected.

It started as a daring plan. But it had become so much more than I ever hoped for.

***

Dana stirred first, waking me. My hand was still on her breast, and between the warmth and sweat, it felt almost glued there.

She peeled it off with a sigh. This time I was the one who whimpered at the loss.

She turned toward me, shifting closer. Draped her leg over mine. Her warm breath against my chest, her skin still flushed from sleep.

I broke the stillness.

"You're quiet," I murmured. "What's on your mind?"

Dana tilted her head back, her green eyes soft but serious.

"I've been lying here thinking..." She hesitated, before she said... "I don't want you to leave."

It hit me hard, slicing through the haze of sleep.

I hadn't expected her to say it.

Not so plainly anyway.

I swallowed, keeping my tone light. "Dana, you know I want to stay. But we both know why I shouldn't."

Her eyes drifted away, like she was lost in thought.

Her hand running down my chest to my hip, her fingers playing absently.

"Why not?" she asked, her voice softer now, but no less stubborn. "Why does it matter what anyone else thinks?"

I exhaled, pressing a slow kiss to her forehead.

"Because it does," I said gently. "If we're both out again tomorrow, people *will* talk. And it's not just talk—it's questions, rumors, the whole thing."

Her brows furrowed, her hand stopped moving.

"So what?" she muttered. "Let them talk. It's none of their business."

"It's not," I agreed, my thumb brushing over the soft curve of her jaw.

"But do you really want to deal with it? We're just starting something good here. I don't want to explain us to anyone when we're still figuring it out ourselves."

She sighed, resting her head against my chest.

"I guess that makes sense," she admitted, her fingers moving lower again.

She reached around to my back and began drifting lightly over my ass.

"You know it does." I grinned, catching her roaming fingers.

She grinned—slipping her hand free and reaching over my hip for my cock.

"Do you think if I hold on tight enough, I can keep you from going?"

I smiled, kissing her deeply.

"You're dangerous, you know that?"

She laughed against my lips, her arm wrapping around my neck.

"But if I call out again, and you're already out, it'll be too obvious," I continued. "We don't need the headache."

She sighed, her reluctant smile not quite hiding her disappointment.

"Okay," she murmured. Then—"But no one will notice if you come over this weekend, right?"

A slow smile spread across my face.

"No, no they won't."

Her eyes brightened.

"Then it's a date?" she asked, giving me a playful squeeze that had me sucking in a breath.

"Absolutely."

She let go, both arms wrapping around me, her head resting on my chest.

For now, we just held each other, the steady rise and fall of her breath against my skin.

She sounded almost... normal again.

We had time to figure this out. Whatever this was.

But for now, we'd stay here, in this moment, a little longer.

Yeah, that sealed it

The next time she stirred, she whispered, "We should get up."

I tightened my arm around her hip, keeping her anchored.

"Not yet."

She laughed softly. "I'll be back in a few minutes," she murmured, leaning in to kiss me before slipping from my grasp.

I cracked one eye open, watching her sit up, the sheet falling away from her bare back.

When she stood, I got a perfect glimpse of her from the side, the soft sway of her hips, the bounce of her breasts as she moved.

She opened her top dresser drawer, pulling out a pair of white lace panties and something else. I smiled to myself, *she hasn't worn panties the whole time I've been here.*

She smiled at me, pausing just long enough for me to appreciate the view.

Then, she disappeared into the bathroom.

The moment she was gone, I exhaled, scrubbing a hand over my face.

God, I didn't want to leave.

When she reappeared, she paused slightly before walking toward me.

Framed by the afternoon light through the window, her damp hair clinging to her shoulders, white lace hugging her hips... bare breasts bouncing with every step. My only thought—

Yeah. That sealed it.

I had no fucking chance against her.

Propping myself up on one elbow, I exhaled before pushing myself upright with a groan.

Dana sighed dramatically, her fingers dragging down my arm—slow, patient—sending shivers through me. I leaned forward and took her nipple in my mouth. She pulled back a little until it slipped out, laughing. *"If* you're leaving, we don't have time for that," she said.

I sighed, forcing myself to move. I stood and made my way to the bathroom. I caught her watching me.

When I returned, her quiet laugh told me she was enjoying the view.

Even as I packed up my backpack, I could feel her eyes on me—tracking my every move. Making no effort to hide it. The way she looked at me, like she wanted me just as much now as she did a few hours ago.

Damn. It had been a long time since I'd felt wanted like this.

As I grabbed my T-shirt, her voice stopped me.

"Wait."

I turned, finding her standing there, bare-breasted. Her playful smile made it damn near impossible to think straight. She reached for my shirt, tugging at it slightly.

"Can I keep this?"

Surprised, I raised an eyebrow. "My shirt?"

She nodded, cheeks coloring just a little. "Yeah, it smells like you."

Something about that hit me. But instead of overthinking it, I just smiled and handed it to her.

She pulled it on, and I immediately liked this decision—because she looked so fucking good in it. The fabric clung in all the right places—barely covering her thighs, her nipples taunting me.

"You look better in that than I ever have," I said, eyes tracing the way it hung on her frame. Then I raised my eyebrows at her. "Though you still look better without it."

She laughed, lifting it up to her chin to flash me. "You mean like this?"

Groaning, I ran a hand down my face. "You really don't play fair."

She grinned. "Nope."

I was missing her already

We made our way downstairs together, moving in sync, her bare legs and swaying T-shirt making it almost impossible to concentrate.

At the door, I set my backpack down for a moment, wanting to hold her one last time.

"I think I'll order some food later," she said, breaking the quiet between us. "I'm starting to feel hungry again."

"Well, promise me you'll wear more than this shirt and those panties when the delivery guy shows up." I winked at her. "Otherwise, you'll give him a hard-on that'll last till the end of his shift."

She laughed, swatting at my chest lightly. "As if I'd answer the door like this."

I chuckled, then pulled her into my arms. The laughter faded—I kissed her, slow and deep, committing the feel of her to memory.

When we finally broke apart, I rested my forehead against hers, reluctant to leave.

"See you in a couple days," I murmured.

She nodded, her green eyes glistening slightly. "See you then."

With one last kiss, I grabbed my backpack and stepped outside. The cool air hit me as the door clicked shut behind me, sealing me away from the warmth of her.

I was missing her already.

Walking to my truck, I replayed the last 24 hours—every kiss, every moan, and every time she made me laugh.

Damn—What had this woman done to me?

Part 2

It didn't happen all at once.
A glance.
A smile.
Moments we noticed—moments that stayed.
We weren't falling yet.
But the ground was beginning to shift beneath our feet.

Chapter 6

A job, not a passion

Dana's world was one of efficiency and routine—carved out behind the scenes at one of the nation's largest big-box chains. As part of the merchandising team, she spent her days orchestrating displays and handling seasonal resets, while most of the store's 165 associates slogged through endless customer interactions. It wasn't a glamorous gig, but it suited her: a steady job that kept her home life separate, a cozy condo waiting at the end of each shift, and the occasional, unremarkable flirtation with dating apps that never quite filled her expectations.

Then, everything shifted—just slightly. Grace, a seasoned team member of four years, announced her transfer to another location to be nearer to family. With her departure came an unexpected vacancy, and four weeks later, on a crisp Monday morning in October, Lind stepped through the door to take her place.

Lind's first day

Before the morning meeting, Brenda—the team's safety captain—introduced Lind to the tight-knit group. One by one, everyone offered their names, tenure, and a little bit about themselves. Pete, with his relaxed smile and easy confidence, clapped a hand on Lind's shoulder. "You're stuck with me for the first week," he said warmly.

Lind managed a sheepish nod, quietly cursing his own forgetfulness when it came to names—thankfully, the mandatory name tags were a saving grace.

The early days were a crash course in store life. Monday was spent shadowing routines with Pete's guidance. Tuesday followed the same pattern.

By Wednesday, Lind found himself in a back room filled with outdated corporate training videos, struggling to stay awake. His chin dipped once, then again, until Pete nudged him with a quiet chuckle. "Don't worry," he said. "Happens to the best of us. These things are brutal, they could put anyone to sleep."

Come Thursday, he was back on the floor, and by Friday, he'd begun finding a rhythm—juggling computer work in the morning with a 62-hour team project that demanded every ounce of focus in the afternoon.

When Lind arrived for the final stretch, Dana was already waiting, clipboard in hand. "Alright, here's your role," she said, efficient and matter-of-fact, as she laid out the plan. Lind repeated her instructions back in his own words—a practice that initially pricked Dana's pride. Had he been testing her? She couldn't tell. But then he dived into the work without a single extraneous question. It was a small thing, but as they broke down boxes and cleared away plastic wrap later that afternoon, Dana couldn't help but admire his no-nonsense approach.

As the team filed out, Lind offered a quiet, "See you Monday. Have a good weekend." His eyes rested on Dana just a moment longer than the rest. Dana felt the weight of his gaze—just a flicker of something—a question perhaps. A possibility, that maybe, just maybe, there was something more to him than "the new guy."

What Dana didn't realize was that Lind had only repeated her instructions because it had been the only way to be sure he'd heard them right. The last thing he wanted was to look like he wasn't paying attention.

Because he was. Just not to her words.

You're a pretty good teacher

By his second week, Lind was rotating through different partners, soaking up every aspect of the merchandising role. On Wednesday, he was paired with Dana. Their task was straightforward—set up a seasonal display, rearrange shelves, and ensure holiday items were set according to the planogram.

Dana pointed out, "Smaller items up top, heavier pieces down low."

"Got it," Lind replied, rolling up his sleeves and joining in.

At first, Dana watched him carefully, half-expecting him to bombard her with questions, or repeat her instructions—but Lind's steady, deliberate pace spoke for itself. When they stepped back to admire their work, Dana allowed herself a small smile. "Not bad," she said.

Lind returned the smile, his voice soft. "Thanks. You're a pretty good teacher."

For a moment, Dana's practiced cool faltered. "You're not the worst trainee I've had," she quipped, and the air between them lightened with their mutual laughter.

In that moment, Dana decided that working with Lind might not be so terrible after all.

Cackling geese

The break room buzzed with its usual hum—a wall-mounted TV droning a tired game show, mismatched chairs clustered around square tables pushed together, and a pair of couches in the corner. The merchandising team had claimed a pair of tables pushed together for their midday break. Near the kitchen area, a trio of outspoken store side associates—Charlene, Debra, and Karen—ruled their domain, their laughter and loud opinions a constant backdrop.

At one of the tables, Dana scrolled through her phone sipping water. Across from her, Lind was halfway through his sandwich when the conversation from the "cackling geese," as he had secretly dubbed them, drifted over.

"Look at him—quiet and mysterious," Charlene chided, waving her fork with theatrical flair.

"Maybe he's saving all his secrets for later," Debra added, nudging Karen, whose quiet smile betrayed her amusement.

Pete, ever the observer, leaned closer to Lind. "Geese are honking," he murmured with a grin.

Lind corrected under his breath, "Cackling geese," careful to let the remark drift to Dana's ears. Her lips twitched as she fought the urge to laugh aloud.

Charlene's fork paused mid-air. "What was that, new guy?" she asked, half-challenging, half-curious.

Lind set down his sandwich, his expression neutral. "Just admiring how lively you all keep things here," he said smoothly.

"Charming, aren't you?" Charlene replied with a playful arch of her eyebrow. "You should come sit with us sometime—get to know the real people behind the scenes."

"Tempting," Lind replied with a measured smile, "but maybe I should wait until I pass my 90 days. Wouldn't want to get too comfortable too soon."

Laughter rippled around the table. By the time lunch wound down Dana nudged him with an elbow as they cleared their trays, her smile softening into something warmer.

"Cackling geese, huh?" Dana remarked, eyes sparkling with amusement.

Lind shrugged, with a small grin. "If the honk fits."

As they headed back to the floor, Dana realized that Lind was becoming much more than just the new guy. Their easy banter and shared moments, however light, hinted at a connection that was quietly growing—a possibility of something more.

Hazelnut. Vanilla. Hope

Dana nodded as Georgette paired her with Lind to complete a few assignments that needed completing by end of day. Nothing hard, just timely.

Brenda looked at her. "You're with Lind today," she said with a knowing smirk. "Team project... Enjoy."

Dana rolled her eyes.

It was Wednesday, mid-January. Post-holiday chaos had finally settled, and the store was easing into its quieter winter rhythm. Dana skimmed the list—seasonal display update, shelf realignment for an upcoming shipment, and back-to-school layout check. Nothing glamorous. Just enough to fill the day.

Lind followed her to the seasonal aisle, travel mug in hand and that easy, unreadable smile on his face.

"All right," she said, gesturing to the shelves. "These go here, then we'll label. Simple enough."

"Got it," he replied, setting his mug aside. "I'll start unboxing."

They fell into a smooth rhythm—she directed, he followed without hesitation. Comfortable silence, the kind that didn't feel awkward. Just steady.

After a few minutes, Dana glanced at the mug he'd parked beside the display.

"You're holding onto that thing like it's keeping you alive."

"It is," he said, grinning. "Early shifts and I don't mix well without coffee."

"Same. But it's gotta be from Brews and Muse for me."

Lind tilted his head. "Brews and what?"

"Technically, Coffee Brews and Muse. Downtown. Cute little place."

He raised an eyebrow. "You mean that artsy place with couches and bad parking?"

"That's the one."

"Hmm. I'm partial to the place on Oak."

Dana snorted. "That shoe box with two coffee options—black and blacker?"

"They roast their beans in-house," he defended, laughing.

"I like my coffee to taste like something. Hazelnut. Vanilla. Hope."

"Pretty sure I saw a caramel option once," he said, teasing. "Might've been seasonal."

"There's no atmosphere. It's so plain Jane."

"It's small," he agreed. "But cozy. Intimate, even."

She arched a brow. "Intimate, huh?"

"You should try it," he said, his voice dipping just slightly into something warmer.

"I have tried it," she replied, lifting her chin.

"Not with me," he said.

She didn't answer, just gave a sideways smile and turned back to the shelves. But the moment lingered.

She couldn't let herself think on that too long—she was afraid if she did, she was going to drop something.

***

The second task—rearranging shelves to prep for a new shipment—took them into one of the quieter corners of the store. The boxes were heavy, so they worked in tandem, sliding them into place and chatting between lifts.

Dana caught herself watching the way he moved—efficient, quiet, muscular. She looked away and busied herself before her thoughts ran off in the wrong direction.

"So," she said, stretching her back, "where'd you move here from?"

"Just the next city over," he said. "Needed a change of pace."

Dana nodded. "Retail merchandising isn't exactly glamorous, but it has its perks. I've been here about five years."

"Five years? You must know this place inside and out."

"Pretty much. I know which aisles get trashed the fastest, which displays are customer magnets, and where to hide for a quick breather."

Lind chuckled. "Noted. Do you have family around here?"

"Not really. Parents are a few towns away."

He nodded. "Mine are out of state. Got a sister. She still lives near them. She's got three kids. We don't see each other much, mostly around the holidays."

Dana grinned. "So, you're Uncle Lind."

"Yep. Lots of energy in those three. Keeps me humble."

"No nieces or nephews for me. But a couple of my friends have kids. I love them to bits—but it's nice to hand them back after a few hours."

They shared a laugh. The ease between them settled in further, like a chair that had finally found its balance.

***

After their lunch, they tackled the final item on the list—checking the layout of the back-to-school section. Dana grabbed a pricing gun while Lind adjusted rows of spiral notebooks.

"So what made you come here?" she asked. "If that's not too personal."

"Not at all," he said. "I used to manage inventory at a small warehouse. Good job. Steady. But I wanted something more people-oriented. Something with a little motion."

She gave him a half smile. "Welcome to the chaos."

"Right? Less predictable. But I like it."

"I landed here on a whim," she admitted. "Retail jobs through college, but no long-term plan. They offered me merchandising and I thought, 'Why not?' Now it's five years later."

"So you just... found yourself here?"

She laughed. "Pretty much. Until something else calls my name."

Their eyes met again—just a flicker of something thoughtful, maybe curious—before they both turned back to the task at hand.

She shook it off, but her grin lingered.

Then—still—she risked one more glance at Lind.

He wasn't looking.

Thank God.

Chapter 7

Cliché romance is the point

The seasonal aisle was alive with the smell of freshly opened cardboard and the sickly-sweet scent of mass-produced chocolates—a heady mix of nostalgia and kitschy romance. Rows of pink and red stuffed animals, glossy heart-shaped candy boxes, and a lazy cluster of foil balloons completed the scene.

Dana crouched beside a half-empty box of plush bears, carefully adjusting the embroidered hearts in their tiny paws. Just across from her, Lind was meticulously lining up small gift bags, his focus almost surgical.

"You're taking this Valentine's setup *way* too seriously," Dana said as she straightened up. "Are you auditioning for Cupid?"

Lind glanced over, one eyebrow arched in playful reproach. "Someone's gotta bring order to the chaos. Otherwise, customers will be tearing through everything in search of the perfect bag of Cliché romance."

Dana grinned. "Cliché romance is the point of Valentine's Day."

Folding his arms, Lind quipped, "Is that your professional opinion?"

"It's my personal opinion," she shot back. Then, picking up one of the bears, she held it out toward him. "Actually... this little guy's got your whole stoic-yet-lovable vibe. Think you could pull it off?"

Lind let out a quiet laugh. "Sure, I could. Just give me a bow tie, and I'll be unrecognizable."

A few minutes later, as Dana loaded her cart with supplies, she paused—her hand frozen over a plain red gift bag speckled with white polka dots. Nestled inside, among crumpled tissue paper, was one of those very bears she'd just teased him about. She glanced toward Lind, who was still working with his characteristic calm. For a moment, she caught the subtle tug at the corner of his lips—a flicker of quiet amusement aimed right at her.

Dana bit back a grin and let the bag remain exactly where it was. Later, as Lind passed by her cart with a pack of foil balloons in hand, she casually plucked a heart-shaped lollipop from the display and dropped it onto his cart. He didn't react immediately; but as he moved away, she caught him glancing down and giving a barely perceptible shake of his head.

By the time they finished setting up, Dana's shoulders ached from bending and lifting. As she stretched near a shelf, she caught Lind watching her with quiet amusement.

"What's up?" she asked, brushing her hands on her jeans.

Lind shrugged lightly. "Just wondering how many other people you're handing out candy to."

Dana's eyes sparkled as she replied, "Hmm... So far? You're the only one who's earned it."

"Good to know," he murmured, his gaze lingering just long enough to send a flicker of warmth through her.

Dana forced herself to refocus on the display, telling herself that this meant nothing. Yet, as she arranged the final items, she couldn't help but think—*it didn't feel like nothing.*

"Fine" isn't good enough

The lunchroom buzzed with its familiar midday shuffle—coworkers drifting in and out, overlapping conversations creating a steady hum.

At their usual table, Dana sat across from Brenda, idly picking at a salad while scrolling through her phone.

"You know, Dana," Brenda leaned forward with a conspiratorial glint, "we really need to find you a boyfriend."

Dana nearly choked on her water. "Why do you care so much about my love life?"

"Because *'fine'* isn't good enough," Brenda replied, mimicking Dana's tone about her morning coffee ritual. "You need a little passion in your life."

"What do you mean by 'fine'?" Dana asked her.

"What do you always say when I ask about dating, men, or anything relationship related?" Brenda chided.

"I'm fine," Dana echoed, making a face.

"Exactly," Brenda said, pointing her fork at her.

From the far end of the table, Pete grinned. "'Fine' isn't going to keep you warm at night. It's still winter, you know."

Dana shrugged. "It's March, and I have plenty of blankets. I'll be *fine*," she mocked.

Then, from the adjacent table came a low, smooth remark that cut through the banter: "Maybe you just need a boy toy."

Dana's gaze flicked to Lind, who was casually finishing his sandwich. His hazel eyes were unreadable yet unmistakably aware of the sudden shift in the room's tone.

"A boy toy..." she mused, tapping a finger against her chin. "I could settle for that."

Laughter burst around the table, yet Lind's smile remained modest—a quiet, telling smile—but it hinted at more than just amusement. It wasn't just what she'd said; it was how she'd said it. Half-joking, half-serious—and somewhat intrigued.

As she looked at Lind, their eyes locked for just a second before she turned away. *Bad idea to play where you work,* she reminded herself.

Casual sex once in a while

The March weather was milder this year than last. The merchandisers were eager to get out and party a little. Friday night at the local bar brought a welcome mix of loud music, clinking glasses, and easy laughter. A few of the merchandisers had claimed a high-top table near the back, close enough to feel the pulse of the room without being swallowed by it.

Dana sat with Brenda, Pete, and Riley, savoring a margarita, while Lind nursed a beer at the end of the table, content to listen.

As the conversation shifted from work Brenda nudged Dana, grinning like a Cheshire. "So, have you found yourself that boy toy yet?"

Dana rolled her eyes, her grin betraying her amusement. "Nope. Apparently, they're in short supply."

Pete snorted. "Boy toys are overrated anyway. Women think they want one, but then they start getting all... possessive."

Riley raised an eyebrow. "You mean like 'We slept together, so now you're mine' possessive?"

"Exactly," Pete replied, taking a long sip of his beer. "That's not a boy toy—that's someone fooling themselves into thinking they don't want more."

Now on her second drink, Dana swirled her margarita thoughtfully before leaning toward Brenda in a lower, measured tone. "I'd like a boyfriend," she admitted. "But I know the difference. Casual sex with the same guy once in a while might be nice—keep me from burning through batteries so fast"

Brenda nearly choked mid-sip, wiping her mouth as laughter spilled over. "Oh my God, Dana!"

Pete and Riley glanced over, but Brenda waved them off. "It's just girl talk."

At the end of the table, Lind maintained a quiet composure. Yet, as Dana caught the slight upward curve at the corner of his lips—a subtle one—she felt a warmth bloom on her cheeks. He'd clearly overheard her, and though his reaction was understated,

Dana saw the corner of his mouth twitch—just enough to make her skin flush.

The night wore on as new faces joined the table—Stephanie and her husband—and the conversation continued to ebb and flow. As the evening wound down, Lind leaned back in his chair, stretching before setting down his empty beer bottle.

"Thanks for the invite," he said, standing. "Had a good time."

Stephanie grinned. "You don't have to leave just because we got here."

Lind chuckled softly. "You know I'm not. But since you're here, someone needs to keep an eye on these guys."

"We'll do our best," Stephanie replied. "See you Monday."

As Lind walked toward the door, Dana found herself watching him go. Maybe it was the alcohol, or maybe it was something else entirely. But as he disappeared into the night, she couldn't shake the feeling that there might be something between them.

I went with a friend

The first warm weekend of spring turned the lunchroom into a vibrant haven of chatter and optimism. Conversations bubbled with talk of barbecues, outdoor plans, and lazy afternoons in the sun.

At the merchandisers' table, Dana idly picked at her salad while Pete launched into an animated retelling of his latest cooking disaster.

"I told my brother-in-law to wait for the coals to heat up completely," Pete declared, grimacing as the table erupted in laughter, "but he just slapped the burgers on anyway. We ended up with what I'd call 'seared tartare.'"

Brenda chimed in, "At least you got outside. We pulled the bikes out of the garage and did a couple loops around the neighborhood. Amazing how out of shape you get over winter."

She shook her head slightly, rubbing one thigh like it still ached. "The first ten minutes were brutal—felt like I needed training wheels. The kids ran circles around us." She laughed. "The husband almost fell... twice!"

From a nearby table, Laura added, "We went to Riverbend Park. The trails were gorgeous, and the river's running so high right now—it was a great day, I didn't want to leave."

Dana's gaze drifted to the end of the table. "How about you, Lind? Do anything this weekend?"

Lind looked up from his quiet reverie. "Yeah. I went hiking too."

"Nice. Where?" Dana asked, genuine curiosity in her tone.

"Pine Hollow," he replied, the name evoking murmurs of recognition. The rugged trails and stunning overlooks of Pine Hollow were well-known—a two-hour drive that promised adventure.

"That's a hell of a hike," Brenda remarked. "You go alone?"

"Not alone," Lind clarified, setting his water bottle down. "I went with a friend. Sam and I like to go there when the weather's good."

Pete raised an eyebrow. "Two-hour drive—was it a day trip?"

"No, overnight," Lind said casually. "Sam lives out that way, so we make a weekend of it."

Dana noticed the quick glance Brenda shot his way and couldn't help but focus on the way Lind said Sam's name—a softness that hinted at something beyond a casual hiking buddy. Pete, ever the inquisitor, prodded, "That's a great hike, but did you do anything else?"

Lind chuckled. "I took some time for myself. Wandered off-trail, found a quiet spot. Nice to just sit and listen, you know? There's nothing like the sound of nothing. And yes—I lazied around, slept in, made breakfast. Took it easy."

Brenda laughed. "That sounds like something you'd do, Lind. Except the 'lazy', 'slept in' and, 'took it easy' parts. Who knew you had it in you?"

Dana found herself picturing Lind alone in the woods, soaking in the silence. It was an image that fit him, she thought. His words stirred a quiet curiosity in her—questions about who he was beyond the routine of work, about the moments he cherished in solitude, and about the friend named Sam.

As the conversation at the table continued, Lind's thoughts drifted back to his weekend with Sam: *the quiet spot off the trail, their intimacy, her laughter, the familiar smell of her apartment, and the way she'd teased him for almost burning the pancakes Sunday morning. Their conversations, their plans. Talking through the music festival in July. She'd rattled off the bands she wanted to see, and the volleyball she missed. The thought of spending a weekend surrounded by music, nature, and Sam's energy brought a small smile to his lips.*

Dana's voice cut gently through his thoughts. "Lunch is over. Back to work. You're with me—we've got to finish that setup."

"Right behind you, Dana," Lind replied immediately.

As he followed her down the aisle he enjoyed the way her hips swayed as she moved.

He smiled to himself, wondering how long he'd wait before asking the questions Dana might not even know were there.

Chapter 8

What's the right question

The receiving area was colder than the rest of the store, even with the weather warming up. Dana shoved the last box into a neat stack, exhaling sharply. "Whoever packed these must hate us," she muttered, eyeing the lopsided pallet still waiting to be sorted.

Lind, working a few feet away, groaned. "At least they're consistent. Every shipment's a fuck-up."

Dana's head snapped up, a glint in her eyes. "Lind! I didn't know you knew that word."

He huffed, rubbing a hand down his face. "Sorry. I usually don't get this frustrated."

Dana brushed off her jeans, casting him a playful glance. "I don't get you, Lind."

Lind glanced at her, brow furrowing slightly. "I said I was sorry."

"That's not what I meant," she clarified. "Sometimes this job just gets to you. Don't worry about that."

He hesitated, looking at her for a second. "Oh. Then what do you mean?"

"You don't talk about yourself much," she said, leaning against the shelving. "Everyone's guessing about what you do when you're not here."

Lind stacked another box onto the cart, the hint of a smile playing on his lips. "Let them guess. Keeps things interesting."

Dana rolled her eyes. "Come on, Lind. You've got to give me something. What's your big secret? Are you a spy? A rock star? What?"

He grinned, hazel eyes flicking to hers. "Nothing that exciting, I promise."

Dana watched him for a moment, arms crossed. "You know, the more vague you are, the more curious I get."

Lind let out a small chuckle. "Is that so?"

"Yep," Dana said, pushing off the shelf. "And I'm not the only one. Brenda thinks you're some kind of wilderness guy, Pete says you're probably hiding a double life, and Laura's convinced you moonlight as a secret chef."

Lind snorted, shaking his head. "Because I go hiking, make a mean breakfast, and—" he paused dramatically— "moonlight as a bouncer?"

Dana blinked, caught off guard. "Wait—seriously?"

Lind grinned. "Hiking and breakfast, yes. Bouncer? No. But I like that one."

Dana laughed, shaking her head. "You're something else, you know that?" She studied him, her expression softening. "So... pancakes or waffles?"

Lind leaned against the cart, considering. "Pancakes. From scratch. None of that boxed mix."

Dana raised an eyebrow, impressed. "Fancy. I'm starting to believe the secret chef theory."

He chuckled, the tension in his shoulders easing. "Not much of a secret. My grandmother taught me. She always said, 'If you're going to feed someone, do it right.'"

There was something in his voice—something softer, more genuine—that made Dana pause. "You're full of surprises, Lind."

He glanced at her, his grin fading into something smaller, quieter. "Maybe. Or maybe people just don't ask the right questions."

Dana tilted her head. "Really? What's the right question?"

Lind hesitated, weighing how much to say. "Something less... surface level, I guess."

Dana leaned in slightly. "Like what?"

He shrugged. "Like... Why hiking?" He met her gaze, hazel eyes steady. "It's not about exercise. It's about getting away from everything. Letting my head breathe a little."

Dana nodded slowly, her expression softening. "That makes sense. This place can be... stifling."

"Exactly. But not just this place—*everyday life*." His face went unreadable for a bit, like he was thinking. But then his smile returned—faint but real. "Out there, it's just you and the world. No schedules, no noise. Just... quiet. And if you're sharing the experience with a good friend, even better."

Dana studied him, something in his words stirring a flicker of curiosity—maybe even something deeper. "That actually sounds... amazing."

Lind looked at her, his usual guardedness slipping just enough to let something honest show through. "It is. There's something about it—no distractions, no expectations. You can just be yourself, you know?"

Dana hesitated, then asked, "Do you go alone? Or do you always have a... good friend with you?" Her tone was light, but the question carried weight.

Lind's pause was brief but telling. "Depends. Sometimes I go alone. But many times..." He trailed off, considering his words. "There's one friend I go with pretty regularly. She's been my hiking buddy for years."

Dana caught the subtle emphasis on *she* and felt a flicker of something—jealousy? Curiosity? It was hard to pin down. "She must be pretty special."

Lind's expression softened. "She is. She's one of those people who just... gets it. No pressure, no drama. Just someone you can be yourself around."

Dana nodded, absorbing his words. "Sounds like you trust her a lot."

"I do," Lind admitted quietly. He lifted another box onto the cart, but his eyes stayed on hers. "But trust isn't something I give out easily."

She felt the weight—the meaning of his words. She wondered if he was referring to her specifically. She wanted to say something light, to break the tension, but instead, she found herself saying, "I get that. Trust *is* hard."

Lind studied her, then nodded. "Yeah, it is." He leaned back slightly, crossing his arms. "But sometimes, you meet someone who makes it feel... worth it."

Dana felt the flush in her cheeks—just for a second—but she covered it with a small laugh. "You're full of surprises today, Lind."

He smiled, his eyes crinkling slightly. "Maybe. Or you're just asking the right questions."

Dana paused, considering his words and what they might mean for her—for them. She shifted the moment back to something playful. "Alright, next question: do you ever bring pancakes on these hikes? Because if not, I'm starting to think you're not as impressive as you seem."

Lind chuckled, shaking his head. "No pancakes in the wild. But if you're ever interested, I'll show you how they're done—properly."

Dana's heart skipped—just a little—but she kept her tone light. "Careful, Lind. I might just take you up on that."

His smile deepened, and for a moment, the receiving area didn't feel quite so cold. "Anytime, Dana."

The sound of footsteps approaching broke the moment, and they both turned as Pete called out from the main floor. "Hey, if you two are done back here, we've got another pallet waiting!"

Dana rolled her eyes, grabbing the cart handle. "Coming, Pete!" She glanced at Lind, grinning. "Guess we'll continue this another time."

Lind chuckled, falling into step beside her as they pushed the cart toward the door. "Don't worry. I'm not going anywhere."

You could let me do it

The seasonal aisle was quiet, save for the faint hum of overhead lights and the occasional squeak of a rolling cart. Dana stood on the top rung of a ladder, her fingers stretching for a box of garden lights perched just out of reach. The ladder wobbled slightly, making her curse under her breath as she shifted her weight, trying to steady herself.

"Need a hand?" Lind's voice drifted up from below, steady and amused.

Startled, Dana glanced down. He stood there, one hand resting casually on his hip, the other poised as if ready to catch the ladder—or her.

"I've got it," she insisted, though the slight tremble of the ladder suggested otherwise.

Lind stepped closer, gripping the sides with both hands. "Yeah, looks like it."

Dana huffed but didn't argue. "Fine. Hold the ladder, and I'll get it."

"Or," Lind said, already stepping onto the first rung, "you could let me do it."

Before she could protest, he climbed up beside her. His height gave him an obvious advantage, and in one smooth motion, he grabbed the box and handed it to her with an infuriatingly smug look on his face. "There. No death-defying acts required."

Dana rolled her eyes, balancing the box on her hip. "Show-off."

"Just keeping you in one piece," Lind said as he climbed back down.

"Need me in one piece, do you?"

"Want you in one piece," he said, turning to her with a grin.

Shaking her head, Dana carried the box toward the display, unable to stop the small smile forming on her lips.

***

Later that day, the two of them stood shoulder to shoulder in front of the same shelf, tackling a reset based on a newly issued planogram. The laminated layout sat between them, crumpled at the edges, already showing signs of Dana's frustration.

"This doesn't go here," she said, tapping the middle shelf with her finger.

Lind raised an eyebrow. "Says who? The planogram is vague."

"It's not vague," Dana countered, arms crossed. "You're just not reading it right."

Lind leaned in slightly, scanning the diagram again. "I'm just saying, if we put this here—" he adjusted a package on the shelf "—it looks better and makes more sense."

Dana studied his adjustment, lips pursed. "...Fine. It's better—but it's still not what they want."

His grin widened as he leaned back. "Better trumps correct. Isn't that a rule?"

"Not in retail," Dana shot back, shaking her head but smiling. "You're impossible."

"Impossibly good," Lind quipped. "Admit it."

Dana laughed, nudging the cart closer. "Maybe. Yeah—okay. But don't let it go to your head. And don't tell anybody I said so."

You're fun to work with

The next morning, the two of them were back in receiving, unboxing new shipments surrounded by stacks of cartons and the familiar scent of cardboard. Dana dragged a box cutter along the seam of a large carton and peeled back the flaps—only to freeze before bursting into laughter.

Lind, lifting a box onto a cart, glanced over. "What's so funny?"

Dana reached inside and pulled out a coffee mug that read, *World's Okayest Boss*. She held it up for him to see, barely containing her amusement. "Pretty sure this wasn't on the list."

Lind took the mug, turning it in his hands as he inspected it. "I mean, accurate for some people."

Dana glanced at him with a spark of mischief. "Think we could slip it into Georgette's office?"

Lind grinned, setting the mug on the shelf beside them. "I dare you."

They laughed, the sound echoing in the otherwise quiet receiving area. Lind looked at her, his expression softened. "You're fun to work with, you know that?"

Dana blinked, a little caught off guard by his tone. "Right back at you."

Lind watched her for a little longer before turning back to his task.

Dana felt a warmth creep up her neck, the air between them suddenly charged with... something. She glanced at the mug, then back at Lind, catching him sneaking another glance at her.

"So," she said, clearing her throat, "should we keep this or sneak it back into inventory?"

Lind chuckled, his eyes crinkling at the corners. "Oh, it's staying. And if anyone asks, it was your idea."

"Coward," she said, but the smile she gave him was still there long after they went back to work.

Where's Lind

The merchandisers gathered in the backroom near receiving, the usual hum of early morning chatter filling the air. Dana stood with

Brenda, sipping her coffee while Pete leaned against a stack of pallets, and scrolled through his phone. Riley fiddled with a clipboard, flipping through pages without really reading them.

"Where's Lind?" Brenda asked, glancing toward the door. "He's never late."

Pete shrugged without looking up. "Maybe he hit traffic. Or overslept."

Dana snorted. "Lind? Not likely. He's been early every day since he started."

Riley grinned. "Maybe he finally got tired of us—and skipped town."

"Doubtful," Brenda said. "He'd at least leave a note."

The conversation stilled as Georgette walked in, clipboard in hand. She scanned the room, then started to speak—but Brenda beat her to it.

"Hey, where's Lind? He's never late."

Georgette's expression remained neutral. "Lind took a personal day."

Dana blinked. "A personal day?"

"Yes," Georgette said. "He hasn't been here long enough to earn vacation time, but he's worked hard. I thought he deserved a little extra time off since he had something personal to do."

A quiet buzz of speculation spread through the room, but Dana barely heard it. Lind took a day off? He never even hinted that he had plans. Her curiosity spiked. He'd shared pieces of himself here and there—his hiking trips, his pancakes—but nothing personal. What was important enough to make him miss work?

She sipped her coffee, lips quirking slightly. *The man of mystery strikes again.*

The meeting continued, but Dana's thoughts wandered, trying to piece together what little she knew of Lind's life outside of work.

DANA'S LOVES

Whatever he was doing today, she couldn't help but wonder... and wish she knew more.

Part 3

Music Festival Weekend

Sometimes you don't know how much you need to breath
*   —until you're finally somewhere that lets you.*
*   And with someone who reminds you how.*
*   This wasn't just a weekend away.*
*   It was a reminder of who I was.*
*   Who I still wanted to be.*

Chapter 9

She wasn't wearing a bra

The sun was bright, the sky a flawless stretch of blue as Lind pulled into the parking lot of Sam's apartment complex. She was already outside, waiting at the curb with a small bag slung over her shoulder, her expression one of barely contained excitement. As soon as he parked, she walked up to the truck, grinning.

Lind stepped out, and without hesitation, they wrapped their arms around each other. Their easy familiarity had always been like this—comfortable, warm, effortless.

"You ready for the great escape?" Lind asked, his grin mirroring hers.

"More than ready," Sam said, sighing dramatically. "If I had to sit through one more Zoom call this week, I might've snapped."

Lind chuckled, pulling her into a tight hug. "Well then, allow me to rescue you." He gestured toward the truck. "Your chariot awaits."

She gave him a quick kiss, then tossed her bag into the backseat, climbed into the passenger side. She stretched her legs out with a contented sigh. Lind took a moment to appreciate her energy, how she had this way of making any moment feel like an adventure before it even started.

"I see you packed light," Lind noted, glancing at her single bag.

Sam grinned. "Took a shower before you got here, put on fresh clothes—the same ones I'll be wearing home on Sunday." She shot him a sideways glance, her smile mischievous. "Because between now and then? I'm wearing nothing. Two days of pure freedom."

Lind let out a satisfied hum. "Now that is what I've been looking forward to."

As they pulled out of the parking lot and onto the open road, the city slowly faded behind them, replaced by rolling hills and endless fields. Sam leaned back in her seat, slipping her sunglasses on as the warm breeze from the open window sent her loose brown hair whipping around her shoulders. Lind stole a glance at her—she was in her element, soaking in the moment.

She wore a loose-fitting, sky-blue button-up blouse. The fabric was light enough to show she wasn't wearing a bra. *Classic Sam*, he thought. Her linen shorts were just as effortlessly casual, and knowing her, she was probably commando.

She propped her bare feet on the dashboard. "So," she said, stretching lazily, "catch me up. What's new in the wonderful world of Lind?"

Lind adjusted his grip on the wheel, a small smile playing at his lips. "Not much, really. Work's been steady. Got the big summer reset done last week. Other than that..." He hesitated for half a second before adding, "There's someone I've been thinking about."

Sam perked up, interest flashing across her face. "Oh? Do tell."

"Her name is Dana," Lind admitted, glancing at her. "We've worked together for about nine months now. Nothing serious... yet, but she's interesting. Smart, funny, keeps me on my toes. She's also got this guarded thing going on, but not in a way that shuts you out—more like she's figuring out whether you're worth letting in."

Sam grinned. "I see. So you like her."

Lind gave a slight shrug. "I think I could. If she's open to it." He exhaled through his nose, considering his words. "But she's not like us. I don't think she's ever considered this kind of life."

Sam hummed, tapping her fingers idly on the armrest. "Traditional, huh?" She didn't sound dismissive, just thoughtful. "Could be a challenge. But if anyone can make someone rethink their whole worldview, it's you." She shot him a look. "Just don't rush it. People only change when they want to, not because someone else wants them to."

Lind nodded. "Yeah. We've both been through that, haven't we? I'm taking it slow. I just hope it's not too slow."

They drove in comfortable silence for a while, the fields passing in a blur of gold and green. After a few miles, Sam stretched again, crossing her arms over her stomach. "Enough about you. Let's talk about me."

Lind laughed. "Oh, by all means."

"Well, while you've been mooning over Dana, I've been busy too," she said. "Jake's been his usual charming self—took me paddle boarding last month. And Brian's been... well, Brian. We've been seeing more of each other lately."

Lind shot her a sidelong glance. "More than usual? I thought you two were on the every-other-week plan."

"We were," she said, shrugging. "Still are, kind of. But he's got it in his head to run a triathlon. So we train together, well, he trains, I'm mostly there as moral support."

Lind laughed. "You must be doing some kind of training with him, you're looking fit."

"You mean because my tummy is smaller?"

Lind chuckled. "You're not pulling me into that obvious trap."

Sam gave his arm a playful shove, then let her hand linger there for a second before pulling away. "You look like you need to take a step back and breathe Lind. Between Dana, work, and whatever else is swirling in that head of yours—when do you actually take time for yourself?"

Lind exhaled, the tension in his shoulders easing just at the thought of what lay ahead. "That's what this weekend's for. Live music, good company, no clothes, and no expectations."

Sam leaned her head back, a satisfied sigh escaping her lips. "Now that is the Lind I know." Then she shot him a playful glance. "Just don't let volleyball distract you. I plan on winning... again."

Lind let out a low laugh. "We'll see about that."

The conversation flowed easily after that—festival lineups, past trips, everything they were looking forward to this weekend. Before they knew it, they were almost there—two days of freedom just a few miles ahead.

As the entrance to the resort came into view, Lind inhaled deeply, feeling his whole body relax. He and Sam made time for each other every few months, and he never missed it. But these festival weekends—just the two of them, away from everything else—always felt different. This was exactly where he wanted to be, and who he wanted to be with.

Sam rolled down her window completely, letting the warm air wash over her face.

"Two days of music, sunshine, and zero responsibilities," she said with a dreamy sigh. "God, I love this place."

Lind smiled. He couldn't help but agree.

This weekend was about more than just music or freedom. It was about reconnecting—*with Sam. With himself.*

You're in Cabin 8 this time

As Lind pulled up to the gatehouse, the air shifted—warmer, lighter, full of anticipation. The hum of an electric guitar drifted from somewhere beyond the trees, blending with the soft chatter of festival-goers already settled in. A staff member, a woman in her forties with sun-kissed skin and a friendly smile, leaned into Sam's window.

"Hey, Michelle!" Sam greeted, her voice full of familiarity.

Michelle grinned. "Sam! Welcome back. You're in Cabin 8 this time—great spot near the main stage."

"Perfect," Sam replied, taking the map and wristbands Michelle handed over.

Lind nodded in thanks as they drove through the entrance. The road wound past groups of people in various states of undress. Some lounged by the pool. Others browsed vendor stalls. A few wandered the paths with towels over their shoulders, moving with unhurried ease. The air felt different here—free, unfiltered, stripped of everything that didn't matter.

***

Their cabin was small but comfortable. A sitting area, a kitchenette, a half bath, and a porch overlooking a winding dirt path leading to the festival grounds. Sam tossed her bag onto the bed and immediately started stripping down. Lind watched as she unbuttoned her lightweight blue blouse, slipping it from her shoulders before neatly hanging it in the small closet.

Then the shorts came off, confirming what Lind had already suspected.

"*Yep. Commando,*" he muttered to himself.

"What was that?" Sam asked, glancing at him over her shoulder, amusement lacing her voice.

"Oh, nothing," he said, shaking his head.

Sam rolled her eyes as she tossed her shorts into the top dresser drawer. She was already barefoot, sandals by the door. Lind, taking his cue, peeled off his own clothes, folding them casually before stretching his arms over his head.

Sam turned to him, hands on her hips. "You done admiring me? Are we ready to go, explore?"

Lind chuckled. "Lead the way."

She grinned as they slipped on their sandals and gave him a playful smack on the ass as she passed. "C'mon, slowpoke."

Throwing towels over their shoulders, they closed the door behind them.

This is what I live for

The festival grounds stretched out before them—a vibrant, sun-drenched space alive with movement. The stage sat at the lowest point of a natural amphitheater. Colorful banners fluttering in the breeze. The grassy hill surrounding it rose gradually, where clusters of people lounged on blankets or low-backed chairs, soaking up the music. Vendors lined the paths, selling everything from handmade jewelry to fresh fruit smoothies.

Sam sipped her drink as they wandered past vendor tents, pausing at one that sold sarongs and woven bracelets. "See? This is what life's about. No pretenses, no stress. Just good vibes and good company."

Lind let his gaze follow hers—toward a group sprawled across the grass, sharing drinks and stories, while a few others danced freely near the stage.

"It's a good reminder," he agreed. "Life doesn't have to be so damned complicated."

Sam bumped her shoulder against his. "Exactly. And it's even better with someone who gets it."

He chuckled, adjusting the towel draped over his shoulder. For the first time in months, he felt the weight of routine and responsibility lift. Here, in this space, there was no schedule to keep, no expectations to meet—just music, sun, and the kind of freedom that felt like breathing fresh air for the first time in too long.

***

The drive had made their first day shorter than they would've liked, but they still managed to squeeze in some water volleyball—where, unsurprisingly, Lind's team lost... again. Now, drying off near the pool, they lounged on their towels, sipping cold drinks and listening to the distant music drifting through the resort.

Sam glanced over at Lind, grabbing his arm to get his attention. "Are we ready to watch some bands now?"

He smiled at her—wet hair pulled back, excitement in her eyes. She looked... beautiful. "Let's go."

As the sun dipped below the tree line, the festival grounds softened under the golden hues of dusk. They swung by the cabin just long enough to grab a blanket and clean towels before heading to the music.

Most of the time, they preferred their low-backed chairs, but tonight, lying out under the stars felt right. They found a spot halfway up the grassy slope—close enough for a good view. Lind spread the blanket, rolling their towels into makeshift pillows.

The second band had just finished and the third was tuning up. A folk music band. The warm evening air felt like a comfortable blanket. Around them, people lay in pairs or small groups, chatting in quiet tones, their laughter carried by the breeze.

Sam stretched out beside him, propping herself up on one elbow. "This," she murmured, gazing at the stage, as she turned her hand in the air, "this is what I live for."

Lind glanced at her—the way her skin glowed under the fading light, the way she looked so at peace here. He inhaled deeply, letting the crisp scent of the woods mix with the distant aroma of campfires and festival food.

Yeah. He lived for this too. Not just the music or the break from work—but for *her*. These weekends weren't often, but they reset him in a way nothing else did.

Chapter 10

What about me

The music swelled gently, its rhythm syncing with the soft hum of voices scattered across the hillside. The air was cooling, a breeze feeling good against their skin. Lind exhaled slowly, the last remnants of tension slipping away.

Sam, stretched out beside him, caught his eye and smiled—a slow, contented look on her face. She reached over, her fingers skimmed lightly over his stomach, tracing circles in his chest hair.

"You look like you're finally relaxing," she murmured.

Lind grinned, tilting his head toward her. "I think I am. This place has that effect."

Sam's fingers trailed lower—playful, familiar. "What about me?"

His grin deepened. "You often have the opposite effect on me." His sheepish tone gave away his meaning as he watched her hand continue its slow, absent-minded exploration.

Sam laughed, low and soft, before rolling onto her back, eyes drifting closed as she soaked in the music. Lind reached for her hand, intertwining their fingers. The warmth of their connection, easy and unspoken.

She pulled his hand onto her stomach, resting her other hand on top. The gesture was simple, but the intimacy of it—wrapped in the music, the fading sunlight, the ease of their environment—reminded him of how this woman had always made him feel... cherished.

As the folk band played its final notes, a ripple of applause spread through the crowd like a gentle wave. Lind turned onto his side, meeting Sam's gaze as she did the same.

"Time to go?" she asked, her voice quiet.

He nodded. After a soft, unhurried kiss, they helped each other up, draping their towels over their shoulders. Sam shook the grass from the blanket while Lind folded it up, then slid his arm around her waist as they made their way back to the cabin, her arm tightening around his in return.

The air had cooled by the time they reached the porch, the distant hum of festival sounds muffled by the trees. Sam leaned against the railing, her hair tousled from the breeze, her face serene. The glow of the porch lights reflected in her eyes.

She glanced at Lind, smiling. "You know, this weekend is exactly what I needed." She nudged him lightly. "Thanks for driving."

Lind leaned beside her, their bare shoulders brushing. "Thanks for inviting me. I mean, we do this every year, but... thanks just the same."

They shared a quiet laugh.

Sam bumped his shoulder with hers, grinning. "Who else would I invite?"

Lind grinned. "I don't know. I can think of at least three other people."

She chuckled, shaking her head, but a thought occurred to her as her laughter faded. She ran her fingers along the porch railing, as she considered how to voice it.

"This is our place," she murmured. "Or at least... it has been."

Lind's expression shifted, sensing where her mind had gone. "Yeah, it is," he admitted. "I always look forward to it."

Her gaze softened. "What happens if Dana works out?"

He exhaled—considering this idea for the first time. "If she ever becomes a big enough part of my world to let her into all of it... she might run for the hills, once she knows everything."

Sam tilted her head, watching him carefully. "You know that's not going to happen," she said, her voice firm but gentle. "And if you don't, I do." She let the words sink in before adding, "There's nothing about you not to love. I know because I've been doing it for years."

Lind's throat tightened, a silent storm of emotion rising in him as he smiled knowingly at her. Meeting her gaze, he spoke softly, "If it works out... I'll have to tell her about you—about all of this," he said, spinning a hand in the air. After a pause, he added, "If it works out... I won't give either of you up."

Sam turned to him, pressing her lips to his, her body warm against his. He wrapped his arms around her, holding her close. She hugged him harder, her skin against his, their bodies fitting together as naturally as always.

The night stretched on, bearing witness to something deeper than love, something more than friendship. A solid—unshakable bond.

Their kisses were unhurried

Sam sat on the edge of the bed, one leg curled beneath her, the other on the floor, her hair spilling over her bare shoulders. Her smile was easy, knowing. She faced Lind as he leaned back against the headboard, his posture relaxed but his eyes and his mind taking her in completely, a hand on her knee.

Damn. He thought.

He admired her—not just for how she looked, but for the way she was. So open. So her. Unapologetic, sensual, completely comfortable in her own skin. He really did love her. Maybe not in the way he once thought love was supposed to look, but in a way that mattered just as much, maybe more.

Sam tilted her head. "You know, moments like this..." She trailed her fingers lightly over his arm, her touch warm and familiar. "I could stay here forever."

Lind smiled, matching her quiet tone. "I think the company has everything to do with that."

Her grin deepened as she moved closer, her hand skimming down his chest before resting on his thigh. Their eyes met, the air between them charged.

Lind reached up, tucking a strand of hair behind her ear, then let his fingers drift lower—over her lips, trailing down her neck, slipping between her breasts before returning to rest lightly against his stomach.

Sam's breath hitched softly as she leaned in, pressing her forehead gently against his chest before looking back up at him.

She leaned in, her lips finding his. Their kisses were unhurried and deep—the way they always started. Her fingertips tracing slowly down his chest, her nails barely grazing his skin before continuing lower.

Lind exhaled through his nose, his muscles tightening beneath her touch.

Sam's breath was warm against his skin as she murmured, "You always take such good care of me."

Her hand found him, wrapping around him with practiced ease, her grip firm yet gentle. With a slow roll of her wrist, she worked him, watching his face, reading every reaction. He knew this rhythm between them well—knew how she reveled in the way his body responded to her, how much she loved pulling those subtle groans from him.

She leaned down, her tongue flicked across the sensitive tip, spreading the thin layer of lubricant over his head with slow, playful movements. Lind groaned, his fingers slipping into her hair as his hips involuntarily tilted toward her.

"Fuck, Sam," he muttered, his voice roughened by restraint.

Reaching over to the nightstand without breaking their connection, she retrieved a condom, tearing the wrapper open with her teeth before pulling back just enough to roll it down over him.

She smiled against him, her lips grazing his length before she moved up his body, pressing her mouth to his. Their kiss deepened, heat pooling between them as Lind took control, rolling them over with ease.

Her legs wrapped around him, her hips adjusting to help him find her.

She had caught the way his eyes noticed—how he'd seen her glistening before they even started. It turned her on even more—being that open and honest with him, that playful and hungry for him.

Her quiet moans filled the space between them—soft, insistent. The sounds that had always been theirs. They moved together in a rhythm they knew by heart, built over years of trust, comfort, and mutual affection.

The urgency was there—raw and undeniable—but beneath it was something deeper. Stronger. A connection unshakable by... well, anything.

Lind pressed his forehead to hers, breathing her in, feeling her pulse race beneath his fingertips. Her hands gripped his shoulders, nails biting into his skin as pleasure coiled tight inside her.

"Lind—" Sam's voice was a whisper as she tipped over the edge, her body shuddering beneath him.

His own release followed a few moments later. His body stiffened as he buried himself deep one last time, a low groan escaping as pleasure surged through him.

With arms and legs, she pulled him down onto her, wanting all of him, his full weight.

For a long moment, neither of them moved. Just the rise and fall of their breaths, heartbeats slowing together.

When Lind finally shifted, Sam let go. He rolled onto his back, peeled off the condom, dropped it to the floor, then turned back to her, pulling her in close against him.

Sam nestled into his side, her fingers tracing patterns across his chest. The night pressed in around them, warm—content—quiet except for the distant hum of someone's music drifting through the trees.

Lind exhaled, his voice low and steady. "I don't take any of this for granted, you know."

Sam's lips curved into a soft smile against his skin. "Neither do I."

Her body fit easily against his, her breathing evening out as she lifted her leg over him, making sure her thigh covered him. She kissed his chest one more time as sleep began to claim her.

Lind stared at the ceiling for a long moment, running his hand across her thigh—his thoughts drifting—not just to Sam, but to Dana.

The two women existed in completely different spaces in his life, yet both mattered in ways he hadn't fully sorted out.

He tightened his hold on Sam just slightly, grounding himself in the moment. There was no rush. No pressure. Just here. Just now.

And for now, that was enough.

Chapter 11

I'm Karen, and this is my husband, Steve

The morning sun filtered through the trees as Lind and Sam walked from the showers back to their cabin, damp towels slung over their shoulders. The crisp air carried the faint scent of pine and sunscreen, though the heat of the day was already creeping in.

Sam tossed her towel over the railing and shook the water from her hair, turning to Lind, she said. "I think you missed a spot on my shoulder."

Lind grinned, reaching over to run his fingers across her damp skin. "I'll make up for it later. Anywhere you need sunscreen, just say the word."

Sam arched a brow, giving him a mischievous grin. "Oh, you know I will."

They grabbed fresh towels and headed out again.

With a soft laugh, they made their way to the café, the aroma of coffee and fresh pastries already drifting toward them. The outdoor seating area was alive with energy—people chatting, the occasional burst of laughter.

After grabbing their breakfasts, they found a table under a wide umbrella. Sam draped her towel over the chair before sitting, the gesture as practiced as breathing. Lind followed suit, stretching his legs out beneath the table.

Nearby, a couple about their age sat with coffee, speaking in low tones. The petite redhead caught Sam's eye and smiled warmly, leaning slightly toward them.

"Hi, I'm Karen. This is my husband, Steve. First time here?"

Sam smiled and gestured toward Lind. "We've been coming for years. Love the music, love the vibe. This is my dearest friend, Lind."

Lind nodded politely. "Nice to meet you both."

Steve grinned. "We love this festival too. Don't get here as much as we'd like, but this weekend—great weather, great music."

The conversation flowed easily, touching on the festival lineup, favorite bands, and activities for the day.

"Are you doing the morning yoga?" Karen asked, eyes bright. "I heard it's amazing."

Sam considered it. "Might check it out. What about volleyball later?"

Steve nodded. "Water volleyball in the afternoon. The music usually pulls most people away, so it's a nice, relaxed game."

Sam grinned at Lind, who rolled his eyes. "We'll see if we can make it."

As the conversation continued, Karen glanced between them. "Where are you two staying?"

"We've got a cabin," Sam said, taking a sip of her coffee. "We always book early."

Karen sighed. "Lucky! We were too late for cabins this year, so we're in our motor home over in the campground."

"Not a bad setup, though," Steve added. "Plenty of space, and we're right near the showers."

Sam nodded in approval. "That's a good spot. Some of the sites can be a trek."

By the time breakfast wrapped up, Karen and Sam had exchanged knowing smiles—an unspoken invitation exchanged between them.

As Lind and Sam walked away, she nudged him playfully. "I like them. Might see if they're up for more than just volleyball later."

"Should I be jealous or relieved?"

Sam's laugh was light and easy. "Both, maybe. I'll let you know."

Lind chuckled, shaking his head as they made their way toward the walking trails, the late morning sun filtering through the trees.

Sam. Hiking. Naked. He grinned. *This was shaping up to be a good weekend.*

I'm taking it slow

The dirt path wound through the woods, dappled sunlight filtering through the trees as Lind and Sam walked side by side. The festival's hum had faded into the background, replaced by birdsong and the crunch of gravel beneath their shoes.

Sam glanced over at him. "You've been quieter than usual this morning. Something on your mind, or just soaking in the peace and quiet?"

Lind chuckled softly, adjusting the strap of his water bottle. "A little of both, I guess. Work... Dana... you."

Sam grinned. "Work how? Annoying coworkers, or is it really about Dana?"

Lind hesitated just a beat too long, and Sam's grin turned knowing.

"Ah, Dana it is," she said, tilting her head. "Trying to figure her out? Because at this rate, you'll be ready for a coffee date by next year."

Lind let out a short laugh, shaking his head. "I'm taking it slow for a reason. She's... different. I don't want to screw things up by rushing in."

Sam nodded, but her voice was firm. "I get it—you don't want to scare her off. But overthinking isn't going to help. She's not psychic, Lind. She won't know unless you tell her. And you don't have to dump everything at once. Just... be you."

Lind exhaled, rubbing the back of his neck. "Yeah. It's just... I don't know if she'll ever be ready for all of me. The nudism, the open relationships—it's a lot for most people."

Sam shrugged. "Maybe. But you won't know unless you give her the chance. If she's a smart girl, she'll at least listen. And you don't have to start with the heavy stuff—ask her to breakfast. Casual, no pressure."

Lind nodded, considering her words.

When they reached a clearing in the woods, they paused, taking in the sweeping view of the resort below.

Not a trio anymore

After a moment of quiet, Lind shifted the conversation. "Enough about Dana. Tell me more about your trio."

Sam paused. "Not a trio anymore. Rick and I called it quits a few months ago. Amicable, but it was time. So it's just me, Jake, and Brian now."

Lind raised an eyebrow. "You've been seeing Brian almost as long as me?"

Sam nodded. "Seven years now. He's solid—practical, funny, always shows up when he says he will. We see each other every couple of weeks. It's comfortable, easy."

Lind shot her a curious glance. "But?"

Sam sighed. "But, like I said, he's training for a triathlon. He's got me biking with him at least once a week."

"I thought you were mostly there for moral support?"

She grimaced. "Yeah, well, biking with him is how I support him."

Lind laughed. "I'm picturing you, fully decked out in spandex, cursing every hill."

"You know it." Sam chuckled.

He tilted his head at her. "Ever think about making it more serious?"

Sam considered for a moment before shaking her head. "We've talked about it. But Brian's not looking for a primary, and honestly, I'm not sure that would work for me either."

She paused. "I think that's why we work. We care about each other, but there's no pressure to be something we're not."

Lind nodded, taking that in before shifting gears. "And Jake? How's he fitting into your life these days?"

Sam's grin widened. "Jake's... Jake. My social butterfly. Always planning something—dinner parties, trivia nights, you name it. He makes every moment feel like an event."

Lind raised an eyebrow. "Sounds exhausting."

Sam laughed. "You'd think, but he balances me out. He's spontaneous, keeps things light. Plus, the guy can cook like nobody's business. Last week, he made this five-course meal just because he was bored."

"Let me guess—you volunteered to be the taste tester?"

Sam nodded, grinning wider. "Obviously. And let me tell you, his tiramisu? Worth every calorie."

Lind studied her for a moment. "So where does Jake see things going?"

Sam hesitated, then shrugged. "Jake doesn't do long-term plans. He's in the moment. And that's what I like about him—he's just... fun. Easy."

Lind nodded. "Sounds like a good balance to Brian."

"Exactly." Sam smiled. "Brian's my rock. Jake's my spark. They're completely different, but they both fit in my life in their own way."

Lind's gaze softened as he looked at her. "Sounds like it's working for you."

Sam nodded, then turned the question back on him. "What about Dana? Think you'd ever want that kind of balance with her?"

Lind paused, considering. "Not quite. With Dana... I want something different. Something more permanent. But it has to include others—especially you. There's too much love not to share."

Sam grinned. "I can vouch for that."

She playfully shoved his shoulder as they reached another clearing. Below them, the resort stretched out in the midday sun, the sounds of festival life drifting up from below.

She nudged him again. "If she's half as smart as you say, she'll figure it out. But only if you speed things up, Mr. Molasses."

Lind shook his head, chuckling. "Yeah, I know."

Been there, done that

By lunchtime, they were back at the café, grabbing a quick meal before heading to the pool area. The sun was high, and the water shimmered invitingly.

Sam pulled her hair into a loose bun as they walked toward the volleyball pool. "You playing this time, or just spectating?"

Lind rolled his eyes. "You dragged me into it yesterday, remember?"

"Dragged? Please. You loved it."

Lind sighed dramatically. "Fine. One more game. But if my team loses again, I'm blaming you."

Sam grinned wickedly as they jumped into the pool, joining the volley ballers.

As they warmed up, Lind glanced around the pool. Sam moved through the crowd like she belonged here—confident, relaxed, already tossing jokes with the guy beside her. He smiled. Yeah. She always knew how to make herself at home.

She glanced back across the net, catching Lind in the serving position.

"You're going down again, buddy," she called across the net, splashing at him.

Lind just murmured. "Been there, done that."

With a wink, he served the ball, and the game was on. Laughter erupted as quickly as the match began, the banter flying as fast as the volleyball.

I'm working on my all-over tan

The weekend was unfolding exactly as it should—good music, good company, and just enough playfulness to keep things interesting.

The rhythmic thrum of bass lines drifted through the festival grounds as Lind and Sam returned from their midday activities, the sun warm on their skin.

Lind unfolded their chairs near the stage, planting their shade umbrella firmly into the soft ground. The crowd had grown, festival-goers scattered in clusters—some sprawled on blankets, others swaying to the music, their movements unhurried. Effortless.

Sam stretched out, letting the warm air kiss her skin as a contented sigh escaped her lips. "This is perfect. The music, the company, and the whole weekend... ours."

Lind tilted his head back against his chair, letting the breeze wash over him. "Hard to beat. Plus, I'm working on my all-over tan."

Sam chuckled, watching as Lind stretched, arms above his head, utterly at ease.

***

As the sun dipped lower, casting long shadows across the grass, Sam's gaze flickered to a familiar pair in the crowd. She motioned toward Karen and Steve, lounged a few spots away, sipping from insulated cups. Their relaxed demeanor mirroring the easy comfort Sam and Lind always enjoyed.

She got up from her chair, tossing her towel over one shoulder. "I'm going to say hi," she declared, a mischievous glimmer in her eyes.

After a while, Sam returned, a curious grin playing at her lips. "They invited us to join them. Karen's into girls, so good for me," she said, her grin widening.

Lind chuckled in response. "And you want to join them?" he said gently.

Sam shrugged lightly. "If you're okay with it. If not, no big deal."

Lind's tone was warm as he reassured her, "Go ahead. I'll be here when you get back."

With that, Sam leaned down to give him a soft kiss before heading back to Karen and Steve. They began making their way toward the campground.

Lind watched them depart, a quiet smile tugging at his lips as he leaned back in his chair.

The next hour unfolded in a pleasant haze of music and distant laughter. Lind observed the ebb and flow of the festival—the dancers moving with wild abandon, couples nestled together in quiet intimacy, and groups of friends sharing snacks and stories.

In that gentle, carefree atmosphere, the bond he shared with Sam felt as enduring and natural as the fading light of day.

This place always reminded him of the best parts of being human. The absence of pretense, the acceptance, the simple joy of connection. Insulated from the outside world.

Nearby, an older couple caught his attention. They stood hand in hand, swaying gently as a slow rhythm pulsing through the speakers. Naked like the rest of them, they moved together with the ease of decades spent in each other's arms.

Lind felt something stir inside him. Admiration, maybe. Or longing. The kind of connection that didn't demand but simply existed. Steady and unquestioned.

His gaze drifted toward the campground. He knew where Sam was, and with whom. A brief flicker of something—nostalgia, curiosity—ran through him, but he let it pass. She was in her element. She was happy. And that made him happy, too.

A warm breeze stirred through the crowd, carrying the faint scent of grass and sunscreen, campfires and pine. Lind closed his eyes and inhaled deeply, sinking into the moment—the sound of laughter. The pulse of the music. The freedom of the night.

Chapter 12

You wanna dance with me

By the time Sam returned, the festival grounds were bathed in nightfall. She dropped into the chair beside him, stretching her legs out in front of her with an easy, satisfied sigh.

Lind glanced over, showing her a small grin. "Good time?"

Sam grinned back. "Good time."

Lind tilted his head. "Safe time?"

She rolled her eyes playfully. "Always safe. You know that."

Lind chuckled, running a hand through his hair. "How good of a time?"

Sam leaned closer, her grin wicked. "Twice."

Lind barked out a laugh. "That's the Sam I know and love."

They lapsed into comfortable silence, fingers interlaced, the last few songs of the night rolling over them like waves. After a while, Lind shifted, glancing at Sam.

"You wanna dance with me?"

She turned to him, eyebrows raised. "Thought you'd never ask."

Lind stood and gently pulled her up. Together, they wandered toward the stage, weaving through the small crowd that had gathered to dance.

The first few songs were fast, energetic. Sam moved like she belonged to the music, her body fluid, confident, while Lind... well, he tried.

"Frog in a blender," Sam teased between twirls.

Lind snorted. "I'll have you know, I am an excellent blender."

When the tempo slowed, Sam slipped easily into his arms, molding against him as they swayed to the gentle rhythm.

ind loved all the things they did together—hiking, swimming, late-night talks—but this? This was his favorite. Holding her, feeling the warmth of her skin against his, moving together like they had done a hundred times before.

Halfway through the second slow song, Sam shifted, turning her back to him, guiding his hands around her waist. They rocked together in an easy rhythm, but the way she pressed against him—her hips shifting, her sly grin evident even without looking—was very much not innocent.

Lind groaned under his breath, then abruptly spun her back around. His hands lower on her back holding her tight against him to hide what she had begun to do to him.

Sam tilted her chin up at him, her expression pure mischief.

He grinned. "Nice try, woman. But we'll have to save that for later."

She laughed, pressing a quick kiss to his cheek as they moved through the last few beats of the song.

Good music, good sex, good friends

They stayed through the final set, letting the music carry them deeper into the night. By the time they returned to their cabin, the air had cooled, the fire pits were burning low, festival goers turning in, and the grounds were quieting down.

Sam wrapped a towel around her shoulders as they stepped onto the porch, stretching before she opened the door. Inside, the space was warm, dimly lit by the glow of the lamp.

Lind pulled the blankets back and Sam flopped onto the bed first, rolling onto her side to watch as Lind followed her and pulled the blankets up over both of them.

"We did good today," she murmured.

Lind chuckled. "What do you mean?"

Sam reached over, her hand resting lightly on his chest, her fingers moving without thinking. "Good music, good sex, good friends, good volleyball. We covered all the essentials."

Lind nodded, his hand covering hers, his thumb brushing over her skin. "And tomorrow?"

She grinned, nudging closer. "More of the same."

Her fingers slid lower, playful and slow, trailing across his skin savoring the feel of him. It was for her own pleasure more than his—just needing to touch, to stay close.

Lind mirrored her pace, his fingertips drifting along the crease of her thigh with quiet affection. Not urgent. Just present.

Their bodies moved lazily, the warmth between them still simmering, but the day's activities had finally begun to claim them.

Gradually, their words faded, replaced by the steady rhythm of their breathing.

Laying together in the hush of the night, Lind let himself relax completely. He didn't need to overthink, didn't need to plan or analyze or second-guess. Here, in this space, with Sam in his arms, things just were.

And that, he thought as sleep claimed him, was enough.

Let's go shower

The soft glow of dawn filtered through the curtains, casting warm streaks of gold across the bed. The air was quiet, save for the slowing rhythm of their breathing. She straddled him, their bodies still joined, her fingers light against his chest as the last wave passed through them—slow, final, fading. The sounds of their pleasure a distant echo.

A lazy, satisfied smile on her lips as she looked down at him. Lind's hands rested on her hips, thumbs caressing her skin, melting into the feel of her.

She leaned forward, pressing a slow kiss to his lips before shifting away. Rising from the bed, she moved with confidence—a playful, mischievous look on her face as her fingers trailed down his stomach.

After holding and stroking him for a bit, she removed the condom, rolling it off carefully before discarding it into the trash can near the dresser. Turning back to Lind, she cupped his face, her thumb tracing his cheek as she kissed him again—softer this time, a whisper of affection.

"Let's go shower and grab some breakfast."

Lind exhaled a slow breath, still catching up with her pace, but he grinned. "Lead the way."

She tossed a towel over her shoulder and walked toward the door and paused. Lind stretched, then swung his legs over the side of the bed, following her with the unhurried ease of someone who had nowhere to be—except exactly where he was.

***

The resort was quiet, most guests still asleep or slowly stirring. As Lind and Sam made the short walk to the showers, the only sound was the rustling of trees in the morning breeze.

Her towel draped over her shoulder, Lind, more strategic, held his in front of him, covering the evidence of their morning activities.

When they reached the showers, they found them empty. Lind turned on the water, testing the temperature, while Sam hung up her towel and stepped inside. Steam rolled around them as they moved through the routine—washing each other's backs, shampooing each other's hair—never in a rush.

By the time they stepped out, drying off, the last traces of their morning had faded. Lind ran a towel over his head, shaking out his damp hair, while Sam stretched, enjoying the cool air against her skin.

The Sunday dilemma, right

The café buzzed with soft chatter, the aroma of coffee and fresh pastries drifting through the air. Lind and Sam chose a table outside under a large umbrella, plates piled with eggs, fruit, and toast.

A festival staff member walked by, posting signs in the eating areas. The list of bands for the day was short—one set at eleven, another at one.

Sam tilted her head, reading the sign. "Looks like a light day for music."

Lind nodded, sipping his coffee. "Makes sense. Everyone's winding down by Sunday."

She took a thoughtful bite of toast. "So, what do you think? Stay for one more set, or head out after breakfast and get a head start on the week?"

Lind leaned back, letting the warm breeze wash over him. The idea of cutting the weekend short didn't sit right. But neither did scrambling to prepare for Monday.

"Depends. Do we squeeze every last drop out of this weekend or leave before we're rushing to unpack and get ready for the week?"

"I'm torn," she said, "part of me wants to stay for the first band—just two more hours of sunshine and music. But the practical part of me knows I'll hate myself later when I'm doing laundry at ten tonight."

Nearby, a couple at the next table overheard and chimed in.

"The Sunday dilemma, right?" The man chuckled. "We always leave after breakfast. And every year, we regret it."

Sam groaned, dramatically resting her forehead on her palm. "You're not helping my decision-making here!"

The woman grinned. "Just saying—you can't take the sunshine and bands home with you."

Lind and Sam exchanged glances, both smiling at the truth of it.

Same time next year

Back at their cabin, Lind folded their towels while Sam grabbed her bag, listening as the distant hum of the first band warming up drifted in through the window.

Sam paused at the door, not ready for it to be over. "Alright, here's the compromise—we'll stay for the first band. One set, then we head out. That way, we get a little more time here but still get home at a decent hour."

Lind nodded approvingly. "Sounds like a plan. You know I'm all about balance."

Sam snorted. "Is that what we're calling it now?"

"What else would we call it?"

"I don't know," she said, "procrastination?"

They laughed, sharing a quick kiss before stepping outside. After dropping off their bags at the truck, they grabbed their chairs and headed back to the festival grounds.

The festival had mellowed. The crowd was smaller, the energy softer. They found a sunny spot near the stage, covering their chairs with towels and sank into them.

The music rolled over them, a last gift from the weekend. Lind stretched his legs out, crossing his arms behind his head, while Sam sat with her eyes closed, soaking in every last second.

As the band wrapped up their set, Lind checked the time and glanced over at Sam, who hadn't moved.

"Alright, sunshine addict. Time's up."

She sighed dramatically, but there was no protest. "Fine, fine. But only because you're driving, and—you know—because we have to."

They gathered their things, waving goodbye to a few familiar faces as they made their way back to the truck. Near the parking lot, they spotted Karen and Steve pulling out.

Karen leaned out the window, waving them down. "Hold up!"

Steve braked, and he and Karen got out, crossing the gravel to meet them.

Sam grinned as Karen caught her by the waist and kissed her—Karen's fingers trailing down Sam's back.

Steve and Lind simply exchanged a look—one of those silent, knowing grins between two men who understood exactly how lucky they were.

Sam gave Steve a hug and a quick kiss before stepping back. "See you next year?"

Karen winked. "Wouldn't miss it."

With final goodbyes, Lind and Sam pulled on their clothes and shoes, and climbed into the truck.

As they drove toward the main road, Sam rested her hand lightly on Lind's arm.

"Thanks for this weekend. I needed it."

Lind grinned, eyes still on the road. "Me too. Same time next year?"

Sam nodded without hesitation. "Absolutely. I'll call the resort when I get home and book a cabin before they're gone."

Lind chuckled. "Smart woman."

The highway stretched ahead, pulling them gently back toward the real world.

But the weekend stayed with them—a pocket of sun-drenched freedom, a reminder of the way life could be when stripped down to the essentials.

And as they settled into the drive, both of them knew: no matter what else changed, they would always find their way back here.

Part 4

I had myself figured out.
I knew what I wanted.
Lind seemed to fit the bill—
with his quiet steadiness,
his unexpected laughter,
his seeing past the version of myself I showed the world.
But Lind was deeper—complicated in ways I wasn't
prepared for.
I didn't know if I could live in his world.
I only knew he made me want to try.

Chapter 13

Look who's back

At the morning meeting, all eyes drifted to Lind. Dana nodded, and he returned it. A quiet acknowledgment, the first of many.

But no one asked—yet.

At first break Lind sat down in his usual seat in the break room, the scent of reheated pasta and over-brewed coffee clinging to the air. He had barely taken a bite of his sandwich when Pete leaned in, eyes sharp with curiosity.

"Well, look who's back," Pete said, grinning. "How was your big three-day weekend? Get into anything exciting?"

Lind smiled slightly, already anticipating the usual round of questioning. "It was good—just a little time out of town. Went to a music festival."

Lisa looked up from across the table, tilting her head. "A festival? What kind of music?"

He kept his tone casual. "A mix of everything. It's more about the atmosphere than the music though."

Pete chuckled. "Let me guess—camping out, you were roughing it weren't you?"

"Not quite." Lind took a sip of water, playing along. "Stayed in a cabin—I like my creature comforts when available."

From the other side of the table, Dana shifted slightly, her attention fully on him now. "Sounds like a nice getaway," she said, her voice easy, but with something thoughtful underneath. "Who'd you go with?"

He glanced at her, measuring his answer carefully. "Just a friend. We've been going for years."

There was a beat of silence—small, but noticeable. He could feel Dana processing his words, weighing them. He kept his focus on his meal, though he could see the faint curiosity sparking behind her eyes.

"What festival is it?" she asked after a pause.

He shrugged like it wasn't anything of consequence. "Small one, out near Cypress. Same crowd every year. Good people."

Dana tilted her head, watching him for a moment longer before letting it go. But Lisa, never one to miss an opportunity, leaned in. "A friend, huh? Not a special friend?"

Lind grinned, unfazed. "All my friends are special, Lisa. I'm just lucky that way."

Pete laughed. "Man of mystery strikes again. What's next on your adventure list?"

Lind leaned back, smiling faintly. "Catching up on laundry after a long weekend. Exciting, I know."

The group laughed, and just like that, the conversation drifted to other topics. Even as Dana joined in, Lind could tell she wasn't done thinking about his answers. She wasn't one to push unnecessarily, but when she wanted to know something, she had a way of circling back at just the right moment.

So, Sam is a woman

A week passed before she brought it up again.

Lind was rearranging a seasonal display when Dana joined him. For a while, they worked in silence—both focused, both comfortable in the quiet.

Then, without looking at him, she said, "I've been thinking about something you said last week."

He glanced at her, curious. "Something from the morning meeting?"

"No," she said flatly as she turned to face him. "In the lunchroom—when Pete was giving you a bad time about your weekend."

Lind let out a small chuckle. "Ah. 'Man of mystery' and all that."

Dana gave a small, self-conscious laugh. "Yeah, that. But seriously, you were so... vague. You said all your friends are special, but it made me wonder if *that* friend was, I don't know, a little more special than the rest."

He hesitated, just for a second. Not because he didn't want to answer, but because he felt the weight behind the question.

"She's someone important to me," he said finally. "We've been close for a long time."

Dana's gaze sharpened, searching his face. "So, Sam is a woman?"

He nodded. "I didn't say it was Sam, but yeah."

Dana grinned at him knowingly. "Is she... like a girlfriend?"

Lind set a box down and exhaled slowly, choosing his words carefully. "Not exactly. It's... a little more complicated than that."

Dana stopped stacking for a moment, her full attention now on him. "Complicated... how?"

He met her eyes. He could tell she wasn't judging—just trying to understand.

"It's not that I don't want to share," he said, his voice softer now. "It's just... unconventional. I try not to... overwhelm people with too much info at once."

Dana's brow furrowed slightly. "Unconventional?"

Lind could see she wasn't going to let this go. He hesitated, then let out a breath. "Sam and I care about each other. But we've always had an understanding that our relationship isn't... exclusive. We both value freedom and honesty more than traditional labels."

For a long moment, Dana didn't say anything. She picked up a small item from the display, turning it over in her hands like she was working through his words.

"So... you're both okay with that? With seeing other people?"

He nodded. "Yeah. It works for us. It feels right for the way we see the world. We don't believe love or connection has to fit into a box."

Dana set the item down, her face unreadable—then a small smile started to form.

"That's... interesting," she murmured. "I don't think I've ever known anyone who thinks like that."

"It's not something that comes up in casual conversation, that's for sure. But even so, you'd be surprised how common it actually is."

Dana tilted her head. "What do you mean?"

"I'd be happy to go over the facts and percentages sometime," he said, amusement flickering in his voice. "It's just how I've lived my life for some time now."

She laughed softly, shaking her head. "Okay, so this weekend... was it part of that? Your... not-fitting-into-a-box thing?"

"Yeah, you could say that," he admitted. "The music festival was just a chance to relax and enjoy the company of like-minded people. It's a space where people can be themselves, without judgment."

Dana's eyes flickered with curiosity. "You're still a bit of a mystery, you know."

Lind smiled deeply. "Maybe. But I like getting to know people slowly—it's less overwhelming that way. For both sides."

"Do you and Sam see each other all the time?"

"No," he said, "not often, but consistently."

She grinned. "You're still dodging a little. But don't think I won't ask more questions later."

"I'd be disappointed if you didn't."

And for the first time, Lind wondered—*hoped*—Dana's curiosity about his world was more than just friendly interest.

Where would I fit... if I let myself

As Dana walked toward her car at the end of her shift, her conversation with Lind replayed in her mind. The afternoon sun beat down on the parking lot, but she barely noticed—too wrapped up in the weight of his words.

Unconventional.

That's how he'd described it. It wasn't a word she heard often—definitely not in reference to relationships. But the way Lind had talked about it... it didn't feel wrong. It didn't feel sleazy or weird. It just felt... *honest.*

She unlocked her car but didn't get in right away, resting her hand on the door handle as she stared across the lot. A steady hum of distant traffic filled the silence.

"Sam and I care about each other."

That part had been obvious. The way he said her name—it wasn't flippant or casual. There was something real there, something steady. *But not exclusive*—that was the part she kept circling back to. *How do you care about someone and not want them all to yourself?*

She leaned back against the car, arms crossed, the warmth of the metal pressing against her through her jeans.

"Freedom and honesty more than traditional labels."

That's what he'd said. And she had to admit—she'd never met anyone who thought like that. Everyone she'd ever dated had been about exclusivity. Or at least, they claimed to be. And look where that had gotten her.

Her thoughts flickered to Al, her high school sweetheart, then to Larry, her last serious boyfriend. Both relationships had their flaws, but mostly, she remembered the weight of expectations. The invisible box they'd tried to squeeze each other into.

Is that what he means by freedom? No expectations. No disappointments?

She exhaled, shaking her head like it might clear the thought away, but the feeling stayed. A pang of something she couldn't quite name. *Curiosity? Envy?* Maybe both.

And then there was the festival. The way Lind had spoken about it—carefully, like he was holding something back.

What kind of music festival is so... freeing? And why do I want to know more?

Finally, she slid into the driver's seat, leaving the door open for a moment. The air inside was stifling from the afternoon sun, thick and unmoving. She didn't start the engine right away.

I'm beginning to see that there's a lot more to Lind than meets the eye.

She'd thought she had him figured out—quiet, dependable, a little reserved. But now? Now she wasn't so sure. And that uncertainty was doing something to her—her curiosity was piqued in a way she hadn't felt in a long time.

What makes him tick? What's his world really like? And where does Sam fit into all of this?

And then, deeper still, another question surfaced before she could stop it.

Where would I fit... if I let myself?

She turned the key in the ignition, the low rumble of the engine grounding her. The AC blasted hot air at first before finally cooling down. As she drove home, the air inside the car grew cooler—but her thoughts didn't.

They kept circling, looping back to Lind, back to that conversation.

It wasn't just curiosity anymore.

It was interest. The kind that made her want to ask more questions. The kind that made her wonder what else Lind wasn't saying.

And why she wanted him to say it.

This puzzle that is Lind

The store was busy, but the seasonal display Dana and Lind were working on was tucked into a quieter section, away from the worst of the noise. Stacking boxes, shifting products into place—it was the kind of mindless task that made conversation flow easily—if you had the right company.

Dana glanced over at Lind as she placed a new box onto the shelf. "So... I've been meaning to ask you something."

Lind didn't look up from adjusting a row of neatly arranged items. "Oh? Should I be worried?"

Dana shook her head, a smile tugging at her mouth. "No, nothing like that." She glanced his way, her voice dipping into something almost playful. "It's just... you're kind of a puzzle, you know?"

At that, Lind turned his head, curiosity flickering in his gaze. "A puzzle, huh? Not sure if that's a compliment or a critique."

Dana grinned, brushing her hands off on her jeans. "Depends on how you look at it. I mean, you're always so calm, even when Pete's grilling you. Like last week, when he wouldn't let up about your weekend. You just—what's the word?—deflected."

Lind's mouth twitched into something between a smirk and a knowing smile. "I like to think of it as privacy."

Dana hesitated briefly, then decided to just go for it. "Well, here's the thing—I like coffee. A lot. And you and I have sparred over which coffee shop in town is the best more than once." She gave him a pointed look. "So, I wanted to see if you'd be interested in meeting me at the *actual* best coffee shop in town—*Coffee Brews & Muse*. You know, downtown."

Lind paused in his work, brow lifting slightly as if the invitation had caught him off guard. But then his expression shifted into something more amused. "Can't say I've been there."

Dana folded her arms, feigning surprise. "Really? I'll bet you haven't. A man of routine like you? I'm guessing you get your black coffee from the same place every time."

Lind's lips quirked as he finally turned to fully face her. "So, coffee. With you. Just us, caffeinating and talking?"

"That's the idea," she said, keeping her tone light. "Call it research. You know, so I can figure out this puzzle that is Lind."

He studied her for a beat, eyes sharp yet unreadable. "You want to try to figure me out over coffee?"

She shrugged, biting back a smile. "Why not? You might even like it."

Lind was quiet for another moment, as if weighing his options. Then, with a slight nod, he said, "It'll take a lot longer than a coffee break to figure me out." His smile widened just a fraction. "But alright. When?"

Dana pretended to think, though she already knew the answer. "How about tomorrow? After work?"

His head tilted, amusement dancing in his eyes. "Tomorrow. Tuesday. You want to go out for coffee with me on a Tuesday? Have you been thinking about this all weekend?"

"I'm not at liberty to say," she replied smoothly.

Lind chuckled, shaking his head. "Okay then. Tomorrow it is."

You mean, like... open

Lind arrived first, standing just inside the door of *Coffee Brews & Muse*, scanning the menu board. The place was cozy, filled with the hum of light chatter and the rich scent of freshly brewed espresso. It wasn't nearly as crowded in the middle of the afternoon as it would be in the morning rush, which he appreciated.

He heard Dana before he saw her—the soft click of boots on the tile, the familiar energy in her step. "I knew you'd be early," she chided, stepping up beside him.

He turned to her with an easy smile. "You say that like it's a bad thing."

They ordered their drinks—Dana's latte, Lind's black coffee—before claiming a small table, in the back corner by the window. Their cups sat steaming between them, the glass window beside them fogging slightly.

Dana took a slow sip of her drink, then leaned back in her chair. "So, here we are. Best coffee in town. You really are one of those 'just black coffee' types."

Lind lifted his cup as if in a silent toast. "Guilty as charged." He took a sip, then made a mock choking sound before grinning. "Not bad."

"Not bad? Really?" Dana said, with mock exasperation. "That's high praise coming from you, Man of Mystery."

Lind chuckled. "Back to 'man of mystery,' huh? You're relentless."

"I can't help it. I'm curious."

His brow lifted slightly. "Curious about what?"

Dana hesitated, then met his gaze. "About you. We've been around each other for almost a year now, and I don't know anything about you, it seems."

Lind studied her, then leaned back in his chair. "Alright. The Puzzle Master is here to put a few pieces in place. What part of me are you curious about?"

Dana felt warmth creep into her cheeks as an uninvited thought flashed through her mind—one that had nothing to do with coffee. She pushed it aside quickly, keeping her tone easy. "You mentioned last week that you've been going to that music festival with your friend, Sam—for years? You've known her a long time, huh?"

Lind took a measured sip of his coffee before answering. "Yeah. Sam and I go way back."

Dana tilted her head, feigning nonchalance. "Back how far? Like—college?"

"No." He met her gaze directly this time, something careful in his tone. "It was long after college. We met when I was still married to Sharon. In fact, Sharon introduced us."

Dana blinked, thrown for just a second. "Oh. So she was... a mutual friend?"

Lind nodded slightly. "Something like that. My ex-wife and I had... an unconventional approach to our relationship. Sam came into my life during that time."

Dana leaned forward slightly, intrigued. "Unconventional? You mean, like... open?"

Lind exhaled slowly, nodding. "Yeah. It wasn't something I planned on. Sharon introduced us to it, and it became part of how we lived. Sam and I connected, and we've stayed close ever since."

"That's... not something you hear every day," Dana said softly, processing.

"No, I suppose it's not," Lind agreed.

"And your ex-wife?" she asked carefully. "Is she still in the picture?"

Lind shook his head. "No. We went our separate ways years ago. But Sam and I—well, we found a balance. I don't see her often, but I do see her."

Dana toyed with the sleeve of her coffee cup, turning over his words. "It sounds like you've figured out something that works for you." She hesitated, then admitted, "I don't know if I'd even know where to start with something like that."

Lind's expression softened. "It's not for everyone. And honestly, I'm still figuring it out. But what I do know is that honesty—real, uncomfortable honesty—is the only way it works. People have to be on the same page and recognize and accept their differences."

Dana nodded slowly, her curiosity deepening. "Differences. Honesty. That's... I don't know. Required, I guess, for any successful relationship."

Lind's mouth curved into a grin. "I'd agree. See? That was an easy puzzle piece to place."

They sat in silence for a while, sipping their coffee and watching people pass by outside.

Dana finally glanced back at him, a small smile playing at her lips. "I can see this puzzle *is* going to take a while to put together."

Lind sighed, tone light. "If you ever get it all figured out, I'd like to see it." His smile was crooked, but there was something else there—something unspoken.

The conversation eventually drifted to lighter topics, but Dana's mind churned on his words. *There was so much more to Lind.* And for the first time, she realized—she *wanted* to know all of it.

Chapter 14

Honesty—real, uncomfortable honesty

Lind's words echoed in Dana's mind as she drove home, the glow of the city lights stretching in blurred streaks through her windshield. He had said it so easily, like it was the most natural thing in the world. *But how many people actually live like that?*

Her fingers tapped against the steering wheel as she replayed their conversation. *Open relationships. A balance with Sam. Unconventional.* The words felt foreign, but not wrong—not the way Lind had described them. There had been no hesitation in his voice, no defensiveness. Just simple, matter-of-fact honesty.

And then there was the part that had caught her most off guard—*Sharon introduced them to it.* Dana had always assumed relationships were about exclusivity, about two people promising to be everything to each other. But maybe that was the problem. Maybe people expected too much, set themselves up to fail.

She exhaled slowly, gripping the steering wheel a little tighter.

There was something about Lind that kept her guessing, kept her wanting to know more. He was so calm, so measured. Like he was carrying a secret he wasn't sure he was ready to share.

And then there was *Sam.*

Dana couldn't stop wondering about her. *Who is she? What does she mean to him?* The way he spoke about her was... different. Not like a lover, exactly. But not *just* a friend either. It was confusing, but that didn't feel wrong either. At least, not to Lind.

Would I ever be able to do something like that? The thought came suddenly, unbidden. *Could I handle... sharing someone?*

A strange flip in her stomach made her grip tighten on the wheel for a second. She wasn't sure if it was excitement or fear.

Dana pulled into her condo complex, shut off the engine, and sat for a long moment, staring at nothing.

Lind is a puzzle, alright. And every piece I find just leads to more questions.

A faint smile touched her lips as she shook her head.

"This is going to take a while to figure out," she muttered to herself, grabbing her bag and heading inside.

Black-coffee-only cult

The seasonal display of quirky coffee mugs was proving to be an unexpected source of entertainment. Dana held up one that read, *I'm not addicted to coffee, we're just in a committed relationship,* and turned to Lind with a grin.

"This one's speaking to me," she said, lifting it for him to see.

Lind glanced at a nearby mug. "'Decaf? No, thank you.' Now that's more my kind of energy."

Dana let out a mock gasp, pressing a hand to her chest. "You know, decaf is coffee's evil twin. It pretends to be friendly, but really, it's just betrayal in a cup."

Lind nodded solemnly. "Spoken like a true coffee connoisseur."

"You know it." Dana set the mug down and shot him a look. "Speaking of—have you recovered from your visit to *Coffee Brews & Muse*? I'm guessing it was a little... overwhelming for someone with your minimalist taste."

Lind pretended to shudder. "It wasn't bad, but I think I aged five years waiting for my coffee. Good thing you were there to keep me company."

She felt a slight warmth in her cheeks. "Come on, it wasn't *that* long a wait. You go to that place where they serve coffee in plain white mugs and don't even bother with foam."

"And that's exactly why I'm inviting you there," Lind countered. "My coffee shop on Oak Street is a place where coffee is just coffee."

Dana lifted an eyebrow. "Oh, so this is about dragging me into your no-frills, black-coffee-only cult?"

Lind laughed. "Not dragging. Not a cult. Just introducing—educating. Think of it as expanding your horizons."

She tapped her fingers against the shelf, pretending to consider. "Alright—but only if you promise not to roll your eyes when I ask for a different kind of coffee, one with actual flavor."

Lind deadpanned, "They *do* have options—'hot' or 'extra hot.'"

Dana let out a laugh, shaking her head. "Fine. You're on." Then she added in a hushed murmur, "I'll bring my own damn flavoring."

Breakfast king & Puzzle master

Lind's favorite coffee shop on Oak Street was the opposite of *Coffee Brews & Muse*. It was small, quiet, with warm lighting and the scent of freshly ground coffee hanging in the air. There were no chalkboard menus listing seasonal flavors, no baristas explaining the *notes* of different beans—just a steady stream of regulars and the comforting hiss of steaming milk.

Dana took a sip of her latte and leaned back in her chair, smiling. "Alright, I think it's only fair I ask—you've been to both my favorite coffee shop and yours. Which one's better?"

"Yours has charm," Lind admitted. "But I would miss the quiet here."

"Spoken like a true introvert," she said. "So, is this place close to where you live?"

"Yeah, about five minutes away. I've got a little apartment—600 square feet. Small, but comfortable."

Dana grinned. "Sounds cozy. I've got a condo—two stories, two bedrooms. Used to have a roommate, but she moved out last year, so now it's just me."

"Do you miss having a roommate?"

"Not really," she admitted. "I mean, it's quieter now, but paying all the bills myself has made things... tighter."

Lind nodded. "That's fair. I keep things simple. My apartment isn't big enough to clutter up, but I do have one indulgence."

She tilted her head. "What's that?"

"My TV. Sixty inches—dominates the place."

Dana's eyes widened in mock surprise. "A sixty-inch TV? What are you even watching on that thing?"

Lind shrugged. "Not much, honestly. I spend more time reading, cooking and tinkering than watching TV."

Dana wondered what he meant by tinkering but she went straight for the obvious. "Cooking?" she asked, raising an eyebrow. "You don't seem like the 'whipping up a soufflé' type."

"No soufflés, but I make a mean breakfast—scrambled eggs, hash browns, pancakes, you name it."

"So you're the *Breakfast King*?"

He mock-bowed. "No, I'm *The Puzzle Master*, but I do breakfast well. Decent dinner, average lunch. But you've gotta try my grilled ham and cheese one of these days."

Dana leaned forward. "Okay, now I'm curious. How'd you get into cooking?"

Lind smiled faintly. "Hello, single guy for a long time. Cook or go broke and fat eating fast food. Breakfast just happens to be my thing." He paused. "What about you? I've noticed you bring homemade lunches every day."

She smiled. "Simple stuff. I like cooking, but I'm no gourmet. I make enough to get by without living on takeout."

"Practical and skilled. I'm impressed."

"Well, don't be," she said, giving him a lopsided grin. "My specialty is pasta with whatever's still edible in the fridge."

"Still, being able to take random ingredients and turn them into a meal is a skill," Lind said.

"High praise coming from the *Breakfast King*."

"*Puzzle Master*," he corrected, grinning. "And it's deserved. You'll have to let me make you breakfast someday."

Dana narrowed her eyes playfully. "I'll hold you to that. But only if there's French toast involved."

"Fine, but my loaded scrambled eggs will steal the show."

She laughed, shaking her head. "What do you even do when you hang out with friends? Pancake cook-offs?"

"Not quite. I like low-key things—like that bar outing with the team a couple months ago. That was fun."

Dana grinned. "Except for Pete's 'let's all do shots' idea. Brenda still blames him for her hangover."

Lind chuckled. "Pete has that effect on people."

Dana's gaze lingered on him. "So... what do you and Sam do when you hang out?"

Lind hesitated, then said, "It depends. Hiking, music festivals, skiing... she's big on the outdoors."

Dana nodded, sensing there was more to the story—but for now, she let it go. She had plenty of time to piece this puzzle together.

The conversation drifted to work-related things—coworker mishaps, and does Georgette ever smile?

When they parted company, a hug was on both their minds, but...

Chapter 15

Pizza, beer, and latte of love

The next week, a nervous Lind asked Dana her favorite kind of pizza. She laughed when he raised an eyebrow and told her pineapple did not belong on pizza.

The pizzeria was warm and bustling, filled with the hum of conversation and the comforting clatter of plates and silverware. Dana and Lind sat across from each other in a red vinyl booth, the scent of melted cheese and oregano drifting between them. A large, warm pizza—half pepperoni and mushroom, half pineapple and ham—sat in the center of the table as Lind poured them each a beer.

As he slid Dana's glass across to her, a grin played at his lips. "So, you've been grilling me about my life and friends. I think it's only fair that I get to know a bit more about you. What's *Dana's* story?"

Dana arched an eyebrow. "Oh, you want the whole story? Hope you ordered a refill on that beer."

Lind gave her a slow, amused wink. "I want to know everything, but I'll settle for whatever you're willing to share—like you have from me."

Dana laughed, shaking her head. "Oh, so you want to hear all about my *latte of love*? Layered, occasionally foamy, sometimes too bitter to finish?" She picked up her first slice of pizza, waving it slightly. "Sure. I've got stories."

Lind leaned back, grinning. "I'm all ears."

Records, rebounds, and red flags

Dana took a bite of her pizza, chewing thoughtfully before launching in. "Let's see... there was Al. My high school sweetheart. Four years together. He was pre-med, so I worked and supported him while he studied. The plan was to get married after he graduated."

Lind raised an eyebrow. "Sounds solid. What happened?"

She shrugged. "He cheated. Twice. First time, I tried to forgive him. Second time? I finally realized you can't fix some things."

"Ouch," Lind murmured. "That's rough."

"Yeah, well. Lesson learned." Dana took a sip of her beer, as if washing away the bitter taste of that memory. "Then there was Larry."

"Larry—?"

"The rebound that turned into a long-term experiment. Three years. We got along great—until he took a job across the country without so much as a discussion."

Lind frowned. "Just up and left?"

"Pretty much." Dana lifted a shoulder. "To be fair, it wasn't exactly the *serious commitment* kind of relationship. I guess he figured I'd just pack up and follow. I didn't."

Lind's grin returned. "Joke was on him, huh?"

"Oh, definitely. Especially since he left all his records behind."

Lind looked amused. "You *kept* his records?"

Dana flashed a quick grin. "Nope. I mailed them back—most of them. But not before listening to all of them first."

Lind let out a low laugh. "All of them? How long did *that* take?"

"About four months. I wasn't in a hurry." She sipped her beer, her eyes twinkling. "I did keep two. He never said anything, so..." She shrugged, feigning innocence.

Lind shook his head in mock disbelief. "Four months? He must've had quite a collection."

"Nope." She reached for another slice of pizza, her sly smile widening.

Lind laughed, raising his glass. "Remind me never to leave anything behind if I move."

Dana clinked glasses. "Smart man."

"Oh, and then there was Wayne," Dana said, shifting gears. "He lasted about three months. Things were actually pretty good... until he decided he wanted to...*spice things up*."

Lind's eyes glinted with curiosity. "Spice things up *how*?"

Dana leaned forward, lowering her voice with a conspiratorial grin. "He wanted a threesome—with another woman."

Lind chuckled, shaking his head. "Classic Wayne. Let me guess. You weren't into it?"

"Oh, I was *curious*," she admitted. "But I told him, 'Sure, if we can also have a threesome with another guy.'"

Lind nearly choked on his drink, laughing. "And how did *Wayne* take that?"

Dana grinned mischievously. "You'd have thought I asked him to stick his dick in a meat grinder. He got all defensive and said, 'It's different.' I told him, 'Not from where I'm sitting.'" Dana sat back and took a sip of her beer. "Yep, that was the beginning of the end."

Lind opened his mouth to say something snarky—but caught the shift in her tone. He smiled instead. "So... Wayne wasn't ready for equality."

"Exactly. He wanted to have his cake and eat it too." She took a sip of beer, tilting her head. "So, I left him to his *fantasy cake*."

A sly grin spread across Lind's face as he let the image play out in his head. "But... *would* you have done it? The threesome, I mean. If he'd agreed to your terms?"

Dana studied him, her expression softened. "Maybe," she admitted. "I mean, I'm not shy about trying new things. But it would've had to feel *right*." She tapped a finger against her glass. "Trust is a big thing for me too."

Lind nodded, his gaze steady.

Dana arched an eyebrow. "Are you taking notes, Lind?"

He smiled back, easy and warm. "Always."

Are you asking about my appliances

Dana leaned back, sighing dramatically. "Hey, I don't mess around when it comes to collecting *stories*."

Lind's expression turned mischievous. "Speaking of collections..." He leaned in slightly. "How big is yours?"

Dana blinked. "Mine? My *collection*?"

Lind leaned in, the corners of his mouth twitching with amusement. "You know. Of... *dead batteries*."

Dana narrowed her eyes at him. "Lind, are you asking about my—*appliances*?"

He gave her an innocent look. "Just curious about your dead battery collection."

Dana pursed her lips in mock consideration. "Well, let's see... two for that one, two more for that one, one for the other..." She tapped a finger on the table, pretending to calculate. Then, with an amused expression, she said, "Yeah, my collection is... *considerable*."

Lind let out a low, appreciative laugh. "Are you sure at least *some* of those guys didn't leave for self-preservation reasons?"

Dana tilted her head, pretending to think. Then, with a deadpan expression, she said, "If you can't take the heat, stay out of the kitchen."

A silence stretched between them—charged, electric, weighted.

Dana was the first to break it.

"Alright," she said, reaching for another slice of pizza, "your turn. Tell me your worst dating story."

Lind chuckled, shaking his head as he took a sip of his beer. "Oh, I've got a few. But fair warning—you might rethink ever dating me after hearing them."

Dana grinned. "Oh, please—try me."

"Well... Sharon—she was my first real love. It was good. More than good. So when she brought up the CNM stuff, it threw me at first."

"C-N-M?" Dana asked, brow furrowed.

"It means consensual non-monogamy. The unconventional relationship we had."

"You didn't start out that way?"

"No," he said. "It was several years in. But she seemed... determined. So I looked into it. Realized I wouldn't be losing Sharon, just adding a little extra now and then."

He paused to sip his beer. "It had its appeal."

"Really? So what happened?"

"She was in it for the sex. The excitement. The thrill. All the things we'd lost over time. She wanted to get that back—while keeping me too. And it actually worked. For a while."

"Why only a while?"

"Remember that demisexual thing I mentioned?"

Dana nodded. She remembered the word, even if she didn't fully understand it.

"Well, Sharon never got jealous over the sex," Lind said, leaning back in the booth, beer in hand. "But the connections? That's what got her. The emotional stuff." He exhaled. "So I told her, 'Let's stop.' And she said, 'You don't have to stop the sex. Just stop the emotional involvements.' I told her I can't. Next thing I know, I'm being served."

Dana blinked. "Holy shit. That seems... drastic. Especially over something *she* wanted you two to do."

"I mentioned that to her."

"And?"

"She said, 'You're supposed to fuck 'em, not love 'em.'" He lowered his beer glass into his lap. "I loved the hell out of her. Did everything she wanted. And still lost her. Got abandoned by her, for doing what she asked."

Dana didn't know what to say. She ached for him.

"I didn't fight the divorce," he said quietly. "But it ripped me up. Been solo ever since, with the occasional... diversion. That was enough pain to last a lifetime."

The silence between them was soft, but carried a sadness.

Then Lind nudged it away with a crooked smile. "But some of those diversions were pretty disastrous."

Dana's smile returned with relief as Lind sat back up to the table, grabbed another slice of pizza, a sip of beer and dove into twenty minutes of ridiculous stories.

They laughed over the barmaid diversion, winced through the girl next door, and couldn't stop laughing about Olivia, who worked in an adult toy store.

And just like that, they were back—the pizza disappearing, the beers going down. The conversation flowed, laughter threading through the air.

Dana had come here expecting a fun evening, maybe some flirting. But what she hadn't expected was the way he let her in tonight—the way he made her feel, like they could say anything to each other, open up about anything, joke about anything. It didn't feel like they were just talking. They were connecting.

She wasn't sure what this was turning into, but she liked it.

A lot.

I like your personality

The last few slices of pizza sat untouched, only remnants of crust left on their plates. The hum of the pizzeria had quieted as the night wore on, the once-packed tables thinning out. Dana leaned back against the red vinyl booth, her beer glass in hand, and let out a small sigh.

"So, yeah," she said, swirling the last sip of beer before finishing it off. "That was my illustrious dating history. A lot of frogs, not a prince in sight."

Lind was grinning as he lifted his glass. "Is that all of them? You had mentioned having one or two over the last couple of years."

Dana blinked, caught off guard. "Who told you that?"

His grin widened slightly. "You did." Lind tapped his ear. "Well, not directly, but I've overheard you and Brenda talking now and then. And that 'boy toy' comment at the bar? Pretty obvious."

Dana groaned, feeling the heat crawl up her neck. "Is it the beer making me so *confessional*?"

Lind didn't answer, just gave her a questioning smile and waited.

With a sigh, Dana set down her empty glass and admitted, "Fine. I *have* tried the 'boy toy' thing a few times over the last couple of years. But they were much more *boy* than *toy*." She shrugged, face warming even more. "So I stick to killing batteries."

Lind smiled, letting her words hang between them for a moment, studying her with a look that made her stomach tighten in a way she wasn't sure she liked. Then, with an easy grin, he said, "Maybe you just need someone who doesn't care that you want pineapple on pizza."

That caught Dana off guard. But then she huffed a laugh. "Or someone who doesn't try to turn my dating life into a personality quiz."

Lind leaned forward slightly, holding her gaze. "I've been around you for about a year now, Dana. I *like* your personality."

She hadn't expected that either—not so direct, not so... *sincere*. Her stomach tightened again, and this time, there was no mistaking what it was.

Dana broke eye contact, glancing down and away as her face grew even warmer. *Jesus, is it possible to actually combust from blushing?*

Lind watched her, caught by how open she was, even if it wasn't on purpose. He had more questions.

"Where did you grow up?" He asked as he poured them both another beer.

Recovering, she said, "About an hour from here, outside a small farming community," her blush almost gone. "My grandparents were farmers, and my dad inherited the house and quite a bit of land. It wasn't hundreds of acres or anything, but... a lot." She paused, the edges of a smile forming as childhood memories surfaced. "It felt like a wonderland to me when I was a kid."

"Sounds like a nice childhood," he said. "Any brothers or sisters?"

"Nope. Only child." She took a sip of her beer.

"Uh oh," he said, with a mock-judgment.

"What is that supposed to mean?" she arched an eyebrow, pretending to be offended.

"Oh, nothing. Just... spoiled rich kid," he said, eyes glinting.

"We were not rich," she shot back, swatting at his arm. "And I'm not spoiled."

"Well, maybe you should be." He grinned at her, slow and deliberate.

The heat rushed back into her cheeks again as she fought back a smile.

Lind was still grinning at her when he asked, "So, were you named after a family member?"

She paused, still flustered by his words. "What do you mean?"

"'Dana'—it's a pretty name. Was it your grandmother's or...?"

"Oh, no," she said with a laugh. "My dad's name is Dan, and my mom is Anna. Tada—Dana."

"Oh," he said, nodding. "That makes sense."

She tilted her head, eyeing him. "And you? What about your family?"

"Grew up near Indianapolis. Nice, middle-class neighborhood. Nothing exciting."

"Siblings?"

"One sister," he said, then frowned. "We don't see each other much—holidays, mostly."

Dana's brow furrowed slightly. "Why's that?"

He shrugged, his tone neutral. "We don't see eye to eye on... a lot of things."

"Sounds like there's some tension there."

"Yeah. A little," he said, not elaborating.

"Well..." she said, taking a sip of her beer, deciding not to push. "So, Lind isn't a name you hear often."

"I was supposed to be a girl," he said, flashing a wide grin. "They were going to name me *Lindsay*."

Dana laughed. "With all the tests and ultrasounds, they thought you were going to be a girl?"

"Apparently," he said.

Dana grinned, playing coy. "Is it really that hard to find?"

"Not anymore," he said, deadpan.

Oh My God. She gasped—nearly choked on her beer, laughing. When she finally caught her breath, she looked up to find Lind smiling at her. There was something different in his eyes—less teasing, more focused. Their laughter quieter now wrapped in something warmer. Her smile faltered just a little, but she didn't look away.

Neither did he.

It wasn't a long moment—but it was enough.

Lind finally glanced down at his glass, clearing his throat like he needed to reset. "They gave the name to me. I took enough shit in school about *Lindsey* that I just started going by Lind."

Dana eased back in her seat, studying him as her grin returned. "Yeah, no. You're definitely not a Lindsey."

Lind chuckled, the tension between them shifting—just enough to turn things playful. And suggestive. They shared a final laugh, the pizza dwindling to just a few abandoned crusts as the conversation moved on to lighter things. But as the evening wound down, Dana knew they both enjoyed those moments—no matter how easily they moved past them.

That wasn't so hard, was it

The warm glow of the pizzeria faded behind them as Dana and Lind stepped out into the cool night air. The parking lot was quiet, the sounds of the city distant but ever-present. Their footsteps echoed lightly against the pavement as they walked together toward their vehicles.

Dana pulled out her keys as they neared her car, flashing Lind a grin. "Well, that was fun. Good pizza, good beer, and even better stories."

Lind nodded. "I'd say the company wasn't bad either."

"High praise from the *Puzzle Master*—I'll take it."

For the first time that night, their easy banter gave way to a comfortable silence.

Lind stuck his hands into his pockets, tilting his head slightly. "Thanks... for... coming out tonight. It was nice getting to know a little more about you."

Dana's smile softened. "Likewise. You're full of surprises, you know."

He chuckled. "You'll have to stick around if you want to solve the rest of the puzzle."

Dana let out a quiet laugh, nodding. "I might just take you up on that."

Before she could second-guess herself, Dana stepped forward and wrapped herself around him in a warm hug.

Lind responded immediately, his arms circling her—strong and steady. But what she didn't expect was the way his hand came to rest at the back of her head, the pressure subtle as he drew her just a little closer to him.

He could feel every part of her.

It wasn't just a friendly hug—it was something else. Something... more.

Dana pulled back slightly, still close enough to feel his warmth. "See?" she said, giving him a wink. "That wasn't so hard, was it?"

Lind grinned. "Not at all. You give pretty good hugs."

Feeling bold, Dana pressed her hand to his chest, pausing just long enough to make her point before stepping toward her car.

She noticed as his breath hitched—as his eyes dipped down.

"Good to know," she said, flashing him one last grin as she unlocked her car door. "Drive safe, Lind."

Lind met her eyes again, smiling. "You too, Dana. See you tomorrow."

As he turned toward his truck, Dana got into her car, still feeling the warmth of his hand in her hair.

When she glanced back, she caught Lind shifting—*adjusting* himself slightly—before opening his door.

Dana bit her lip, smiling to herself. *Oh yeah—he definitely noticed.*

As she pulled out of the lot and onto the road, a small but undeniable feeling hit her. No matter how she tried to ignore it, she couldn't—*something* had shifted between them.

And she liked it.

***

The following week passed in a slow, mutual dance of exchanged glances at work and late-night texts that ranged from ridiculous to flirty without either of them acknowledging just how much *more* was creeping into the space between them.

By Friday night, they had made a plan: a morning hike, before the weather turned too cold.

October had arrived, and with it, the quiet anniversary of his first year working at the big box store.

Chapter 16

Ready for this hike

The Sunday morning air was crisp as Dana pulled into the trail head parking lot. The sun was just beginning to warm the horizon, golden rays filtering through the trees.

Lind was already there, leaning against his truck, holding two cups of coffee and a paper bag with pastries.

Dana stepped out of her car, inhaling the scent of cinnamon and espresso as she took the offered cup. "Look at you—all prepared. Should I be worried you'll start charging for these coffee runs?"

He handed her a cup. "Not unless you start ordering something more complicated. This is still within my budget."

She took a sip, sighing happily. "My lattes aren't *complicated.* They're *refined.*"

"I'll take your word for it," he grinned, nodding toward the trail. "Ready for this hike?"

Dana peeked into the bag, inspecting the pastries. "As long as there's enough sugar in here to fuel me, sure."

They shared a laugh, falling into step as they started up the trail. The sound of leaves crunching beneath their feet mixed with birdsong as they made their way deeper into the woods.

It was easy, this thing between them.

And Dana wasn't sure if that scared her—or if it was exactly what she'd been waiting for.

Yeah. He's definitely a man

The trail stretched ahead of them, winding through the dense trees, golden morning light filtering through the canopy. The air was crisp now, but Dana knew it wouldn't stay that way. The steady incline and the rising sun would warm her soon enough, so she had chosen her layers carefully—a snug, light jacket over a thick cotton pullover, fitted jeans, and her favorite hiking boots.

Still, as she took another sip of coffee and fell into step beside Lind, she could already feel the cold morning air working against her. She wasn't oblivious to how the cold hardened her nipples beneath her pullover—or to the way Lind's gaze flickered down, however briefly, before he looked away, as if forcing himself to focus on the trail ahead.

Yeah. He's definitely a man.

Did she mind that he noticed? Did she want him to notice? Did she want him seeing her, being distracted by her? So many questions ran through her mind, and the only person who could answer them was her—and she wasn't sure she could—yet.

***

Lind walked ahead of her, the bag of pastries swinging in one hand, his coffee in the other. She let her eyes drift lower, watching the way his jeans fit—well-worn but sturdy, moving effortlessly with each long stride. He walked like someone completely comfortable in his own skin—steady, unrushed.

Unlike me, Dana thought, biting her lip slightly. She wasn't impatient exactly... but she was starting to wonder what holding Lind back.

They hiked in comfortable silence for a while, the sounds of their footsteps mixing with the occasional rustle of leaves as small creatures darted through the underbrush. The cool air carried the scent of damp earth and pine, a sharp contrast to the cinnamon still clinging to her fingertips from the pastry she'd eaten earlier.

When the trail narrowed, she stepped ahead, leading the way up the incline.

Lind let her pass, but he wasn't above taking in the view.

Her jeans hugged her curves in a way that made it damn near impossible not to look. She was fit, strong, but there was a softness to her too—one that made something stir deep in his chest. He swallowed and turned his gaze slightly upward, pretending to admire the trees instead.

What are you waiting for, Lind?

The voice in his head was more of a challenge than a question.

Still being careful. Fine. Frustrating man

The trail evened out into a wide, open overlook, the valley below still shrouded in morning mist. Dana sighed, stretching her arms above her head before resting them on her hips. "Now *this* is a view."

Lind took a long sip of his coffee, standing beside her. "Not bad, not bad at all," he said, his voice casual, but his attention wasn't on the valley.

They stood close, the space between them narrowing as they both gazed out at the rolling landscape. At first, it was just a shared quiet, both of them absorbing the stillness. Then Dana felt it—the lightest brush of skin, the back of his hand barely touching hers where they both rested their arms at their sides.

It was nothing, really. Just a small, fleeting point of contact.

But she didn't move—and neither did he.

The warmth of him seeped through the spot where their hands met, an almost imperceptible connection.

Dana exhaled, turning her head slightly toward him. "You're being careful," she murmured, not quite a question.

Lind didn't respond right away. He just glanced over at her, his expression unreadable. "Shouldn't I be?"

She tilted her head. "Is that a real question?"

A small smile played at his lips, but he didn't answer.

They stood like that for a few more moments, neither moving away but neither pushing further. Then Lind cleared his throat and nodded toward the trail. "We should keep moving before we lose the morning light."

Dana watched him for a second longer before sighing and turning back toward the path.

Still being careful. Fine. Frustrating man.

They had been walking for nearly thirty minutes without stopping when Dana abruptly turned to Lind and planted a hand on his chest.

"Whoa." His brow lifted slightly, but he didn't step back.

Dana's palm pressed flat against the solid heat of him, feeling the steady thump of his heartbeat beneath her fingers. "I was just checking," she said, her voice laced with amusement. "Your heart rate's normal. Impressive, considering we've been hiking uphill for a while now."

Lind smiled, one brow arching. "Is this just an excuse to touch me?"

Dana's lips twitched. "*Maybe.*"

He looked at her, watching her fingers spread slightly before she pulled them away, slow and deliberate. His skin burned where she had touched him, but he forced himself to stay still, to not react too much.

He didn't know why he was holding back anymore. Maybe it was caution. Maybe it was self-preservation.

Or maybe it was just fear.

He had gone through hell after Sharon. And he knew himself too well—if Dana became as important to him as he already suspected she might, there'd be no walking away unscathed if things fell apart.

But he also knew something else.

If he let this moment pass, if he let her pass, he'd regret it.

Lind exhaled, rolling his shoulders. "You done with your medical exam?"

Dana grinned. "For now."

As he turned to start back up the trail, his hand drifted to his chest—right where hers had been. He didn't even realize he was smiling.

As they continued along the trail, whenever she walked ahead, he didn't even try to look away.

Chapter 17

You were taking too long

By the time they made it back to the parking lot, the sun was fully up, casting warm golden light across the clearing.

Dana shrugged off her jacket, tying it around her waist as she turned to face Lind. "Thanks for the coffee, pastries, and the hike. You *might* spoil me into expecting this every week."

"Let's plan it. I'll start rotating the pastries."

Dana laughed softly, stepping closer. "You're trouble, you know that?"

Without hesitation, she wrapped her arms around him.

Lind's arms circled her waist immediately, his hold firm, warm, solid. And just like before, he rested his hand at the back of her head, fingers tangling in her hair.

Only this time, he didn't let go right away.

Dana pulled back slightly, their faces inches apart. "You're overthinking this," she murmured.

Lind exhaled, shaking his head. "I don't think we should rush this, Dana. It's... important."

She tilted her head, her voice soft but teasing. "Lind, if we were moving any slower, we'd be going backwards."

Caught off guard, Lind chuckled, shaking his head. "Okay then."

And he kissed her.

Soft at first, slow. Just a press of lips, careful but sure.

Then, as if something inside him finally gave way, he deepened it—his fingers tightening just slightly against the nape of her neck.

Dana responded instantly, leaning into him, her hands gripping his shoulders before one slipped down, her palm flattening against his chest again—only this time, she wasn't pretending.

When they finally broke apart, their foreheads touching, Lind let out a breathless chuckle. "That was... nice."

Dana grinned, her voice slightly breathless. "You were taking too long."

Lind closed his eyes as he brushed his nose against hers. "Noted."

She reached up, tapping a finger lightly against his chest. "So... does this mean I *finally* get to see the rest of the puzzle?"

Lind exhaled a laugh, shaking his head as he tucked a loose strand of hair behind her ear. "Stick around, Dana." His voice dropped just a little, something more behind the words. "And I'll show you everything."

Dana smiled. "I'm counting on it."

As she stepped back, Lind instantly noticed her nipples—only this time, it wasn't the weather, her cheeks were flushed, her eyes bright. He knew it was him, it was them. There was no point in fighting it anymore.

She cupped his cheek as she gave him one last quick peck. He closed his eyes to feel every ounce of it. When he opened them Dana was looking quizzically at him.

He smiled at her, the hesitation thick between them, before he said, "See ya tomorrow."

He watched her walk back to her car as he wandered toward his truck. *What now Lind?* He thought, *This is the last stop before there is no stopping. Brakes or no brakes—decide!*

This man is going to drive me crazy

That kiss...

Her heart was still racing, the warmth of his lips and the slow brush of his nose against hers making her entire body hum with 'that' energy. She gripped the edge of her car door to steady herself, pulse pounding in her ears.

I almost lost it right there. Almost.

Who was she kidding? If he'd kissed her again, if he had even leaned in the slightest bit closer, she would have *jumped him*—right there, in broad daylight, in the middle of the damn parking lot.

Forget coy—I'm ready. Right here, right now. And he just says 'see ya'? What the hell is he so afraid of?

This man is going to drive me crazy—And I'm letting him.

Dana's not going to let me do slowly anymore

That was... perfect. More than.

Dana hadn't even hesitated. The way she looked at him after—the heat in her eyes, the way she *melted* into him—he could see everything she was holding back. Everything *they* had been holding back.

A small smile played on his lips as he unlocked his truck, his thoughts already moving ahead.

I should start planning what's next. Dinner at my place, maybe? Something personal. Comfortable...

His mind drifted to the image of her in his kitchen, wine in hand, her laughter filling the space as the evening stretched into something quieter. Something softer. Maybe even a morning where she was still there.

Yeah. It's time to move forward. Slowly...

He exhaled, gripping the steering wheel as he started the engine.

Who am I kidding? Dana's not going to let me do slowly, anymore.

No brakes.

Both drove away, the taste of the kiss still on their lips, the feeling of it still humming in their bodies. The spark between them had officially caught fire—too strong to ignore now.

For Lind, it's them. For Dana, it's him.

You're just scared of a little complexity

Monday night, Dana sat cross legged on her couch, scrolling absently through her phone. The glow of the screen flickered over her face as a notification popped up—a text from Lind.

Lind: I finally figured out why you love fancy lattes. It's the algebra, isn't it? Pastry + foam art = happiness.

Dana's grin formed instantly as her thumbs moved.

Dana: That's not algebra, Lind. It's logic. You're just bitter because black coffee has no personality.

Lind: Black coffee is efficient. Yours comes with an instruction manual.

Dana: That's what makes it interesting. You're just scared of a little complexity.

There was a short pause before his reply came through.

Lind: Complexity isn't the problem. It's pretending something isn't complicated when it is—that's where people get lost.

Dana stared at the screen a moment longer than she expected to. Then...

Dana: Okay, philosopher barista. Are we still talking about coffee here?

Lind: Are we ever just talking about coffee?

She rolled her eyes, smiling.

Dana: It's not that complicated. You're just overthinking it.

Lind: You're the one who overthinks everything.

Dana: Obviously not the only one. Right, Lind?

She watched the screen. *"Typing..."* blinked once, then vanished. *Uh huh. Thought so.*

Then it returned.

Lind: *Yeah... maybe I am.*

Dana: *Mm-hmm. And not texting back when I'm right is classic avoidance.*

Lind: *Guilty. You caught me.*

Dana: *Good. Now stop thinking, go to sleep — and don't make me text first tomorrow.*

Like you even know what subtle means

By midweek, their workday interactions carried that same energy. In the break room, their conversations stretched longer. In passing, so did their glances. It wasn't obvious—at least, not to everyone—but Dana caught Pete giving them a look more than once, and it only made her smirk.

Dana was straightening a display when Lind walked by, slowing just enough to glance around before speaking.

"You're going to get us both in trouble, you know."

Dana arched a brow, feigning innocence. "Me? I'm just working here."

Lind leaned slightly closer, the corner of his mouth twitching up. "The way Pete keeps side-eyeing us, you'd think we were passing state secrets."

Dana grinned, barely looking up from the shelf. "Maybe he's jealous. Or maybe *you* should stop staring at me across the lunchroom."

Lind chuckled under his breath, stepping back. "Fair point. I'll be more subtle."

Dana shot him a playful glance, lowering her voice. "Like you even know what *subtle* means."

Lind gave a small shrug as he walked away, flashing her a grin. "You'll see."

She shook her head, biting back a smile. *Yeah, right.*

Dinner at my place. You in

By Thursday Lind couldn't hold back any more. They were side by side, straightening shelves at the end of their shift when Lind spoke casually, keeping his tone even.

"Hey, Dana."

She hummed without looking up, still focused on arranging a display.

"Saturday night. Dinner at my place. You in?"

Dana stilled for a second, then turned, arching an eyebrow. "Just like that? No lead-in? No witty banter?"

"You told me to stop being slow, stop overthinking—I'm taking notes."

She narrowed her eyes, amused. "Fair." A pause. "What's on the menu?"

He adopted a mock-serious expression. "That's classified. But I *will* say this—you'll leave impressed."

Dana folded her arms, giving him a slow once over. "Bold claim. Guess I'll have to see if you can back it up."

I'm fine, Dr. Lind

Dana slumped onto her couch. Her laptop opened in front of her. Her fingers hovered over the keys, but the words on the screen blurred. She yawned, rubbing her eyes, feeling a dull ache creep into her temples.

Her phone buzzed beside her.

Lind: *Looking forward to Saturday.*

She smiled faintly, typing back.

Dana: *Me too.*

But as she hit send, her body slumped, a heaviness setting in. She exhaled, trying to ignore the nagging sensation in her throat. *Just a long week. That's all.*

***

Dana sat at a break room table, stirring her tea with a sluggish motion. Across the room, Lind entered, coffee in hand. His gaze flicked over her, immediately catching the shift in her usual energy.

He crossed the room and stopped by her table, frowning slightly. "Tea instead of coffee? That's a red flag."

Dana sniffled, waving a hand. "Ugh, I think I'm catching something. Hoping it's just allergies."

Lind didn't look convinced. He set his coffee down, tilting his head. "Allergies don't usually make you look this tired. You okay?"

"I'm fine, Dr. Lind. Just need more caffeine."

He leaned against the table, studying her. "Or maybe you need to take it easy."

Dana let out a soft huff. "Fine. When I get home, I'll take a couple aspirin and go straight to bed."

Lind gave a small shake of his head, but his smile stayed warm. "Sounds good. But seriously, Dana—I'm concerned. Maybe check in with a doctor?"

She waved him off. "I'll be fine."

But as she took another sip of tea, her throat burned, and she suddenly wasn't so sure.

That's what you said yesterday

Dana woke to the sound of her own coughing. Her head pounded, her body felt heavy, and even the effort of lifting her phone felt monumental.

With a sigh, she typed out a message.

Dana: *Hey, I hate to cancel tonight, but I'm not feeling great. Definitely don't want to bring germs into your kitchen. Rain check?*

Lind's response came almost immediately.

Lind: *Rain check for sure. Let me know if you need anything, okay?*

She smiled faintly, typing back.

Dana: *I'm fine, but thanks! :)*

He frowned.

Lind: *That's what you said yesterday.*

She groaned, tossing her phone onto the blanket beside her. *Annoyingly observant man.*

***

Wrapped in a blanket, Dana curled up on the couch, her laptop forgotten on the coffee table. Her chest felt tight, her head stuffy. A box of tissues sat beside her, half empty.

Her phone vibrated again—another text from Lind.

Lind: *Checking in. Any better this morning?*

Dana sighed and decided to be honest this time.

Dana: *Feeling worse. Coughing now, too. But I'll live.*

A pause. Then his reply.

Lind: *Do you need me to bring anything? Soup, meds?*

Dana: *No need. I don't want to infect you, Puzzle Master.*

A moment later, his response appeared.

Lind: *Okay. But don't be stubborn. If you need anything, say the word.*

She smiled faintly, her heart warming despite the fever.

No, you're not fine

Monday morning Dana was pushing through her shift, she tried to ignore the bone-deep exhaustion weighing her down. Every movement felt heavier than usual, and her cough was getting worse.

She wasn't the only one who noticed.

Georgette appeared at her side, arms crossed. "Dana, you look awful. Go home."

Dana waved her off. "I'm fine. It's just a little cold."

Georgette's expression hardened. "No, you're *not* fine. And if you don't see a doctor, you're not coming back tomorrow. Go. Now."

Defeated, Dana sighed, grabbed her bag, and headed toward the exit.

As she reached her car, she pulled out her phone, typing a quick message.

Dana: *Georgette sent me home. Guess I'm officially sick.*

The reply came almost instantly.

Lind: *Let me know if you need anything. I mean it.*

She exhaled slowly, staring at the screen for a moment before typing back.

Dana: *I will.*

And this time, she actually meant it.

Part 5

I didn't mean to fall for him.
I just kept saying yes.
Yes to another hour.
Yes to another night.
Yes to another piece of my heart.

Chapter 18

I come bearing sustenance for thy lady

Lind had been at the store for less than a year when I really started to get curious about him. He was good at the job—quick to learn, efficient, and always steady, which made him a solid addition to the team. He wasn't one for small talk, but when he did speak, his words carried weight. He had this way of dropping into conversations at just the right moment—never the center of attention, but always aware.

There was something about him that intrigued me, an intelligence mixed with restraint that made me wonder what went on behind those sharp, thoughtful eyes.

I thought about asking him more personal questions now and then, but work was always busy, and I wasn't the prying type.

About nine months in, I finally caved and asked him to grab coffee. It was nice—easy, low-stakes. A few days later, he asked me out for coffee too. That's when I started to wonder: maybe there's something here after all.

Coffee was simple, easy. He was a little better at small talk one-on-one, but I could tell he was still holding back. It was like he had a whole world inside him that he wasn't ready to share just yet.

And honestly? It was a little frustrating. The coffee dates didn't lead anywhere. No suggestive flirting. No stray touches. Not even a maybe. I started wondering—were the girls on the store side right? Was Sam a boyfriend? Was Lind gay? I already knew that wasn't correct, but still.

Then he asked me out for pizza.

That was different. This time, the conversation went deeper. He told me about his divorce, how it had gutted him, how he was still piecing himself back together. He liked me, he admitted, wanted to see me more, but hoped he wasn't moving too slow.

And that was the moment—right then—that my brain short-circuited for a second. Too slow? I'd been single for a couple of years now, and this was starting to feel like a crawl. What about holding hands? Hugs? Maybe—oh, I don't know—kisses? Something that actually led somewhere? Because, at this rate, I was single-handedly keeping the battery industry afloat.

The thought made me laugh later, but at the time? It just left me frustrated.

And then—I got sick.

It hit me like a freight train—an upper respiratory infection that knocked me flat on my ass. I never get sick, so this was new and absolutely unwelcome. Monday morning, I managed to drag myself to work, but by ten, even my supervisor was insisting I go home. That's when I knew it was bad—I never called in, never left early. The drive home was a blur, and by the time I collapsed into bed, I barely remembered the rest of the day.

Tuesday morning, I felt just as miserable but woke up starving. I stopped for a breakfast sandwich on my way to urgent care, took one bite, and that was it. Covid test—negative.

Antibiotics—prescribed. List of over-the-counter meds—handed to me like a sad consolation prize. Hydrate, rest, don't die.

**

Back home, my phone buzzed. Lind.

He was checking in.

I told him I was fine, just needed rest.

He offered to bring me something, and I... declined. *Why?* If I was being honest with myself, I wasn't sure how to let someone take care of me. Women are always the ones looking after everyone else—when is it our turn?

But for just a second, I let myself imagine it. Someone showing up with soup, fluffing my pillows, making me feel looked after.

I pushed the thought away.

So when a knock sounded at my door later that afternoon, I ignored it. Probably a package.

Then came a second knock—firmer.

I groaned, dragging myself out of bed, too hot and miserable to grab a robe. The meds hadn't kicked in yet, and I shuffled my way downstairs, feeling like a zombie. I cracked the door open, squinting against the light, and there he was.

Lind.

Standing there, looking like himself—calm, steady, and entirely too capable—holding a deli bag.

My brain took a second to catch up. He came. I hadn't asked him to, and that made me feel... warm. And mildly annoyed. Because now he was seeing me like this—sweaty, disheveled, wrapped in pajamas that did not do me any favors.

His eyes flickered with concern, then—briefly—to my chest.

Shit.

I realized what my pajama top was doing (or, more specifically, what it wasn't doing) and quickly threw an arm across my chest, clearing my throat.

"Hi," I croaked, my voice rough from too much coughing and not enough dignity. A small, tired smile tugged at the corner of my mouth anyway. "What are you up to?"

Lind tilted his head slightly, the beginnings of a grin forming. "I come bearing sustenance for thy lady," he announced, voice dipped in mock-heroic flair.

For a second, I just stared at him. Really? The whole 'medieval knight' routine? I didn't know whether to roll my eyes or laugh, but—okay, fine. It was cute. And a little unexpected.

He stood there, waiting, looking almost... hesitant.

I had a choice.

I could send him on his way.

Or I could let him in.

Something in me wanted him there. Maybe it was the fever. Maybe it was just exhaustion. Or maybe... it was everything else—the way he'd shown up, the way he'd cared enough to check, to come, to bring something without me having to ask.

I stepped back, opening the door.

Lind crossed the threshold, and I motioned toward the kitchen. As he walked in, I glanced down at the backpack he'd left by the door, my foggy brain barely registering what that might mean.

I followed him into the kitchen, rubbing my arms against the chill, already feeling the weight of his presence. Lind. Here. Now.

And I wasn't sure how I felt about that yet.

I'll eat in the kitchen

Lind set the deli bag on the counter. "I brought you chicken noodle soup and a sandwich," he said, his voice calm and steady, like this was just a normal thing for him—showing up, taking care of people. "Where are your bowls? I'll heat some up for you."

For a second, I considered just pointing him in the right direction and dragging myself back to bed, but something in me resisted. Letting him take over like that felt... vulnerable. I wasn't used to someone looking after me. And more than that, I wasn't sure how I felt about him being upstairs in my space.

I grabbed the throw blanket from the couch and wrapped it around myself as I eased into a chair at the table.

I pointed to the cabinet. Lind retrieved the bowls, pouring the soup, placing them in the microwave. He barely needed direction, moving easily through my kitchen. He looked, I pointed again, he grabbed the spoons and paper towels without hesitating, as if he'd done this a hundred times before.

Something about that made my chest tighten.

Sitting across from him, cradling the warm bowl in my hands, I felt the first real sense of relief I'd had since getting sick. Not just from the food, but from the presence. The fact that I wasn't alone. That Lind was here, of all people.

Had I wished for this? Had I somehow made this happen?

Or was this just luck? Maybe bad luck. Maybe a setup for disaster. But then...

I pushed the thought away. *Stop thinking. Stop overthinking. Just eat the damn soup.*

I gave him the rundown from the doctor, keeping my voice light, as if this fever and exhaustion hadn't completely wrecked me. He asked about the meds, if I had the over-the-counter stuff urgent care suggested. He even offered to pick up more.

I had to stop myself from getting emotional.

It wasn't just the offer—it was the way he meant it. Like he actually wanted to help. Like it wasn't an obligation or something he'd begrudgingly agreed to. It was so simple, but something about it lodged itself in my throat.

"I have most of it." Not willing to admit to him I hadn't gotten everything they suggested. Lind didn't need to know that.

When I finished eating, he took my bowl to the sink.

"Leave them, I'll get to it later," I mumbled, suddenly a little self-conscious about the mess—coffee cups, a couple of plates stacked in the sink, the usual signs of a few sick days.

But Lind ignored me, rinsing the bowls like he was in his own kitchen. That quiet, matter-of-fact way of doing things—just taking care of what needed to be done—sent another wave of vulnerability through me.

This is different, I thought.

And the best part? It was Lind.

Then he turned, looking at me. "Want me to tuck you in?"

I shot him back a look. *Really?*

He was already grinning, but there was something almost... hesitant in his expression, like he wasn't sure how I'd take it. Like he was offering, but would back off if I wanted him to.

Something in me almost said no. I could have made a joke, waved him off, kept things at arm's length where they were safer.

But safer from what?

The last asshole I'd dated was more than a year ago. Lind wasn't him. Lind wasn't anyone I'd ever dated before.

What did I actually want right now?

Maybe it was the need to not feel so... alone.

I nodded. "Okay."

Lind followed me upstairs.

I climbed into bed and burrowed under the blankets, pulling them tight around me, trying to shake the chills that wouldn't let go.

Then, as I rolled onto my side, I heard the rustle of fabric. His shoes hit the floor. The bed shifted.

My heart kicked up a little. Lind is in bed with me.

Not *in* bed, exactly—he was on top of the covers, but still. The weight of his body on the mattress, the sheer presence of him, made something in my chest flutter—uncomfortably?

I wasn't sure how I felt about it in that moment.

Then he moved closer.

The warmth of his body seeped through the blankets, his arm draped over me gently... carefully. My body tensed on instinct—what does he want? But Lind didn't move beyond that.

Just... held me.

For a long, quiet moment, I stayed rigid, waiting for something else.

Nothing.

No pressure. No expectation.

Just being there.

And slowly—bit by bit—I relaxed. My body softened. My breath evened out. His warmth worked its way into me, easing the cold ache of fever.

A small, tired smile on my lips.

He's not moving too slow now, I thought hazily, as my eyelids drifted closed.

Or maybe I was just too tired to care.

Chapter 19

None of my fantasies

I wasn't sure how much time had passed when I heard his voice.

Soft. Hesitant. "You need anything?"

I thought for a second, trying to pull myself out of sleep.

"Water," I murmured.

Hydrate, hydrate, hydrate—the nurse's voice echoed in my head. My throat felt dry from breathing through my mouth.

Lind didn't say anything. He just got up. I heard his footsteps moving downstairs.

A minute later, he was back, pressing a cold bottle into my hand. I took a few sips, the coolness soothing against my raw throat, and set it on my nightstand.

He placed a second bottle on his side.

I hesitated—*his side*—the intimacy of it caught me off guard.

The thought of it made me smile though.

Then, in the quiet. "Mind if I use the bathroom?"

I let out a small laugh. "Of course."

It was strange—this whole thing. Navigating the space between coworkers, friends, maybe something more—while I was sick and exhausted and feeling entirely not like myself.

And yet... it didn't feel wrong. It felt... nice. Like we were finally moving.

When Lind came back from the bathroom, I was still lying in the same position, back to him, my body relaxed but my mind buzzing with uncertainty again.

I heard him moving, the quiet rustling of fabric, the soft clink of metal against wood. What is he doing?

Glancing over my shoulder, I caught sight of him unbuckling his belt. Oh, shit—is he getting undressed? My heart skipped, my muscles tensed. Then he sat on the edge of the bed, taking off his socks. He pulled his keys, wallet, and phone from his pockets and set them on the nightstand.

I inhaled slowly, my pulse steadied. Right—just getting comfortable.

Still, when he lay down behind me again, shifting to claim whatever blankets I hadn't already cocooned around myself, I could feel the difference.

He was closer now. Not just near me but right there, his warmth pressing into my back.

Instinctively, my arms folded tighter over my chest. Why? Protection? From what? My shivering had mostly stopped, so this wasn't about warmth anymore. It was something else—some knee-jerk reaction I hadn't expected.

And I had to admit, none of my fantasies about Lind had ever involved protecting my chest from him.

WTF, Dana?

Then—without really thinking—I reached back, my hand finding his thigh.

Just for a second. My fingers rested on his thigh briefly. Fabric. Pants.

I wasn't sure why I did it—maybe I needed to know. Confirm something. Reassure myself? Maybe. But the second I felt the soft, worn fabric of his jeans beneath my fingertips, two feelings hit me at the same time—relief... and disappointment. In equal measure.

I pulled my hand back quickly, tucking it under my chin. *What the hell was that?*

But instead of retreating, I shifted a little closer to him.

Something about knowing he was there—solid, steady, warm—made me feel safer. This is okay. He's here. He's not pushing—we're still moving slowly.

Was I comfortable with that? A small, wry smile began to form. *Not going down that rabbit hole tonight.*

I sighed quietly, my body melted into his, and Lind just held me. He didn't say anything. Didn't shift. Didn't expect anything. And that was... comforting.

***

I drifted in and out of sleep for a few hours, waking to the sound of steady breathing behind me. The fog in my head was lifting slightly—not enough to feel normal, but enough to feel more aware of the moment. My body still ached, but the fever had eased.

I shifted, testing my limbs, and felt Lind stir behind me. He was awake too.

We started talking—soft, unhurried. Nothing heavy. Just the kind of conversation you have when there's nothing else demanding your attention—work, family, random thoughts that didn't need conclusions.

One arm under my head, the other rested across me, his fingers grazing my stomach, my thigh, my arm—small, absent movements as he adjusted, got comfortable. Casual, easy.

And yet, I found myself sharing things I hadn't planned to. The warmth between us felt natural. Safe.

For a moment, I hesitated before saying, "I think I'm a little hungry." Lind shifted slightly, his voice still thick with drowsiness. "Are you asking me to get you more soup?"

I didn't want him to move. I wanted to stay tangled up like this, wrapped in warmth and the quiet intimacy of it. But... yeah. Food sounded good too.

Without hesitation, Lind rolled off his side of the bed. "I'll heat up the rest of it. Would you like the sandwich too?" I smiled into my pillow.

"Yes, please," I murmured. "And could you bring it up here? I don't want to go up and down the stairs again tonight."

Lind grinned sideways. "Anything for thy lady."

I groaned. "No more medieval knight shit today, please."

He chuckled, heading for the door. "Whatever the lady of the house wishes."

Ugh!

As soon as he was gone, I propped myself up, adjusting the pillows behind me, trying—for no damn reason at all—to look a little more put-together before he got back. Which was stupid. I was still sick. Still a mess. But maybe I didn't want to look quite so... miserable.

When Lind returned, he was carrying two bowls of soup, the sandwich, quartered neatly, and a small pack of crackers balanced under his arm.

His eyes met mine, and he smiled. Not at me. Not at the way I looked. Just... at *me*.

And I liked that.

***

I ate propped up in bed while he sat on the edge, facing me, our conversation easy, warm.

But at some point, I realized the way Lind was watching me.

Not intensely. Not in a way that felt demanding. But curious. Admiring. His eyes moved over me, lingering here and there, and suddenly I was aware of my pajama top—the way the fabric clung to my chest, outlining the shape of me.

For a brief second, I thought about pulling the blanket higher.

But I didn't. His gaze wasn't intrusive. It didn't make me uncomfortable. It just was.

And, if I'm being honest with myself, I didn't mind it. This... was not unlike several other fantasies.

***

When we finished eating, Lind took the dishes downstairs. I listened to him moving around my kitchen, the clink of bowls, the soft rush of water. The sound of someone taking care of things.

Taking care of me. Because he wanted to.

After visiting the bathroom I fell back into bed. I sank into my pillows, warmth spreading through me. I let myself really feel it—this moment, this feeling of being cared for. Not just by someone. But by Lind.

And when he came back, setting his backpack quietly by the doorway, something inside me fluttered.

It wasn't just the fact that he brought his things upstairs. It was the confidence in it. The quiet certainty that he didn't need to ask. That he was here. That he was staying.

And at this point... I couldn't imagine him not staying.

The warmth of our bodies pressed together under the blankets created a cocoon that was almost *too* comfortable. For the first time in days, I wasn't shivering. The fever chills that had rattled through me earlier seemed to be fading, and instead of being caught in that miserable, achy cold, I felt warm. *Safe.*

Sleep tugged at me, my mind drifting in and out, but something else itched at the edges of my awareness. A thought. A small, nagging desire.

A shower.

I mumbled something about it, barely registering my own voice. "Later," I murmured, mostly to myself, already sinking back into drowsiness.

I don't even think Lind heard me.

What are you wearing

At some point, I don't know how much time had passed, Lind shifted behind me. "Bathroom," he said, his voice low, already half up before I even managed an acknowledgment.

I heard the faint sound of his backpack zipper. My brain flickered with mild curiosity, but exhaustion weighed me down too much to open my eyes and see what he was up to.

I must have dozed off again, because the next thing I knew, the bed dipped as he got back under the covers.

Warmth. Immediate, surrounding, comforting.

Without thinking, I reached back, resting my hand on his leg. A reflex, more than anything. Just checking in, I supposed. But my fingers found a softer fabric. Pajama pants?

I exhaled, barely conscious of the small, lazy question that left my lips. "What are you wearing?"

Lind propped himself up on an elbow. His voice held quiet amusement as he answered, "Pajama bottoms. I was getting hot under the covers."

That answer made me smile, despite myself. "You came prepared?"

I opened my eyes just enough to catch the glint of humor in his expression as he shrugged. "I didn't know if you'd let me stay, but... you know. Just in case."

The way he said it—light, almost sheepish—sent a small, unexpected flutter through me.

I let my hand rest on his thigh for a moment before pulling it back, folding my arms across my chest again, tucking my hands under my chin. Then, without thinking, I pressed myself closer.

My bare skin, the heat of my body—separated from his by only the thin fabric between us.

I shifted slightly, adjusting against him, feeling the pressure of him there, the way the fabric did nothing to mute the sensation. I smiled.

A quiet hum left my lips, but the awareness was exciting. He must have felt it too, as he adjusted himself against me as well.

Lind's warmth, his... presence, it was...I didn't know. Needed. Wanted. Desired maybe...

Outside, the sky was dimming. It would be dark soon.

***

As the minutes blurred into the next few hours, I drifted in and out of sleep, my body easing into his.

Lind stayed with me, solid and steady, my head resting lightly against his arm, his other arm draped over me, warm and there.

At some point, I became aware of how much better I felt. The fever was gone—I could tell. My body still ached, my chest still tight, but the crushing exhaustion had lifted some. My sinuses were still stuffed, and I knew the cough wasn't done with me yet, but I wasn't drowning in sickness anymore.

I wasn't better. But I was better than before.

Lind shifted slightly, and I let my hand drift to his arm, my fingertips idly tracing against his skin, almost without thinking.

At some point, my fingers found his hand. I held it, just for a moment, feeling the solid warmth of it, the quiet assurance in his touch.

A part of me wondered—was this too much? Too intimate for something still so undefined?

But then I thought back to the end of our hike—Lind saying he was taking things slow because it mattered. Because I mattered. *Important*, he said. *I was important.*

I told him if we were moving any slower, we'd be backing up. Then he leaned in and kissed me.

The memory of that kiss had me wondering—was this really too much? Too intimate? Was this really still undefined?

I reached back, my fingers trailing lightly over his leg and hip. I wasn't in a hurry—just touching.

It wasn't necessarily an invitation—I didn't have the strength for that. But it was something.

A thank you? A silent acknowledgment? A way of saying: *I see you. I feel you. And I'm glad you're here.*

I wasn't even sure myself. But I *was* happy he was.

Chapter 20

He's naked

The faint glow of the nightlight softened the room into warm, hazy shadows.

I hardly noticed Lind move at first. The shift in weight, the subtle lift of the blankets, the absence of warmth behind me.

Then, realization.

My stomach tightened—a brief, instinctive flicker of worry—but before I could fully wake, I heard it.

The bathroom.

The soft sound of running water.

I let out a slow breath, my body easing again. *Good. Still here.*

The thought of Lind standing there, washing up, made me smile faintly. I imagined the way he probably ran his fingers through his hair, sighed as he stretched his neck.

But I didn't move. Didn't open my eyes.

I was so tired.

***

The bed shifted again as Lind returned. I felt him slip in behind me.

His arm under me, the other draped over me as I pressed back against him.

The steady rhythm of his breathing soothing against my back.

I barely processed it, my body sinking further into sleep—into warmth, comfort, presence—but as I reached back again, my fingers grazing the side of his hip, something was different.

No soft fabric.

No pajama pants.

Just bare skin.

My heart skipped.

I froze, pulling my hand back—as if I'd touched something forbidden.

I curled in on myself, tucking my arms across my chest, my hands under my chin. Tighter.

He's naked.

My mind raced.

Wait. Had I missed something? Some cue? Had he thought—?

But then, I stilled. *Slow down, Dana, don't overthink it.*

What is he doing... anything?

No.

No movement. No pressure. No expectation.

Just Lind.

Just this moment.

The swirl of emotions inside me—embarrassment, intrigue, uncertainty, want—clashed together, all tangled up.

But beneath it all, I thought...

Did I mind? Was this OK with me?

A slow breath. A pause.

A smile, a whispered truth:

Maybe I don't mind... Hell, isn't this almost exactly my fantasy?

Except in that one... I was naked too.

Does this man know my fantasies

After a moment, I realized I needed space to think—space to process.

"I need to use the bathroom," I murmured, keeping my voice steady even as my mind swirled.

I sat up, immediately aware of his warmth still clinging to my skin, the weight of his presence behind me. Lind didn't move, didn't say anything—just lay there, silent, steady, waiting.

I slipped out of bed, feeling the cool air against my skin where his heat had been. I headed to the bathroom.

His pajama pants and T-shirt sat neatly folded on top of his backpack.

Of course they were.

A small smile formed on my lips. *This man.*

Shutting the door softly behind me, I leaned against the counter, exhaling slowly.

The bright glow of the bathroom light illuminated my reflection.

Flushed cheeks. Tousled hair. Barely parted lips.

Was it the fever, or was it him?

Did I know the answer?

I turned the faucet, letting cool water rush over my fingers before splashing it against my face, chasing away the haze.

He's naked. With me.

And instead of fear or hesitation, a slow, mischievous grin took over my lips.

We're moving now, aren't we?

The truth was clear.

I didn't want him to leave... because I *did* want him.

I peeled off my pajamas, running a damp washcloth over my body, letting the warmth of it sink into my skin. A quick swipe of deodorant, then I slipped back into fresh fabric, the cotton cool, grounding.

Turning the knob, I stepped out, pausing as the dim glow of the night light caught his silhouette.

Lind still lay on his side, waiting.

I paused.

DANA'S LOVES

Does this man know my fantasies?

I flicked off the bathroom light, my steps slow and deliberate as I wandered back to my side of the bed.

My side.

A small, secret smile on my lips.

My fingers played with the hem of my pajama top.

The room was too dim to see his expression, but I felt it—the weight of his gaze, the quiet pull of anticipation between us.

And then, without overthinking, I pulled my top over my head, the cool air kissing my skin in its absence.

My bottoms followed, slipping to the floor, forgotten.

My pulse quickened as I climbed back into bed, pressing bare skin to bare skin.

A ripple of heat. Awareness.

My back fit against his chest, the slow rise and fall of his breathing syncing with mine.

I tangled my legs with his, letting our bodies align.

His response was immediate.

Not rushed. Not greedy.

Just... there.

I've been with men who would have been all over me by now.

Grabbing. Touching. Feeling. Poking.

Lind wasn't.

Was I happy about that? Or confused?

I tested him.

Pressed my hips back. Felt him press right back.

A slow rhythm.

Searching. Finding. Exploring.

His fingers flexed against my hip, responding to the movement. Feeling it. Becoming part of it.

His touch traveled lower, skimming down my thigh, then back up, then back down.

When his other hand reached over and found my breast, a sharp inhale caught in my throat.

I didn't hesitate.

I reached down, took his hand from my thigh, and guided him to mirror the first, my touch firm, certain, wanting.

This. I wanted this. I wanted him.

His lips pressed against my shoulder, the warmth of them sent shivers down my spine, the kind that had nothing to do with my fever.

I leaned into him, tilting my head, offering more.

His lips pressed against my neck, his breath warm against my skin.

He let go of my breast. I missed his touch the second it was gone.

But as his hand traced down my body I knew where he was headed.

Yes, Oh God, YES.

I draped my leg back over his, opening myself to his touch.

My heart raced, anticipation curling low and insistent.

This wasn't just physical.

Of course, it was.

It was also the way he moved.

Slow. Intentional. As if he was asking.

My answer was yes.

Yes to this.

Yes to him.

Yes to letting him see me, touch me, know me in a way I hadn't let anyone in a long time.

I reached down to cover his hand with mine. The sensation...

Feeling his hand explore me, the pleasure doubled—what he was doing, what he was making me feel, the heat of his touch itself.

I pressed closer, wanting more.

Was he waiting for me

After a moment, I let go of his hand and reached back, searching for him.

I wanted to feel him. Play with him. Show him how much I wanted him.

His cock was firm in my hand—the feel of it, the smoothness of his skin, the sensitivity of his head.

The moan that slipped from him, the want in his tone, the way he flinched as I played... it sent a rush through me.

I wanted more...

Anticipation thrummed through me. Was he waiting for me?

Because if you are, you're still backing up.

He must have read my mind, because in the next breath, the only thing stopping him from being inside me was my hand.

So I let go.

The lightning strike of pleasure as he pushed into me erased everything else.

Our rhythm started slow but quickly built, my body trembling with pleasure I hadn't felt—from another person—in so long.

But even as desire flared, my breath caught for another reason.

The wheezing. The congestion pressing into my chest.

Exhaustion and desire clashing.

Damn it! It's not like I'm on top doing cowgirl. I'm just laying here enjoying him!

He knew. Our rhythm slowed.

Lind felt it before I could say it.

When he pulled away, I felt his absence immediately—a pause, a shift in his focus.

My body resisted, my legs tightening around him, my hand reaching back for his hip to hold him there.

Stay.

But he pulled away again—just enough—rolling me onto my back.

Yes, I thought, *yes.*

I let him move me, my legs wrapping around him again, my breath ragged, my body aching for him to keep going.

But he didn't. *Why did he stop?*

His gaze met mine, and I could see it—the heat, the want, the hesitation.

Confusion flickered through me. Was he waiting for me to say something?

Why isn't he continuing? And then—his lips.

The warmth of his mouth on my neck, trailing lower. The question dissolved.

Each kiss stoked the fire, replacing doubt with sensation.

Collarbone. Chest. Nipples.

My back arched, hands in his hair, on his shoulders, anywhere I could reach.

My legs stayed locked around him, refusing to let him go.

But he wasn't rushing back inside me. He was changing course.

He kissed lower, and lower still, and then I realized.

My grip on him loosened, realization sinking in like a slow, delicious revelation.

I think I stopped breathing when it hit me. He's not done pleasing me. He's just steering us into something else.

His kisses slowed at my belly button, lips grazing my skin, sending small electric shocks through me.

Anticipation built.

His hands gripped my hips, slid beneath me, like he was serving me up to him.

The way he moved—the way he looked at me—I felt both vulnerable and cherished at the same time.

I closed my eyes, letting it take me.

First stroke of his tongue

The first slow pass of his tongue made me gasp.

My head tilted back, fingers clenching the sheets.

Oh my God.

It had been too long.

Too long since I'd been seen like this, pleasured like this.

Each movement of his mouth was purposeful, measured, exploratory.

He was learning me. Savoring me.

I could hear myself—breathless, uneven, a little raspy.

The soft, desperate noises escaping me, mixing with the sound of his breathing, his lips, his tongue.

One hand gripped the bed, keeping me from floating away.

The other—buried in his hair, tangled in him, anchoring me to him.

This wasn't just pleasure. It was the way he watched me.

The way he listened to my body, read my reactions, adjusted.

The way he made me feel like I was the only thing in the world right now.

I'd rarely had this kind of attention before. It made me feel... special.

***

When his tongue ventured even lower, carefully exploring places I'd never allowed anyone else, a fleeting moment of hesitation flickered through my mind.

But it was brief, quickly eclipsed by the gentleness of his touch, the slow, easy pressure of his tongue, and the way his fingers brushed softly, knowingly, over places I'd kept private, places that had only ever belonged to me.

175

He didn't insist. He didn't push. His movements were invitations—slow, patient, asking rather than taking—and I accepted without reservation.

The vulnerability I felt was tempered by the care and tenderness he showed.

His mouth returned to my clit, this time firmer, surer.

And the pleasure coiled tighter, hotter, sharper.

His hand reached up and cupped my breast, kneading my nipple. I placed my hand over his, encouraging more, harder.

And then I came... hard

The tension spread through me, like fire, like lightning.

Every nerve, every cell caught in the ecstasy of him.

The sounds spilling from me—uncontrolled, unfiltered.

Lind didn't stop, didn't slow—kept me right on that edge, right where I wanted to be.

And then—I came... hard.

My body arched, tensed, released—the pleasure tearing through me so forcefully that I cried.

The walls might have muffled it.

The neighbors might have heard.

I didn't care.

Lind's tongue and hands stayed with me, coaxing me through it, drawing every last pulse, every last spark from me.

Until I couldn't take any more.

I reached down with the other hand too, and used both to gently push his head away.

Too sensitive. Too much.

I rolled onto my side, the aftershocks still rolling through me, making me tremble.

My breathing was ragged, strained, uneven. Then—a cough.

It broke through the haze of pleasure, and for a brief second, I felt embarrassment creep in.

But Lind wouldn't care. Of course he wouldn't.

The fading glow of my orgasm left me feeling weightless, half-floating in the warmth of the bed.

I wanted to feel him

When the tremors subsided, I rolled onto my back, knees bent, legs open, waiting for him.

My chest rose and fell unevenly as I tried to catch my breath.

He was looking at me.

And something in that gaze reached me deeper than I expected. I felt... cherished, important.

Even as the pleasure still hummed through me, I wanted more.

I knew my body couldn't handle more—but I wanted it.

I wanted him—inside me—again.

Lind watched me. He could see the want in my eyes. But he could hear the labored breathing too.

He reached out and gently pushed my knees to one side, to make space for himself.

He lay down beside me. No urgency. No rush. Just there.

I was still wanting, I knew he had to be too.

But he put that aside for me, at least for now... and that was a kind of care I wasn't used to.

As we lay side by side, I became acutely aware of my breathing again.

Each inhale still labored, still rasping.

I felt his fingertips trailing down my stomach to my hair, playing with it idly.

A small, affectionate intimacy. Not a demand. Just a touch. A simple, quiet connection.

And before I could think too hard about it, my own hand drifted down below his belly, seeking to share in the same intimacy he was offering.

Nothing more. Just this. Just us. Just this moment.

Chapter 21

No one had ever done this for me

When my breathing steadied, Lind put his arm under my head and guided me onto his chest.

I let myself rest there, my body draping over his, my thigh resting on top of his erection.

The rhythmic rise and fall of his chest against my cheek was comforting, and with each slow inhale, the last remnants of tension melted away.

I traced the lines of his jaw, the curve of his lips, fingertips moving without thought, without purpose—just feeling.

For once, I wasn't thinking about the past or the future.

Just this.

The warmth of his body against mine.

The quiet, uncomplicated comfort of simply being held.

After a while, Lind shifted.

The bed dipped as he got up, but I stayed where I was, half-awake, half-drifting, listening to the soft sounds of him in the bathroom.

I wondered what he was doing, but I was too tired, too content to move.

When he returned, he brought a warm washcloth and a towel.

I blinked up at him, confused but curious.

Without a word, he rolled me gently onto my back, easing my legs a little.

His movements were careful—tender.

When he placed the warm cloth between my legs, my breath caught.

A rush of emotions—surprise, gratitude, curiosity, confusion, fascination.

I watched him silently, my chest tight—not from exertion, but from the unfamiliar intimacy of it.

No one had ever done this for me before.

It left me feeling open, and exposed in a most beautiful way.

When he finished, he leaned down, his breath ghosting over my skin before he placed one last playful kiss between my legs—a quick nip. One slow lick that sent a sharp jolt through me.

My body jumped in surprise, a soft cry escaping before I could stop it.

Lind's grin spread across his face, completely unrepentant.

Despite myself, I couldn't help but smile back.

As he went back to the bathroom, I lay there, still feeling the warmth of his touch, the feel of the washcloth against my skin.

When he returned, he pulled the covers up from the floor, draping them over me before getting under them himself.

We lay there, face to face, in comfortable silence.

When we talked, it was soft, unhurried, our hands occasionally exploring each other, knowing, smiling.

My eyes grew heavier, the weight of sleep pulling at me again.

When I finally rolled over, his arm wrapped around me, and I nestled into him, our bodies fitting together naturally in our usual spooning position.

Penis-cillian

The shrill sound of Lind's alarm broke the quiet of the early morning, pulling me from sleep.

I groaned softly but didn't move, keeping my back to him as he fumbled for his phone.

The bed shifted as he sat up, and I heard the faint tapping of his fingers on the screen.

Half-asleep, I mumbled, "Are you going to work? Who are you texting?"

His voice was low, steady. "Texting Georgette."

Pause.

"Letting her know I won't be in because I'm warm and comfortable in bed with Dana, taking care of her and giving her shots of penis-cillin."

That snapped me awake.

I whipped around to face him, eyes wide, my brain scrambling to process what I'd just heard.

His expression unreadable, except for the tiny smirk tugging at the corner of his mouth.

"You told her what?" I demanded, half-shocked, half-amused.

He wouldn't actually text that... right?

Lind let me hang for a bit. Then...

"I told her I ate something from the fridge that had been there too long and wasn't feeling well."

Relief washed over me, quickly followed by mock indignation.

"That's not funny," I muttered, swatting his shoulder.

But I couldn't stop the grin creeping across my face.

Lind chuckled, rolling back over, pulling the blankets tighter around us.

I could still hear the amusement in his voice.

Maybe it was a little funny, I thought, fighting the urge to laugh as I closed my eyes again.

The morning after

When I woke again, sunlight streamed through the blinds, warming the room. I stretched slightly, careful not to disturb Lind, but I knew he was awake.

I could feel his gaze on my back. My chest tightened—I needed a moment.

Slipping out of bed, I moved toward the bathroom. I didn't look back.

Inside, I shut the door quietly and leaned against the counter. The mirror reflected a mess of hair, flushed skin, faint circles under my eyes.

The morning after. A soft huff left my lips. I hadn't had one of those in a long time.

Cool water rushed over my fingers before I splashed it onto my face, hoping to steady myself. Last night, the memories—they came all at once.

The way he touched me—attuned to what I needed.

Like I was something fragile, but not weak. It wasn't just sex. It felt like more.

Lind had adjusted to me, to my body's limitations, with patience and care.

That meant something, didn't it?

My mind was swirling.

What does this mean?

Lind wasn't like anyone I'd been with before. The way he cared—it wasn't just about the physical.

It was about me. *That* thought was both comforting... and unsettling.

I grabbed a washcloth, ran it under warm water, and pressed it to my face.

Does this mean we're together now? Or was this just... a boy toy thing?

God. The words from the bar crept in: *Women always say they want a boy toy, but the second they sleep with him, it's 'you're mine now.'*

I'd laughed at the time, insisted I knew the difference.

But now?

My stomach twisted. *I'm not one of those women... Am I?*

No. This was more than that. Lind *made* it more than that.

The fear of overthinking crept in, but I couldn't stop the questions. *What if last night was the start of something real?* Something I swore I wasn't looking for.

But then, another voice whispered—

Would he really go this far if it was just about sex?

I shook my head, pushing the thought away.

For now, there were no answers. I wasn't sure if that was exciting or terrifying.

I dried my face, and wrapped myself in a towel.

As I reached for the doorknob, I made a decision. I didn't need all the answers...

What I needed was to take the next step—whatever that looked like.

Chapter 22

Let's make breakfast

When I stepped back into the bedroom, Lind was still lying in bed, his eyes tracking me as I crossed the room. I caught the faint flicker of disappointment as he took in the towel securely wrapped around me, and I couldn't help the smirk on my lips.

"What?" I asked.

"Oh, nothing..." he said with a trace of playful defeat.

But beneath the humor, I felt the pull of something more.

I moved toward the dresser, the cool air against my damp skin. I could still feel him from last night. The echoes of his touch. Whatever this was—whatever it *might* become—I couldn't deny the flicker of hope that it could be something worth holding on to.

I pulled out clean pajamas as Lind sat up, stretching. Then, he got up, crossed the room to his backpack near the door, and grabbed his T-shirt and pajama bottoms before heading into the bathroom.

I watched him.

Nice. *Very nice,* Lind.

A slow smile spread across my face, admiring the view.

But my stomach was rumbling.

"I'm starving," I called after him. "Let's make some breakfast."

He nodded just before his perfect, bare ass disappeared behind the bathroom door.

Oh, really? I bit my lip. *Is that your little revenge for me covering up?*

I thought back to the flicker of disappointment on his face and let my smile grow.

Wow. *Did I really want to see him in all his glory as much as he wanted to see me?*

The answer... it was already written in my smile.

But first—*food*.

So, you're playing it cool now

I slipped into the clean pajamas and headed downstairs.

The ache in my muscles reminded me that I wasn't over this, but I felt better than yesterday.

As I reached the bottom of the stairs, I surveyed the damage.

My living room looked like it had been hit by a small tornado.

I started straightening up, picking up a few stray blankets, tossing crumpled tissues into the trash.

Even small things, like tidying up, made me feel like I was taking back control.

The sound of Lind's footsteps on the stairs pulled my attention back.

I glanced up briefly, taking in the yellow cotton fabric of his pajamas.

They clung just enough to hint at the outline of his body underneath.

My stomach did a little flip.

The man cleaned up well—even in pajama pants.

I barely looked up from folding a throw blanket. "Want some coffee? Got instant."

"Yep." Lind nodded, and I set two cups of water in the microwave.

As the whir of the microwave filled the silence, I returned to tidying the living room.

I bent to grab another blanket, folding it, letting my mind wander.

I'm sure my top shifted every time I moved, the way it fit loose and soft against me.

And as I bent over I could feel the cool air against more than I probably should have been showing.

Part of me knew Lind was looking.

His gaze felt almost tangible.

But I didn't rush to adjust myself.

Was it intentional? *Maybe.*

Was I comfortable knowing he noticed? *Yes.*

I straightened up, smoothing the hem of my pajama top, and caught Lind's eyes for a brief second before he looked away.

His expression carefully neutral—too neutral.

So, you're playing it cool now?

He looked back at me and caught the corner of my mouth turning up.

If this morning was a game of subtle glances and quiet teases, I wasn't sure who was winning.

But I was starting to enjoy it.

What am I working with here

The microwave beeped, snapping me back to the present.

I added two scoops to each, his—black. I added a little creamer to mine.

"Here you go," I said, handing Lind his cup while keeping the other for myself.

I took a sip, the warmth comforting in my hands, though my mind was still buzzing from the quiet tension in the room.

Lind glanced around the kitchen, his gaze sweeping over the counters and fridge with the air of someone taking inventory.

Then, after a moment, he set his mug down and walked to the fridge.

"Okay," he said, tilting his head, "what am I working with here?"

I grimaced, taking another sip.

"Not much," I admitted. "I've been sick, remember? I didn't get to go grocery shopping this weekend. But there should be eggs, hash browns, cheese... maybe some other stuff."

He opened the fridge, scanning the contents with a level of focus I wouldn't have expected for a casual breakfast.

Then, triumphantly, he pulled out the carton of eggs.

"Alright," he said, pleased.

He found the cheese and frozen hash browns, holding them up like a trophy.

"This is a good start," he announced, his head still buried in the fridge.

"What about green pepper? Red pepper? Yellow pepper? Onion? Ham? Bacon? Sausage?"

He rattled off the list so fast I didn't have time to answer between questions.

"I'm sure some of that is in there," I said, amused. "But I don't know how good it is."

A beat later—"Found some onion."

I turned just in time to see him pulling the yellow onion from the drawer like a kid finding an Easter egg.

"Oh God, throw that out," I laughed. "It's ancient."

By the look on his face, he agreed. Into the trash it went.

He rummaged deeper, then held up a small pack of ham over the fridge door.

"Here's a little ham," he said.

"Yeah, but it's not enough for both of us."

"I'll make it work," he bragged.

With part of a red onion he'd also found, and a few more finds, he started prepping.

"Gourmet breakfast coming right up."

I raised an eyebrow. "Gourmet?"

"You're making scrambled eggs, Lind. Let's not get carried away."

He grinned, the corners of his eyes crinkling in a way that made my stomach flutter.

"Trust me. I make the best scrambled eggs you've ever had."

I arched a brow. My smirk was evident too.

"I see bread over there," he nodded toward the counter.

"Well, don't get too ambitious," I said, "I don't even know if I have butter."

Lind opened the fridge again, then grinned.

"Yep, you got butter," he declared, holding it up like another victory.

He shot me a smug smile. "This definitely became a gourmet breakfast."

I rolled my eyes. "Oh, did it now?"

Maybe he did make a mean breakfast

I grabbed the bread, popping slices into the toaster while Lind set a pan on the stove.

The sharp sound of eggs cracking filled the air, followed by the soft sizzle of oil in the pan.

I watched as he moved through the kitchen with quiet efficiency, dicing peppers, chopping the ham, and—Wait. Mushrooms? I blinked.

"Where did you find those?"

Lind shot me a look over his shoulder. "They were in *your* fridge," he said, as if it were obvious.

"Wait, when did I buy mushrooms?"

He shrugged. "I don't know, it's your fridge—and they're still good."

Just then the toast popped up. I pulled the slices onto a plate, buttering them while they were still hot.

I watched as Lind grated cheddar cheese into the eggs, and stirred it together with everything else. It made me rethink my earlier sarcasm.

Okay... maybe he could make a mean breakfast.

***

We sat at the table, the warmth of the morning sun spilling through the windows.

The eggs were fluffy, rich with cheese, and full of texture and flavor—each bite better than the last.

I closed my eyes after the first bite, savoring the flavor.

"Okay," I admitted, nodding. "You win. These are amazing."

Lind chuckled, his gaze steady on me as he forked another bite. "Told you."

For a while, we ate in comfortable silence, but the tension between us was unmistakable.

I could feel his eyes on me.

The way he focused on my face, on my neck—the shifting of my pajama top.

The memory of last night was still fresh. I could feel his restraint—his patience—but his body language was giving him away.

It wasn't just in his expression. It was in the way he leaned toward me.

The way his voice was just a little rougher when he spoke.

Yes, that one

As I finished my toast, Lind set his fork down, his expression shifting.

"Dana."

His voice was low, almost hesitant.

I looked up at him.

"Yeah?"

His lips curved into a slow, wicked smile.

"Do me a favor?"

I raised a brow. Here we go.

I knew this was going to be something sexual, but since it was Lind asking, it was more likely sensual.

But let's see what he wants before I categorize it.

"Probably not."

A lie. And we both knew it.

"Please?" He tilted his head slightly, voice playful, coaxing, like a child begging for a toy.

"What?" I asked, feigning impatience.

He gestured lightly toward me. "Unbutton your top a little. Just that button right there." He pointed.

His eyes flickered to the button between my breasts.

Oh.

That button.

"This one?" I asked, toying with it. His eyes darkened just slightly.

"Yeah. That one."

Heat flushed through me—not from embarrassment but from the way he said it.

Not demanding. Not pleading. Just... horngry.

My first instinct was to play with him a little.

But the truth? I didn't mind.

I was still humming from last night, still wanting.

And the thought of giving him what he wanted—of letting him look—sent a thrill through me.

But instead I said, "No, I don't think so."

But as I toyed with the button—and the idea—I think my smile gave me away.

Lind knew exactly what I was thinking.

For a moment, neither of us moved.

I could feel the quickening thrum of my heart, the weight of his gaze.

And then, with a slow exhale, he leaned back slightly, pulling himself back just enough to keep from tipping over the edge.

"Let's clean up," he said, his voice still low, but lighter now.

Like he was giving us both a second to breathe.

Still wanting, huh

I nodded, our hands bumping against each other as we gathered the plates.

As we moved around each other in the kitchen, his yellow pajama betrayed the effect our little game had on him. The moment I saw it, heat flared inside me—instant, undeniable.

I wondered...

How long could we keep holding back before it all spilled over—again?

Trying to push that thought aside, I stacked the plates neatly on the counter while Lind took care of the pans.

It was such a small thing—cleaning up after breakfast.

But watching him scrub the skillet with easy efficiency made something in my chest tighten.

There was no hesitation. No halfheartedness.

He wasn't just doing this because I was sick.

He was doing it because it needed to be done.

How many men just do the damn dishes without being asked?

I hid a small smile as I set our mugs on the counter next to the sink.

When I offered to help, he shook his head.

"I've got it. Go upstairs, take your meds."

"I'm going to shower while I'm at it."

He nodded, "Good idea. It'll help you feel better."

I turned to go, but my gaze flickered downward—just for a second.

The telltale strain against the soft cotton of his pajamas, showing.

Still wanting, huh?

The thought sent a shiver through me—a longing.

Chapter 23

Did I want him to

The shower felt incredible.

Hot water cascading over me, washing away the stiffness, the heavy feeling of being sick.

I closed my eyes, letting the steam surround me, my mind wandering back to Lind.

The way he'd watched me in the kitchen.

The quiet restraint in his movements.

It wasn't just desire. It was something deeper, more patient.

He wasn't rushing me. He wasn't demanding *anything*.

But the tension between us was undeniable.

And then I realized—

I hadn't locked the door.

I never did, living alone. I barely even bothered to close it.

But the idea of him walking in... of seeing me...

A fresh heat spread through me.

Would he?

Did I want him to?

My cheeks flushed.

I bit my lip, shook my head, trying to push the thought away.

Stop overthinking, Dana.

When I stepped out of the shower, he wasn't there. The door was still closed.

Damn.

I wrapped myself in a towel, taking my time getting dressed. Pajama bottoms. A loose top. Soft. Comfortable.

I caught a glimpse of myself in the mirror.

And I looked...

Happy.

Content, even.

The thought stayed with me as I opened the bathroom door.

One orgasm wasn't enough

Lind was lying on the bed, his head tilted slightly toward the ceiling, but when he saw me, his eyes softened, a broad smile took over his lips, and there was something more...

Anticipation?

"I'm going to jump in the shower," he said, already reaching for his backpack.

I wasn't sure if that was a statement or a question, "You better." My voice was light, and tinged with my own anticipation as I reached out and grazed his chest as we passed.

He glanced back at me just before the bathroom door clicked shut. I let out a slow breath.

I could hear the soft hum of the shower, I sat down on the edge of the bed, my thoughts racing.

The memory of his arousal earlier crept back into my mind. The weight of his desire doing things to me I liked.

I mean, it wasn't just his. My body was still humming. Still remembering the way he touched me.

One orgasm wasn't enough. And I knew it. But it wasn't just about the sex.

The way he moved through my space—cleaning the kitchen, touching me so gently, giving me time to feel better without pushing for more—it was different.

It made me feel seen, cared for... wanted.

His hunger matching my own

I leaned back, my damp hair cool against the pillow, and stared at the ceiling.

The shower stopped. My heart kicked up a little. The door would open any moment, and Lind would walk back in.

Would he look at me the same way he had earlier? Would we let this tension build until it finally snapped?

I didn't have the answers. But I could feel the pull of expectation.

Lind walked out of the bathroom in his pajama and T-shirt, setting his backpack down in the same spot. He laid down on his side facing me, his presence warm, steady.

I reached out, fingers grazing his shoulder, then moving up to his jaw. I traced the outline of his face, marveling at how something so simple could feel so intimate.

His hand found its way to me, gliding lightly along my pajama top, focused, deliberate. From my shoulder to my hip, a slow, exploring touch that sent a shiver through me. When his hand slipped beneath my pajama top, I sucked in a breath. His fingers gently moved along my stomach, waist, and lower back.

Each touch warmed my skin, his presence soothing and electric all at once.

I moved without thinking—rolling over on top of him, my hips pressing into his, my lips finding his. There was no mistaking what we both wanted.

I slid my top over my head, my bare skin pressing into the warmth of his chest. Lind's lips parted against mine, his hunger matching mine.

His mouth moved to my ear, soft nibbles sending waves of heat down my spine.

Lower—to my neck.

Every kiss sent a rush of warmth through me, a quiet sigh escaped me.

His hands roamed—my back, my waist, my hips—like he was learning me piece by piece.

When his lips found my breasts, my fingers curled into the fabric of his T-shirt.

The pleasure was sharp. Electric.

I could feel his arousal pressing against me. It sent a thrill through me.

I reached for him, my hands moving down his chest, his stomach—I needed to feel him.

I needed to feel the hardness of him in my hand. He pushed his pajama bottoms off, and my hand stopped short. He took my hand into his, guiding me, urging me.

I wrapped my fingers around him. Stroking softly, feeling all of him.

He let go of my hand, his fingers skimming over my hips, my thighs... he began pulling at my pajama bottoms.

And then—

He rolled me onto my back, slowly, gently.

The cool air kissed my skin as he pulled my pajama bottoms off completely, leaving me bare beneath him.

I should've felt exposed—vulnerable. But I didn't. His gaze made me feel beautiful, wanted, adored.

He sat up, his knees framing my hips.

I wrapped my legs around him, pulling him closer, needing him.

His hand reached down, guiding himself against me.

He circled—rubbed, played—until I began to moan.

Each stroke sent another pulse through me.

My head fell back, another quiet moan slipping past my lips.

It wasn't just the physical sensations. It was the way he looked at me. Like I was the only thing in the world that mattered.

And when he finally pushed inside me—everything tightened. I arched. I heard myself let out a soft cry.

The fullness of him, the way he moved, sent waves of pleasure rolling through me.

My hands found his shoulders, his arms, his back—holding onto him, anchoring myself to our rhythm.

Each thrust was intentional, steady—Lind wasn't rushing. He was feeling me, knowing me.

My eyes fluttered shut, overwhelmed.

Then I forced them open again. I wanted to see. I lifted my head to watch. The way we fit together. The way his body moved with mine.

Beautiful.

And when I caught his gaze—I saw it. The same thing I felt. Connection. Desire. Want.

The room felt smaller, quieter. As though nothing else existed but the two of us. And for the first time in a long, long time—I felt alive.

This wasn't just sex

Lind's hands gripped my ankles, his fingers firm, stretching me wider than I expected. It wasn't forceful—just sure.

He watched as he thrust into me, his gaze dark with hunger, with need. With him holding my ankles, I couldn't see what he saw, but I could feel it—

It turned me on even more, him watching—how much he was enjoying it.

I wanted to see too, to watch the way he moved inside me, but the pleasure was overwhelming. My head tipped back, my eyes fluttering closed as I gave in, let go, let myself feel everything.

I was completely exposed. Completely vulnerable. Completely seen...

And I loved it.

My hands fisted the sheets. Gripping them like they were the only thing keeping me from floating away.

My voice filled the room—louder now, pleasure raw, uncontrolled.

His rhythm quickened. My body met his, needing more, wanting more.

And then—a cough. A sudden, involuntary interruption.

Another cough, and then—laughter.

I couldn't help it, the absurdity of the moment breaking the tension, but not the connection.

Lind let go of my ankles and I wrapped my legs around him again.

His movements slowed, his body pressing into mine. He leaned forward, his weight supported on his arms as he hovered over me.

His lips brushed my neck, soft, caressing. A reminder.

This wasn't just sex.

The warmth of his kisses spread through me, and I tilted my head, silently asking for more.

And Lind—he listened.

His lips moved lower, trailing down my chest, the heat of his mouth sending new sparks through me.

When his tongue found my nipple, my breath caught again.

I held onto him, fingers gripping his shoulders, his back—pleasure. Consuming.

Weightless.

His tongue, his lips, his teeth—

Each sensation perfectly timed, perfectly placed.

And then—A shift.

I noticed the change in his rhythm. He had stopped moving inside me.

But he was still there.

Still filling me. Holding still, as though he wanted to savor the moment. And God help me, I wanted that too.

The way he slowly pulled out of me made me shiver, the absence of him just as electrifying as his touch.

A shaky breath escaped me, my body trembling from both the aftershocks of what we'd shared and the anticipation of what was coming next.

Lind's lips traveled lower, each kiss sending a wave of anticipation through me.

When he paused at my belly button, feeling his soft nibbles and the playful strokes of his tongue, I laughed—giggling really.

A brief, lighthearted second in the midst of so much intensity. But it didn't last. Because his hands found my hips.

His grip grounded me, held me still, held me open.

And in that moment—I let myself sink into the trust of his touch.

As he continued downward, my body tightened, every nerve on edge.

The first touch of his mouth against me sent a shock through me, a delicious sensation that had me pressing his head between my thighs for a second.

Each stroke of his tongue, each flick—I couldn't stop the moans spilling from my mouth. I didn't want to.

When he sucked me into his mouth, the intensity nearly undid me.

His focus was sure, every feel of his tongue—a slow unraveling.

I could feel it—his patience. His dedication to every reaction he drew from me.

It wasn't just about touching me. It was about understanding me. About reading me, knowing me.

And fuck, it was exhilarating. Terrifying. Overwhelming.

His touch was deliberate

His tongue moved in slow circles, his hands guiding me, encouraging me to move with him.

And I did. My hips lifted, seeking more. His grip tightened, meeting me halfway.

I reached down, my fingers tangling in his hair, gripping, anchoring. Not to guide him. Just to hold him there.

My body moved against him, chasing the release he was so effortlessly giving me. And he encouraged it. With his hands, his mouth, his body.

One of his hands found my breast again, his fingers pinching, tugging at my nipple. The sharp pleasure of it shot through me, layering over everything else.

The pleasure building, the need tightening, coiling inside me.

His touch was deliberate, every movement precise.

His fingers slipped inside me, found the spot that sent ripples of pleasure through me.

The rhythm of his touch—steady. Insistent.

I moved with it, without thinking, without hesitation. Shifting, chasing, desperate for more.

And then his other hand—roaming lower, touching, exploring. Soft, feather light strokes that sent shivers through me.

I bit my lip, caught between a moan and a plea.

And then—lower still. A flicker of nervousness. A moment of uncertainty.

But his touch was so light. So noninvasive. So full of care.

The tension melted away. Because I trusted him. And that realization—let me sink even further into the moment.

When Lind pulled his fingers from me, a soft whimper escaped my lips, the loss of him—sudden. Unwelcome.

But before I had time to miss him—his hand pressed against me again.

His thumb finding my clit, each slow stroke that sent fresh waves of pleasure through me.

And then—his tongue replaced his fingers inside me.

The heat of him and an unhurried rhythm that made my head press back into the pillow.

The sensation of his tongue—reaching the same spot his fingers had found—

It was almost too much. My body arched toward him, thighs trembling, as his hand held me steady.

His thumb never lost its rhythm. Every stroke, every slow flick of his tongue pushed me higher and higher.

I couldn't hold back the sounds spilling from my lips. Didn't want to. When his mouth moved back to my clit, my body was already teetering on the edge.

The steady, rhythmic strokes of his tongue. The warmth of his breath against me. They sent me spiraling, breaking, falling.

My fingers tangled in his hair. Holding onto him to keep me from floating away. The tension inside me coiled tighter, tighter—until—I shattered.

The orgasm hit like a wave, stealing my breath, making me tense and then releasing a rush of pleasure so intense it left me feeling weightless.

My cry filled the space between us. And Lind never let go.

He adjusted seamlessly, his tongue moving lower, prolonging the pleasure.

But when the sensitivity became too much, I released the sheets, reached down, gently pushing his head away.

I squeezed my thighs together, trying to catch my breath. My body still pulsed with the aftershocks, as I rolled onto my side.

I looked down at him, my breath uneven—a quiet intensity in his gaze.

This wasn't just physical. It was something more.

I felt it. And I knew he did too.

Fire and electricity racing through me

I lay on my side, my body still trembling from the aftershocks. Lind moved closer, his hands gently encouraging me to roll onto my stomach.

I let him guide me, feeling the softness of the sheets beneath me as I shifted to the middle of the bed.

His touch was careful. Like he was giving me time to breathe.

When he straddled my legs, his weight was warm and anchoring.

I sighed, my body sinking into the mattress.

His fingers moved lightly across my back. Each touch, soothing, and intimate. A quiet kind of connection.

His weight shifted, the light pressure of him rubbing against me—my thighs, my ass—sending little jolts of anticipation through me.

My body reacted instinctively. My hips moved beneath him, wanting more, needing more. His hands gently parted me.

And then he pressed into me. Slick. Easy. Wanted. My hips moved up and back, needing all of him. And when our bodies met I could feel the soft tap of him against my butt.

I don't know how loud I was becoming, but I didn't care.

He filled me, moving slowly at first. Letting me adjust. Letting me feel everything.

The combination of his touch, the motion of his hips, and the way I met him halfway sent fire and electricity racing through me with every thrust.

I pressed my forehead into the pillow, unable to stop the moans. The sound of my pleasure filled the room. Blending with his low, rough breaths.

His hands gripped my waist. Holding me in place. Grounding me. Owning me. Wanting me.

Each deep stroke, gliding over that spot, again and again—my moans grew louder.

My body tightened.

The pleasure overwhelmed me. Consumed me.

And then—

The words were out before I could stop them. "Oh God, cum in me, Lind. Cum in me."

I felt the change in him immediately. His movements became less measured. More urgent.

A low, thick groan. My name on his lips. The sound sent another wave of pleasure through me.

I closed my eyes, I felt him fall. His body tightened against mine. His breath ragged, uneven.

And then—my second orgasm washed over me.

That was as close as I had ever come to a simultaneous orgasm with anyone.

And it felt out of this world.

For a moment, the world was still.

The only sound—our breathing. Ragged. Uneven. Contented.

Lind's weight was warm against me. His body still wrapped around mine. And the connection between us—real.

I liked it. I really, really liked it.

***

Lind leaned over me, his warmth against my back. But he kept most of his weight off me.

Still careful. Still considerate.

His lips warm against my skin. Soft, tender kisses along my shoulders, my spine. Keeping me in the moment.

As his breath slowed, I closed my eyes, letting myself soak in everything we had just shared.

When he shifted, sliding his arm under me and pulling us onto our sides, I instinctively melted into him, our bodies fitting together like they belonged that way.

I could feel him inside me—wanting him there, needing him there, even as his body began to relax, his erection slowly fading.

Neither of us spoke.

The silence between us—full of the weight of what we'd shared.

I stayed pressed against him, not wanting to break the moment.

Not wanting him to move, to leave, to let go.

Then—I coughed, and he was out.

The sound cracked through the quiet, unexpected and absurd, and in an instant, the tension shattered.

Lind's chest shook behind me as his laughter rumbled through his body, and I couldn't hold mine back either.

It bubbled up, uncontrollable, spilling over, and we both laughed until we were breathless again—the humor of it, the absurdity.

Our laughter filled the room, dissolving everything else, leaving only warmth, only joy.

Only us.

Chapter 24

It wasn't just practical—it was tender

Lind got up, murmuring he'd be right back. I turned onto my back, staring at the ceiling, a faint smile on my lips. A moment later, the sound of running water filled the room, and I let out a quiet chuckle. *Of course* he's cleaning up. That small, predictable habit of his stirred something warm in me. He was always thoughtful, and in ways I hadn't expected, that made me feel cared for.

When he returned, a warm washcloth and a towel in hand, I immediately knew what he intended. This time, I didn't hesitate. I spread my legs for him, the simple gesture of trust feeling just as intimate as everything we had done. The cloth pressed against me. It felt good—the heat sinking into my skin.

His touch was steady, unhurried. He cleaned me with the same quiet attentiveness he always seemed to have. It wasn't just practical—it was *tender*. And when he leaned down to give my clit a quick, playful lick, I swatted at him with a laugh.

"Jesus—Lind," I groaned, half a protest, half a warning.

He grinned, unapologetic. He reached for my hand, placing it over the washcloth so I could finish. That simple act sent a rush of emotion through me—he didn't take over, didn't assume, just *offered*.

When I was done, he dried me and then took the towel and washcloth back to the bathroom. I pulled the covers up around me, sinking into the warmth, feeling content in a way beyond just sex. When he climbed back into bed, I pressed myself tightly against him, my back flush to his chest. His arm came around me, strong and sure. I took his hand and put it on my breast, and I held him there.

For the first time in a long time, I felt *safe*.

I don't want you to leave

A while later, after we dozed a little, I turned to face Lind. Lying there with him, his warm body against mine, I let my fingers wander over his chest, tracing the contours of muscle, feeling the steady rhythm of his breathing.

Every now and then, his hand would drift along my hip, up my waist, tracing along the edge of my breast. Each touch of his fingers sent a ripple of heat through me, raw and insistent. The last twenty-four hours had been incredible, but maybe... maybe this could be the beginning of something more.

I tilted my head, my fingers trailing lower. "I've been lying here thinking..." My voice was softer than I meant it to be. "I don't want you to leave."

The words hung in the air between us, heavier than I expected. Saying it out loud made it real. It made the idea of him walking out that door harder to accept.

I watched the flicker of longing in his eyes, but behind it was something else—caution. "Dana," he said, voice steady but warm, "you *know* I want to stay. But we both know why that's a bad idea."

I sighed, already knowing where this was going, but refusing to let it go. "So what?" I propped myself up on one elbow, letting my hand drift down to his hip. "Why does it matter?"

"It *does* matter," he said, holding my gaze. "And you know it. If we're both out again tomorrow, people will talk. You know how they love to talk."

I groaned, flopping back onto the pillow with an exasperated sigh. "Let the trio gossip all they want. It's none of their business."

"It isn't," he agreed, his hand resting on my cheek. That small touch calmed me even as frustration bubbled just beneath the surface. "But do you *really* want to deal with them? The questions, the rumors? We're just getting started here. I *want* this. I *want* you, Dana. But I don't want us to have to explain ourselves before *we* even know what this is."

His words landed hard, like a weight dropped on me. *Damn it, I hated that he was right.*

I let my head fall against his chest, my hand drifted around to his back, down to his butt. "I *guess* that makes sense," I muttered reluctantly.

"You *know* it makes sense," he said, his tone lighter now, and then he chuckled, the sound vibrating against my cheek. His hand slipped down to my hip. "Believe me, it's not easy. *Especially* with your hand on my ass."

I grinned, feeling the mischief spark in me again, and before I could stop myself, my fingers slid around to the front, wrapping gently around him. "Do you suppose if I *hang on real tight,* I can keep you from going?"

His eyes darkened, hunger flickering there, heat rising between us again, and he leaned in, kissing me—deeply—slowly, like he wanted to savor every second. "You're dangerous," he murmured against my lips, his voice low and full of warmth. "But if I call out again, and *you're* already out... we *don't* need that headache."

I sighed, loosening my grip, but refused to let go. "Fine," I said quietly, but I was still disappointed.

And then a thought, "No one will know if you come over this weekend, will they?"

His hand found mine, lacing our fingers together. When he looked at me, there was something in his expression—care, warmth... love?

"No," he said grinning. "They won't."

"Then it's a *date?*" I gave him a playful squeeze, feeling him stir slightly in my hand.

His eyes widened a little. "Yes," he answered. "It's a date."

I nestled closer, resting my head against his chest, my fingers still curled around him, as if holding on could make him stay. He let go of my hand and wrapped his arms around me, solid and sure, and for a moment, it felt like that thing I saw in his eyes was real.

I didn't want him to leave. But I knew he was right.

We had time—plenty of time.

And the way he held me, the way he kissed me, made me believe it.

What is this man doing to me

I sighed softly, nestled against Lind, my fingers wandering along his arm as he draped it over my waist. I didn't want to move, didn't want to disturb the quiet bubble we'd built in these last few hours. But my body had other ideas, and I felt the telltale pressure reminding me it was time to head to the bathroom.

"I should get up," I murmured, more to myself than to him.

He stirred slightly, his hand tightening around my hip. "Not yet," he mumbled sleepily, his voice muffled against my hair.

I smiled, shifting just enough to turn my face toward his. "Just a few more minutes," I kissed him softly before pulling away.

As I sat up, the cool air was a stark contrast to his warmth. I swung my legs over the edge of the bed, moving slowly, reluctant to leave his arms. But as I stood, a sensation stopped me—a slow, unmistakable trickle down my thigh.

Oh. Right.

I glanced down, a small laugh bubbling in my throat at how something so simple could evoke such a strange mix of emotions. Normally, this would be an irritation—how many times had I found myself rolling my eyes, feeling like I was always the one left to deal with the mess? But with Lind... it didn't feel that way at all.

This was different.

This wasn't just anyone's cum—it was *his*. And for reasons I couldn't quite explain, that realization filled me with an unexpected happiness. A flicker of excitement, even warmth, that his presence stayed with me in a way that felt oddly intimate. My cheeks flushed, and I shook my head slightly, trying to make sense of it all.

What is this man doing to me?

I'd never said those words before—never told anyone to "cum in me." It wasn't something I planned, it just *slipped out*—a truth I hadn't even known I was holding. And I'd meant it. Every word.

What was it about Lind that made me so... open? So *raw*?

I stepped over to the dresser, pulling open the top drawer to grab a pair of panties. As I held them in my hand, I hesitated. This wasn't just about necessity anymore—it felt like something more. I wasn't just cleaning up. I was carrying a part of him with me, *holding onto him*.

The thought made me smile as I grabbed a light pad from the back of the drawer and turned toward the bathroom.

The cool tile was a welcome contrast beneath my feet as I closed the door softly behind me. I moved through the motions of cleaning up, but my mind kept drifting back to Lind. To his hands. His voice. The way he'd looked at me. The way I felt right now.

When I was done, I caught my reflection in the mirror. My hair was a mess, my skin still flushed from the hours we'd spent tangled together—but I didn't mind. There was something *softer* in my face, a quiet contentment I hadn't expected to find.

I opened the door and stepped back into the bedroom, my heart fluttering at the sight of Lind still lying there, watching, waiting for me. Whatever this was—whatever we were starting—I wanted more of it.

More of *him*.

Chapter 25

You're really going to leave me

I slipped back under the covers, pulling them up as Lind wrapped an arm around me, pulling me in close. The room had cooled now, the warmth of the afternoon fading into evening, and with it came the creeping reality of his leaving.

He stretched, his hand grazing so gently against my breast—probably not an accident—as I caught the small smirk on his lips.

"You're *really* going to leave me, aren't you?" I reached out and put my hand on the side of his face, my eyes locking with his.

He gave me a lazy, lopsided grin. "Unfortunately, yeah. Work waits for no man—or woman."

He propped himself up on one elbow, groaning as he sat up all the way. "I need to get moving."

I let out a dramatic sigh, my fingers trailing down his arm as he swung his legs over the side of the bed. He stood, heading to the bathroom—I watched him the whole way.

His bare back. His hips. That *squeezable* ass.

I propped myself up on one elbow, watching shamelessly as he disappeared behind the bathroom door. And when he emerged a few minutes later, walking toward his backpack, I had one very pressing thought:

Really? You're going to walk around naked with that beautiful face, broad shoulders, pudgy little waist, and that... swinging around... and expect me to just let you leave?

I bit the inside of my cheek to keep from laughing. The man was *dangerous*.

He grabbed his backpack and walked it right up to the bed, right to where I was sitting. And *damn it,* how was I supposed to keep my hands to myself?

I watched as he started packing—his pajamas, his toiletries—moving with the same quiet efficiency he always had. He wasn't in a hurry, but he didn't waste a second either. There was something mesmerizing about it.

Or maybe it was just *him.*

The moment he reached for his jeans, I sighed and got up out of bed. *Show's over, I guess.*

As he grabbed his T-shirt I caught his attention. "Wait."

He paused, tilting his head.

I reached for it, pulling at the fabric. "Can I keep this?"

He arched a brow, amusement flickering in his eyes. "Sure... why?"

I hesitated for half a second before answering, "Because it smells like you."

The blush crept up my neck as the words left my lips, but I didn't take them back.

His lips quirked into a slow smile, and he handed it over without hesitation.

I slipped it over my head, the fabric soft against my skin. It hung loose and comfortable, reaching just above my thighs, a perfect pairing with my panties.

He watched me for a long moment. Then he shook his head with a quiet laugh.

"What?" I asked, feigning innocence.

"Nothing," his voice warm with amusement. "You just look better in that shirt than I ever have." He paused, then gave me a slow, knowing smile. "Of course... you look *even better* without it."

I grinned. "You mean like this?"

Before he could react, I lifted the shirt to my chin, flashing him.

He blinked, swallowed, and ran a hand down his face.

"You *really* don't play fair," he muttered, shaking his head, but there was no fight in his voice. Only *want*.

I dropped the shirt, smiling as I sat back on the bed.

"I *never* said I played fair."

See you Friday

We made our way downstairs together, his backpack slung over one shoulder, my fingers entwined with his as we walked. At the front door, he turned to me, his expression soft, deep. I could feel it in the way he looked at me, the way his hands rested lightly on my hips—this was more than just a goodbye.

"I think I'll order some food later," I said, breaking the silence. "I'm starting to feel hungry again."

He leaned in, his voice low. "Just promise me you'll put on something more than my T-shirt and your panties before the delivery guy shows up. Otherwise, you'll give him a hard on that will last to the end of his shift."

"Oh My God—As if I would."

He grinned at me. "I'm just saying—if you answered the door looking like that, I'd give *you* the tip."

The heat in my face was instant. "You already did."

Grinning—his eyes locked with mine, as he slowly licked his lips and I about lost it.

Then he pulled me in and kissed me. A slow, deep kiss that curled my toes and left me breathless. It wasn't rushed. It wasn't restrained. It was full of everything the last 24 hours had given us.

When we finally broke apart, my heart pounded, my breath uneven.

"See you Friday," he murmured.

I kept him close—screaming in my head—*What about right now? You can't just do that to me and leave.*

But I just nodded, holding his hand for just a moment longer before he pulled away and stepped outside. The cool air rushed in, giving me welcome relief for the heat.

I shut the door behind him, leaning against it as I tried to steady myself. My cheeks were still flushed, my mind spinning. I *already* missed him, and he hadn't even reached his truck yet.

As I pressed my back against the door, I was imagining him walking through the parking lot, his backpack slung casually over one shoulder, his easy stride carrying him away from me. The further he got, the more I felt his absence.

My hand drifted over the fabric of his T-shirt, my fingers tracing over my stomach, up to my breasts, brushing over my nipples.

I smiled, shook my head, and asked again... *What has this man done to me?*

My mind flickered back to his teasing about the delivery driver. As if I'd answer the door like this. He knew I wouldn't. But the fact that he could joke about it—that he wasn't jealous or possessive—set him apart. Any other men I'd been with would've had something to say about it.

But not Lind.

He knew I wouldn't do anything like that.

And that trust felt... *intoxicating.*

Did he care about me? Everything about the last 24 hours screamed *yes.*

And yet, it was the quiet, steady way he *showed* it that left me breathless. The way he cleaned up after breakfast. The way he ran his hands over me like he was memorizing me. The way he held me after, not just because it felt good, but because it *mattered.*

This man was unlike anyone I'd ever known. And I couldn't get enough of him.

I pushed off the door, heading back upstairs to lay in bed for a little while longer. Maybe I'd scroll through some food delivery apps.

Or maybe I'd reach into the nightstand drawer and relive every moment of the last 24 hours, wrapped up in his T-shirt, his memory, and his scent.

Part 6

<u>What If..</u>

What if this thing is real?
  What if I'm not too much?
  What if he really sees me?
  What if that doesn't scare him off?
  What if he means it—every word?
  What if I let it be easy, just this once?
  What if I let him in, and it changes everything?
  What if he's already all in—and I just can't see it?

Chapter 26

It's just Lind

Dana had been up since 6:30 a.m.

Even after years of 6:00 a.m. shifts at the big box store, she still wasn't a morning person, but the anticipation of Lind showing up had kept her restless.

She'd paced the condo long before sunrise, showered, dried her hair, and spent an embarrassing amount of time debating between casual-but-put-together or just-rolled-out-of-bed. In the end, she chose leggings and an oversized sweater. Comfortably braless, Lind wouldn't be able to tell... *Mm-hmm.*

The knock came right at 9:00 sharp. She froze mid-step, took a breath.

Act normal. You're fine. It's just Lind.

She opened the door—and there he was. A plastic grocery bag in hand, and a lopsided grin on his face. Same faded jeans from earlier that week, paired with a gray hoodie that somehow made him look softer. Her stomach did something annoying and fluttery, and she did her best to push the feeling down.

"I was hoping you'd still be in pajamas," Lind said, his eyes flicking over her outfit.

Dana rolled her eyes, leaning against the doorframe. "You don't strike me as the *bunny slippers and bathrobe* kind of guy."

"True," he said, stepping inside. "But you'd look cute in bunny slippers."

She grinned, closing the door behind him. "Flattery isn't going to get you out of making breakfast, you know."

"I wouldn't dream of it," he said, holding up the grocery bag. "Where's the kitchen?"

"Same place it was three days ago."

First-night sleepover test

Lind moved easily around the now-familiar kitchen, pulling out eggs, sweet peppers, onion, ham, cheese, and bread from the bag.

"I forgot mushrooms. Do you have any?" he asked.

"Nope. We used them up."

He glanced at the counter, nodding approvingly. "At least you have coffee going."

"Yeah," Dana said, leaning against the counter. "Thought I'd actually use the coffee maker this time."

She had her arms crossed—not in a defensive way, more like she was holding herself together.

Lind cracked the eggs into a bowl and started whisking. "So," he said, a grin playing at his lips. "What's the verdict? Did I pass the first-night sleepover test?"

Dana blinked, caught off guard. "Is that a thing?" she echoed, half-laughing.

"Of course," Lind said. "Rule one: don't hog the blankets. Rule two: make her breakfast. Rule three..." He paused, his tone softening. "Make sure she wants to see you again."

Her heart gave an unsteady thump. She ducked her head, hiding a small smile. "You're like five out of three on the sleepover test," she admitted, blushing.

Lind paused mid-whisk, shooting her a smile.

What's on your mind

As Lind cooked, the air between them grew quieter, heavier.

Dana shifted her weight, biting her lip. She didn't want to ruin the easy vibe, but the words were already bubbling up.

"Lind," she said, her voice quieter than she intended.

He glanced up from the stove. "Yeah?"

She hesitated, her arms tightening around herself. "I'm glad you're here."

His brow furrowed slightly. "But?"

She sighed, stepping closer. "But I think we need to talk about... this. Us. Everything."

Lind set the spatula down, turned the heat down, and faced her. His expression was steady, calm. "I figured you might be anxious or conflicted. What's on your mind?"

Dana looked at him quizzically. "Why did you think I was anxious?"

"You mean just because you canceled Friday night's sleepover"—He sighed—"and rescheduled it for a Saturday morning meeting instead?"

Dana paused. "That's fair."

Lind waited... but then asked again, "So what's on your mind?"

Dana hesitated. "A lot. I mean, for starters, I'm freaking out about work. Like, are we going to act weird around each other now? Or worse, are other people going to notice and start gossiping?"

Lind leaned back against the counter, "That wasn't bothering you Wednesday afternoon," he said, folding his arms as her face blushed.

He looked at her for a beat longer, reading her expression, "Is that what's bothering you the most?"

"No," she admitted, barely above a whisper. "I'm... worried about other stuff too. Like..." She glanced at the eggs on the stove, feeling heat rise to her face. "We didn't think things through before..."

Lind's gaze softened, but he waited for her to finish.

"I know it's probably fine," she rushed on, "but I can't stop thinking about all the what ifs. "Like..." She hesitated, choosing her words carefully. "What if Sam *is*... your girlfriend? Where would that leave me?"

Lind straightened slightly, his expression serious but not defensive. "Dana, I'm not hiding anything. Sam's a friend—someone I care about—but she is not a girlfriend. That hasn't changed—and neither does what happened between us."

Her chest tightened. "And what exactly is *our* relationship?"

Lind turned back to the stove, choosing his words carefully as he spooned the eggs onto their plates.

"I think that's something we should continue to explore. Together."

Dana liked the sound of that, but... it also left things uncomfortably open.

Vasectomy? Wait, what

A quiet pause stretched between them as Dana shifted in her chair, nudging the eggs on her plate with her fork. She could feel Lind's gaze on her, patient but expectant, waiting for her to speak.

You have to say it, Dana. Just rip the band-aid off.

She exhaled sharply and set her fork down. "Lind," she started...

He glanced up from his plate. "Yeah?"

She hesitated, not knowing quite how to begin. "I've been thinking about... you know, our time together. And how maybe we weren't as careful as we should've been. That we didn't *exactly think things through.*"

Lind's brow furrowed slightly. "You said that already. What exactly are we talking about?"

"Well," Dana started. "*All of it,* I guess. Like, what if something happens? What if..." She bit her lip, feeling ridiculous but pushing forward anyway. "What if I get pregnant?"

Lind leaned back slightly, his hands resting flat on the table. His expression remained calm, but his voice was careful. "I thought you said—"

"That I can't have kids, yeah," Dana interrupted, shaking her head.

Lind gave a slow nod, watching her.

"But still," she continued, her fingers fidgeting against the table. "I don't know. *Things happen.* Doctors can be wrong, or..." She trailed off, feeling stupid for even saying it out loud, but the worry still clung to her.

Lind reached for her hand, his fingers warm as they covered hers. When he spoke, his tone was gentle but firm. "Dana. I get it. I do. But I promise you—pregnancy is *not* something you need to worry about."

She blinked at him, still uncertain. "How can you be so sure?"

He gave a quiet smile, like he'd been waiting for this question. "Because years ago... after Sharon, I decided not to bring kids into this world."

Dana frowned slightly, confused. "What do you mean?"

"Vasectomy," Lind said without hesitation.

Dana blinked. "Wait, *what?*"

He shrugged. "Doctor assured me it's reversible if I ever change my mind. So far?" He tapped his fingers against the table. "No change of mind."

Dana stared at him, her mind catching up to what he'd just said. "You *could* have told me that *before* I had a mild panic attack."

Lind squeezed her hand. "I *did* tell you. More than once."

Dana opened her mouth, then hesitated.

Lind raised an eyebrow, waiting.

"...I don't remember that," she admitted.

His lips quirked, amused. "It was months ago. I mentioned it twice while you were close enough to hear, but apparently you didn't?"

Dana wracked her brain, and after a second, a vague memory surfaced. Her stomach dropped. "Oh."

Lind frowned slightly. "And *how* did you forget?"

Dana groaned, leaning back in her chair. "Because I overthink *everything*."

"Bingo," Lind said, smiling.

She shook her head, letting out a slow breath. "Well. That's one less thing to obsess over, I guess."

Lind squeezed her fingers gently. "Good. Because this isn't just about *you*, Dana. It's about *us*."

She squeezed his hand again, her pulse quickening.

Careful, Dana, she warned herself. *You're falling pretty quick.*

As she thought it, both joy and fear seized her at the same time. She nodded slowly. "Yeah. *Us*."

Lind's smile softened. "Exactly."

You mean STIs

There was a short silence as Dana stared into her coffee. She swirled it, watching Lind finish his eggs. Her stomach churned—not from the food, but from the words sitting heavy on her tongue.

She had the kind of nervous energy that builds when you know you have to say something but don't know how to start.

Clearing her throat, she finally forced it out. "So, uh... we need to talk about something else."

Lind looked up, fork pausing midair. "Okay. What else would you like to know?"

Dana hesitated. "Well, I'm not really sure what they call them these days," she started, her cheeks already warming. "We used to say 'diseases,' but I think now they're mostly called infections."

Lind frowned slightly, confused for a beat. Then the realization dawned on him. He set his fork down.

"You mean STIs?"

Dana nodded quickly, gaze darting anywhere but his face. "Yeah. I mean, I *know* it's not exactly a romantic topic, but... I need to know. Are you... you know... *okay?*"

Lind's expression softened, and he leaned back in his chair, looking at her with quiet reassurance. "I'm okay. That's the other thing you don't have to worry about."

Dana narrowed her eyes. "How do you know?"

"I got tested," Lind said simply.

Dana blinked, caught off guard. "Oh. Really? When was that?"

"About three weeks ago," he replied, his tone calm but matter-of-fact.

Her curiosity got the better of her. Looking him in the eye she asked, "Why did you think you needed to be tested?"

Lind huffed a little, glancing down at his coffee mug before answering. "I didn't think I *needed* to," he said, looking back up to meet her eyes. "I got tested because I've had a few casual encounters over the last couple of years. I've always been careful—always condoms—but I wanted to be sure."

Dana tilted her head, studying him. "Sure about what?"

Lind exhaled, glancing at his coffee as he set it down.

Looking back up at her with his usual calm self, his voice quieter. "I wanted to be sure... just in case what happened between us... *happened between us.*"

Dana's fork hovered in midair, her brows drawing together. "Wait... you mean—"

"I got tested because you're important to me," Lind said, cutting her off gently, "and I wanted to make sure *you* were safe."

Dana froze, her heart thudding in her chest.

It's a good thing I'm sitting down, she thought. *Because if I wasn't, I'd probably fall over right now.*

She managed to speak, though her voice came out a little shaky. "But... Why? You couldn't have known this was going to happen."

Lind's eyes stayed locked onto hers, steady and unwavering. "Because of how I've gotten to know you over the last year," he said, "these last few months especially."

He let out a slow breath, like he was choosing his next words carefully. "I've been cautious for a long time, Dana. But with you..." His voice lowered slightly, more certain now. "I was willing to take the chance again. *I wanted to be ready.*"

Dana stared at him, her mind racing to catch up.

"A chance? On me?"

Lind nodded. "Yes." His voice was firm, no hesitation. "It isn't just that I *want* you." His fingers slid lightly over hers. "I mean that... I want *you.*"

Dana's breath caught, her body suddenly feeling too small to hold the wave of emotions crashing through her.

His words echoed in her mind.

I want *you.*

She set her fork down carefully, realizing her hands were trembling slightly.

"Lind..."

He reached across the table, his fingertips barely grazing hers—a silent reassurance.

Lind smiled at her. "I just wanted you to *understand* that."

But Dana swallowed the lump in her throat and slowly shook her head. "It isn't just *me* taking this chance," she said finally, her voice trembling slightly. "We *both* are. And... I've never had someone..."

She trailed off, searching for the right words, but she wasn't sure they existed.

For the first time that morning, Lind's full smile appeared—slow and unmistakably relieved.

"Yes, we both are," he said softly. "And it's *worth it.*" His thumb brushed against the back of her hand. "I think... *you're* worth it."

Dana's lips curved into an almost disbelieving smile. Her doubts melted like morning fog in sunlight.

She felt lighter. Freer.

"Well," she said, attempting a teasing tone to break the tension, "that makes two of us."

Lind chuckled, shaking his head. "So, in case you didn't catch it... *I did exactly think things through.*" His voice turned playful, but there was also something solid behind it.

Dana squeezed his hand, her voice still catching slightly. "Yeah, I guess you did."

Chapter 27

Dana, you're still overthinking

As the conversation drifted, Dana found herself voicing more worries before she could stop them.

"I just keep thinking about work," she admitted, pushing her coffee mug in slow circles across the table. "What if people notice? What if someone says something? I mean, you know how Lisa is. She'd turn this into lunchtime gossip in a heartbeat."

Lind smiled as he lifted his coffee to his lips.

"I'm serious," Dana pressed. "What if it gets weird between us? Or worse, what if this—" she gestured between them, "—doesn't work out?"

Lind set his mug down, his expression softening. "Dana, you're still overthinking."

She huffed. "I can't help it. That's just how I am."

"I know," he said, leaning forward. "But you're not in this alone. We'll figure it out. One day at a time."

Dana blinked, caught off guard by his certainty.

"You make it sound so easy."

"It's not easy," he admitted. "But, I really do think it's worth it."

Her heart gave an unsteady beat at that.

Dana inhaled deeply, steeling herself. "Okay. If we're doing this—whatever this is—we should probably talk about what we want. Like... what are we even doing—here?"

Lind tilted his head, considering her. "You mean, are we dating or just playing?"

She nodded, cheeks warming. "I guess... yeah. Or—well, are you still seeing Sam?"

Lind's expression remained thoughtful, steady. "Sam and I are still friends. We always will be. We've been close for a long time—that's not going to change."

Dana felt the weight of that.

"But right now," Lind continued, "I'm focused on us."

Her heart skipped again.

She swallowed, her pulse kicking up. "What does that mean to you, Lind?"

"It means dating you. It means building a relationship with you."

Dana studied him, watching his face for any hesitation.

"Do you mean that?"

Lind nodded. "Yes... I do."

She leaned back in her chair, letting his words wash over her.

Her mind still spun with questions, but she nodded slowly.

"Okay. I... I like the sound of that."

I don't know what I'm doing

His words hung in the air, solid and certain.

Dana traced the rim of her mug with her finger, grounding herself. "It's just... this is all new to me. Not just you, but the idea of being with someone who's... open like this. I don't know what I'm doing."

Lind leaned forward, resting his forearms on the table. "Dana, no one starts out knowing. It's okay to feel unsure. What matters is that we're honest with each other. We'll figure it out together."

She swallowed hard, her voice quieting. "I like the sound of that. Because I don't want to mess this up. Or get hurt—or hurt you."

"You won't," Lind said gently. "Not if we keep talking like this. That's how it works—communication, trust, and a lot of patience."

Dana let out a shaky laugh. "Patience isn't exactly my strong suit."

"I've noticed," the corner of his mouth lifted knowingly.

She looked up at him, heart knocking against her ribs. "You accept that about me?"

"Yeah," he said simply. "You're real. You don't hide how you feel, even when it's hard. It's kind of cute—most of the time."

She grinned, but his words landed. He saw her. Accepted her. And that was terrifying and comforting all at once.

I'm trusting you

The warmth in Dana's chest spread, but a flicker of doubt remained.

"You make it sound like you have it all figured out," she murmured. "Like nothing fazes you."

Lind's smile faltered.

"That's not true."

Dana tilted her head, studying him. "You always seem so... calm."

He exhaled, running a hand through his hair.

"That's because I've had a lot of practice." His voice dropped slightly. "Hiding how I feel. Giving vague answers. Deflecting when people get too close. Not giving up too much."

He hesitated. Then, quieter—

"Because if you don't show too much of what's inside... people can't hurt you. They can't judge you. They can't ostracize you."

Dana's breath caught. She wasn't expecting that.

She studied his face, taking him in like she was seeing something new.

"But that's not what you're doing now, is it?"

Lind met her gaze, holding it. "No," he said quietly. "Not with you. Not with this. It's all too important."

He paused—then...

"I'm trusting you with more of me, right now, than most people will ever see."

Another breath.

"And more of my heart than I even thought I had left."

Dana's stomach flipped, something fragile and powerful twisting inside her.

"Why me?" she asked, voice barely above a whisper.

Lind held her gaze, his walls cracking just a little more.

"Because I *see* you," he said. "And what I see makes me want you. You're strong, honest, and messy in the best ways. You don't pretend to be anything you're not. That feels familiar," he said with a crooked grin.

Then his face went still. "I want to let you in, and that scares the holy hell out of me."

They sat in silence for a moment, as Dana considered all that those words might mean.

Dana reached across the table, covering his hand with hers. "I'm scared too," she admitted. "But I do want to figure this out—with you."

Lind nodded, turning his hand over and interlacing their fingers. "We will."

She let out a slow breath, the tension in her chest finally easing. It felt like they were on the same page.

"So," Lind said, picking up his fork again. "How about we eat before the eggs get cold?"

Dana grinned, putting a fork full of eggs in her mouth. "Too late."

Lind grinned. "Microwave."

Zombie apocalypse

Dana exhaled, rolling her shoulders as if physically shaking off the heaviness of their conversation. She managed a smile, as the microwave beeped.

"Okay, that got way too serious for breakfast."

Lind chuckled, leaning back in his chair. "Agreed. Next time, let's stick to lighter topics—like, I don't know, which one of us would survive a zombie apocalypse."

Dana arched an eyebrow, amused. "Oh, that's easy. Me. No question."

Lind tilted his head, his voice laced with playful skepticism. "Oh really? And what makes you so confident?"

She grinned, crossing her arms. "Because I'm scrappy."

Lind laughed, shaking his head. "Scrappier than *me?*"

"Well, yeah," she said, "After all, *I* have to trip *you* to slow the zombies down."

Lind scoffed, feigning offense. "*Wow... Using me as bait?* I see how it is."

Dana shrugged. "Survival of the fittest."

Her grin gave her away, and Lind chuckled, shaking his head. "Noted. I'll remember that."

Normal? With you? Not a chance

The laughter softened the mood between them, and Dana leaned back in her chair.

"Okay, but seriously... work. How are we going to play this? Are we pretending nothing happened?" She hesitated. "Or—*nothing's happening?* Because that's going to be impossible."

Lind leaned toward her a little. "How about we just act normal and not make it weird?"

Dana rolled her eyes. "Normal? With *you?* Not a chance."

"Hey, I resemble that remark," Lind said with a grin.

She shook her head, amused. "But seriously. You think we can just pretend *this*—" she gestured between them, "—doesn't exist?"

"I think we'll be fine," Lind said with a shrug. "We've worked together for over a year without anyone catching on to the fact that I..." He trailed off, catching himself.

Dana arched an eyebrow. "That you *what?*"

Lind hesitated, rubbing the back of his neck. "That I might've *liked* you."

Dana's lips curled into a slow grin. "'*Might've?*'" she repeated. "So, what, you were *pining* for me this whole time?"

Lind huffed a laugh. "I wouldn't call it *pining* necessarily..."

"Uh-huh." Dana leaned forward, voice dropping slightly. "You *totally* were."

Lind pointed a finger at her. "Don't flatter yourself."

Dana leaned back, grinning. "Oh, I don't have to. Lisa's going to have *so* much fun with this."

Lind's expression faltered immediately. "Lisa doesn't *know* anything."

Dana laughed. "Relax, I'm just *kidding.*"

Lind didn't quite laugh along with her, his expression still cautious.

The conversation eased as they started clearing the table. Dana rinsed the dishes while Lind grabbed a towel to dry. He moved easily around her kitchen, as if this was something they'd done a hundred times before.

"You're *surprisingly* good at this," Dana said, nodding toward the neatly stacked dishes beside him.

"Don't sound so shocked," he said, tossing the towel over his shoulder. "I *do* own a dish towel, you know."

Dana chuckled. "Just *one?*"

Lind hesitated, narrowing his eyes slightly before giving her a look of surrender. "You're *really* going to make me admit that, huh?"

Dana laughed, shaking her head, a glint in her eye, "I'll let you use mine any time."

Lind's grin widened as he reached for her, pulling her in for a slow kiss.

Damn. I knew I should have brought my pack

With the kitchen clean and the air between them warm, they drifted toward the front door. Lind slipped into his jacket, his movements unhurried.

"Thanks for breakfast," he said.

"Thanks for *cooking*," Dana replied, leaning against the door frame. "I might have to keep you on kitchen duty."

Lind chuckled. "Fair trade. You keep the coffee flowing, and I'll handle the eggs."

As Lind opened the door, Dana's voice stopped him.

"So... what do you have planned for the rest of the day?"

Lind paused, his hand still on the door. "Not much," he admitted, his lips twitching into a small smile. "I kind of left it open. *Just in case.*"

Her brow furrowed slightly. "Just in case *what?*"

Lind turned back fully, his smile widening. "Just in case you *wanted me to stay.*"

Dana's heart fluttered, the room suddenly feeling warmer.

She crossed her arms, her tone casual. "Well, aren't *you* presumptuous."

"You didn't say no," Lind murmured, his voice low, gravelly, confident.

Dana held his gaze for a beat, then stepped forward, hooking a hand behind his neck. She pulled him in, kissing him slow—unhurried, like they had all the time in the world.

With her other hand, she reached for the door—and pushed it closed.

Her fingers found his, lacing them together. "Come on," she whispered, tugging him toward the stairs.

Lind followed, grinning.

Damn. I knew I should have brought my pack.

Part 7

We called it slow.

But in a week, he knew what made me laugh, what made me shiver, and how I liked my coffee.

In a week, I'd slept beside him more nights than not.

It didn't feel like falling—it felt like choosing.

But when someone starts to feel like home, is there really a choice?

We were going pretty damn fast for slow.

But we're not hiding because we're ashamed.

We're hiding because we're not ready for anyone else to touch what we're building.

Chapter 28

Earth to Dana

The hum of morning chatter filled the air as Dana stood in the middle of the room near Brenda, her usual spot for the morning meeting. The routine was familiar, yet something about it felt different—like her world had subtly shifted over the weekend, leaving her slightly off balance. She folded her arms loosely, offering polite smiles to coworkers as they trickled in, but her mind was elsewhere.

"How are you feeling, Dana?" Brenda's voice was casual, but her sharp, motherly instincts always had her checking in.

Dana managed a small laugh. "Mostly better. Just a stubborn stuffy nose clinging for dear life..." She sniffled lightly for effect, looking down to avoid Brenda's eyes.

Brenda patted her arm. "That time of year. Glad you're better."

Before Dana could respond, Pete chimed in. "Hey, did you try that ginger tea I told you about?"

"Not yet," she admitted. "But it's on my list. The over-the-counter stuff seems to be doing the trick, though."

The small talk swirled around her, providing an easy distraction—one she needed, because just a few feet away, Lind stood in his usual spot leaning against the wall. Close enough to be noticed. Far enough to pretend nothing had changed.

Dana didn't dare turn to look at him directly—too obvious, too risky. But her peripheral vision was sharp, and every now and then, she caught glimpses of him—hands in his pockets, head tilted slightly, that casual-but-not-really posture that sent a flutter through her stomach.

She pretended to listen, the small talk giving her cover to glance over her shoulder now and then. One of those glances landed directly on Lind.

Their eyes met.

Briefly.

Her breath caught. She turned quickly, heat creeping into her cheeks. If she hadn't known better, she'd swear he almost smiled.

"Earth to Dana?" Brenda's voice cut through the haze, pulling her back.

"Sorry, what?" she asked, forcing an apologetic smile.

"I said, did you catch the game last night?" Pete repeated.

"Oh, uh... no." She hesitated. *Busy* was one way to put it. "But I heard it was good?"

Pete launched into an enthusiastic recap, giving Dana a much-needed escape from her own thoughts. She let the chatter fill the space between her and her swirling emotions, keeping her gaze locked on the supervisor's desk as Georgette approached, clipboard in hand.

"Alright, let's get started," Georgette announced, her voice cutting through the murmurs.

Dana exhaled softly, shifting her weight from one foot to the other. She couldn't help but wonder, was Lind feeling just as tense as she was? Did anyone notice?

From his spot, Lind kept his expression carefully neutral, but inside, his thoughts raced just as fast. The weekend had been unforgettable, and now, here they were—back to '*normal*', surrounded by coworkers, pretending nothing had changed.

And *normal* had never felt more complicated.

As the meeting started, Dana fidgeted with her pen, trying—failing—to keep her mind from wandering. She focused on Georgette's words, but a single thought looped in the back of her mind.

We'll figure this out. We have to.

Georgette scanned her clipboard, her voice steady and matter-of-fact as she read through the day's assignments.

"Dana, Brenda, and Lind—you'll be working on the seasonal reset for Aisle 7. It'll take most of the morning, so pace yourselves."

Dana's stomach tightened. *Of course.*

She flicked a glance at Brenda, who gave her a quick smile and nod. From his spot, Lind straightened slightly, his head tilting in acknowledgment. His face remained neutral, but Dana caught the flicker of awareness in his eyes. He didn't look at her—not directly—but she knew he'd registered the pairing.

"Got it," Brenda said cheerfully. "Come on, team, let's make some magic happen."

Dana mustered a weak smile and followed as the meeting dispersed.

Straight into the fire.

Something you want to share, Dana

Brenda led the way to the seasonal section, chatting as they walked. Dana mostly listened, her thoughts preoccupied with Lind's footsteps behind them.

Lind, meanwhile, had his own distractions. This morning wasn't going to be easy, he thought, adjusting the cuffs of his sleeves. But at least it's just Brenda. And if he had to follow Dana down an aisle, well...it *was* the best view in the store.

The air in the seasonal section was thick with the scent of cardboard and shrink wrap. Resetting displays wasn't complicated, just tedious—dismantling old setups, unboxing new stock, carefully arranging everything into place.

Brenda set her hands on her hips, surveying the mess. "Alright, let's divide and conquer. Dana, start clearing the old stock on the left. Lind, take the pallets on the right. I'll sort and organize the middle."

Dana nodded quickly, grateful for the clear instructions—and the space—between her and Lind. She moved to her section, hyper-aware of every time he stepped near.

Brenda kept the conversation light as they worked, rambling about her kids' soccer games and the disastrous batch of cookies she burned over the weekend. Dana half-listened, trying to ignore the pull to glance in Lind's direction.

"So, Dana," Brenda's voice took on a teasing tone as she cracked open a box of decorations. "Any fun plans this week?"

"Not really," Dana replied, stacking items into a cart. "Just catching up on stuff at home. You?"

"Oh, you know. Wrangling kids, keeping my husband in line." Brenda huffed.

Lind, who had been quietly unpacking a box of string lights, spoke up unexpectedly. "Sounds like a full-time job."

Brenda shot him a knowing look. "You're not wrong, Lind. But hey, someone's gotta do it."

Dana risked a glance at him. Her pulse quickened, and she quickly looked away, forcing herself to focus on the wreaths she was arranging.

Brenda's eyes bounced between them, the corners of her mouth twitching. She didn't say anything, but Dana could feel the gears turning in her head.

A couple of hours passed in a steady rhythm of unpacking, sorting, and arranging. Every so often, Dana and Lind's paths crossed—brushing past each other, exchanging quick, professional-sounding comments about shelf placement. But every movement felt charged with an energy both of them were trying to ignore.

And Brenda wasn't missing a thing.

"So, Lind," she said after a while, her voice too casual. "What did you get up to this weekend? Anything exciting?"

Dana froze mid-reach for a box of garland.

Lind didn't pause. "Not much. Took some time to relax."

Brenda hummed, clearly unimpressed by his vague answer. "Relaxing's good. We all need that sometimes."

Dana kept her head down, her heart pounding.

By mid-morning, they had made significant progress. Dana stepped back, pushing a strand of hair back into place, and turned—only to find Lind standing much closer than expected.

"Looks good," he murmured, nodding toward her work.

"Thanks," she replied, matching his neutral tone.

For a split second, their eyes met again. The world shrank.

Then, just as quickly, the moment passed, and Lind returned to his side of the bays without another word.

Dana exhaled, turning back to her work—only to catch Brenda watching, her lips twitching with a suppressed grin.

"Something you want to share, Dana?" Brenda asked lightly.

Dana forced a laugh. "Not really. What do you mean?"

"Oh, nothing," Brenda said, turning back to her work. "Just... noticing."

Dana sighed.

It's going to be a long day.

Oh, come on, Dana. I'm not blind

The first half of the day had flown by faster than Dana expected. By lunchtime, the seasonal reset was nearly complete, with only a few finishing touches left. She had kept her interactions with Lind minimal, but that hadn't stopped Brenda from watching her with a knowing look more than once.

After lunch, Georgette gathered the team for reassignment. She tapped her clipboard with her pen and spoke crisply. "Alright,

Lind, I need you over in Receiving to help with the new shipment. Dana and Brenda, you'll be tackling the clearance section—there's a lot to sort and organize, so I'm counting on you two to get it done."

Dana felt a mix of relief and apprehension. Relief that she wouldn't have to spend the next few hours navigating her feelings around Lind. Apprehension because, well... Brenda.

"Got it," Brenda said brightly, nudging Dana as they walked away. "Clearance, here we come."

***

The clearance section was a disaster—mismatched items, open packages, and a few broken displays in desperate need of attention. It was going to take a while to put it all in order, but Dana welcomed the distraction.

Brenda, however, had other plans.

"So," she said casually as she straightened a row of marked-down blenders, "you and Lind seemed... cozy this morning."

Dana's hand froze mid-reach for a misplaced toy. She quickly resumed moving items, keeping her voice neutral. "Cozy? I don't know what you mean."

Brenda chuckled, shaking her head. "Oh, come on, Dana. I'm not blind. The way you kept sneaking glances at him—and don't even get me started on the way he was sneaking glances back at you."

Dana felt her cheeks heat. "I wasn't sneaking glances."

Brenda gave her a pointed look. "Really? Because from where I was standing, it looked like you two were in some kind of silent conversation. You know, the kind that says, I'm trying really hard not to look at you, but I can't help it."

Dana sighed, setting down the toy and turning to face her. "It's not like that."

Brenda raised an eyebrow. "Oh? Then what is it like?"

Dana hesitated, choosing her words carefully. "We... talk outside of work now. That's all. It's not a big deal."

Brenda folded her arms, watching her closely. "Not a big deal," she repeated. "Girl, you've got it bad, and he's not exactly subtle either. So, what's the holdup?"

Dana glanced at her, unsure how much to reveal. "It's complicated."

Brenda tilted her head, her expression softening. "Complicated how? He's single, you're single, and you clearly like each other. What's stopping you?"

Dana hesitated. She wanted to say it wasn't serious yet, but that's not how she felt. Not anymore. Not after this weekend.

Dana bit her lip. "I guess... I'm just trying to figure out where this is going. And I don't want to mess things up at work."

Brenda nodded slowly, her gaze narrowing thoughtfully. "Fair enough. But let me give you a little advice—life's too short to overthink everything. If you like him, and he likes you, maybe it's worth taking the risk."

Dana managed a small smile. "Maybe."

Brenda grinned, leaning in like she was sharing a secret. "Just promise me one thing."

"What?"

"If this turns into something, I will be the first to know. And I expect all the juicy details."

Dana laughed despite herself, shaking her head. "You're impossible."

"And you love me for it," Brenda said with a wink, giving Dana a playful nudge.

As they turned back to their work, Dana felt a little lighter. Brenda always had a way of cutting through her tension, and for the first time all day, she allowed herself to consider the possibility that maybe, just maybe, things with Lind didn't have to be so complicated after all.

Chapter 29

Demisexual

The early evening sun stretched long shadows across the dirt path, golden light filtering through the trees. The crisp air carried the scent of pine and dirt. Quiet and still.

After Dana and Lind had met at the trail head, after a quick kiss and hug, they started up the trail.

They walked side by side, their steps crunching softly against the gravel.

The silence wasn't uncomfortable, but it carried weight—unspoken thoughts, unanswered questions.

Dana glanced at Lind. His hands were tucked loosely into his jacket pockets, his posture relaxed, yet his expression was thoughtful. He always seems so calm. *How does he do that?*

She inhaled, steadying herself. "So, I was thinking... we didn't even know each other that well before we ended up in bed."

Lind let out a quiet laugh. "You don't say."

She rolled her eyes, nudging him lightly. "I just mean—it's crazy, right? How fast it all happened?"

Lind slowed his pace slightly, his voice easy but certain. "Not crazy. Not for me."

Dana frowned, tilting her head. "What do you mean?"

He glanced at her before looking ahead again. "I don't do casual—not really." He paused, "Didn't you say I was moving so slow we were backing up?"

Dana was caught off guard. "I guess... yeah. But still—you weren't slow last week."

"And you were?"

Dana blushed. "Okay, maybe this isn't so fast..."

"I really like you, Dana. And I have for... well, a while now," Lind said, choosing his words. "I don't do casual... often. It's not how I'm wired." He paused again. "We talked about this over pizza."

"Over pizza?"

"Yeah, remember what caused Sharon to leave me? 'You're supposed to fuck 'em, not love 'em.'"

"Oh, yeah, I remember."

"There's actually a word for that," he said. "Demisexual."

She blinked. "Demisexual?"

He nodded. "It means I don't feel sexual attraction unless I have an emotional connection with someone. It's not that I can't have sex without one—it's just not my preference. It's not how I'm wired."

Dana was silent for a moment, processing that.

She'd never thought much about the why behind attraction—hers had always been immediate, physical first. But with Lind...

She'd wanted him before she'd even realized it.

Isn't that how their relationship grew? The flirting at work. The way he made her laugh. The way he looked at her sometimes, like he already knew her.

Maybe it wasn't just about sex. Maybe it had never been.

"That actually makes sense," she said quietly, kicking a stray pebble along the path. "I think I've been feeling that way with you too. I just didn't know how to explain it."

Lind reached out, and without hesitation, Dana slipped her fingers into his. Their hands intertwined naturally, his warmth connecting with her.

They walked on in comfortable silence. It felt good, walking like this—knowing they were okay.

Lind broke the quiet first. "So... what do you see happening next? Short-term, I mean—besides the sex."

Dana smiled, giving his hand a playful squeeze. "I don't know yet. I think... just spending more time together. Seeing where this leads."

Lind nodded, his thumb tracing slow circles against her knuckles. "That sounds like something I would say," he chuckled. "But, yes, no pressure, no rushing. Just... us."

She glanced at him, her smile flirty. "And long-term? Any big plans I should know about?"

He chuckled softly. "Let's just say I'm open to possibilities. But it's way too early for anything concrete."

"I like possibilities with you," she said, hugging his arm.

And for the first time since the weekend, Dana felt comfortable—not with certainty, but with knowing they didn't need certainty just yet.

They just needed this.

Survive is a strong word

Dana and Lind continued along the trail in silence for a bit, until Dana broke it with a small laugh.

"So," she said, glancing sideways at Lind, "how'd you survive *your* first Monday back?"

Lind's lips quirked into a half-smile. "*Survive* is a strong word. Let's just say it was... an exercise in self-control."

Dana raised an eyebrow, intrigued. "How so?"

He kept his gaze on the trail ahead, his voice thoughtful. "The morning meeting, for one. Watching you answer everyone's questions about how you were feeling, standing there like nothing had changed—like this weekend hadn't turned everything upside down for me, for us—that was tough."

She blinked, caught off guard by his honesty. "You seemed calm. I thought you were fine."

Lind chuckled softly, the sound low and warm. "Oh, I was anything but fine. You were standing there, smiling, talking, and all I could think about was... us. I wanted to walk over and—" He stopped himself, shaking his head slightly. "Anyway, I think I deserve an award for restraint."

Dana squeezed his hand, her laugh light. "I know what you mean. Every time I glanced back at you, it was like this... pull. And I had to keep reminding myself we were at work, surrounded by coworkers."

"Yeah," Lind agreed, his tone quieter now. "It's a weird balance, isn't it? Wanting to see you, talk to you, but knowing we have to be careful, deciding we have to be careful."

They walked in thoughtful silence for a moment before Dana added, "I think the assignment with Brenda might have given us away."

Lind raised an eyebrow. "How so?"

Dana hesitated. "She said something today that made me wonder if she's catching on."

"Brenda? Catching on?"

Dana sighed. "Yeah. She made this comment about us exchanging glances and then gave me that look."

Lind chuckled knowingly. "Ah, the look."

"She didn't outright say anything, but I don't know... she watches everything. She's sharp."

Lind nodded. "Brenda is sharp. But if she was really onto us, she'd already be asking pointed questions."

Dana exhaled. "You're probably right. Still, it's weird knowing someone might be noticing."

Lind gave her hand a light squeeze. "We knew this would happen eventually. But we're fine. We'll just keep doing what we're doing."

They continued walking, falling back into comfortable conversation.

After a moment, Lind said, "Being reassigned in the afternoon gave me a little breathing room myself. But—I missed being near you."

Dana glanced at him, her expression softening. She squeezed his hand lightly. "I missed you too."

Lind continued to rub his thumb gently over her knuckles.

Dana's thoughts drifted back to Brenda's comment—the way it hinted at something being different—and the small jolt she'd felt when it first landed. Not because she didn't want people to know eventually, but because she wasn't used to having something that mattered this much.

She exhaled, letting the thought go. "You know," she said, glancing at Lind, "talking to Brenda made me realize something."

Lind glanced at her. "What's that?"

Dana hesitated, choosing her words carefully. "That I don't want to hide this—not forever. I know we have to be careful at work, but... I don't want this to be a secret. I want us to feel like we can just... be."

Lind stopped walking, turning to face her fully. His hazel eyes held hers, steady and reassuring. "We'll get there," he said. "But we'll take it one step at a time. No rush, no pressure. We'll figure it out—together, right?"

Dana nodded.

He hesitated, "Though I am dreading the store gossip when it gets out."

Dana groaned. "Oh my God, the cackling geese are going to be relentless."

"Exactly," Lind chuckled.

Dana paused, looking up at him with warm eyes, her fingers tightening around his. "But I like what you said—us, figuring it out together."

She stood there for a second, just looking at him, feeling the quiet certainty in his presence. Then, without overthinking it, she stood on her toes and pressed a quick, soft kiss to his lips.

Dana exhaled, watching the trail curve ahead of them. The last of the sunlight flickered through the trees. She'd been so focused on wanting things to move forward, and now... now she was realizing just how much had changed in a matter of days.

"I know I said things felt slow before," she admitted, glancing at him. "But after this weekend, I guess I'm realizing... maybe it's moving faster than I expected. Or faster than I thought I'd be ready for."

She glanced at Lind, half-expecting him to look concerned. But his expression remained calm, steady. "It's okay to feel that way. There's no rule book here. We're figuring this out as we go, at whatever pace feels right."

His words soothed the tension curling in her chest, but she couldn't help the small laugh that bubbled up. "It's just funny, you know? You were right, I was complaining in my head about how slow you were moving before... and now I'm the one worried about going too fast."

Lind smiled. "I wouldn't call it 'too fast,'" he said. "Tomorrow makes it a week. Yes, a lot has happened in that week, but it doesn't feel rushed. It feels like we've just... stopped holding back."

Maybe he was right. Maybe they were just ready. She thought.

They resumed walking, their hands still intertwined, their conversation flowing as naturally as the trail stretching out before them. The day's events felt distant now, fading into the background. Out here, it was just them—no coworkers, no assignments—just the two of them figuring out what this was and what it could be.

They found themselves talking easily about the week ahead, making casual plans for the weekend, tossing around ideas for places they might visit together. Small steps... forward.

As the trail looped back toward the parking lot, the last light of day was fading, Dana felt lighter. Clearer.

They kissed goodbye, a quiet goodnight exchanged between them. It was late, and by the time they got home, it would be straight to bed.

4:30 AM... comes awfully early.

Chapter 30

Morning, sunshine

The energy Tuesday morning was more subdued compared to Monday, as everyone got back to their routines. Dana and Lind kept to their usual spots, maintaining the balance they'd established from the first day Lind started working there.

Dana felt steadier this morning, though she was still hyper-aware of Lind's presence. As Georgette read through the assignments, Dana snuck a glance in his direction. Lind caught her eye for the briefest moment, the corner of his mouth twitching into a faint smile—small, subtle, but enough to send a thrill straight through her.

When the meeting ended, Brenda sauntered up beside her, grinning. "Morning, sunshine. You're looking awfully chipper today."

Dana gave a nervous laugh. "It's called caffeine, Brenda. Lots of it."

Brenda raised a brow, her tone full of mischief. "Really? Were you up late last night?"

Dana smirked, shaking her head. "No, Brenda. In fact, I went to bed a little early... alone."

She tried to keep her expression neutral, but she couldn't help a small smile from creeping in. Brenda gave her a slow, knowing nod. "Mmm-hmm."

Dana rolled her eyes, already knowing exactly what was spinning in Brenda's head. She wouldn't press—not yet—but the wheels were turning.

***

Dana and Lind were assigned to separate areas, which was a relief.

Being apart made it easier to focus—no looks from Brenda, no temptation to glance Lind's way when she should be working on markdowns. But even with the distance, Dana found her thoughts drifting. *Was he thinking about her too?*

Across the store, Lind was focused—but not immune. He caught sight of Dana pushing a cart of supplies past his aisle, her head down, her hair falling over her shoulders. His gaze followed her for a few seconds before he turned back to the shelves, a quiet smile tugging at his lips.

An hour later, she was kneeling near the top of the pet aisle, restocking the bottom shelf, when Lind appeared at the far end. Hands in his pockets, looking around like he might've wandered there by accident—then started down the aisle like a man on a mission.

As he reached her, he said, "Hey."

Dana glanced up. "Hey."

"I was wondering... what kind of music do you like?"

The question caught her off guard. She blinked. "Uh... classic rock. Some contemporary stuff, but mostly older songs. Why?" Her brow started to lift.

"No particular reason," he lied smoothly.

Dana glanced around, making sure no one from their team was nearby. "What kind of music do *you* listen to?"

"There's only two kinds worth listening to," he said with a straight face. "Country and western."

She rolled her eyes. "Of course there are."

Then narrowed them again. "But why are you wondering about this *now*?"

He took a slow step back, already turning. "Just thinking about this last weekend."

The flush hit instantly, heat rising up her neck. She looked around quickly, like she'd just been caught with her hand in the cookie jar.

He paused just a bay away and tilted his head toward the ceiling. "You catch what's playing right now?" he asked, nodding slightly toward the overhead speakers.

Only then did she actually stop to listen to the music trickling down from the intercom.

Bum bum bum bum bum... Wild thing...
Bum bum bum bum bum... You make my heart sing...

Her eyes widened. Her blush deepened. Lind gave her a wink and kept walking, cool as a cucumber.

Dana stared after him, her cheeks burning. *Oh God, everyone is going to know. My face is on fire. It's so obvious. Brenda's going to—*

She shook her head. *Get a grip, Dana. Nobody knows anything. You're fine. Act normal. Nobody's around.*

A couple of deep breaths later and her flush started to fade.

Until Lind reached the end of the aisle. He glanced back and hit her with one more grin before disappearing around the corner.

The heat came rushing back like a second wave.

Damn it, Lind!

Brenda, don't start

The lunchroom hummed with the usual midday chatter. Dana and Lind sat at separate tables, surrounded by their usual groups, but the space between them buzzed with awareness.

Brenda plopped into the seat beside Dana, eyeing her over the rim of her soda can. "So," she said, too casual, "how's your day going?"

"Good," Dana replied quickly, taking a bite of her sandwich.

Brenda's grin widened. "I'll bet it is."

Dana shot her a warning look.

"Brenda, don't start."

"I'm just saying," Brenda teased, lowering her voice. "Lind's looking extra... focused today. Wonder what's on his mind."

Dana fought the urge to glance toward his table. "Probably work," she said, keeping her tone light. "You do remember Lind, right? Always focused."

Brenda laughed and leaned back in her chair. "Alright, alright. I'll leave you alone—for now." Their conversation shifted to safer ground.

Across the room, Lind was only half-listening to Pete's long-winded story about his weekend. His gaze drifted toward Dana's table just once. He caught her mid-laugh, her head tilted back, smiling at something Brenda had said. He smiled faintly before turning back to Pete.

***

The afternoon brought an unexpected twist—Dana and Lind were paired together for an inventory reconciliation project, which meant they'd be working side by side the rest of the shift.

At first, it was all business. Their voices stayed low, their conversation strictly about numbers and stock counts. But as the hours passed, the comfort between them returned.

"You missed a box," Lind murmured, tapping the tablet's screen.

Dana glanced up, her lips curving into a quiet smile. "That's what you're here for, right?"

"To keep you on track?" Lind said, catching her eye. "Always."

"To keep *us* on track." She shot back. Their banter was light, subtle enough not to draw attention—but unmistakably theirs.

At one point, Dana leaned closer to show Lind something on the screen. Their shoulders brushed, sending a ripple of warmth through her. She didn't pull away right away.

Neither did he.

***

As the workday wound down, Dana and Lind found themselves walking out of the store together. They did most days, but this afternoon... it felt different.

"How'd today go for you?" Lind asked as they stepped into the cool afternoon air.

"Better than yesterday," Dana admitted, smiling up at him. "I think we're getting the hang of this."

"Agreed," Lind said, his gaze steady. "It's only the second day, but yeah... I agree."

They shared a quiet moment at Dana's car. Neither of them seemed in a hurry to leave.

Finally, she said, "See you tomorrow?"

Lind nodded, a soft smile on his face. "See you tomorrow."

As Dana drove home, anticipation hummed through her, mingling with something quieter. Something deeper. They'd shared so much over the past week.

And she wanted it again.

And again.

And again.

The ride home was a blur, her thoughts replaying the day—the glances, the smiles, the closeness. Before she knew it, she was pulling into the condo complex.

Had the drive home always been this short?

You miss me already

The faint hum of traffic drifted through the windows of Lind's apartment as he leaned back on the couch, scrolling absently through his phone. Work had been easier today, less tense, and he felt cautiously optimistic about how things were starting to feel real with Dana.

His phone buzzed in his hand, and a small smile tugged at his lips when her name lit up the screen.

"Hey, Dana."

"Hi," she said, her voice warm but hesitant. "I hope I'm not interrupting anything."

"Not at all," Lind replied, shifting forward. "What's up? You miss me already?"

"Well... yes, actually," Dana admitted, her tone softening. "I was just thinking... if you're not busy, maybe we could go out to dinner tonight. My treat."

Lind chuckled, the sound low and warm. "You don't have to bribe me with food, you know. I'd love to have dinner with you."

"Great," she said, relief in her voice. "I'd really like to spend more time together today."

"Agreed," Lind said, already mentally deciding what to wear. "What place did you have in mind?"

"I was thinking that little Italian spot downtown," Dana suggested. "It's cozy and quiet. We could actually talk without shouting over music."

"Sounds perfect," Lind said. "What time should I meet you there?"

There was a pause, then Dana added, almost shyly, "Actually... I was wondering if you'd want to come back to my place after dinner. We could have a glass of wine or something. And, um... maybe you should bring your work clothes for tomorrow."

Lind raised an eyebrow, the corners of his mouth twitching. "You know," he said, "just a couple of hours ago, you were saying things might be moving a little fast. And now you're inviting me to a school-night sleepover?"

Dana let out a quiet laugh. He could almost picture her biting her lip. "Okay, yeah. I might be sending mixed signals. But I thought about it and... I don't know. Spending time with you feels right. I want to see you some more. I don't want to overthink it."

Her honesty hit him in the chest—it always got him how open and real she was.

"Well, when you put it that way," he said, his voice softening, "how could I say no?"

"So that's a yes?" she asked, hopeful.

"Yes, Dana," Lind said. He paused for a beat, considering. "Actually, if you're okay with it, why don't I come pick you up? That way we can drive together. Easier, don't you think?"

Dana hesitated, then smiled. "That's... a great idea."

"Alright," Lind said. "Give me twenty minutes, and I'll swing by. Sound good?"

"Perfect," Dana replied, her smile clear in her voice. "See you soon."

As the call ended, Lind stood and headed to his closet, the same small smile on his lips.

Whatever pace they were moving at—it felt natural. And that was all that mattered.

Chapter 31

It's only been a couple of hours

Lind pulled his truck into a spot in front of Dana's building, cutting the engine and slinging his backpack over one shoulder. He glanced up at her lit windows, a slow grin pulling at his lips as his pulse picked up.

The sound of his boots crunching on the walkway filled the quiet as he made his way to her door. He lifted his hand to knock—

But before his knuckles could connect, it swung open—Dana already waiting for him.

Dana stood there, her hair loose around her shoulders, green eyes lighting up when they met his.

"You're fast," Lind said, grinning.

"I saw you pull in," she replied, stepping back to let him inside.

He'd barely set his backpack down when she threw her arms around him, pulling him close. His hands found her waist as she pressed her cheek to his chest.

"I missed you," Dana murmured.

He tightened his arms around her. The feeling was mutual.

"It's only been a couple of hours," he said, kissing the top of her head.

"Still," she said, tipping her face up, her eyes bright. "I missed this. Us. Being close."

"I couldn't agree more," Lind said with a grin.

"And having you so close at work and not being able to touch you," she paused slightly, "is harder than I thought it would be." She buried her face in his neck. "I want more of this."

Her words were all the invitation he needed. He pulled her head back just a bit and captured her mouth in a kiss that started soft but deepened as she leaned into him. The weight of the day—the careful distance they'd kept at work—fell away, just the two of them, here, now, alone.

Dana's fingers trailed up his neck, tangling in his hair as their kiss turned urgent. Lind shifted, leaning back against the wall for balance as she pressed into him. His self-control was quickly fraying at the edges, and after a beat, he forced himself to break the kiss, resting his forehead against hers while they caught their breath.

"Dana," he said quietly, his voice edged with restraint. "We really should go to dinner first."

"Why?" she asked, flashing him a wicked smile.

"Because," Lind murmured, "if we don't, we're not leaving this condo anytime soon. And I want the whole evening with you. Not just—this."

Dana tilted her head, searching his face. "You're saying you want more than just the fun part?"

"It's all fun parts," he said, his smile warming. "I also want to talk with you, laugh with you, enjoy a good meal with you. Let's do those parts first. Then..."

"We'll see where the evening goes," she finished, mischief in her eyes.

"Exactly."

She let out a soft laugh, but there was a question in her eyes as she slid her hands down to rest on his chest. "You're kind of impossible, you know. I thought you would—*but* you keep surprising me, Lind."

"I hope it's in a good way," Lind replied. "But I mean it. I want the whole evening. Not just the highlight reel."

Dana sighed, over dramatic. Then she smiled. "Fine. Dinner first. But you owe me a second round of this when we get back."

Lind chuckled, stepping back, though he didn't let go of her hand. "Deal. You ready to go, or do you need a minute to... regroup?"

Dana shook her head, already reaching for her purse. "Nope. Let's go before I change my mind and tackle you again."

Lind laughed as they headed for the door. "Every guy at the restaurant's going to enjoy the view."

"Why?" Dana asked as she glanced down, following his gaze. Her eyes widened. "Oh God," she muttered a curse, quickly crossing her arms.

Then she straightened, stretched her arms out, giving him a taste of just how much he affects her. "I guess you'll just have to walk behind me. Maybe use your hands. Make sure no one sees."

"You really like trouble," Lind said, as he turned her to the door. "It's going to be a long night."

"If I have anything to say about it, it will."

She threw on a light jacket against the cool night air, and together they stepped outside.

Lind felt it as they walked—the excitement, the energy, the anticipation.

Pretty damned fast for slow

The small Italian restaurant Dana had suggested was everything she hoped for—cozy, quiet, and tucked away from the downtown streets. Soft candlelight flickered on their table as they settled in.

They'd already gone through the pleasantries—ordering their food, commenting on the charm of the place—and now the conversation had shifted into something quieter. Easier.

There was no work, no coworkers, no weight to carry here.

Dana toyed with her fork, watching it twist idly through the air before she set it down. "I was thinking earlier," she said, glancing at Lind. "What if you had said no?"

Lind smiled, his eyes warm as they met hers. "You had to know I wouldn't turn you down?"

She laughed softly, shaking her head. "It's just... I feel like I want this every day, you know? To come home, see you, be with you. It's hard not to want that when this feels so... easy."

Lind's mouth curved slightly, but his gaze turned thoughtful. "You ever notice how sometimes *'love at first sight, can't get enough of each other'* relationships burn the hottest—and crash the hardest?"

Dana tilted her head, intrigued.

"I've seen it happen," he went on. "Two people fall fast. It's all late nights, constant texts, barely coming up for air. But eventually, it starts to suffocate. You skip the slow part—the part where you build something real—and before you know it, you're out of fuel. Burned up. Or worse, burn each other up."

Dana nodded slowly, her smile fading into something more reflective. "Yeah. I've seen that too."

He paused, watching her for a moment. "That's what I want to avoid. I want this to last, Dana. I want you. But rushing into this too fast..." He gave a small shake of his head. "It's like building a bonfire too big. It burns hot and bright, but it'll destroy everything." Lind met her eyes, voice quieter now. "I don't want that."

She held his gaze, the weight of that simple truth gave her pause.

Dana tilted her head, considering. "So you're saying we need to take it slow?"

"Not just take it slow," Lind said with a faint smile. "Take it *intentionally* slow. And right now, my beautiful, sexy woman, we're moving pretty damned fast for 'slow.'"

Dana laughed, her cheeks warming. "Yeah... you're not wrong. But it's hard not to want more when everything feels... like this."

"I know," he said, his voice soft but sure. "But slow and steady. Not because we're unsure. Because it matters."

Lind reached across the table, taking her hand. "It does feel good. And I want more too. But we don't have to cram everything into every moment. We see each other every day at work, even if we can't exactly act like this there." His thumb grazed the back of her hand. "But the weekends, they're wide open."

"Yeah, yeah, I know," Dana smiled, her gaze softening. "You're making sense. As usual."

Lind chuckled. "I have my moments."

They fell into an easy silence, sipping their drinks and watching the slow bustle of the restaurant. The candle between them flickered gently, catching Dana's attention for a moment.

Finally, Dana looked away from the candle. "So," she said, a playful lilt in her voice, "if we're being intentionally slow, does that mean you'll make me wait until the weekend to spend the night?"

Lind's brow lifted. "Depends. Are you inviting me over every night this week?"

She laughed, leaning in so no one else could hear. "I am tempted to have you–you know, over every night this week, yes." She grinned wickedly. "But I'll just have to pace myself. If you weren't so damn good... at... everything, it would be easier."

"Thank you, Dana," Lind said quietly, his grin softening as his fingers traced slow circles over her hand. "As much as I'd love to be had by you every night this week, I want to savor this. I want to savor you. To build something that lasts."

Dana's heart softened at that.

"Me too," she said, her voice quiet but sure. "I want that too."

Maybe we could go someday

As the plates of pasta arrived, the air filled with the warm, familiar scent of garlic and basil. Their conversation shifted naturally into something quieter, more thoughtful. The soft clinking of silverware and the low murmur of other diners became a kind of backdrop—cozy, steady, and far from everything else.

Dana twirled a forkful of linguine, glancing at Lind with quiet curiosity. "Have you ever visited a place that just... stayed with you? One that replays in your mind, even years later?"

Lind set down his glass, his smile thoughtful. "Yeah, a few. But one that always sticks with me is the Grand Canyon. My parents took me and my sister when I was about ten or eleven. I remember standing on the edge, just... in awe. It was so massive, so overwhelming. It made me feel small, but not in a bad way. More like I was part of something bigger."

"That's a beautiful way to put it," Dana said, her eyes lighting up. "I've never been, but it's on my list. Did you hike any of the trails?"

"A little," Lind said, smiling faintly. "Mostly short ones. My parents weren't exactly the 'rugged outdoors' type, but they gave me enough of a taste for it."

Dana leaned forward, resting her elbow on the table. "Where else have you been that you really loved?"

Lind hesitated for a second, then smiled. "A few years ago, I went to the Pacific Northwest—Seattle and Portland—with Sam."

Dana's brow lifted slightly, but she nodded for him to go on.

"It was amazing," Lind said, his tone casual but warm. "The air felt cleaner, the weather was cooler. And the food scene in Portland? Unbelievable. We spent most of the trip eating and wandering through little neighborhoods."

"That sounds incredible," Dana said honestly. "I've always heard great things about the Pacific Northwest, but I've never made it that far west."

Lind nodded. "It's worth it. I'd go back in a heartbeat. Maybe we could go someday—hit the food trucks, do a little hiking."

Dana smiled, the thought warmed her. "I'd really like that."

She twirled her pasta again, her expression softening. "For me, it's the beach. We used to go to the Outer Banks every summer when I was a kid. My mom would spend hours collecting shells. My dad built these ridiculous sandcastles with me."

Lind's smile widened. "That sounds like a great childhood memory. Have you been back?"

"Once," Dana said, her voice quieter now. "With Al, my first serious boyfriend. The summer after high school. It was fun at the time, but now... now it feels complicated."

"Because of the breakup?" Lind asked gently.

Dana nodded. "Yeah. It's hard to separate the place from the person sometimes. But I'd like to go back and make new memories—ones that aren't tied to him."

"I get that," Lind said, his tone understanding. "Seeing a place with fresh eyes—or with someone new—makes all the difference."

"What about you?" Dana asked after a moment. "Any place you'd want to revisit?"

Lind thought for a moment. "There's a cabin in the Smoky Mountains I stayed at once. Quiet, tucked away in the trees, with an amazing view. I'd love to go back, but... with the right person."

Dana could picture it. "That sounds perfect. The mountains. The quiet. I think I'd like that too."

They sat quietly for a moment, the conversation so easy and comfortably between them. Then Dana asked, "What about places you haven't been yet? Any dream destinations?"

"Alaska," Lind said immediately, his eyes lighting up. "The wilderness, the wildlife, the northern lights. I've always wanted to see it for myself. You remember telling me about Greg and his Arctic documentaries you hated?"

Dana laughed. "Oh God, those! Yeah, I remember." She frowned. "Alright, we'll add Alaska to our 'someday' list."

"Deal," Lind said with a soft chuckle. "What about you?"

"Europe," Dana said without hesitation. "Italy, France, maybe Greece. I've always dreamed of wandering through old streets, eating amazing food, and soaking it all in."

Lind chuckled. "I can see it. You, glass of wine in hand, wandering through the streets of Paris like you own the place."

Dana laughed, shaking her head. "I'll take that as a compliment."

"It is," Lind said, his voice quiet but sure.

The conversation flowed from there—family road trips, high school adventures, awkward vacations with early relationships. They laughed, they shared, but beneath it all was something deeper.

The quiet certainty of connection, of understanding.

By the time the plates were cleared and the check arrived, it was there between them.

They'd shared pieces of themselves—past and future—and left room for the possibilities ahead.

Chapter 32

Wherever we decide there is

As Lind navigated the quiet streets, the low hum of the truck's engine filled the space between them. Dana leaned back in her seat, her hands resting loosely in her lap as the darkened storefronts slipped by. The passing street lights flickered across the windshield, casting shifting patterns of light and shadow inside the cab.

"You're really patient with people at work," she said suddenly, breaking the quiet.

Lind shot her a brief glance, curious. "What makes you say that?"

"The way you handle everyone," Dana replied, turning toward him. "Even the cackling geese don't seem to get under your skin."

Lind chuckled, his mouth twitching. "I've learned not to take people like that too seriously. They don't mean any harm—most of the time, they just have their opinions."

Dana tilted her head, thoughtful. "I don't know how you do it. I try to keep my cool, but some days... it's hard not to let them get to me."

"I think it's because I don't give them that power," Lind said simply. "I'm not saying it's easy, but it's not worth the energy to get upset over people you can't change."

Dana nodded slowly, his words giving her perspective. "That's... a good way to look at it. I guess I care too much about what people think. About me, what I do, who I am."

Lind's voice softened. "Caring isn't a bad thing. It just means you have a big heart. But maybe save that energy for the people who really matter."

She smiled at that, a quiet warmth inside her. "I like the way you see things," she admitted. "It's steady. Solid. I could use more of that."

Lind shrugged, his voice light. "Well, you're stuck with me, so maybe some of it will rub off."

Dana laughed softly. Her gaze drifted back to the road ahead, but her thoughts played on his words.

After a moment, she spoke again, her voice hesitant. "So... when you and Sam do stuff together, is it usually hiking? Or do you do... other things?"

Lind's hands stayed relaxed on the wheel, his tone easy. "Hiking's a big one. We've always enjoyed that. Sometimes we check out a new town or try quirky restaurants. She's got a thing for food trucks."

Dana nodded, keeping her tone measured. "That sounds fun. But it's... different from what we do, right? I mean, you and I have our own thing."

"Completely different," Lind said without hesitation. He glanced at her briefly, his eyes steady. "What I have with Sam isn't like this. With you—it's more."

"More?" Dana echoed, her voice softer.

"More present," Lind clarified. "More day-to-day. With you... I want to build something that is part of my everyday life. Not just moments here and there."

Dana's chest tightened, his words catching her off guard. "I like hearing that," she said quietly. "Because this—whatever we're doing—I want it to feel real. Like it's going somewhere."

"It is," Lind said firmly. "But we're figuring it out as we go. No rush. No pressure. Just us... going there, wherever we decide *there* is."

Dana smiled faintly, her fingers playing with the seatbelt. "You're good at that. Keeping things steady."

Lind grinned, his tone lighter. "Someone's got to keep you from getting too worked up over the cackling geese."

Dana laughed, shaking her head.

Lind's smile widened as he turned onto her street.

Every time with this man

As Dana and Lind climbed the stairs, anticipation thick between them, she led the way, holding his hand. This felt so easy for her, so natural. *What is it about this man, why do I feel like this about him?*

They stopped near the bed, hands searching, fingertips tracing, exploring. Dana's fingers ran along the back of Lind's neck, sending a shiver through him, and he answered with a slow caress along the side of her face, savoring the warmth of her skin. Their kisses started soft, but as each kiss deepened the want sharpened, stretching time between them. The heat of his mouth, the tickle of his breath, sent a fresh ripple through her body.

Dana pulled back, a quiet smile tugging at her lips. She ran her hands down his chest, her touch light. She reached the hem of his shirt and began undressing him—slow, sensual, savoring the feel of his skin under her fingers. Each time he moved to help, she swatted his hands away.

"I want to do this," she murmured, her voice thick with want.

She took her time as she revealed him to her. His body, familiar and desired, felt like something she wanted to explore all over again. Her fingers traced the lines of his muscles, igniting sparks between them. When he was fully bare, she stepped back, just for a moment, drinking him in.

Lind reached for her, but she stayed just out of reach, her smile playful as she began to undress herself. Slowly, letting each piece fall away. She was keenly aware of his gaze following every movement, the tension between them tightening with each second.

When she was finally bare, she stepped in to kiss him, deep, wanting. He responded in kind. Her breasts pushed tight against him, he swore he could feel her nipples poking his chest. She pulled away just a bit and she pushed him onto the bed and climbed onto him, her body pressing close. She rocked her hips, teasing him, loving the feel of him hard beneath her. She'd known what she wanted the moment he walked through her door, but now it was more. This wasn't just raw need—it was connection, and the way they moved now was deliberate, meant to make this moment last.

Her lips found his—soft, then deep, then hungry. Her fingers tangled in his hair as she kissed her way down his neck, his chest, tasting him, memorizing him. His groan rumbled through her as his hands gripped her hips, his control slipping the longer she moved against him. When she moved up again, her breasts brushing against his mouth, he took full advantage, lips, tongue and teeth—until she shivered.

She rose higher, straddling his head between her thighs, one hand gripping the headboard, the other threading through his hair. His eyes—dark, focused—were the only part of him she could see when she looked down, and that look alone made her pulse race.

Every nerve in her body was lit up. It had been that way all night—waiting, wanting. And now the tension was coiling, tighter and tighter, every movement of his mouth bringing her closer and closer until it finally snapped. Lind held her in place, his mouth learning what made her come undone—and how to keep her there.

As the sensitivity crested, she pulled away a bit, gasping for breath, her body shuddering with the aftermath. Lind watched her, waiting as her focus returned.

Dana slid back down his body, catching his mouth in a deep kiss. She tasted herself there. *More, I want more*. It wasn't just hunger—it was something deeper. *Every time with this man.*

She reached for him, guiding him into her—and they moved together. Slow at first, finding rhythm, until the pull between them grew urgent. Hands grasped, lips searched, bodies tangled. The room faded away until all that was left was sensation and the steady beat of them, together.

They stayed like that for a long while, moving with a rhythm that was unhurried, building toward something they both already knew was inevitable. When Dana came again, it was quieter this time—a deep, body-heavy release that left her clinging to Lind, her face tucked into the curve of his neck, her breath warm against his skin. He followed a few moments later, his arms tightening around her as he buried his face in her hair, exhaling her name like a promise.

Lind ran his hand slowly down her spine, smoothing the damp strands of hair at the nape of her neck before easing her onto her back. He pressed a soft kiss to her shoulder before getting up out of the bed.

Dana watched him go, she listened to the quiet sounds from the bathroom—the water running, this now familiar routine. She smiled to herself, knowing what he was doing.

When Lind returned he had a towel and a warm, damp washcloth in hand. He eased her thighs apart to clean her. His gaze flicked up to hers more than once to make sure she was okay.

Dana reached down, laying her hand over his wrist. "You always do this," she murmured.

Lind gave a small shrug, his thumb grazing the inside of her knee. "I like taking care of you."

And he did. She could feel it in every careful stroke of the cloth, in the way he smoothed it over her skin without hurry. When he finished, he pressed another kiss to the inside of her thigh before slipping the cloth aside. He grabbed the towel and dried her gently.

He took them both back to the bathroom, rinsing and hanging up the cloth and towel.

He smiled at it, resting on the neatly folded towel—long ago air-dried. As he left the bathroom, he ran his fingers lightly over it.

Back in the bedroom he pulled the covers over them.

No rush. No hesitation. Just them.

Not my fault you're distracting

Lind's arm heavy across Dana's waist, their bodies fitting together easily. The steady rhythm of his breathing, the warmth of his chest pressed to her back, lulled her into sleep almost instantly. The last thing she remembered was the tickling of his breath in her hair.

The alarm shattered the quiet far too soon. Lind groaned, reaching blindly for his phone on the nightstand to shut it off. Dana stirred, rolling over to face him, her hair a tousled halo around her face.

"Damn," she muttered, voice thick with sleep. "What time did we even get to bed?"

"You mean *to sleep,* you really don't want to know," Lind mumbled, rubbing his eyes with the heel of his hand.

Dana groaned, stretching lazily. Her bare skin rubbing against his, and Lind's hand drifted to her hip without thinking.

"So... who's taking a shower first?" she asked, voice still drowsy.

"If we're going to be ready on time," Lind said, with a slow grin, "we might want to take it together."

Dana's lips twitched into a sleepy smile as she propped herself up on one elbow. "If we take it together, we won't make it to work."

"I think we should chance it."

She laughed, shaking her head. "You're not helping."

But after a beat, he added, "You'll need more time to get ready," he said, relenting. "You go first."

Grumbling, Dana slipped out of bed, making her way to the bathroom, shivering as cool air met her bare skin. Lind stayed where he was for a minute, listening to the soft hiss of water before climbing out of bed and heading after her.

As he stepped toward the shower curtain he noticed the neatly folded towel on the counter, along with its contents, was gone. He smiled.

Inside, Dana was lathering shampoo into her hair when she heard him come in. She resisted the urge to peek around the curtain, but she didn't have to—Lind had no such reservations as he pulled it back a bit.

"Are you sure you don't want me in there?" he asked, his grin unapologetic.

Dana startled a little. She turned toward him, shooting him a warning look. "I'm serious. If you step into this shower with me, we're not making it to work. Then what will Brenda say?"

Lind sighed dramatically and backed away. "Fine."

When Dana finished, he was waiting with a towel. She stepped out and grabbed it, but not before wrapping her damp arms around him in a wet, impromptu hug. He chuckled, kissing her hair as she pressed herself against him.

By the time Lind shut off the water a few minutes later, Dana was at the sink, naked, brushing her teeth with one hand and towel-drying her hair with the other. Lind paused after pulling the curtain aside, watching her for a moment, the swaying of her breasts—with every movement—giving him ideas they didn't have time to entertain.

"Stop staring," Dana said, catching his reflection in the mirror.

"Not my fault you're distracting," Lind replied, his voice warm.

He dressed quickly and headed to the kitchen, throwing together scrambled eggs, hash browns with cheese, and toast. Dana joined him a few minutes later, damp hair twisted into a bun, sipping coffee as she leaned against the counter.

Now you owe me the details

They walked out together but stuck to the plan—Dana drove ahead, and Lind followed a few minutes behind. The streets were quiet this time of day, the sky still holding on to the last traces of night.

Dana arrived first, coffee in hand, slipping into her usual spot at the morning meeting. Lind walked in a few minutes later, taking his usual place against the wall. His hands tucked in his pockets, his expression easy.

But Brenda's sharp eyes caught everything. She leaned toward Dana with a mischievous grin. "Now you owe me the details."

Dana blushed, her gaze flicking to Lind in spite of herself. He didn't look their way, but the practiced nonchalance was telling.

This was going to be a long day.

Part 8

<u>First 3 Months</u>

Work was one world.

Secret glances. Stolen touches. The text messages we pretended not to send.

Home was another.

At night, there was no pretending.

Just us. No them.

And every time I thought I might be getting the hang of it...

He'd smile. And I'd forget to be careful.

Chapter 33

Don't play innocent

Dana shot Brenda a look, trying and failing to suppress the warmth climbing up her throat. Damn it, Brenda. She flicked another glance at Lind, only to catch him already looking away, cool and composed as ever. *How does he do that?* Her poker face was barely holding, and there he was, looking like nothing had happened.

Brenda nudged her elbow. "Don't even try to brush me off, girl. You owe me."

Dana leaned back, voice quiet. "There's nothing to tell." She took another sip of coffee, the heat no help at all.

Brenda gave a soft snort. "Oh, come on. Don't play innocent. I may be old-fashioned, but I'm not blind. You two have a vibe today." Her grin widened. "And you're smiling like the cat that got the cream."

Dana rolled her eyes, the smile on her face making her feel *exactly* like the cat that got the cream. "You're imagining things."

"Oh sure," Brenda said, voice dry with disbelief. She tilted her head toward Lind. "I bet he's imagining things too."

Dana's stomach flipped. Brenda wasn't entirely wrong.

Before she could reply, the door creaked open. Georgette strode in, clipboard in hand, all business. "Alright, folks, let's get started."

The room quieted. Brenda gave Dana one last look, her grin promising the conversation was far from over.

Dana exhaled slowly and fixed her gaze on Georgette. Across the room, Lind stood by the wall, arms crossed. Not a single crack in his composure. *We've got this. Just stay calm.*

I've got questions, you've got answers

Once the meeting wrapped up, Georgette started running down the assignments. Dana kept her head down, studying her clipboard like it held the secrets of the universe. Lind jotted notes, his expression steady.

Dana risked another glance his way—only to find Brenda watching her instead.

Brenda nudged her shoulder. "Smooth," she muttered.

Dana pressed her lips together. Lind's playing it cool. She could too.

"Dana and Brenda," Georgette called. "You're handling the seasonal aisle reset today. Clear out the old stock, reorganize shelving, and get the end caps set up. Let's have it done before lunch."

"Yes, boss," Brenda chirped, giving a mock salute.

Georgette rolled her eyes but moved on.

Lind made a quick note on his clipboard. As Georgette gave him his assignment, his gaze flicked to Dana—brief, steady—before turning away again.

As the group broke apart, Brenda bumped Dana's elbow. "Just us, huh? Lucky me." She grinned. "I'm sure this'll be a productive morning."

Dana groaned inwardly. "It's just shelves, Brenda. No need to make it dramatic."

"Oh honey," Brenda said as they headed for seasonal. "The shelves are fine. But I've got questions. And you've got answers."

Friends? Girl, if that's friendship

The seasonal aisle still clung to fall—half-priced wreaths, leftover pumpkins, and a few sad boxes of unsold candy corn. Brenda handed Dana a roll of tape, brandishing her box cutter like a weapon.

"Alright," Brenda said, slicing into a box of garland. "Spill. What's going on with you and Lind? And don't think about dodging me."

Dana sighed, kneeling to unpack a box of snowflake decals. "There's nothing to spill. We're friends."

Brenda snorted. "Friends? Girl. If that's friendship, I've been doing it wrong."

Dana kept her focus on peeling labels. "Brenda—"

Brenda held up a hand, cutting her off. "Not judging," she said, her voice softer now. "If you two are a thing, good for you. He's a good guy. But why all the sneaking around?"

Dana hesitated, checking the aisle before answering. "We're keeping it professional. That's all."

Brenda raised an eyebrow. "Uh-huh. And how's that working out?"

Dana huffed a quiet laugh. "Not as smooth as I'd hoped."

Brenda's grin softened into something more curious. "So... you like him. You really like him."

Yeah, Dana thought, *REALLY is exactly the right word to describe it.*

Dana's hands stilled on a roll of ribbon. "Yeah," she admitted, her voice low. "I do. It's different with him. Easy. Real. But..." Her throat tightened. "It's complicated."

Brenda tilted her head. "You said that before, complicated how?"

Dana exhaled. Not here, not now. "We're figuring things out."

Brenda studied her, then nodded once. "Fair enough. But when you're ready, I want details. Until then, I'm just gonna assume you're getting more action than the rest of us combined."

Dana rolled her eyes. "You're relentless."

"I'm persistent," Brenda corrected, tossing ornaments into a nearby bin. "Now let's finish this before Georgette gets twitchy."

As they worked, some of Dana's tension eased. Brenda's teasing was relentless, but never cruel. She wasn't digging for answers Dana wasn't ready to give—just poking at what was already obvious.

Still, as Dana taped up the last box of fall clearance, one question stuck with her.

How long can we keep this under wraps?

What does this mean for us

Dana's days felt fuller now, each moment with Lind carving its own space in her mind. At work, they were careful—sometimes too careful. A glance here, a shared joke there—always measured, always under the radar. The weight of their secret pressed against the edges of their carefully constructed normality. Every unguarded moment outside of work felt like a breath she no longer had to hold.

Lind carried that weight differently. Compartmentalizing came easily to him. He wore indifference like a uniform, but every now and then—when Dana's laughter escaped too easily, or she looked at him a little longer than she should—the mask slipped. Hopefully, no one noticed.

Still, it was worth it, Dana thought. Every fleeting touch. Every quiet thrill of a text exchanged between them, on the floor or in the break room. Those little moments turned the long workdays into something more.

And outside of work? Outside, they could just be.

Hey yourself

Some days, Dana forgot where they were.

She rounded the corner of aisle 23, scanning for signage tape to finish her bay. The late-morning lull of shoppers softened to background noise.

She wasn't expecting to see Lind coming from the other direction, a box of shelf brackets balanced in one hand.

Their eyes met, and the familiar rush stole her breath for just a second.

Dana smiled—warm, instinctive. "Hey," she said softly, shifting to the side as he approached.

"Hey yourself," Lind replied, his voice low, familiar in a way that made her stomach flutter. He set the box down on a nearby shelf, taking his time like he needed a reason to stay there. His gaze flicked toward the ends of the aisle. Too risky. Be careful.

Dana followed his glance—empty, for now. A rare pocket of privacy.

She really wanted to reach for him, and before she even knew it, her hand was traveling lightly along his forearm. Warm skin under her fingertips sent a quiet thrill through her. Lind's mouth twitched, the faintest smile breaking through.

"Careful," he murmured, hazel eyes catching hers.

"I know," she whispered. "It's just... nice to see you."

He exhaled, the sound soft. "You see me every day."

"You know what I mean." Her voice low, but her heart thudded unevenly in her chest.

Lind watched her for a beat longer. Then he shook his head, his expression fond. "We should get back to work."

"Yeah," Dana agreed. But she was slow to step back. Slow to let the moment go.

He picked up the box again and turned toward his bay. Dana hesitated, watching the easy line of his shoulders, until footsteps echoed down the aisle.

Her heart leaped into her throat. She snatched her hand back just as Pete rounded the corner, clipboard under his arm.

Pete passed Lind first, offering only a muttered, "Excuse me," before moving past Dana without so much as a glance.

Dana ducked her head, suddenly fascinated with realigning a stack of shelf labels. Her pulse hammered at her temples. She risked a quick glance at Lind. He threw her a playful look over his shoulder.

Heat rose in Dana's face, and she bit the inside of her cheek to keep from laughing. Thank God Pete saw Lind first—because if he'd caught her expression, the game would've been up.

But that was close

Later, in the break room, Dana sat across the room from Lind, her phone in her lap. She sent him a pair of laughing emojis, remembering Pete's almost-catch.

Across the way, she watched Lind's phone buzz on the table. A slow smile breaking as he ran a hand across his forehead. *Whew*, he seemed to say without words.

Dana smiled to herself, fingers flying over the screen.

Okay, I'll stop. But that was close.

His reply came fast.

Yeah—insatiable. That was close.

She rolled her eyes, cheeks heating again.

Can't help it—and you wouldn't want me to.

This time, Lind didn't hide the color that touched his face. He leaned back in his chair, fingers tapping out his next message.

We still going to see that movie on Friday?

Dana's chest warmed in a different way, something softer.

Yes. Thank God that's tomorrow!

Lind's grin deepened.

Another weekend with you. Thank God indeed.

Chapter 34

Oh, it's war now

The theater was pretty empty for a Friday, the soft hum of pre-show ads filling the dim space. Dana had her feet tucked beneath her, the bucket of popcorn wedged between her knees like a prize she wasn't planning to share.

"You're hogging it," he whispered, nudging Dana's arm.

"You're imagining things," she replied smoothly, grabbing another handful without even glancing at him.

Lind narrowed his eyes. "Imagining, huh?" He plucked a single piece from the top of the pile and flicked it at her.

The popcorn bounced off her shoulder. Dana froze, slow-turning to look at him.

"Oh, it's war now," she murmured, her voice low and teasing.

Before he could retreat, Dana struck. Her fingers found his side, tickling without mercy. Lind let out a strangled laugh, twisting away from her. The popcorn bucket wobbled dangerously, nearly tipping into the row ahead. People turned to look.

Dana caught it just in time, grinning like she'd just won.

"Truce," he gasped, still laughing.

She lifted the bucket like a trophy. "We'll see."

The lights dimmed then, signaling the start of the movie.

Lind was still smiling, put his arm around her as the first scenes played out on the screen.

***

The theater buzzed with low chatter as the credits rolled. Dana stretched, her feet still tucked beneath her, and glanced over. Lind was crumpling the now-empty popcorn bucket with deliberate care.

"That was better than I expected," she admitted.

Lind's eyes flicked to hers, narrowing in mock warning. "Yeah, but you still owe me, popcorn flicker."

She laughed, grabbing her coat. "You started it, popcorn hoarder." Outside, the crisp night air bit at her cheeks.

Lind pulled open the passenger door of his truck. His expression, gentler than usual.

"Thanks for tonight," Dana said as she stepped into his truck.

He leaned in for a quick kiss. "Thank you for reminding me why I don't share popcorn." She swatted his arm, laughing as he closed the door. The drive back was quiet in the best way—comfortable, familiar.

When they reached her building, Lind parked without a word and leaned over, kissing her softly. Then he got out, walked around, and opened her door like it was the most natural thing in the world.

They walked arm in arm to her condo, through the front door and up the stairs, neither of them in a hurry to say goodnight.

The cook wants some lovin'

Morning came slow, winter sunlight creeping in through the blinds. Dana stretched beneath the covers, the warmth of Lind's body beside her too tempting to resist. She rolled onto her side, brushing a kiss against his lips.

Lind groaned softly. "Hmm."

"Time for breakfast."

"Breakfast?" His voice was thick with sleep. "Who's making it?"

"You are," she replied, poking his ribs.

His eyes cracked open, slow and lazy, his mouth tipping into a grin. "Then it's not time for breakfast yet... because the cook wants some more lovin.'"

Dana barely had time to squeal before he pulled her on top of him, her laughter muffled against his shoulder.

"You know," she murmured, fingers combing through his hair, "at this rate, we won't have breakfast. Or make it to the rink."

Lind pulled her closer, breathing hot into her ear. "Which would you rather do?"

Dana giggled. "You know the answer to that." She pushed away from him. "But... I'm hungry. And I haven't been skating in forever. Plus, you promised you'd try it for me today."

He groaned. "Fine. I'll settle for eating food and playing with slippery ice."

"When you say it like that, I almost want to stay here," she grinned, leaning back down to kiss his jaw as she got out of bed.

This is worse than skiing

The outdoor rink buzzed with life, Dana felt the crisp air on her cheeks as she laced up her skates. Kids shrieked, couples laughed, and the glow of twinkling lights reflected off the ice.

Lind sat beside her on the bench, eyeing the scene with mild suspicion. "When's the last time you did this?" Dana asked.

"College," he said. "It didn't end well."

She smirked. "Lucky for you, I'm an expert." She stood, offered him her hand. "Come on."

He took it without hesitation but the second his skates touched the ice, his arms flailed.

Dana bit back a laugh. "Careful," she warned. "Don't take me down with you."

"If I go, you're going," he muttered, as his grip tightened on her hand. Their first loop was slow, Lind stiff as a board, his jaw set with

281

concentration. Dana coaxed him along, their hands linked tightly. By the time they circled the rink again, he'd relaxed enough to let go—though he stayed close.

"See?" she said, skating backward ahead of him. "You're not half bad."

He shot her a look. "I'll take that as a compliment... I think."

Dana laughed, skating backward a few more paces before spinning away with easy grace. Lind watched her, both impressed and mildly annoyed that she made it look effortless.

"This is worse than skiing," he grumbled, pushing off to follow.

"Come on, tough guy," she called over her shoulder. "Catch me if you can."

He narrowed his eyes. "You do realize I outweigh you."

"Yeah, but you'll have to catch me for that to matter." She teased, darting ahead, weaving through the crowd.

Lind swore under his breath but pushed off harder, determined not to be left behind. He was shaky, sure, but he wasn't about to let her disappear on him.

"Unfair advantage!" he called after her.

Dana's laughter drifted back over the ice as she skated away.

Once you stopped torturing me

Later, when their cheeks were flushed and their legs ached in that pleasant, used kind of way, Dana tugged Lind toward one of the benches near the rink. She plopped down first, laughing as she wrestled with the laces of her skates.

"I think my ankles are going to hate me tomorrow," she said, breathless.

"Mine too," Lind replied as he sat beside her, working at his own laces. His movements were slower now, but there was an easy looseness in his shoulders. He shook his head. "Skating *is* worse than skiing."

Dan raised a brow. "Oh really? You ski?"

He gave a wry chuckle. "No. Well... yes. If you count the bunny hill."

Her eyebrows lifted, amused. "Bunny hill, huh?"

"Sam keeps trying to teach me," Lind admitted. "But I just can't get the hang of it. My coordination's fine on solid ground, but you strap things to my feet and put me on something slick, it's game over."

Dana laughed, leaning against him. "I thought you did pretty good out there today."

He gave her a chuckle. "Yeah? I really did start to get the hang of it, didn't I?" He bumped her shoulder gently. "You're a good teacher. Once you stopped torturing me."

"I was motivating you," she corrected, nudging him back.

Dana smiled, but her eyes dropped slightly as her thoughts wandered.

Sam keeps trying to teach me, he'd said it casually. Easy. Like discussing who takes out the trash or what to make for dinner.

She pushed the thought aside and took his hand in hers, their fingers intertwining easily—like they always had.

He gave her a long look, something softer hiding behind the teasing. "I guess skating's easier than skiing. Especially with you."

Dana's chest warmed. She didn't press, didn't call him out on the quiet weight of his words. Instead, she squeezed his hand lightly.

They sat like that for a few moments, watching the skaters glide across the ice. The cold bit at their cheeks, but neither seemed in a hurry to leave.

Finally, Lind said, "We should get cocoa."

Dana squeezed his hand again. "Yes, let's. Then I can warm my hands on you afterward."

He huffed a quiet laugh. "Always looking for an excuse to touch me, aren't you?"

"Always," she grinned.

They stood, hands still linked as they walked toward the concession stand. Nothing about the moment was grand, but it felt real, something she wanted to hold on to.

You know, besides

The glow from the TV flickered across Dana's living room, soft shadows shifting against the walls. She lounged on the couch, legs draped comfortably over Lind's lap. His hand traced slow, absentminded patterns along her calf, the warmth of his touch soothing her as the movie played on—neither of them really paying attention.

"We still good for next weekend at your place?" Dana asked, breaking the quiet.

"Yeah," Lind said. His thumb skimmed along the inside of her ankle. "You want to head over Friday night?"

"Works for me," she replied, fingers toying with the edge of the blanket draped across her lap. A playful glint sparked in her eye. "What are we going to do, you know... besides...?"

Lind's fingers began tracing lightly up toward Dana's thigh. "Do we have to do anything else... besides?"

She giggled softly. "You know me."

"Yes, I do," he said, his voice low. "Insatiable."

"Complaining?" she challenged, her brows lifting.

"Not a chance." No hesitation. Just certainty.

For a moment, they let the quiet stretch between them, easy and familiar. Dana's hand rested lightly against his arm. Then, she asked, "How about the weekend after?"

Lind's fingers stilled. The shift was subtle, but Dana felt it. "That's my weekend with Sam," he said carefully, watching her face.

"Oh." Dana blinked. "Right. I forgot."

He studied her for a beat longer. Not cold, not detached. Just... watchful. "Didn't you say you were thinking about seeing your folks that weekend?"

She hesitated. "Yeah. I guess I did mention that."

"Might be good," he said, his tone easy but weighted all the same. "It's been a while, hasn't it?"

Dana's gaze drifted back to the TV, though she wasn't seeing it. "It has," she admitted. "I guess I could call and see if they're free."

Somewhere in the back of her mind, she remembered saying it once before. After Thanksgiving, maybe. Talking about future plans—trips, weekends, all the things they wanted to do together. Then Sam's name had come up, and Lind had mentioned January. She'd said it then, hadn't she? *Maybe I'll go visit my folks that weekend.* Had she meant it? Or had she just been making room for him without realizing it?

Lind resumed his slow, soothing patterns back down on her calf. His thumb traced a gentle line against her skin. "You said it has been a while since you've been home."

Dana forced a small smile, keeping her tone light. "Yeah, it has."

He chuckled. "Just trying to look out for you."

She smiled back, but something tightened in her chest. *Why does it feel like he's pushing me away?*

She knew he wasn't. Rationally, she understood—he was trying to make sure she wouldn't be left sitting at home while he was with Sam. It was thoughtful. Considerate. In a strange kind of way.

But it didn't stop the slow, creeping ache. The weight of it pressing against her ribs. Why does it always feel like I'm the one adjusting?

Except... that wasn't true. Not entirely. She knew that. *Nothing was the same for him anymore either—because of her, everything was different.*

Lind's fingers squeezed gently around her ankle, grounding her again. "You okay?" he asked quietly. His tone was soft, full of understanding.

"Yeah," Dana said too fast. She cleared her throat. "Just tired. Long day."

He watched her for another second, as if debating whether to call her out on it, but then nodded and let it go. His attention shifted back to the TV.

Dana leaned her head back against the couch, staring up at the ceiling, trying to loosen the knot in her chest.

Might be good for you to visit, he'd said.

Maybe it would be. Maybe she did need the distraction.

But the question lingered in her mind long after he let it go.

What does this mean for us?

I love you too

When the movie ended, they wandered off to bed, their routine easy and familiar. But tonight, Dana was quiet in a way that Lind noticed right away. She slid in beside him, pressing close—not playful, not wanting. Just close.

Without a word, he wrapped his arms around her, holding her steady against him. He kissed her shoulder, then the back of her head, his breath warm against her skin. "I love you," he murmured.

Dana's breath caught, but she answered softly, "I love you too."

And yet, as she closed her eyes, the thought slipped in through the cracks.

Then why are you going to spend time with her?

The tears didn't come. But the sadness was there just the same.

She wanted it from Lind

Sunday morning began with a kiss and ended with Lind rinsing out the washcloth, hanging the towel neatly on its rack.

He returned to bed, stretching out beside Dana. She lay on her back, her gaze drifting toward him. When he leaned in, she met him halfway, their lips connecting softly in the quiet light.

They stayed there for a while, knee against her hip, but when she reached down to touch him, he shifted back, making space for her.

It wasn't playful. It wasn't teasing. It was about them—about connection, about love. Dana's fingers moved slowly, exploring the familiar landscape of his body.

Lind's left hand, caught between them, rested at her waist, tracing softly over her skin. His right arm lay too far away to be of use, but he didn't mind. Neither did she.

This moment wasn't about doing anything. It was about *being*.

Her fingers traced down to his hair, and she smiled softly, remembering trimming it last weekend. The shower afterward. How they'd laid wrapped up in each other, her head tucked under his chin, the world outside quiet and far away.

Her hand slowed and stilled, resting over him. Lind exhaled and pressed his palm over hers, connecting them both in the simple weight of that touch. Every so often, her thumb shifted, a small, slow caress that sent quiet pulses of pleasure through him.

He cherished these moments. When she wasn't searching for more, when she was just there, giving freely, deepening what was already theirs.

But the day was waiting.

Dana showered while Lind made breakfast, the scent of coffee and eggs warming the condo. Midway through rinsing shampoo from her hair, she laughed to herself.

He washed me up, and now I'm cleaning myself again. Really?

287

But even before the thought finished, she understood. The washcloth, the towel—it hadn't been about cleaning. It had been about *care*. About the quiet, wordless ways he showed love.

And she wanted that. She wanted it from Lind.

Chapter 35

We've got time

The workweek returned with its usual balance of stolen glances and restraint. Dana walked the line between excitement and frustration—being near Lind without being *with* him.

Some days, she dreaded working the same assignments. Too tempting. Too hard to hold the line. Other days, she craved it, if only for those flickers of closeness that no one else seemed to catch.

And then came Wednesday. Their night.

They'd agreed to take things slow. *Sort of.* But Wednesdays belonged to them.

Lind cherished those midweek nights, no matter how they spent them. Sometimes they kept it simple—early dinners followed by movies, curled up on the couch with nowhere else to be. Other nights, they did something different.

Darts at the bar—Dana getting better, but still no match for him.

Bowling—where laughter did nothing to improve their scores.

Coffee shop conversations—where hours slipped by unnoticed as they talked, planned, dreamed.

Each night, in or out, felt like a new chapter in this life they were building.

"We've got time," Lind reminded her often. When they made plans, when they talked about the future. "We've got time."

And then there was the lovin'. Sometimes slow. Sometimes not. But always theirs. Always more than just sex.

Dana was excited for the weekend ahead. She had plans, things she wanted to do with him.

But the excitement was tinged with something quieter. Sam was looming in the back of her mind.

By Thursday, Brenda noticed. Dana had gone quiet in a way Brenda didn't like.

When she asked about it, Dana only shrugged and said, "It's complicated."

By Friday, Brenda had decided she was done waiting for answers.

That's your favorite word lately

Dana and Brenda worked side by side, organizing the end cap displays for the latest sale. The store was still quiet, the early hour offering a rare pocket of calm before the usual rush.

Brenda adjusted a row of cereal boxes, stealing a sideways glance at Dana. Something was off.

Her usual sharp focus, the occasional spark of mischief in her eyes—it wasn't there.

And then Lind walked by.

Pushing a pallet jack loaded with boxes, he passed the end of their aisle, his presence effortless, familiar. Dana's gaze followed him a second too long, her expression unreadable.

Brenda noticed.

A few minutes later, Lind passed by again. This time, Brenda didn't let it go.

She leaned in. "Alright. Spill it." Her voice was low but teasing.

Dana blinked, snapping her attention back to the shelf she was arranging. "What?"

Brenda's sharp eyes stayed on her. "You keep watching Lind like he's about to sprout wings and fly away. But you don't have that usual sparkle. What's going on?"

Dana sighed, setting down the box in her hands. "It's... complicated."

Brenda tilted her head, arms crossing. "That's your favorite word lately."

Dana gave a half-smile, but it didn't reach her eyes. "It fits."

Brenda waited, but when Dana stayed quiet, she nudged. "You spent last weekend at your place. Just the two of you."

Dana nodded. "Yeah."

Brenda raised an eyebrow. "And that's a problem, why?"

Dana hesitated. "It's not. But next weekend..."

Brenda's expression sharpened. "But next weekend what?"

Dana bit her lip. "He has... other obligations. I'm going to see my parents."

Brenda adjusted a display item, keeping her tone casual. "That sounds like a nice break. A weekend with your folks could be good for you."

"It should be," Dana admitted. "But it's... complicated."

Brenda studied her for a long moment, her expression shifting to quiet understanding. "Okay. I'm not going to push. But can I give you some advice?"

Dana nodded, though her reluctance was clear.

Brenda's voice softened. "Stop worrying about next weekend. Or next month. Or next year. Focus on now. Focus on this weekend with Lind." She nudged Dana's shoulder. "You're going to drive yourself crazy if you keep thinking about what's ahead instead of enjoying what's right in front of you."

Dana exhaled, the weight of her thoughts pressing heavier. "I know you're right. It's just... hard."

Brenda's gaze softened. "I get that. But if you keep living in fear of the future, you'll miss the good stuff happening right now. And from what I've seen? Lind's good stuff."

Dana couldn't help the small smile. "He is."

Brenda grinned and went back to stacking shelves. "Then enjoy it. Focus on now."

Dana nodded, but the ache in her chest didn't quite go away.

Lind passed by the aisle one last time, offering Dana a quick smile before disappearing around the corner.

Oh my God, Brenda's still drilling her, he thought. *I hope she's okay.*

Dana's heart felt a little lighter as she straightened a row of boxes. Brenda's words echoed. *Focus on now.*

She wasn't quite okay. But she was better.

When Dana arrived home from work, Brenda's advice was still circling in her head. *Focus on now. This weekend. Today.*

She couldn't silence the thoughts about Sam completely, but she was determined to push them aside. This weekend was hers—and she intended to make the most of it.

Packing for the weekend

Tossing her coat onto the couch, Dana pulled out her backpack and started packing.

Jeans. Sweaters. Toiletries. Pantyliner.

She went through the motions, but her mind wandered.

A trip to the snow-covered waterfall.

Sledding on the big hill nearby.

Breakfast out Sunday morning.

She smiled to herself. *Lind always made the best breakfasts. But he deserves a break—just this once.*

And five steps this way

As she folded her clothes, a memory surfaced—the first time she'd gone to Lind's apartment.

"Come on in," he said, stepping aside. She'd set her backpack down, eyes scanning the space.

"Let me give you the grand tour," Lind said with a grin, sweeping his arm around the living room.

"We're standing in the spacious living area—big enough for a full-sized couch, a coffee table, and a recliner."

Dana scanned the space. It was small but inviting—tidy, masculine, with the huge TV dominating one wall.

On a small bookshelf, nestled between a few how-to books and a worn field guide, she noticed a collection of mechanical odds and ends—something half-taken apart. Tiny gears rested on a folded cloth, lined up like they were waiting their turn.

"You mess with those?" she asked, tilting her head.

Lind glanced over. "Yeah. I tinker with them sometimes."

She shook her head. He was full of quiet surprises.

Lind grinned, motioning dramatically toward the kitchen. "And five steps this way—the kitchen!"

"Oh, where the magic happens."

"No, no," Lind shot back, pointing toward the bedroom. "That's where the magic happens."

Her cheeks had flushed, her gaze flicking toward the door. But Lind caught it—the flicker of nerves. His grin widened.

"The bathroom's next to it there," he continued. "And that's the laundry room off the kitchen. Full-service establishment."

Dana, trying to shift the subject, asked, "You doing laundry?"

"A quick wash—some new hand towels and washcloths," he'd answered smoothly.

"For later?" she'd asked, raising an eyebrow.

"Yes," Lind said, mock serious.

"Later today or tomorrow?"

"Yes." His grin turned mischievous.

Dana's blush had deepened. "You seem pretty confident."

"I had no idea how confident, until we started seeing each other," he'd said, tone matter-of-fact—but his eyes told her everything else.

Dana had turned her head, laughing softly.

Even now, the memory made her smile as she folded the last of her clothes.

I really do love him, she thought, warmth blooming in her chest.

I'm giving my man a morning off

Lind was running behind.

He had just returned from the grocery store and was rushing to put everything away before Dana arrived. A quick glance at the clock—4:30. She'll be here in half an hour. *Maybe I can shower before—*

A knock at the door cut off the thought.

He opened it to find Dana standing there, backpack slung over one shoulder, a sly smile playing at her lips.

"Howdy, cowboy," she said, her tone playful.

Lind cocked an eyebrow. "Cowboy? Where's that coming from?"

"Later," she winked and stepped inside.

Lind chuckled, shaking his head as he headed back to the kitchen. "We're still going out for breakfast Sunday, right?"

"Yep," Dana said, dropping her backpack near the couch. "I'm giving my man a morning off."

"Love you for that," he replied, glancing over his shoulder with a warm smile. "Dinner's simple tonight—gourmet grilled ham and cheese with tomato soup. Want a salad with it?"

"No salad," Dana said, wandering toward the kitchen. "Are we talking about your famous grilled cheeses?"

"Nothing but," Lind confirmed.

"Yum." She was already imagining that first bite.

Lind kissed her on the way to the bedroom. "First, I need a shower."

Dana watched him disappear into the bathroom, then grabbed her backpack and headed to the bedroom to unpack. As she passed the bathroom door—left ajar, as usual—she paused.

He didn't even close it, she mused. *He's such a nudist.*

You were watching me

Curiosity got the best of her.

She nudged the door open a little wider, peeking inside just as Lind stepped under the spray. The clear curtain hid nothing.

Her eyes watched, a mischievous grin spreading across her lips for a moment.

Tempted... but she behaved. Mostly.

She left the door cracked just a little wider than he did, and wandered back to the living room, sitting in his recliner. The best vantage point in the apartment—*for this kind of thing*.

When Lind finally emerged, towel slung low on his hips, he found Dana exactly where he expected—curled up in his chair, watching him with far too much amusement.

"You were watching me, weren't you?"

"Maybe," Dana replied, twirling the hem of her blouse in her fingers.

He leaned down, kissing her slow and warm. "You're trouble."

As he turned to head toward the bedroom, Dana's hand shot out—grabbing the towel and giving it a sharp tug.

It came off in her hand without protest.

Lind paused, glancing over his shoulder, lips lifting at the corners.

Dana stayed right where she was, bunching the towel up in her hands, eyes roving freely.

Nice view, she thought, with a sudden rush of... but... somehow managed to stay put.

Lind just shook his head and kept walking.

Howdy, cowboy

Dinner was easy—Lind's grilled ham and cheese sandwiches lived up to the hype, and they cleaned up together, bantering as they moved around his tiny kitchen.

Later, they sank onto the couch, a movie playing in the background that they weren't watching.

Lind's arm draped around her shoulders. Dana leaned in, resting her hand on his chest. Their conversation was quiet, full of shared looks and easy laughter.

It didn't take long before they found themselves in the bedroom, clothes abandoned in a trail that led from the living room.

They wrestled playfully for control—Dana finally pinning Lind beneath her, straddling him, her hands firm on his chest.

She leaned in close, her hair falling around their faces, voice low. "Howdy, cowboy."

Lind's laugh rumbled against her hands. "You've been waiting all night to say that."

"Maybe," she said, shifting her hips just enough to make him groan.

His hands steadied her, hazel eyes dark and hungry. "You *are* trouble," he said, his breath catching.

"Complaining?" she murmured, lips meeting his.

"Not a chance."

They lost themselves in each other, a perfect tangle of desire and heat, passion and play. When they finally stilled, Dana's body softened against his. She closed her eyes, letting herself get lost in the feel of him.

Lind slid out from beneath her and returned with a warm washcloth and towel, tending to her with the same quiet tenderness he always did.

When he returned, he pulled her close, his arms wrapping around her as they lay face to face.

But even in his arms, Sam's name flickered at the edges of Dana's thoughts. The reminder of Lind's weekend plans sank into her chest, sharp enough to make her tense.

Why am I thinking about this now?

Lind noticed immediately.

His hands stilled on her back. "You okay?" he asked softly, his voice full of quiet concern.

Dana hesitated. "Yeah," she said quickly, forcing a smile. "Just... a lot on my mind."

He didn't push.

He only tightened his arms around her, his voice low. "You're allowed to have a lot on your mind."

And just like that, some of the pressure eased. She pressed her face into his neck, breathing him in.

Focus on now, she told herself again. *Focus on now.*

A hot shower together

Saturday flew by in a blur of snow and laughter.

They visited a nearby waterfall, its frozen cascades glistening like crystal in the winter sunlight, fresh snow blanketing the landscape.

Later, they joined the locals at a sledding hill, taking turns racing down the slope on an old sled Lind had borrowed.

Dana's shouts of exhilaration echoed across the hill, and Lind couldn't help but smile at her.

By the time they returned to his apartment, cheeks flushed and clothes damp from the snow, they were exhausted.

A hot shower together turned into playful banter, with soap suds, stolen kisses, and a bit of extra time under the warm spray.

Dinner was a team effort—spaghetti with garlic bread and salad.

They laughed over clumsy moments in the kitchen, Dana's unimaginative salad fixings, and nearly burning the garlic bread.

But the best part of dinner was each other.

The food wasn't bad, either.

Just doing my part

Dana woke first, the golden morning light filtering through the blinds.

She turned, finding Lind still asleep, his face relaxed, peaceful.

A playful smile crept across her lips as she leaned closer, brushing a soft kiss along the line of his jaw.

"Mmm," Lind murmured, stirring slightly. His hand found hers under the blanket. "Morning."

"Morning," Dana replied, her tone light. She pressed another kiss to his neck, her hand slipping up to rest on his chest.

"You know," she said, tracing patterns on his skin, "I was just lying here thinking..."

"Dangerous," Lind muttered sleepily, cracking one eye open, his mouth twitching into a smile.

Dana laughed softly.

"I was thinking it's a good thing you're here, or I'd have to find other ways to keep myself entertained this morning."

Lind chuckled, shifting to pull her closer.

"Other ways, huh?" His voice was low, teasing. "That's one problem I'm happy to help you with."

His lips found hers, the kiss slow and unhurried.

"You're very good at problem-solving," Dana murmured against his mouth, a soft laugh escaping as he rolled her onto her back.

He smiled down at her. "Just doing my part."

"You always do," she replied, pulling him back in for another kiss.

Lind took his time, ensuring she felt every moment of it.

***

Later, as the sunlight crept higher, they showered and dressed, heading out to breakfast at a cozy diner nearby.

The smell of coffee and pancakes filled the air as they sat in a corner booth, sharing stories, stealing glances, and dreading the work week ahead.

But at least they would still see each other every day.

Chapter 36

Sam loomed like a storm cloud

The warmth of the weekend still clung to Dana like an invisible glow.

Brenda caught it immediately during their coffee break, a bright knowing smile lit up her whole face.

"You've got that *post-weekend shine*, girl. Must've been a good one." She arched an eyebrow over her steaming cup.

Dana managed a laugh, and a vague comment about relaxing and catching up on sleep.

But Brenda wouldn't let it go. "Oh, come on, girl. You gotta give me more than that."

"Yes, Brenda, it was nice," she said, as she gave Brenda an annoyed grin.

"Seems like all of your weekends have been nice lately, huh?" Brenda prodded.

Dana gave her a smile with a little too much glow to hide. But in the back of her mind, she thought, *Not all of them.*

As the week progressed, Dana's glow began to dim.

The anticipation of Lind's weekend with Sam loomed like a storm cloud.

***

On Tuesday, Dana was quieter than usual during their lunch break.

Even when Lind leaned in with a quiet joke, her laugh was slower, her gaze distant.

Brenda began to notice the change.

***

By Wednesday, the tension crept into her work.

She fumbled simple tasks, caught herself zoning out, her mind a tangled mess of thoughts she couldn't silence.

Brenda spoke up.

"You sure you're okay?" she asked softly as they worked side by side, sorting merchandise.

Dana forced a smile. "Just tired."

Brenda didn't look convinced.

Lind, ever perceptive, noticed the shift.

He didn't need to ask what was wrong—he knew.

Even their midweek date, usually filled with laughter and teasing, felt off.

Sensing Dana wasn't in the mood for much, Lind suggested takeout and a quiet night on the couch.

She leaned into his arms, pretending to watch TV, but her usual spark was missing.

When the night ended without their typical intimacy, Lind didn't press.

Instead, he held her a little closer, offering quiet reassurance.

He respected her need to process, though it wasn't easy not to reach for her—but he hated the distance it created.

For now, he stayed patient, hoping to show her that she was safe with him.

She had him—he was hers in a way no one else could take away.

Except her.

At her door, Lind kissed her goodnight, his hand warm against her cheek.

"I'm looking forward to seeing you tomorrow," he said softly.

"Me too." Dana managed a small smile, as he stepped out through the doorway.

She closed the door behind him, leaning her forehead against the cool wood.

Her hand tightening on the knob, her chest heavy.

She missed him already.

And he had hardly even left.

***

By Thursday, Dana snapped at a coworker, then immediately felt guilty.

The knot in her stomach tightened, making it harder to meet Lind's eyes when they passed.

Every glance at him reminded her of the coming weekend without him.

He's seeing someone else

By Friday, Dana's shift in demeanor was undeniable.

Brenda—who had been holding back all week—finally cornered her in the stockroom.

"Alright, enough is enough. What's going on with you?" she demanded, her tone firm but kind.

Dana blinked, caught off guard.

She opened her mouth, then hesitated.

"It's complicated."

Brenda raised an eyebrow. "Girl, you've used that line too many times. I know you're scared but whatever it is—say it. We're standing next to a pile of ugly lamps. No one's gonna hear us."

Dana looked down at the toe of her boot, then blew out a breath. "He's seeing someone else."

Brenda's eyes widened a little, but she didn't respond.

Dana's eyes flicked up. "Did you hear me?"

"I heard you," Brenda said, tilting her head. "Is this something new?"

"No." Dana shook her head. "She was there before me. I knew about her when we started... I just didn't realize how much it would get to me."

Brenda was quiet, her expression unreadable for a moment. Then she asked, "He's honest about it?"

Dana nodded. "Yeah. Completely. It's not cheating or anything. It's just... it's part of his life. It's just how he's built."

Brenda's voice softened, but her tone stayed grounded. "And you thought you could be okay with it."

"I did," Dana admitted. "At first, it didn't seem real. It was all new, and fun, and we weren't serious. But the longer we're together, the harder it gets. She's not a girlfriend, exactly, and they don't see each other very often. But she is someone he cares about, that he loves even. And I'm really trying to be ok with it."

"You keep saying 'she', does she have a name?" Brenda asked.

"Sam," Dana said.

"The same Sam he mentioned hiking with? The one from the festival?"

Dana nodded slowly. "Yeah. That Sam."

"Let me ask you this. Has Lind shared with you what kind of relationship he wants with you?"

Dana nodded. "He says I'm his girlfriend. That he's in this for the long haul. That we'll figure it out together, day by day."

Brenda gave a small nod. "Then what's making you question it? Is it Sam?"

Dana looked away. "I believe him," she said softly. "I do. But if he has me, why does he still need her?"

Brenda was quiet for a moment, then said gently, "You're focusing on the wrong things, Dana. Focus on today. On what's right here in front of you."

Dana's voice cracked just slightly. "But he's not here, Brenda. He's spending the whole weekend with her."

Brenda stepped closer, voice softer now. "He's not leaving you. He's just spending time with someone else who's part of his life—but you *are* his life. You're not being replaced. He loves you."

Dana looked down, her fingers twisting at the hem of her shirt.

"You've seen him, been with him every day for months now," Brenda continued. "And when he gets back, you'll still be with him. Nothing's changing that. Unless *you* do."

Brenda's words landed like a truth Dana wasn't ready to hear.

Brenda gave her a second, then added, "Don't let the fear of what he shares with Sam ruin what *you're* building with him. Focus on today. Stay present. Lind was upfront with you. You went into this with your eyes open."

Dana's chest tightened.

"It's just not that simple," Dana said quietly.

"I know," Brenda said. "But simple or not, you love him. And he loves you. That's something worth fighting for—even if it takes a little time to figure it out."

After a long pause, mulling over her words, Dana resolved to try and focus on the positives, reminding herself of Lind's honesty and their agreement to take things one step at a time.

But it was hard to ignore the ache growing in her chest—the gnawing sense that she was being left behind.

Even if only for a couple of days.

This was the hardest part—the waiting, the uncertainty.

And as she headed home that evening, the shadow of the weekend felt a little lighter thanks to Brenda.

But even as she looked forward to a quiet weekend with her folks, deep down, she wondered whether it would be enough.

I forget how quiet it is here

The scent of freshly brewed coffee and the faint hum of the local radio station greeted Dana as she stepped into her parents' kitchen.

Her mother stood by the stove, flipping pancakes like she'd been doing it her whole life, while her father sat at the table, glasses perched on his nose, reading the newspaper.

"Morning, honey," her mom said brightly, turning to smile at her.

"Hope you slept well."

"Like a rock," Dana replied, choosing a chair across from her dad.

"I forget how quiet it is here."

Her dad chuckled, folding the paper.

"City life getting to you?"

"Not exactly," Dana said, pouring herself coffee. "Just... different."

***

The morning passed easily, the warmth of home wrapping around her like a well-worn blanket.

Later, as she helped her mom fold laundry, Dana found herself treading into uncharted conversational territory.

"Mom," she began carefully, folding a towel into a neat square,

"When you and Dad were dating, did you ever feel like... you weren't on the same page?"

Her mom glanced at her, eyebrows raised.

"What do you mean?"

Dana hesitated, smoothing the towel in her lap.

"I guess... did you ever feel like you had different expectations? Or like you wanted different things?"

Her mom's expression softened, and she set down the shirt she was folding.

"Of course we did. *Everyone does at some point.*"

"Your dad and I didn't agree on everything right away—sometimes we still don't."

"But we always talked things through."

"That's the key, Dana, you have to be honest with each other, even when it's hard."

Dana nodded, her throat tight.

"Yeah. That makes sense."

Her mom reached over, squeezing her hand.

"This about you and Lind?"

Dana froze for a second, then forced a small smile.

"Maybe, a little."

Her voice was quiet when she added,

"I *want* it to work." She told her mother.

I really want it to work. She told herself.

Her mom smiled knowingly but didn't press further.

Dana exhaled slowly, grateful for the reprieve.

But her mind buzzed with uncomfortable thoughts.

Honesty.

Even when it's hard.

I like watching you show off

The lodge smelled of cedar and melting snow, the fire crackling in the corner, casting a warm glow over the room.

Lind leaned against the counter in their suite, watching as Sam unpacked her gear.

Her skis stood propped against the wall, a testament to her enthusiasm for the slopes.

"Thanks for coming," she said, glancing at him with a smile.

"You don't have to thank me," Lind replied, tossing her a playful grin.

"I like watching you show off on the mountain."

Sam laughed, pulling on her gloves.

"Don't think I don't notice you sticking to the bunny hill, as always."

"Hey, I'm just trying to keep the emergency room out of our plans."

Her expression softened as she stepped closer, brushing a hand against his arm.

"I don't mind taking it slow with you." Her tone as inviting as her touch. "Half the fun is spending time together."

"Go." He said, "have fun on the slopes. Before I don't let you go." He gave her a quiet sigh. "I'll meet you for lunch."

She leaned in and kissed him softly. "Can't wait."

***

The day passed in easy rhythm—Sam carving graceful lines down the mountain while Lind navigated the bunny hill with caution.

They met for lunch in the lodge, laughing over shared stories of falls and near-misses, mostly his.

She spent the rest of the afternoon trying to teach Lind—for the umpteenth time—but skiing just wasn't his thing.

"This is better than ice skating though." He told her, with a wry grin.

She just laughed at him.

But he isn't here for the skiing, he's here for Sam, which is good, because she's here for him.

***

After a nice dinner and good conversation, catching up on the last few months, Sam finally asked,

"So... tell me more about Dana."

Lind's fork paused for a second before he set it down.

"I *did* tell you about her," he said carefully.

"You did. Briefly," she looked at him warmly. "But I can tell she's becoming important to you."

Lind hesitated, then nodded. "Yeah... she is."

Sam studied him thoughtfully, a small smile on her lips.

"I know it's a big risk you're taking with your heart again," she said.

She reached across the table, giving his hand a gentle squeeze.

"I applaud you for it. And I have to say—she sounds wonderful for you."

Lind glanced at her, his smile deepening.

Sam had always been supportive of him, always wanted the best for him.

And he appreciated that more than she knew.

Maybe that's why his words came so easily now.

He told her about the agreement he and Dana had made to keep things quiet for now, and how awkward that made things at work. How a few times, they'd almost gotten caught, Dana's fault, of course. Which made Sam chuckle.

He told her about their Wednesday nights—darts, bowling, trying new restaurants. How Dana laughed when she won, and swore when she didn't.

Sam gave him an approving grin.

And he told her, more quietly, how nice it was to wake up next to someone you love... again.

Sam listened, her expression softening as she spoke. "Besides me, you mean."

Lind gave her a look, "You know what I mean." He stated.

She laughed as she reached out and cupped his face with a tenderness that hadn't changed.

"Sounds like you're really settling in with each other," she said, approval in her tone.

He smiled faintly, nodding. Putting his hand over hers on his cheek.

He didn't tell her how Dana was still having trouble accepting Sam in his life.

Some things were better left unsaid, at least for now.

You're worth it

That evening, back in their suite, the warmth of the fireplace wrapped around them as the snow fell softly outside.

"Still no interest in tackling the big runs with me?" Sam teased, her tone light as she sipped her drink.

"None," Lind replied with a smirk, stretching out on the couch.

"But I'll always cheer you on from the bottom."

Sam chuckled, setting her glass down.

She moved to sit beside him, her hand gently cupping his face.

"You're a good sport, you know," she said softly.

"This really isn't your thing, but you come up here every year with me and spend half the day alone in the cold."

Lind met her gaze, his expression softening.

"You're worth it," he said as he leaned in and kissed her.

She slid off him

The conversation faded into a comfortable silence, the fire crackling softly in the background as the warmth of their connection wrapped around them.

It wasn't rushed or planned—it was natural, unfolding with the ease of two people who truly knew and cared for each other.

Sam straddled Lind in the oversized chair, kissing him deeply, her body pressing against his, igniting the familiar spark between them.

As she rocked against him, she felt his arousal, the heat of it even through their layers of clothing.

Her hands moved with intent, reaching down to unbutton his pants.

She slid off him as he shifted to help, lifting his hips so she could pull them away.

The intimacy between them was undeniable, familiar and cherished.

Lowering herself onto her knees, she took him in her hands, teasing him with her mouth, her tongue.

She smiled inwardly at the way his breath hitched, at the soft groan that escaped him as he tilted his head back, eyes closed.

It had been a while since she'd done this for him, and she wanted him to feel every bit of her attention.

Lind's hands tangled gently in her hair, his moans deepening as she pushed him toward release.

As his climax built, he tipped his head forward, watching her—
The sight of her only intensified the moment.

When it finally hit, she stayed with him, her hand stroking, her tongue teasing, coaxing every last wave of pleasure from him.

When it passed, she stayed with him—playing in his release, her fingers moving through it slow and unhurried.

She cherished these moments, knowing they didn't happen often, knowing they meant something different to both of them.

It felt raw and real—another layer of connection.

Lind stood, pulling her gently to her feet.

"Let me clean up," he murmured, kissing her cheek.

She smiled against his lips, though she knew better than to push for more in this moment.

When it became too much

He was gone only a few minutes, but when he returned, Sam was already lying on the bed, completely bare, her skin bathed in firelight.

She raised a hand, crooking her finger in a playful invitation.

Lind crawled onto the bed, meeting her with a deep, consuming kiss.

Her hands framed his face, pulling him onto her, her legs wrapping around his waist, anchoring them together.

She rubbed against him, her movements slow and intentional.

His lips traveled down her neck, pressing at the curve of her collarbone before moving down.

He bit, sucked, and soothed in a slow, rhythm, his breath fanning heat over her sensitive skin as he claimed every inch of her breasts with his mouth.

Sam arched beneath him, her fingers threading into his hair as his mouth traced down her stomach.

Lind was methodical, taking his time—teasing her, avoiding the most sensitive spots.

Building her up. Holding her right at the edge.

Until she couldn't stand it any longer.

When his tongue finally found her, her body arched in response.

The first wave of pleasure hit quickly, her hands gripping the sheets as she moaned his name through gritted teeth.

Lind held her steady, mouth tight against her, prolonging her pleasure, driving her higher with every flick and stroke.

When it became too much, she tugged at his hair, pulling him up to meet her lips.

She kissed him deeply, the taste of herself on his mouth only heightening the intimacy.

With a soft growl, she rolled him onto his back, her body moving fully on top of him.

For a while, she simply lay there, her head on his chest, listening to the steady rhythm of his heartbeat.

His arms wrapped around her, his fingers lightly stroking her back.

Neither of them spoke.

The silence between them was full.

There was no need for words—only the warmth of their affection, the comfort of their bond.

Here, in the glow of the fire, in the safety of each other's arms—everything else fell away.

Parallel Reflections

Dana

That evening, Dana sat by the window in her childhood bedroom, gazing out at the familiar backyard.

The stillness brought comfort—But also questions.

Honesty, she thought again, the word heavy in her chest.

How much honesty can I handle?

Lind

At the lodge, as Sam dozed, her head resting on his chest, her arm draped over his hip, Lind stared at the fire.

Its glow casting shadows against the walls.

His thoughts drifted—to Dana.

Was she surrounded by warmth, the way he was here?

How much can I ask of her?

I don't want to lose her.

But... I don't want to lose me either.

Part 9

<u>I love you, Dana</u>

We were deeper in it now. His hands, his eyes, his love—steady.
  But steady didn't mean simple.
  Not when fear kept pacing the floor of my heart.
  I wanted to be enough.
  I wanted to believe I already was.

Chapter 37

Elephant in the room

Lind's apartment was cozy and unpretentious, but its warmth was dimmed by the tension between them. The remnants of their takeout dinner sat on the coffee table—two half-empty plates of Thai curry, a crumpled napkin.

Dana tucked her legs beneath her on the couch, cradling a mug of tea, while Lind leaned back in his recliner, his hazel eyes on her. She shifted, her gaze flicking from her tea to him, then away again. Her thoughts wouldn't stop—her worries rustling around in the silence.

"Work felt weird Monday." She tried to be casual, but the words came out too deliberate. Too stiff.

Lind picked up on it immediately, leaning forward. "Yeah, I noticed. You kept avoiding eye contact in the lunchroom. Pretty much everywhere." His voice was soft, but laced with curiosity.

Dana exhaled, setting her mug on the table. "I didn't know what to say. You'd just gotten back, and I... I don't know. It felt like there was this giant elephant in the room that only I could see."

Lind tilted his head. "I get that. It's not like I can bring up my weekend with Sam over coffee at work. But you don't have to tiptoe around me, Dana. If something's on your mind, say it."

She hesitated, then blurted, "Okay, how was your weekend with her?"

The second the words left her mouth, she regretted them. Her cheeks flushed, pulse quickening. But Lind didn't look uncomfortable. If anything, he looked steady. It felt like that should have annoyed her.

"It was nice," he said after a pause. "Relaxing. We spent time on the slopes—she skied the mountain, I stuck to the bunny hill. We had dinner by the fire. Talked. Nothing crazy. Just a quiet weekend to catch up."

Dana swallowed. "Is that all you did?"

Lind held her gaze. "No. It wasn't."

Her stomach twisted. The answer didn't surprise her. But hearing it—hearing it spoken aloud—still hit harder than she wanted to admit.

She studied his face, searching for hesitation, discomfort—something to hold onto. There was nothing. Just quiet honesty.

"I thought I'd be okay with this," she admitted, her voice barely above a whisper. "In theory, I am. But actually living it... feels different. Being at work with you Monday, pretending nothing happened—it was harder than I expected."

Lind leaned in, forearms resting on his knees. "I understand that. It's a lot to process. And I know it's not easy for you. But Dana, I'm here with you. Because I choose you. It took a year of getting to know you to make that decision. But I made it."

She wanted to believe him. She did believe him. And yet, the same question gnawed at her. *If he chose me, why does he still need her?*

"I don't want to feel like I'm competing with her," she said quietly. "Like I have to prove I'm worth being here."

Lind's expression softened. "You don't. There's no competition. Sam is her own thing, separate from us. Comparing doesn't make sense. They're not the same."

Dana nodded, but the words didn't land the way he intended. To her, it did feel like a competition. One she was losing.

She glanced down at her hands. "Brenda told me I need to stop overthinking everything. She said if I keep doing that, I'll miss what's right in front of me."

Lind smiled faintly. "Brenda knows? Sounds like she's got good advice."

She felt the warmth of his fingers brushing lightly against hers.

"Can we try something?" he asked gently. "Let's just focus on this. Right here. Us. Forget Sam. Forget work. Just for tonight. Can we do that?"

Dana lifted her gaze to his, searching. After a long pause, she gave a small, hesitant smile. "Yeah. I think I can do that."

The tension softened, and the space between them closed, quieting into something warm and mutual. Later, when it was time to leave, their usual intimacy was replaced by something quieter—a gentle goodbye. She pressed a soft kiss to his cheek, murmuring goodnight.

Lind squeezed her hand. "I'll see you tomorrow. And I'm looking forward to our weekend."

Dana hesitated, her heart and mind still at odds. She forced a small smile. "Me too."

But the words felt hollow.

And Lind noticed.

Do you talk about me with Sam

Friday night's dinner filled the kitchen with the warm scent of garlic and ginger, the soft hiss of stir-fry breaking the quiet. Lind stood at the stove, stirring vegetables, the easy rhythm of cooking relaxing him. Across the room, Dana sat at the table, a glass of wine in front of her, untouched. She swirled it absently, thoughts churning.

The silence stretched a moment too long before she finally spoke.

"Do you... ever talk about me with Sam?"

Lind glanced over his shoulder, surprised but unbothered by the question. "Of course. I let her know how much I like being with you. She said it sounds like I've found someone special."

Dana blinked. "She said that?"

Lind turned, leaning against the counter, a small smile touching his lips. "Yeah. She told me, 'Sounds like you've found a good one—hang on to her.' And I told her, 'I intend to.'"

Something flickered in Dana's chest—validation, warmth. But it was fleeting, quickly smothered by the familiar weight of doubt.

"That's... nice of her to say."

Lind moved closer. "Dana, you don't have to worry about what Sam thinks. I'm with you because I want to be."

Dana hesitated, fingers tightening around the stem of her glass. "I know. It's just... sometimes it's hard to wrap my head around."

Lind tilted his head, his eyes softening. "Then let me help. You're my priority. And if there's ever anything you want to ask or talk about, I'm here."

He turned back to the stove, the easy rhythm resuming, but Dana's mind wasn't quiet. She watched him, her heart pulling in two directions.

He makes it sound so simple. But it's not simple for me. Sam isn't just some abstract figure—I feel her presence even though she's not here. I know he cares about me, but will that ever be enough to quiet this ache?

She picked up her glass and took a slow sip, hoping the wine would help quiet her thoughts.

For now, she wouldn't bring it up again.

But the thought of it weighed on her.

***

317

The stir-fry was good, rich and flavorful, the easy rhythm of their dinner conversation smoothing the edges of Dana's lingering doubt. By the time they moved to the couch, their wine glasses in hand, she felt lighter.

The TV played softly in the background, though neither of them were watching. Lind wrapped an arm around her shoulders, and she leaned into him, pressing her cheek against the soft fabric of his shirt. His warmth, his scent—steady, familiar.

"This is nice," she murmured. "Just being here with you."

Lind pressed a kiss to the top of her head. "I feel the same. I've been looking forward to this all week."

Dana shifted slightly, her head resting against his chest, the steady thrum of his heartbeat beneath her ear. "Me too." This time, the words felt sincere.

Being Here Helps

When the program ended, Lind reached for the remote and turned off the TV. The quiet wrapped around them in the soft light of the living room. He looked down at her, his smile warm, tender.

"You look tired," he murmured. "It's been a long week."

Dana gave a faint smile. "Yeah, but being here helps."

Lind leaned down, his lips meeting hers—soft at first, then deepening. The slow, unhurried pull of it wrapped around her. She let herself lean into him, her hands drifting up his chest, fingers resting against his collarbone.

When Lind pulled back, his voice was low, a whisper against her lips. "Do you want to go to bed?"

For a moment, she hesitated. But as she met his gaze, the earlier doubts faded—eclipsed by the comfort of this. Of Lind. The way he looked at her, like she was the only thing in the world.

"Yeah," she said softly. "Let's go."

That She Was His

The bedroom was dim, the bedside lamp casting an amber glow that softened everything—the edges of the furniture, the quiet distance between them. Lind pulled her close, his hands a steadying presence at her hips. His kiss was slow, deliberate, as if mapping every inch of her.

Dana melted into it, letting the weight of her insecurities fade beneath the stroke of his hands along her sides. Every touch, every kiss, felt intentional—like he was reminding her, over and over, that she was here, that she was his.

His lips traveled lower, to her neck and then her shoulders, nibbling at the sensitive skin of her breasts. A soft sigh escaped her as he took his time, as if savoring the way she arched beneath him.

When his mouth found her clit, she drew a sharp breath, her fingers tightening in his hair. The first slow stroke of his tongue sent heat unraveling through her, her body reacting instantly to the familiar, practiced rhythm of him. He knew her well—how to make her fall apart, how to pull her to the edge and keep her there until she was pleading.

Her climax took her in waves, leaving her breathless. She whimpered, pushing at his head as sensitivity took over, and he relented, pressing a soft kiss against her inner thigh before resting his cheek on her mons, taking in the tremors as they subsided.

Lind's fingers wandered lightly over her skin, no intent—just closeness, just them.

Dana's fingers found their way into his hair, twisting and untwisting the strands, grounding herself in the small, simple moment.

When he finally lifted his head, she met his gaze, her breath catching at the look in his eyes.

Love?

Lind kissed his way back up her body, slow and intentional, pausing to play at her breasts before capturing her lips again. This kiss was deeper, consuming, her hands roaming over his back, pulling him closer.

When he finally entered her, her whole body flinched, instinctively arching to meet his. The way he filled her, the way he moved—it was everything. The slow, steady rhythm of their bodies, the way his breath mingled with hers, the way he whispered her name like it was something sacred.

There was no Sam.

No work.

No doubts.

Just this.

Dana let herself be here, let herself believe in the warmth of his arms, the quiet certainty of his touch.

Lind's rhythm grew more urgent, his breath uneven, his body trembling against hers as he reached the edge. His orgasm came with a throaty moan, her name spilling from his lips as she held him tighter, wishing she could make the moment last longer.

And for a little while, she let herself believe that it could.

I Love You, Dana

They lay entwined, their breathing the only sound in the quiet. Dana rested her head on Lind's chest, his fingers skimming gently over her arm.

"You're incredible, Dana. You know that, right?"

She glanced up, her heart catching at the sincerity in his eyes. "I don't always feel that way, but... thank you."

"You don't have to feel it," he said, reaching out to play with a strand of her hair. "I'll remind you... often."

A prickle of tears burned at the edges of her vision. She blinked them away, pressing a soft kiss to his chest. His words warmed her in a way she hadn't expected.

For the first time in weeks, she wasn't thinking about Sam.

Wasn't thinking about competition.

Wasn't wondering if she was enough.

In Lind's arms, she simply was.

She swallowed past the lump in her throat. "Thank you for this. For... being you."

Lind kissed the top of her head, his hand stroking her back in slow, soothing circles. "I'm just glad you're here. You mean a lot to me. I love you, Dana."

She should've said it back. He deserved to hear it.

She knew he meant them. But a small part of her still wondered—*am I enough?*

Is this?

Lind slipped out of bed, disappearing into the bathroom. A moment later, he returned with a warm washcloth and a towel, tending to her with the same quiet care as always. He rinsed the cloth, hung it neatly by the sink, then climbed back into bed, pulling her into his arms once more.

Dana nestled into him, the steady rhythm of his breathing lulling her toward sleep.

For tonight, she pushed aside the questions, the doubts, the ache in her chest.

For tonight, she let herself believe.

Chapter 38

Coffee Brews & Muse

Dana woke to the muted glow of morning light filtering through Lind's curtains. The aroma of freshly brewed coffee filled the air. She stretched lazily, the residual warmth of his bed tempting her to stay cocooned in the blankets.

But the smell of coffee was too inviting.

She pulled on one of Lind's oversized t-shirts and wandered into the kitchen, where he stood at the counter, pouring coffee into two mugs.

"Good morning," Lind said, glancing up with a small smile.

"Morning," Dana murmured, her voice still thick with sleep. She leaned against the counter, holding the warm ceramic mug he handed her. The heat seeped into her palms.

Lind watched her over the rim of his own mug, a hint of amusement in his eyes. "I was thinking we could hit that coffee shop you love—Coffee Brews & Muse. Grab some breakfast, maybe walk around downtown."

A slow smile formed on Dana's lips. "That sounds perfect."

***

The coffee shop hummed with its usual weekend energy—soft acoustic music playing overhead, the low murmur of conversation, the comforting scent of fresh ground coffee and pastries wrapping around them. A fire crackled in the stone fireplace near their table, its warmth a welcome contrast to the bite of January air outside.

Dana held the steaming mug of espresso up, letting the rich steam fill her senses. "This is cozy."

"It's perfect," Lind replied, his eyes reflecting the golden flicker of the fire as they met hers.

They shared a plate of croissants, the flaky layers melting in Dana's mouth, buttery and warm. Conversation flowed easily, laughter slipping between sips of coffee and stolen bites of pastry. For a little while, the light snow falling outside felt like a world away.

After breakfast, they bundled up against the cold and wandered downtown, the fresh powder crunching beneath their boots. Lind reached for her hand, tucking their gloved fingers together as they passed shop windows glowing with twinkling fairy lights.

"Ready for some window shopping?" he asked, grinning.

Dana laughed, pulling her scarf tighter. "Lead the way, my mountain man."

Hand in hand, they wandered through the streets, their laughter mixing with the crisp winter air.

For the first time in days, Dana allowed herself to just *be*. No spiraling thoughts, no gnawing doubts—just the simplicity of a winter morning with Lind.

Shower? Together? Well yeah.

By the time they returned to Lind's apartment, the sky was streaked with hues of burnt orange and dusky pink, the last light of day casting a soft glow over the snow-covered streets. Dana's cheeks were flushed from the cold, her fingers stiff despite the thick gloves she'd worn.

"Cold doesn't even begin to describe it," she muttered, unwinding her scarf and kicking off her boots.

Lind rubbed his hands together briskly, flashing a grin. "I have an idea."

She arched a brow. "Oh?"

"Yeah," he said, "how about a shower?"

Dana's lips quirked. "Together?"

Lind's expression was playful. "Well, yeah."

She shook her head, chuckling. "Let's do it, my mountain man."

They quickly shed their layers and stepped into the bathroom, where the sharp chill of the air made the steaming shower all the more enticing. Lind adjusted the water temperature until it was just right, then pulled her in beneath the warm cascade.

The first rush of heat sent a sigh spilling from Dana's lips, her muscles unwinding as the water soaked into her hair and skin.

Lind reached for the body wash, lathering it in his hands before smoothing his palms over her shoulders, down her arms, and along her back. His touch was slow, as he savored the simple act of caring for her.

"Warm enough yet?" he murmured, his lips pressing against the damp skin.

Dana hummed in response, reaching for his hands and guiding them up to her breasts. His thumbs played at her nipples, sending a ripple of pleasure through her. She tilted her head back against his shoulder, a soft sound escaping as she covered his hands with hers, losing herself in the sensations.

The weight of her in his hands, the firmness of her nipples and the surrender, the want, in her invitation had him feeling like them again.

She turned to face him, her palms pressing against his chest, feeling the steady drum of his heartbeat beneath her fingertips. The heat of the water, the warmth of his skin—it coiled into something more than just body heat.

Dana tipped her head up, kissing him then she reached for the body wash. Lathering her hands, she let them glide down the length of him, moving slowly, methodically—not to rush, not to push forward, just to feel.

Lind's breath hitched, but he let her set the pace, let her explore. They touched, felt, caressed, mapping familiar territory. There was no urgency, no goal—only the intimacy of touch, and quiet trust.

When the water began to cool, they reluctantly stepped out, wrapping themselves in thick towels. Lind grabbed another to dry Dana's hair, his movements tender as he ruffled the damp strands.

"You're like my personal heater," she said, grinning up at him.

"Always," he murmured, pressing a kiss to her forehead before drying himself off.

They pulled on their coziest pajamas—Dana in one of Lind's flannel sets, the fabric hanging loose on her frame, and Lind in his usual thermal shirt and lounge pants.

As they sank into the couch, a blanket draped over their legs, Dana leaned into Lind's side, her fingers slowly tracing the lines of his palm.

This is what I want.

The thought was both warm and certain.

Movie night

Dana tucked her legs up under her as Lind carried over a bowl of popcorn and two steaming mugs of hot chocolate. The scent of cocoa mingled with the traces of woodsy cologne lingering on his hoodie, which wrapped her in an easy comfort.

"Movie night?" he asked, holding up a few options.

Dana pulled the blanket tighter around her shoulders. "Something funny. I think we've earned a little laughter after braving the tundra out there."

Lind chuckled, starting a classic comedy before cuddling under the blanket with her. His arm wrapped around her shoulders as she leaned into him, her body molding easily into the comfort of his warmth. The quiet of the snow falling outside only added to the cozy warmth between them.

Laughter filled the room as the movie played. Dana felt lighter, more present. The doubts in the back of her mind fading away.

Lind's voice was a quiet murmur against her hair. "Comfortable?"

She exhaled softly. "Very."

He kissed her temple, a soft kiss. The light touch sent a slow building warmth in her chest, spreading lower, tugging at her focus.

"Let's go to bed," he said, his hazel eyes meeting hers, more of a question than a statement.

Dana hesitated—just long enough to acknowledge the way her body was already answering.

She nodded, standing and slipping her hand into his. "Let's finish what we started in the shower."

Lind's brows raised slightly. "Oh yeah?"

"Oh yeah."

Tonight she was in no rush

By the time they reached the bed, they had thrown off the last of their pajamas. Lind threw back the comforter and top sheet, but before he could guide her onto the mattress, Dana pushed him back instead.

He landed against the sheets with a surprised chuckle, his expression shifting from curiosity to something deeper when he saw the way she looked at him.

Her slow smile left no room for doubt.

She straddled him, letting the heat between them simmer before she moved. She took her time, dragging her fingertips down his chest, hungry kisses along his collarbone, his shoulders, and hips.

Tonight, she was in no rush.

And neither was he.

You Deserve it

The smell of pancakes and maple syrup pulled Dana from sleep. She stretched beneath the warmth of the blankets, sore in the best way, before slipping out of bed, throwing on one of Lind's tee shirts and heading to the kitchen.

Lind stood at the stove, flipping golden pancakes onto a plate. Eggs and ham were already waiting, the spread simple but warm, thoughtful—like him.

He glanced over his shoulder, smirking when he saw her. "Good timing. Breakfast is ready."

Dana hummed in approval. Stepping closer, she wrapped her arms around him, palms on his chest. "You didn't have to do all this."

Lind shrugged, his hand sliding down to cup her ass. "You deserve it."

Dana grinned at him as she turned to sit, Lind brought their plates over and set them down.

They ate together at the small kitchen table, the easy rhythm of conversation filling the space between bites. It felt... effortless. Natural, like something they could do every Sunday for years to come.

When they'd finished, Lind leaned back in his chair, stretching. His expression softened, a flicker of something wistful beneath the lightness of his voice.

"These weekends always feel too short."

Dana rested her chin in her hand, offering him a small smile. "Guess that's what makes them special."

Lind reached across the table, taking her hand. "It is. And I'm glad we have them."

Dana's throat tightened—

"Me too."

Thanks For Inviting Me

The Sunday sky streaked with pink and orange as she gathered her things. Lind walked her to the door, wrapping her in a warm hug before she could even reach for the handle.

"Thanks for spending the weekend with me," he murmured against her hair.

Dana pressed closer, feeling the warmth of his words. "Thanks for inviting me."

Like most Sundays, they were unwilling to say goodbye without a fight.

When she finally stepped outside, the crisp air filled her lungs, sharp and grounding. She glanced back at him, offering a small wave.

For now, she chose to carry the quiet joy of their weekend, leaving the weight of her worries behind.

But she knew they'd find her again.

Chapter 39

Dana let herself believe

The cold winter months unfolded over the city in thick blankets of snow. Dana and Lind fell into a comfortable rhythm—weekends spent exploring museums, trying out new recipes, binge-watching shows, nestling on the couch.

Some days Sam crept around in the back of Dana's mind, like a shadow moving in the dark.

But at other times, when Lind reached for her hand in public or pressed a kiss to her temple just because—Dana let herself believe. This is what matters. This is enough.

That's still a few months away

One evening, Dana and Lind stood at the sink, the sound of water running as they washed and dried the dinner plates. It was an easy, shared task—one that had become second nature between them.

Lind rinsed a plate, then, almost casually, said, "Sam and I usually plan a weekend getaway around April or May. I wanted to give you a heads-up." His tone was light, but there was a watchfulness in his gaze.

The dish in Dana's hands nearly slipped beneath the soapy water.

She forced herself to stay still and not react.

"That's... still a few months away." Her voice was even—too even.

"Exactly," Lind said, placing the plate on the drying rack. His tone was light, but his eyes flicked toward her, careful. "It's the end of January. I figured with plenty of notice, it wouldn't catch you off guard. We've got so many plans of our own between now and

329

then… and beyond." He turned to her fully, resting his hand on hers. "I want to make sure we're focusing on us."

She nodded, searching his eyes.

He's not wrong. It's months away. It doesn't matter yet.

She let go of his hand, swirling her fingers through the warm, soapy water.

But it did.

"You're right," she said finally. "No point worrying about something so far off."

Lind dried his hands on a towel, his voice softer. "Dana, I know this isn't easy. But I want you to know—you're my priority. I'll keep saying it as many times as you need to hear it."

She wanted to believe him.

She wanted to accept that.

And maybe, for now, she could.

She managed a small smile. "Thanks, Lind. I just… need time to get used to all this."

Lind ran his fingers over her arm—a quiet reassurance. "And I'll give you as much as you need."

Dana let out a breath.

I hope that's true. Because this is going to take a while.

And that weekend in April was going to come, whether she was ready for it or not.

She's Not Your Competition

The comforting aroma of freshly brewed coffee enveloped Dana as she sat across from Brenda in the corner booth. The café was familiar and warm—the kind of place that usually calmed her. But today, her thoughts churned too fast—too loud.

Brenda, ever perceptive, didn't waste time. "So, how are things with Lind?" she asked, stirring sugar into her latte.

Dana cupped her mug between her hands, watching the steam as it disappeared into the air. "Good, actually." She hesitated. "He mentioned his usual weekend with Sam coming up. It's months away, but..." She sighed. "I'm trying not to let it bother me."

Brenda tilted her head, studying Dana. "What about it bothers you, exactly?"

Dana frowned slightly, the question forcing her to pick apart feelings she wasn't sure she wanted to face. "I guess... it's the idea of them being together. Just the two of them. Sharing moments I'm not a part of."

Brenda leaned forward, her elbows resting on the table. "What do you think happens on those weekends that makes you feel this way?"

Dana hesitated. "I don't know." The words were quiet, like a confession. "Maybe their connection is stronger than ours. Or maybe... what if their sex is better? What if she knows how to make him happier than I can?"

Brenda's gaze didn't waver. "Do you think Lind would leave you for her?"

Dana blinked, the question hitting her like a splash of cold water. "No." The answer was immediate. But then... "At least, I don't think so. But I do feel like Sam has this hold over him that I don't understand."

Brenda tapped her fingers against her mug, her voice calm but pointed. "Do you think Lind belongs to you? Are you at a point in your relationship where he's yours and yours alone?"

Dana opened her mouth, then closed it. The words should have been easy, but they weren't. "No! Of course not," she said, a little too quickly. "That's not what I'm saying."

"Then what is it?" Brenda pressed, her tone gentle but unyielding. "If it's not about possession, and it's not about him leaving you, what is the real issue here?"

Dana looked down at her tea, fingers tightening around the warm ceramic. *What is the real issue?*

Her voice was softer when she spoke again. "I guess... it's the feeling of not being enough for him. Like, no matter what I do, I can't measure up to the history they have or the connection they share."

Brenda reached across the table, giving Dana's hand a reassuring squeeze. "That's a valid feeling, Dana. But has Lind ever made you feel like you're not enough?"

Dana thought back over the months they'd been together. His patience, his steadiness, the way he always reassured her without hesitation. She shook her head slowly. "No. If anything, he's been incredibly supportive. He's always trying to make me feel loved."

"Then maybe," Brenda said, her voice soft but firm, "it's not about how he feels about you. It's about how you feel about yourself in this situation. And that's something you'll need to work on—whether you're with Lind or anyone else."

The truth of that hit her—hard. Not just because Brenda was right, but because Dana knew it was something she couldn't outrun. Not with Lind. Not with anyone.

It wasn't just about Sam. Or sharing. Or even Lind's love.

It was about the voice in her own head—the one that whispered *you're not enough,* no matter how many times he told her otherwise. And now, Brenda had handed it to her straight: this wasn't Lind's work. It was hers.

Work she'd have to do whether she stayed with him or not. And that terrified her. Because what if she couldn't?

Brenda offered a small smile. "You've come a long way, Dana. You're handling this better than you think. And if Lind is the guy you believe he is, he's going to meet you halfway, more than halfway. But you've got to stop comparing yourself to Sam. She's not your competition."

Dana let out a breath, a glimmer of resolve sparking beneath the uncertainty. "Thanks, Brenda. I really needed to hear that."

Brenda winked. "Anytime. Now, let's stop talking about Lind and Sam. I've got some good gossip from work that'll make you forget all about them."

For the first time in days, Dana let out a genuine laugh, grateful for her friend's presence.

Chapter 40

What's that supposed to mean

The week leading up to Valentine's Day carried a quiet charge, a weightless anticipation Dana hadn't felt in a long time.

She and Lind had finalized plans to escape for the weekend—a charming bed-and-breakfast in the countryside, secluded and quiet.

Over dinner one night, as they went over plans, Dana caught the small, knowing smile playing at Lind's lips.

"What are you grinning about?" she asked, narrowing her eyes in mock suspicion.

"Nothing." The grin widened. He leaned back in his chair, fingers drumming against the table. "Just thinking about this weekend. I think you're going to like it."

Dana arched a brow. "Oh?" Her curiosity piqued. "What's that supposed to mean?"

He shrugged, trying and failing to look nonchalant. "You'll see."

"Lind..." she warned, though her lips curving into a reluctant smile.

"Relax." He said as he reached across the table, taking her hand. "Let's just say I've been planning something for a while. You'll find out soon enough."

Dana's heart fluttered, a slow warmth building in her chest.

He planned something. For her.

She exhaled, shaking her head. "You're maddening sometimes, you know that?"

Lind squeezed her hand, his hazel eyes holding a softness that made her stomach flip. "So I've been told."

Dana tried to fight back the grin tugging at her lips, but it was no use.

For the first time in weeks, she let herself fully lean into it—the anticipation, the excitement, the way Lind made her feel.

Whatever he had planned, she was ready.

God, I love this man

The bed-and-breakfast was even more enchanting than Dana had imagined. Nestled among rolling hills dusted with snow, the cottage-style building exuded warmth, its ivy-covered facade illuminated by soft string lights. Inside, the air was thick with lavender and woodsmoke. A fire crackled in the cozy common room.

Their suite was intimate—almost dreamlike. A four-poster bed draped in gauzy white fabric stood as the centerpiece, its delicate canopy shifting with the softest breeze. A stone fireplace flickered warmly beside a small sitting area, and French doors led to a private balcony overlooking the snow-covered countryside.

Dana spun slowly, taking it all in. "This place is beautiful."

Lind watched her with quiet intensity, his eyes reflecting exactly what he was feeling. "You're beautiful."

She barely had time to react before he stepped forward, cupping her face in his hands, and kissed her—slow and deep, lips lightly pressing against hers with a tenderness that sent warmth cascading through her.

Her fingers curled into the front of his jacket as she kissed him back, hard and wanting.

God, I love this man.

Lind smiled against her lips before pulling back. "We have lots to see..." His hands rested at her waist, his breath warm against her mouth. "Before we settle in."

Dana let out a small, reluctant sigh but grinned. "Fine. But don't take too long playing tour guide. I have plans for you later."

Lind's chuckle was rich, promising. "Yes, Ma'am."

They spent the day exploring the surrounding area, indulging in a leisurely lunch at a charming café before strolling hand in hand through snow-dusted trails. The cold air left Dana's cheeks flushed, but Lind's presence kept her warm.

Lind... it's beautiful

That evening, they returned to the B&B's quaint dining room for a private candlelit dinner. The space was cozy, filled with the low hum of conversation and the faint crackle of the fireplace. Their table, set near the window, was adorned with fresh roses and flickering candles, casting a golden glow over the linen tablecloth.

Lind seemed thoughtful, his attention unwavering as they talked and laughed over the meal. But Dana could tell—he was holding something back.

As dessert arrived—a decadent chocolate fondue with fresh strawberries—Lind reached into his jacket pocket, pulling out a small velvet box.

He placed it on the table between them.

Dana's breath caught. "Lind..." Her eyes darted between him and the box, her heart suddenly hammering. "Shouldn't you be down on one knee?" she teased him.

"It's not that kind of box," he smirked. "Open it," his voice warm, steady.

With a nervous chuckle and trembling fingers, she lifted the lid, revealing a delicate gold chain adorned with a small, sparkling diamond. The candlelight caught the facets of the stone, making it shimmer brilliantly.

She swallowed hard. "Lind... it's beautiful."

He reached across the table, lacing his fingers with hers. His eyes held her there, anchoring her. "I wanted you to have something to remind you of how much you mean to me." His voice dropped, softer now. "The sparkle you bring to my life..." He exhaled a small, self-deprecating chuckle. "I had a whole speech planned, but apparently, I forgot most of it."

Dana blinked against the sudden sting of tears. "It's perfect. Thank you."

"Let me put it on you." Lind stood, moving behind her.

Dana gathered her hair to one side, shivering slightly—not from the cold, but from the sensation of his hands brushing against the bare skin of her neck as he clasped the necklace.

"There," he murmured, pressing a soft kiss to the back of her neck. "Perfect."

Dana touched the diamond, heart swelling with affection. "I love it." Her voice was barely above a whisper.

Lind returned to his seat, watching her. The softest smile played at his lips. "And I love you."

Every moment, every thought

Later, after their shower, they sat together by the fireplace in their suite, wrapped in the thick robes provided by the B&B. The flames cast flickering light across the room, gilding their skin in soft gold.

Dana's fingers hovered over the diamond on the necklace, its cool touch keeping her in the moment.

"You really surprised me tonight." She leaned against him, her voice quiet, but full of warmth. "I thought you didn't do sparkly things and all that."

"I don't, but you do " Lind said, with a knowing smile.

"It's beautiful," she repeated, feeling the warmth of his hug.

"I like keeping you on your toes." Lind's arm tightened around her, his usual smile laced with something deeper. His voice softened. "But seriously, you're worth it, Dana. Every moment, every thought. I just want you to know that."

She tilted her head up, her eyes locking onto his. "I don't know what I did to deserve you."

"Just be yourself." His voice was steady, full of conviction. "That's all I want."

The weight of his words made her feel seen. Wanted. Cherished.

Dana pressed a slow kiss to his lips, pouring all of her gratitude, all of her feelings into it. Her heart felt lighter than it had in weeks—and for once, the doubts seemed distant.

Lind stood and reached for her hand. Dana took it, her fingers lacing through his without hesitation.

When he pulled her to her feet, his other hand cradled the side of her face, he kissed her again—deeper this time. More deliberate.

Then, he moved to the sash of her robe.

The knot slipped free, the soft fabric parting.

Dana let him look. Let him take her in.

Lind's gaze roamed her slowly, reverently, his expression shifting to something deeper—awe, desire, something she could feel down to her bones.

The way he looked at her made her feel beautiful. Desired.

And when his eyes finally lifted back to hers, she stepped closer.

Her fingers found the knot on his robe, untying it just as slowly. As the fabric fell open, his response to her was immediate—undeniable.

She smiled, that playful, naughty smile he loved so much.

Her hands traced the path of fine hair on his chest that trailed to his stomach and disappeared below.

Lind shrugged off his robe, letting it pool at his feet.

By the time they reached the bed, Dana's robe lay next to his.

Both forgotten on the floor.

Chapter 41

For as long as you let me

Nestled beneath the soft sheets and the weight of the comforter, their bodies pressed close, warmth growing between them. Every touch was unhurried, reverent, with a tenderness that spoke without words.

Dana pulled Lind over her, her hands gliding over his back, feeling the tension in his muscles, the heat of his skin against hers. She kissed him deeply, sinking into the slow burn of him, the way he fit inside her—not just physically, but completely. He wasn't particularly large or thick, but the way he moved within her felt uniquely perfect—a rhythm, a connection, a pleasure only they could create together.

They moved in a languid rhythm, their bodies speaking in soft whispers of heat and friction. There was no rush, no desperation—only savoring. The warmth of his breath ghosted over her neck, his lips pressing slow, passionate kisses against her skin.

"I want you... just love me," she whispered, her voice barely more than a breath.

Lind's response was immediate, his lips tickling her ear. "I do. And I will—for as long as you let me."

His words wrapped around her like a second layer of warmth.

They shifted, rolling together, and Dana was on top, straddling him. The firelight flickered over her bare skin, sparkling off the diamond dangling between them. Her rhythm slow, full of want and desire with every stroke.

The comforter, the sheets—too warm, too much. She shoved them aside, leaving them both exposed and open. The air between them thickened, charged.

She moved over him, her hips setting the pace. Her hands pushing against his chest, holding him there, connecting herself to him. Their bodies aligned, perfect in their unhurried urgency.

Her green eyes locked onto his, searching, holding.

Lind reached up, taking her face in his hand. His fingers trailing down her cheek, over her collarbone, and over the delicate gold chain of the necklace.

"You're beautiful." His voice was thick with a mix of love and desire.

A soft, knowing smile touched her lips. "You make me feel that way."

And for a long time, they just stayed like that—moving, feeling, holding each other. It wasn't about proving anything, or reaching a finish line. It was about presence, about breathing together, about being seen and felt in a way no one else ever had.

When release finally claimed them, it was a slow, unraveling wave—a quiet culmination of everything they had built together. Lind held her tightly as she trembled against him, his arms strong, steady, a place to land.

***

Later, as they lay tangled beneath the covers he'd pulled back up over them, Dana rested her head on his chest, listening to the steady rhythm of his heartbeat. His hand wandered slowly along her back, patient and familiar, a rhythm she'd come to crave.

"I love you," Lind murmured, his voice just above a whisper.

Dana tilted her head up, meeting his hazel eyes in the dim firelight. "I love you too." The words flowed easily this time—no hesitation, no uncertainty.

For the first time in weeks, she felt completely at peace. No comparisons. No wondering if she was enough. No weight of Sam lingering in the back of her mind.

With Lind, in this moment, she simply was.

And that was more than enough.

As the fire burned lower, the last flickers of gold casting soft shadows over the room, they drifted into sleep, wrapped in the warmth of their connection.

And this time, Dana didn't feel like she was waiting to fall.

Those would look great on you

Weeks passed, and Dana found herself sinking into the quiet joys of her relationship with Lind. Their weekends unfolded like a well-worn novel—each chapter filled with laughter, stolen kisses, shared experiences, and the kind of contentment lovers know. Late-night comedy shows, trying new restaurants, talking over coffee and homemade breakfasts on Sunday mornings—the simple, easy rhythm of them.

For the first time in a long while, she wasn't thinking about Sam.

One crisp March afternoon, the promise of spring in the air as Dana and Lind wandered downtown, the streets humming with life. The first craft fair of the season had popped up in the nearby park, a telltale sign that winter was finally releasing its grip. Vendors lined the pathways, booths bursting with handmade pottery, watercolors, woven scarves, and intricate carvings.

Lind paused at a stand selling hand-carved wooden figurines, picking up a small dog—a short-haired terrier, its features smooth from careful craftsmanship.

"Think he'd fit on your bookshelf?" he asked, grinning as he turned it over in his hands.

Dana laughed, shaking her head. "He's cute. And it's about as close as I'm going to get to having a dog anytime soon."

Lind chuckled, nodding. "Yeah, same. This is about as close as I want to having the responsibility of a real dog."

Dana nodded her agreement.

They wandered further, their fingers touching occasionally but never quite lacing together, a quiet closeness threading between them.

At a small stand featuring delicate handmade jewelry, Lind stopped, his eyes catching on a pair of gold drop earrings, tiny crystals winking in the late afternoon light.

"Those would look great on you," he murmured, tilting his head toward them.

Dana's cheeks warmed. She reached up instinctively, and ran her fingers over the necklace he'd given her on Valentine's Day. It had barely left her neck since.

"You think so?"

"Absolutely," he said. "They'd match your necklace perfectly."

For a moment, she considered the earrings, running her fingers over them, imagining how they'd feel against her skin. But then, she shook her head. "Maybe next time."

Lind didn't press. But his expression remained soft, warm.

"I'll remember them," he said with a wink.

Then let's make it happen

They continued their stroll, stopping at a cozy corner café where the scent of coffee and fresh pastries filled the air. Lind grabbed their drinks while Dana picked out two warm cinnamon rolls, their sticky-sweet aroma too tempting to pass up.

Outside, the sun peeked through thinning clouds, the bite of winter fading as they meandered through the streets.

Dana took a slow, indulgent bite, sighing as the buttery cinnamon melted on her tongue. "So, once it really warms up—where would you want to go?"

Lind took a sip of his coffee, his gaze thoughtful. "I've always wanted to hike up to Hidden Falls. It's not too far, but I've heard it's beautiful in the spring."

"I've never been." Dana perked up, the idea of escaping into nature with him, just the two of them, suddenly so appealing.

Lind's smile deepened. "We should make a weekend of it. Maybe rent a cabin nearby, spend a couple of days exploring."

Dana swallowed another bite, already imagining mornings wrapped in blankets with coffee on a cabin porch, evenings by a crackling fire.

"That sounds amazing. I've always wanted to do something like that."

Lind nudged her playfully. "Then let's make it happen."

He paused, tilting his head. "What about you? Anywhere you've been dying to visit?"

Dana brushed a few cinnamon-sugar crumbs from her fingers. "I've been wanting to check out that botanical garden everyone talks about. The one with the walking trails and butterfly sanctuary."

Lind's face lit up in recognition. "I know the place! It's beautiful. Let's add it to the list."

Dana grinned, something light and warm unfurling in her chest. "Deal."

As the afternoon stretched on, they wandered through the streets, peeking into shop windows, stopping to admire local artists' work.

The chill of winter loosening its grip, and with Lind beside her—his hand in hers—Dana felt lighter than she had in weeks.

No overthinking. No quiet doubts.

Just this.

And for the first time in a long time, Dana let herself believe in it.

Chapter 42

My weekend with Sam is coming

The soft glow of the corner floor lamp cast shadows across Lind's living room as they sank into the couch, Dana tucking her legs beneath her. Lind grabbed a small notepad from the coffee table, flipping through the pages as he spoke.

"Alright, let's map out our plans for the next few weeks."

Dana leaned back, watching as he marked a few dates with his pen, his brow furrowing slightly in concentration. The casual domesticity of planning together should have been comforting.

Then he said it, like he was telling her about breakfast.

"Oh, I almost forgot—it's almost April. My weekend with Sam is coming up in a couple of weeks."

His tone was neutral, matter-of-fact. He glanced at her over the notebook, unaware of the way the words clenched her stomach like a fist.

Dana's pulse skipped, then quickened.

She fought to keep her expression neutral, her voice even. "Right," she said softly. "I guess it's that time already."

Lind set the notepad down and turned toward her fully, reading her like he always did. "I wanted to remind you so it doesn't catch us off guard as we plan." His eyes were steady, kind, giving her space to react.

She forced a smile, though it felt like a fragile thing, barely holding its shape. "Of course."

For a moment, neither of them spoke.

The silence wasn't heavy, but it wasn't easy, either.

Then Lind, ever anchoring, picked up the notepad again, shifting the mood just enough. "Okay, so what are we thinking for next weekend?"

Dana exhaled slowly, pulling herself back. Back to them. Back to now.

"I was thinking we could revisit that Italian restaurant downtown on Friday," she said. "And maybe go for a hike on Saturday? The weather's supposed to be nice."

Lind's smile returned, easy and genuine. "I like it. Low-key and outdoorsy. Perfect."

She watched him, the way he jotted down her words. He always made her feel like she mattered.

But the ache was there, haunting her, and before she could stop herself, the words tumbled out.

"Let's wait until after your weekend with Sam to plan anything else."

Lind's pen hovered over the paper. Slowly, he set the notepad aside, tilting his head as he studied her. His voice softened, caution threading through it.

"Dana, are you sure that's what you want?" He didn't push, but there was concern behind the question. "I don't want us to stop planning things for us just because of one weekend."

Her cheeks warmed. "It's not that." She hesitated, searching for the right words. "I just... feel like it's better if I don't think too far ahead right now."

Lind didn't answer right away.

Instead, he reached for her hand, resting his palm over hers. "I get it," he said gently. "But I need you to hear me on this—Sam's weekend doesn't change what we have. It's one weekend, and when it's over, I'll be right here with you. Like I always am."

Dana swallowed hard, nodding slowly. "I know. It's just hard to remember that sometimes."

"That's okay." Lind squeezed her hand, reassuring but firm. "Don't let this take away from the good things we've got going."

Dana stared down at their joined hands, tracing the veins on the back of his hand with her fingertips.

He was right.

She knew he was right.

But knowing and feeling weren't always the same thing.

Still, she forced a small smile. "I'll try not to let it."

Lind leaned closer, his voice warm, grounding. "No trying, Dana. We're planning our weekends because we enjoy being together, not because we're filling time before something else. Let's focus on what's in front of us, okay?"

Something about the way he said it made her stomach twist—like Lind needed her to believe it just as much as she needed to hear it.

Because it sounded like something Brenda would say.

Still, she nodded. "Okay."

Lind returned her smile, lifting her hand and pressing a soft kiss to her knuckles. "That's my girl."

The warmth of his lips sent a flicker of hope through her.

She resolved to hold onto it.

For herself.

For them.

He wasn't leaving her

That night, sleep eluded her.

She stared at the ceiling, listening to the soft, steady rhythm of Lind's breathing beside her.

It should have been soothing.

But her mind wouldn't stop.

The progress she had made over the last few months—the stability, the ease—felt like it was unraveling, thread by thread.

Why did it still hurt?

Why did the thought of Lind spending a weekend with Sam stir something so deep inside her that she couldn't seem to name it without choking on it?

She turned her head, watching him sleep.

He wasn't leaving her. He wasn't choosing Sam over her.

He had said so. Repeatedly. He had shown her. Repeatedly.

And yet.

The quiet insecurities—the ones she had worked so hard to bury—were creeping back in the dark.

And tonight, they were louder than ever.

What's really bothering you

The lunchroom hummed with its usual midday energy—clinking utensils, quiet conversations, the low hum of vending machines. But Dana barely noticed any of it as she stirred her coffee, her gaze distant.

Brenda sat down in the seat across from her, her sharp gaze taking in Dana's silence. "Alright, what's going on?"

Dana exhaled, pushing her coffee aside. Leaning in, she quietly said. "Lind reminded me last night about his weekend with Sam coming up. I thought I was okay, but now... I'm not so sure."

Brenda leaned forward, her tone measured but knowing. "What's really bothering you? Is it their history? The sex? Their connection? I thought we talked about all that?"

Dana hesitated, "I know... but," her voice quieter. "Maybe it's all of it. I keep wondering if I'm enough... or if they have something I can't give him."

Brenda's expression softened, but her words were firm. "Listen, Lind chose to build something lasting with you. Whatever he shares with Sam doesn't take away from what he has with you." She let that sink in for a moment before adding, "But you have to ask yourself—are you letting this 'competition' idea distract you? Keeping you from actually building something special with Lind?"

Dana blinked, caught off guard by the question. "I don't want to compete, but... it's hard not to feel like I have to prove myself."

"You don't." Brenda's voice was unwavering. "You're enough because you're you. Focus on that—and maybe plan something fun for yourself while he's gone. You deserve a break too."

Dana let out a faint smile. "Thanks, Brenda. I needed that."

Brenda winked. "Anytime. Now finish your coffee. You've got this."

Then let's plan something

That evening, Dana was stretched out on the couch, absently scrolling through her phone when a text from Brenda popped up:

"How are you holding up?"

Dana smiled faintly, grateful for her friend's intuition. Instead of typing a response, she hit call.

Brenda picked up on the first ring. "I was just thinking about you. What's up?"

Dana hesitated briefly. "I've been thinking about what you said at lunch. I need something to do that weekend, Sam's weekend. I don't want to sit around stewing about it."

Brenda's voice lit up instantly. "Then let's plan something! A girls' weekend—spa, wine, the works."

A flicker of excitement replaced the tightness in Dana's chest. "You think the others would be up for it?"

"Are you kidding?" Brenda laughed. "Give me ten minutes, and I'll have everyone on board."

True to her word, Brenda rallied the group, and by the end of the night, they had a plan—a lakeside resort cabin, complete with hiking trails, a hot tub, and plenty of space to unwind.

"This is exactly what you need," Brenda said. "A weekend to focus on yourself. No distractions, no overthinking. Just us girls."

Dana felt a weight lift off her chest. "Thanks, Brenda. I really appreciate this."

"What are friends for?" Brenda said with a grin. "Now let's make this weekend one for the books."

As Dana hung up, she found a renewed sense of purpose.

Having something to look forward to—something just for her. She wasn't just coping, she was choosing, and that made the thought of Lind's weekend with Sam a little easier to bear.

Chapter 43

You did good, woman

The restaurant glowed warmly, candles flickering on each table, soft music weaving through the air. The smell of garlic, tomatoes, and fresh herbs wrapped around Dana like a comforting embrace.

Lind held the door open, flashing his signature easy grin as Dana stepped inside.

"Coming back here is perfect," she said, taking in the cozy décor. "I've been craving their pasta all week."

"I am pleased as well. We had a great time last time we were here." Lind smiled as the hostess led them to the same corner table.

As they browsed the menu, their conversation flowed easily—stories about work, lighthearted debates over their favorite TV shows, playful banter about who could finish more garlic bread.

But as their meals arrived, Dana's laughter faltered briefly.

The looming weekend sat just on the edge of her thoughts, trying to wedge itself between them.

Lind noticed but didn't call her on it. Instead, he effortlessly steered the conversation, launching into a story about a stockroom mix-up at work that had their whole team in stitches.

Dana grinned despite herself. "I can't believe we manage to get anything done with all the chaos."

"Sometimes it feels like herding cats," Lind admitted, his eyes crinkling with amusement. "But it keeps things interesting."

As the evening wore on, Dana let herself relax, the warmth of Lind's presence soothing the tightness in her chest.

She reached across the table, resting her hand on his. "This was a good idea," she murmured. "Thanks for making tonight happen."

Lind leaned back slightly, his smile easy. "It was your pick, both times. The food's great, and I love the atmosphere. You did good, woman."

She laughed, noticing a tiny spot of sauce on his chin.

For a moment, she thought about reaching over to wipe it off.

Then a different idea crossed her mind.

Maybe I'll lick it off later.

A slow grin tugged at her lips as the evening stretched on.

Guess we'll experience it together

Dana woke to the distant sound of soft clattering, and the aroma of bacon.

She stretched, listening to the low hum of the stove vent, the rhythmic sizzle of eggs in the pan, the comforting sounds of a slow morning.

Slipping out of bed, she threw on one of Lind's T-shirts, the fabric soft and familiar against her skin, before wandering into the kitchen.

Lind stood at the stove in his boxers and a T-shirt, spatula in one hand, a pan in the other. His hair was slightly mussed, the comfortable ease in his stance making her smile.

"Good morning, chef." Dana's voice was still husky from sleep.

Lind glanced over his shoulder, grinning. "Morning, sleepyhead. Thought I'd get breakfast going. Hope you're hungry. We're gonna need energy for our hike."

"Starving." She stepped closer, sneaking a piece of bacon from the plate.

Lind swatted at her hand with the spatula. "Hey. That's for the meal, not the pregame."

Dana popped the bacon into her mouth anyway, grinning. "It's quality control."

She sat down at the table, the warmth of the coffee mug seeping into her fingers as she took her first sip.

Lind brought over two steaming plates and set one in front of her before taking his seat. The food was simple but perfectly done—fluffy eggs, crispy bacon, hash browns, and thick slices of buttered toast. His usual.

She took another sip, sighing in approval. "Okay, okay—this looks amazing."

Lind grinned, digging into his own plate. "I try."

For a few minutes, they ate in comfortable silence, the soft scrape of utensils and the occasional satisfied hum from Dana.

After a few bites, Lind nodded toward her. "So, what's the plan for after the hike? You still want to check out that little café?"

Dana lit up. "Yeah! We've talked about going there a few times. They're supposed to have the best homemade pies, right?"

Lind nodded, taking a sip of his coffee. "And killer sandwiches. Figured we could grab lunch there after the hike, maybe sit outside if the weather holds up."

Dana speared a bite of hash browns, considering. "That sounds perfect. What's the hike actually like? I know it's got a waterfall, but how long is it?"

Lind set his fork down, thinking. "About four miles round trip. Nothing crazy. Steady incline in the beginning, but once we hit the falls, it levels out. It's worth it, though—views are amazing."

Dana chewed thoughtfully. "You've been before?"

"Once, years ago. But I barely remember it." He flashed her a grin. "Guess we'll experience it together for the first time."

Dana liked that idea.

She snagged another piece of bacon, smiling. "Okay, so: hike, café, and then what?"

Lind leaned back, stretching. "I dunno. What do you feel like? We could hit up the farmer's market if we're back early enough.

Or..." He began to grin. "We could just come back here and, you know, be lazy."

Dana laughed, nodding. "It's a lot of work being lazy with you," she said with a wink. "Let's see how we feel after lunch."

Lind's grin widened as he lifted his coffee mug. "Deal."

She took another bite, savoring the last few moments of breakfast, the warmth of the meal matching the warmth in her chest.

Lind shook his head, chuckling. "Go take a shower before I make you help me with the dishes."

Dana gave him a mock-offended look, popping one more piece of bacon into her mouth. "A couple more bites and I'm done."

Lind just smiled, sipping his coffee, waiting her out.

***

The warm water washing over her woke her completely.

By the time she returned to the kitchen, Lind was already rinsing dishes, his back to her.

Dana smiled at the sight of him. "You really are a domestic god." She leaned against the counter, watching him.

Lind quirked a brow. "Only on special occasions." He nodded toward the door. "Go get dressed. I'll finish up here."

Dana gave him a mock salute, her grin returning. "Yes, sir. Just gotta do my hair first."

And just like that, the weight in her chest lifted.

This weekend was theirs.

And for now, that was enough.

A moment later, Lind stepped out

Steam blurred the mirror's edges as Dana ran a brush through her damp hair. The scent of warm water and Lind's soap filled the space, familiar and comforting.

Behind her, the shower shut off with a final splatter of droplets. A moment later, Lind stepped out, towel in hand, shaking the water from his hair.

Before she could move, his hands slid around her waist, then up, palms warm against her breasts as he pulled her back against him.

"Good morning again," he murmured, pressing a kiss to the top of her head.

Dana smiled at him in the mirror, tilting her head slightly. "Morning, again."

Lind gave her a playful squeeze before stepping back. He grabbed a towel, ran it gently down her back, before turning it on himself.

By the time he finished, Dana had already disappeared from the bathroom.

Lind followed the faint sounds of movement to the bedroom, where Dana was already dressed in hiking gear, seated on the edge of the bed, lacing up her boots.

Her expression was one of quiet focus.

"You're quick," Lind said, leaning against the doorway, watching her with amusement.

Dana looked up, admiring the view. "You're slow."

"I call it thorough," he countered, stepping to the dresser for a pair of boxers.

"I call it slow."

Lind chuckled, slipping into his pants. "Looks like you're ready to hit the trail?"

Dana tied off her last knot, giving it an extra tug before standing. She grabbed her sweatshirt from the chair, just in case. "Almost."

He watched her smooth down her shirt, adjusting the fit out of habit, then flash him an expectant look.

"Okay. Now I'm ready."

Lind laughed, finishing his own routine. "Alright, boss. Lead the way."

As they stepped outside, Dana glanced back at him, her smile softened as their eyes met.

For the first time in days, something inside her felt light.

But this? This is ours

The trail curved through pockets of golden light, the sun filtering through the treetops. Dana adjusted her footing on the rocky incline, her boots pressing into the damp earth as Lind led the way ahead of her.

His walking stick tapped lightly against the ground, a steady rhythm blending with the rustle of leaves and the distant bird calls.

Then, Dana spoke.

"Do you and Sam ever hike when you go to the cabin?"

Lind glanced over his shoulder, his pace never faltering. "If the weather's good, yeah. It's hard to resist being outdoors in a place like that."

Dana nodded slowly, her gaze drifting ahead. "You said Sam likes the outdoors?"

"She does." Lind's voice was even, unrushed. "I think I mentioned that."

Dana tried to keep her tone casual. "Makes sense. Seems like the kind of thing you'd enjoy doing together."

Lind paused, leaning on his walking stick for a moment before turning to face her.

"We do," he admitted, then gestured to the path, to her. "But this? This is ours."

His words warmed her despite the cool morning air.

She wanted to hold onto that.

But somewhere deep inside, a flicker of doubt remained.

She pushed it away, focusing instead on the crisp air filling her lungs, the steady rhythm of their steps... and Lind.

I have plans

As they reached a wider stretch of trail, Dana ran her hands over her leggings, shaking off the strain of the climb.

"By the way," she said, keeping her tone light. "I have plans for your Sam weekend, too."

Lind shot her a curious glance. "Oh? What's on the agenda?"

"Brenda and I are going on a girls' trip." Dana stepped carefully over a gnarled tree root. "We're staying at a cabin—kind of a resort area."

"Sounds nice. Just the two of you?"

"No, I think Shirley, Ann, and Becky are going too."

Lind grinned. "Full crew. Sounds like fun. What kind of area is it? Near a town?"

Dana laughed softly, her tone playful. "Brenda says there's enough around to get into trouble if we wanted. But I told her I wasn't looking for that much of a distraction."

"A little trouble might be fun."

Dana shot him a look. "I think she was talking about men and alcohol."

She watched him closely, waiting for his reaction.

Any other man she'd been with would have had something to say about that.

Lind's expression, however, remained calm, unreadable.

"Oh really? And?"

Dana arched a brow. "That's not the kind of trouble I need. I've got enough with you."

Lind chuckled under his breath. "A little flirting wouldn't hurt."

Dana rolled her eyes. "I'm not that kind."

Lind's voice softened, "I know. But still..."

She frowned slightly. "You really think I would do that?"

Lind turned his head, his expression turning serious for the first time.

"No, Dana." His voice was firm, unwavering. "I don't think you're that kind."

The silence stretched between them, filled only by the rustling wind and the sound of their footsteps crunching against damp leaves.

Finally, Lind broke it, his tone lighter again.

"But it does sound like fun times with the girls."

Dana smiled, feeling the tension ease from her shoulders. "Brenda says there are a couple of good coffee shops and some neat little places to browse. But I'm pretty sure it'll mostly be wine and bonfires."

Lind smirked. "Sounds like a solid plan."

His voice was easy, steady. Just like him.

"You'll come back with some good stories, I bet."

Dana nodded, inhaling the crisp mountain air.

She wasn't sure what story she was writing for herself just yet.

But for now, this moment felt enough.

Hungry? Starving

As they made their way back to the trailhead, the parking lot came into view, a handful of cars scattered under the midday sun. Dana stretched, feeling the pleasant ache in her legs, the kind that came from just enough exertion.

"Hungry?" Lind asked, tossing his walking stick into the back of his truck.

Dana wiped her brow, the heat of the midday sun pressing down on her. "Starving."

"That little café we were talking about is just down the road," Lind said.

Dana nodded easily. "Yep, let's give it a try."

Chapter 44

Just thinking about next weekend

The café was quaint, its rustic charm inviting, with a small patio shaded by bright umbrellas. A light breeze stirred the air, carrying the scent of fresh bread and roasted coffee.

They found a table near the edge, the hum of conversation and the occasional clink of dishes providing a cozy backdrop.

Dana picked at her turkey club, her appetite waning slightly as her thoughts wandered.

"Penny for them?" Lind asked, sipping his iced tea, as he watched her.

Dana shook her head with a small smile, pushing her thoughts away. "Just thinking about next weekend. I want to make sure I pack enough wine for Brenda."

Lind chuckled, setting his drink down. "She's lucky to have you as her planning partner."

Dana's smile widened.

"Didn't know you had a moving truck though?" Lind winked.

Dana tilted her head. "For what?"

"Brenda's wine," he chuckled.

Dana swatted at his shoulder. "She doesn't drink that much."

They shared a laugh at the absurdity of it.

The knot in her chest loosened as she let herself sink into the moment, savoring the easy rhythm of their day.

Next weekend could... wait.

***

They pulled back onto the main road with the windows down, the wind tousling Dana's hair as she leaned her elbow on the door frame. Her legs still ached pleasantly from the hike, and even the air felt heavier, lazier now that lunch was over.

Lind tapped the wheel with one hand. "Still want to hit the farmer's market?"

Dana groaned lightly, smiling as she rolled her ankle in a slow circle. "Only if you plan to carry me through it."

He laughed, glancing over at her. "That bad?"

"Let's just say I've hit my step count for the week." She stretched, then let her hand drift across to rest on his thigh. "I vote we go home, shower, and be lazy the rest of the day."

Lind nodded, his grin easy. "Lazy with you? That's the best kind."

They drove in companionable silence for a few minutes, the road stretching out ahead of them, sleepy and sun-warmed.

***

Back at his place, they kicked off their shoes, the rhythm of the afternoon slowing around them.

After their shower, Dana had sunk into the couch in Lind's soft pajamas, wine in hand.

Lind stirred a pot of soup on the stove, the rich aroma of simmering vegetables and herbs filling the air, mingling with the faint buttery scent of freshly baked biscuits from the café.

At the table, Dana arranged a wooden tray with an assortment of meats and cheeses, laying out crackers between them with slow, careful movements.

"This is nice," she murmured, looking up from her task.

Lind glanced over, ladling the soup into bowls. "Simple but good. Sometimes that's all you need."

They ate at the small kitchen table, conversation flowing easily—bits and pieces of their day woven between spoonfuls of soup and bites of bread.

Dana leaned back with a satisfied sigh, grinning as she dabbed at her lips with a napkin. "You could probably make this at the café and sell out."

Lind shook his head. "Nah, too much pressure. Cooking for you is a lot more fun."

He knew what weighed on her

Later, they sank into the couch, a comedy show playing in the background.

Dana rested her head against Lind's chest as his arm draped loosely around her shoulders.

She laughed at a particularly silly scene, the warmth of Lind's body soothing her.

And yet—her mind slipped.

Does she laugh with him like this?

The thought came unbidden, sharp and unwelcome.

She forced her focus back to the screen, willing herself to stay present.

Lind chuckled beside her, the quiet vibration of his chest under her cheek pulling her back.

For a moment, just a moment, she let herself believe that none of it mattered.

Lind, however, noticed her occasional quiet spells.

He didn't say anything. Didn't press.

Instead, he tightened his hold around her ever so slightly—a small, quiet reassurance.

Her laughter sounded a little forced tonight.

But he let that go too.

He knew what weighed on her.

And he knew she was doing everything she could to hold on.

Lind's warmth surrounded her

By the time they straightened up and headed to bed, Dana felt the signs of exhaustion tugging at her.

The comfort of their routine—brushing teeth, dimming the lights, slipping under the covers like muscle memory.

Dana climbed in first, the sheets cool against her skin.

Lind followed, pulling the blanket up, slipping his arms over her waist as they turned to face each other.

Dana's fingers wandered absently, tracing the angles of his face—his ear, his jawline, the bridge of his nose.

Lind smiled faintly, his own touch mirroring hers—gentle strokes along her neck, shoulder, down the side of her breast, the curve of her waist.

When he reached for her hip, his grip firm but unhurried, Dana covered his hand with her own, holding it there for a long, quiet moment.

Then, softly, she brought his hand to her lips, pressing a kiss against his knuckles.

She rolled onto her side, their usual spooning position, pulling his arms tightly against her body.

She pressed herself into him, seeking the warmth, the familiarity.

Lind exhaled softly, pulling her tight to him.

"Goodnight," he murmured softly.

"Goodnight," Dana whispered, her voice soft but steady.

She held onto him like a lifeline, her grip firm but tender.

Lind's warmth surrounded her, but her thoughts remained tangled.

The ache in her chest hadn't left.

It had only quieted.

Lind lay awake for a few moments longer, feeling the tension in her... even in her sleep.

She was nestled into him almost protectively, her fingers still wrapped around his.

He pressed a soft kiss to the back of her head, a silent wish.

If only he could quiet the doubts.

Glad you approve

The savory scent of biscuits and sausage gravy pulled Dana from sleep. She stretched lazily, then slipped on one of Lind's T-shirts before making her way into the kitchen.

Lind was already at the stove, his movements calm, practiced, familiar.

"Biscuits and gravy," he announced, setting a steaming plate in front of her with a satisfied grin. "The best you've ever had, guaranteed."

Dana sat in her usual spot, cradling her warm coffee mug, watching steam roll out in disappearing swirls.

Lind placed a plate in front of her, a generous serving of gravy poured over the soft, buttery biscuits.

She took a bite, her eyes widening. "Okay, you weren't lying. This is amazing."

"Glad you approve."

She took another bite, savoring the rich, creamy warmth. "Where did you learn to make it like this?"

"My grandmother." His response was matter-of-fact, simple—just truth.

They ate in comfortable silence, the occasional soft hum of approval escaping Dana as she sipped her coffee.

But even as she smiled, Lind could sense it—the undercurrent of unease still coiled inside her.

When she suggested heading out early, he didn't want her to.

But he didn't object.

"No problem," Lind said easily. "We can save our usual Sunday plans for next time."

Next time.

Her grip on her coffee mug tightened.

Next time for us is two weeks from now.

Next time, you'll be with her.

She—couldn't help it.

As much as she wanted to, she couldn't stop the thought from invading.

She took her time, gathering her things slowly.

She didn't want to miss time with Lind.

But the thoughts... the intrusion... the next weekend. It wouldn't leave her alone.

Goodnight Lind

Back at her condo, Dana kicked off her shoes, stripping out of her jeans before climbing straight into bed.

Exhaustion—both emotional and physical—washed over her.

She lay there staring at the ceiling, her limbs heavy, the bed too big.

Then, sleep came swiftly, pulling her under.

When she woke, the light outside had dimmed, shadows stretching across her walls.

The familiar ache—the longing in her chest.

Missing Lind.

Missing his touch.

She sighed, rolling onto her side. Then, almost without thinking, she reached for her nightstand.

A familiar toy in hand.

She settled back into the sheets, her eyes drifting shut, her mind slipping into the only place she wanted to be.

Lind's hands. His mouth. The warmth of his body against hers.

The release came fast, leaving her breathless, but only momentarily satisfied.

After cleaning up and setting the toy out to air-dry, she climbed back into bed, pulling Lind's pillow against her bare skin, pressing her face into the faint scent of him.

"Goodnight, Lind."

Her voice was small, breaking slightly.

A single tear slipped down her cheek, vanishing into the pillowcase.

And finally, sleep claimed her again.

But the ache never left.

About you going away

The store buzzed with the usual Monday morning chaos—carts rattling, announcements crackling overhead, coworkers joking in the aisles.

Dana stood at the end of an aisle, methodically arranging bottles of sunscreen on a summer display. The cheerful beach images mocked her.

The thought of Lind's upcoming weekend pressed against her ribs like a weight.

From the corner of her eye, she saw him approaching. Clipboard in hand, he navigated the busy aisle effortlessly.

"Morning," Lind said, his voice warm but casual.

Dana forced a small smile, barely glancing up. "Morning."

He stopped beside her, leaning slightly against the shelf. "Everything okay?"

She hesitated, aligning the bottles in perfect rows, avoiding his gaze.

"It's fine." Quick. Clipped. A little too sharp.

"Dana." His voice softened, searching. "What's going on?"

Her hands stilled. Slowly, she turned to face him.

"It's nothing." She hadn't meant for it to come out sharp, but the words tumbled out too fast.

Then, after a beat: "Just... thinking about this week. About you going away."

Lind's expression softened, his eyes steady on hers. "I get it," he said, voice low, just for her.

"I know this is tough. I won't pretend it isn't. But I'm here now. And I'll be here when I get back."

Her chest tightened.

I know.

She wanted to believe it.

"I just... I don't know what to do with how I feel about it."

Lind didn't hesitate. "Talk to me."

Simple. Certain.

Dana swallowed hard, managing a faint smile. "Thanks, Lind."

Got any fun plans

By lunchtime, Dana's nerves were frayed. She sat at the far end of the break room table, half-listening as coworkers laughed about customer horror stories and weekend recaps.

Lind sat diagonally across from her, close enough to notice her quiet demeanor but far enough to give her space.

He glanced at her a few times, reading her without pressing.

Then—a coworker's voice cut through the noise. "So, Lind," they grinned. "Got any fun plans this weekend?"

Dana's stomach dropped.

She focused hard on her fork, pushing lettuce around like it was the most fascinating thing in the world.

Lind hesitated.

Just a flicker.

Then, smoothly, he answered, "Just a little getaway. Nothing too crazy."

Dana felt the words land inside her like a stone.

They shouldn't have hurt.

But they did.

She waited for someone to press further, to ask for details—but Lind didn't give them a chance.

"What about you?" he asked, his voice easy, redirecting. "Got any big plans?"

The coworker launched into a camping trip story, their enthusiasm drawing the group's attention.

Lind nodded, asking just the right follow-up questions to keep the spotlight off himself.

Dana risked a glance at him.

Their eyes met. *Did he do that for me?*

Did he know how much I needed that topic to die?

When the break ended, Dana hesitated a few extra seconds, letting the others file out first.

Lind waited for her near the door. As they walked back toward the floor, she murmured, "Thanks."

Lind played innocent. "For what?"

A small, knowing smile. "You know." *For not making it worse.*

Lind's expression softened. "I'll always try to make it better, Dana."

A pause.

"Always."

Chapter 45

Just the same Lind stuff

The bar was cozy, its warm lighting casting a soft glow over polished wood and amber-filled glasses. A low hum of conversation filled the space. Light crowd for a Tuesday night, but the blend of laughter, clinking ice, and the occasional burst of music from the speakers felt familiar. Near the window, Dana and Brenda sat across from each other, their small table scattered with cocktail napkins and empty glasses.

Brenda lifted her drink. "Cheers to surviving another workday."

Dana clinked her glass. "I'll drink to that."

They started with harmless chatter—work gossip, their boss's latest ridiculous request, a coworker's disastrous attempt at flirting. Dana swirled her drink slowly, her smile slipping as her gaze drifted toward the window.

Brenda set her glass down and leaned in.

"Okay," she said, her voice low but pointed. "Spill."

Dana hesitated, running a finger along the rim of her glass. "It's nothing, really. Just... the same Lind stuff."

Brenda arched a knowing brow. "'Stuff' doesn't sound like nothing."

Dana sighed, setting her drink aside. "It's just this weekend. The fact he's going away with Sam again."

Brenda nodded, already familiar with this pattern. "You were handling that pretty well, I thought."

"I was trying." Dana exhaled slowly. "And I still am. But it's getting to me again. He mentioned they're going to a remote cabin this time."

Brenda tilted her head. "Remote like middle-of-nowhere?"

Dana shook her head. "Not really. He said it's six minutes from town, about two hours from here. Just quieter than their usual spot."

Brenda took a sip, studying her. "And how do you feel about that?"

Dana gave a small shrug, her voice softer now. "Better than before. At least, I think so. But the thought of them together... it's like this little knot in my chest I can't untangle."

Brenda leaned back, arms crossed. "That's why we planned our girls' weekend for the same time. Distraction therapy."

Dana mustered a small smile. "Yeah. Just you, me, and the others. Two days of laughing, wine, and questionable dancing. That should keep my mind off things."

"Exactly." Brenda's tone was firm. "I even picked up extra wine. You'll be having too much fun to think about Lind."

Dana chuckled. "Here's hoping."

Brenda set her glass down with purpose. "Listen, Dana. You're doing the work—mentally, emotionally. And Lind isn't just off on some vacation without a care in the world. If he's the guy you say he is, he's probably thinking about how to make this easier for you too."

Dana tapped the rim of her glass. "That's the thing. He does try. He checks in all the time, makes sure I'm okay. I just can't get out of my own head."

Brenda's gaze softened. "Then maybe it's time to trust the effort he's putting in. And the effort *you're* putting in. This isn't about whether you're enough for Lind. It's about whether you're enough for yourself."

Dana blinked, her throat tightening.

"You're annoyingly good at this, you know that?"

"It's a gift." Brenda said, lifting her glass. "Now, cheers for the girls' weekend and all the questionable decisions we'll make."

Dana laughed, some of the tension in her chest loosening. "How many questionable decisions can we even make in a cabin in the woods?"

Brenda grinned. "Plenty. There are other cabins nearby. And the local town is five minutes away—they've got a great bar. We could get into all kinds of trouble."

Dana rolled her eyes. "You know that's not going to happen."

Brenda clinked their glasses. "I know. But isn't it nice to know it's an option?"

They both laughed. As their conversation shifted to lighter topics—what to pack, which wine to bring, and Brenda's insistence on resurrecting their old karaoke playlist—Dana felt a flicker of hope. Maybe, just maybe, she could navigate this after all.

You've been busy

The smell of roasting chicken filled Dana's kitchen. She adjusted the silverware on her dining table for the third time, an attempt to tame the nervous energy bubbling inside her.

Lind arrived right on time, a bottle of red wine in hand, his easy smile disarming as he stepped inside.

"You've been busy," he said, glancing around the spotless space.

Dana shrugged, laughing softly. "If I'm going to cook, I might as well make it look like I know what I'm doing."

He lifted the wine. "This is my contribution," he said. "Thought it might impress the chef."

Dana took the bottle, smiling. "You've already impressed me by showing up on time. That's more than most people manage."

Lind chuckled, leaning down to press a light kiss to her cheek. "High praise. I'll take it."

***

Candlelight flickered over the table, casting a glow against the deep red of their wine. Lind cut into his chicken, his fork pausing mid-air.

"This might actually rival my cooking."

Dana snorted. "I know you're lying, but I'll take the compliment."

"Maybe," Lind admitted, grinning. "But you've outdone yourself. This is really good."

Their laughter filled the small space, the clink of glasses punctuating their conversation. After dinner, Dana gathered their plates while Lind uncorked the wine, pouring them each a generous glass.

"This feels almost fancy," she mused.

Lind lifted his glass toward hers. "To midweek date nights."

"To not burning the chicken," she countered, clinking her glass against his.

They sipped in comfortable silence, the warmth of Lind's presence easing the knots in Dana's chest. But as the quiet stretched on, her thoughts stirred.

And does Sam cook

"So," Dana began, keeping her tone casual as she swirled her wine, "have you and Sam stayed at this cabin before?"

Lind nodded, resting his glass on the armrest. "Yeah, a few years ago. It's a nice spot—small, but it has everything we need. Plus, there's a lot of public land behind it for hiking."

Dana traced a fingertip along the stem of her glass, keeping her voice steady. "Is it remote enough that there's no cell service?"

"It used to be," Lind said. "The first time we went, it was completely off the grid. But now it has decent reception. Still feels pretty secluded, though."

"Sounds peaceful." She forced a small smile, though her chest tightened at the image forming in her mind—Lind and Sam, alone in a cozy cabin, their world shrinking to just the two of them. "Do you ever go into town while you're there?"

"Not usually," Lind said. "It's a small town—just a couple of shops, a coffee place, and a café with good breakfast. We mostly stick to the cabin. Hiking, talking, catching up."

Catching up. The phrase stuck, twisting in her. There was a comfort in it, an ease she wasn't part of.

"And does Sam cook?" she asked, aiming for lighthearted but feeling anything but.

Lind chuckled. "She's okay at it, but she doesn't bother much when I'm there. Cooking's kind of my thing."

Dana nodded, filing away the image of Sam leaning against the counter, watching Lind move around the kitchen with practiced ease. It shouldn't hurt—this was just a part of his life. A routine. A tradition.

"It sounds nice," she admitted, though the words tasted bitter.

"It is," Lind said quietly. His gaze didn't waver. "What Sam and I have is nice. But you and I—this—it's different Dana. This is something special, something lasting. I don't want to lose that."

She smiled faintly. *Something special?* She wanted to believe him, wanted to trust in what they had. But her mind spun with images of the cabin—Sam's laughter, their shared bed, the quiet moments between them that she would never see.

Tonight's About Us

Lind seemed to sense the tension in her. He reached over, resting his hand on hers. "Hey," he said softly. "Let's not let the weekend hang over us. Tonight's about us."

Dana swallowed hard and nodded. "You're right. Sorry. It's just... hard to ignore sometimes."

"I know." His hand covered hers, warm and grounding. "But we'll get through it—together."

His voice was steady, filled with certainty, and for a moment, she let herself believe it. Taking a deep breath, she leaned into him, allowing the warmth of his presence to soften the edges of her doubts. They let the conversation shift—work stories, old memories, easy banter that made her laugh despite the knot still coiled in her chest.

For tonight, she told herself, this was enough.

***

As the night wound down, Lind walked her to the door and he kissed her deeply, his palm warm against her cheek. "Thanks for dinner," he murmured. "And for everything else."

Dana smiled, her heart aching with a mix of love and quiet fear. She watched as he walked away, the solid weight of his presence slipping from her grasp.

Closing the door behind her, she leaned against it with a sigh. The silence of her condo smothering her, and with it, the reality she'd been pushing aside. No matter how much she tried to distract herself, Lind would still be leaving in a few days.

For now, she let the warmth of their evening carry her to bed.

He's not blind

Outside, Lind paused by his truck and tilted his head back, staring up at the scattered stars. His breath fogged in the crisp air, vanishing into the dark.

Dana's smile had been there tonight—soft, beautiful—but it hadn't reached her eyes the way it usually did.

He hated seeing her hurting—even more so because there wasn't a simple fix.

He stood there for a long moment, the night air cold against his skin, the ache of wanting to make it better burrowed deep in his chest.

He would keep showing up.

He would keep holding her.

Holding *them.*

For as long as she let him.

Part 10

I Know He Loves Me

I kept showing up.
To his bed.
His kitchen.
His life.
His world.
And every time, I asked myself the same quiet question—
Is there room for me here?

Chapter 46

Tomorrow, she would have distractions

Dana sat on the couch, scrolling through her phone. She'd spent the day trying to keep busy—cleaning, watching half a movie before turning it off, picking up a book only to stare at the same page for ten minutes.

But as the evening stretched on, her thoughts drifted back to Lind. Was he packing already? Had he left? Was he thinking about her?

Her thumb hovered over his name in her contacts. She debated calling, just to hear his voice, to anchor herself in something real. Instead, she set the phone down, her chest tightening. *I'll see him when he gets back,* she told herself.

But the reassurance felt hollow in the silence of her condo.

Her phone buzzed, breaking through her thoughts. Brenda.

You packed up yet?

Dana frowned as she typed. *Absolutely.*

Good, because we're leaving early—like 8:00! A grinning emoji followed.

Dana rolled her eyes, typing back. *8:00? Half the day will be gone by then.*

8:00 is half the day if we're at work. We're not! Be ready.

She laughed softly, tapping out her reply. *I am ready.*

It was a lie.

But it was easier than admitting she was still sitting here, staring at her phone, trying to pretend she wasn't unraveling.

See you tomorrow.

Setting the phone aside, Dana exhaled slowly. Tomorrow, she would have distractions. Laughter, wine, questionable karaoke choices.

Tonight, she had nothing but the quiet, and the thoughts that refused to let her go.

Okay, ladies, we need wine

The quaint little town buzzed with life, its main street lined with brick storefronts and colorful awnings. Locals and tourists mingled, weaving in and out of shops, their laughter blending with the occasional clang of a shop bell. The air carried the warm scent of freshly baked bread from the corner bakery, mingling with the rich aroma of coffee drifting from a nearby café.

Dana and the four other women strolled along the sidewalk, pausing to admire handmade crafts and delicate trinkets displayed in shop windows.

Brenda, as usual, led the charge, her stride purposeful. "Okay, ladies, we need wine, cheese, crackers, and something sweet. Oh, and maybe some olives. What else?"

"I thought you brought wine?" Shirley asked, turning to Dana.

"I did, but not enough," Dana said, glancing around at the charming storefronts. "We'll need two more bottles, maybe three."

"Are you sure we need more than you already brought?" Shirley asked, playfully. Laughter rippled through the group.

Dana shot a quick look to Brenda.

"Yes, Shirley, I'm sure." Dana said.

Ann grinned. "Let's not forget the sweets. There's a chocolate shop two doors down that's calling my name."

Shirley pointed toward the café across the street. "And coffee. We're going to need it for tomorrow morning if we want to survive."

Brenda chuckled. "Not a bad idea. But didn't one of you say you wanted to try that coffee shop up the street? The one with the huge chalkboard menu?"

Becky nodded enthusiastically. "Yes! I saw it online. They do pour-overs and have some kind of signature cinnamon latte. We have to go."

Dana tilted her head, smiling at their enthusiasm. "We'll need to come back into town tomorrow anyway, right? We can grab coffee before heading back home."

"Deal," Brenda said, steering them toward the wine shop. "But first, priorities. More wine and snacks. Then we get settled in at the cabin."

Inside the shop, the women split up, wandering through rows of bottles. Dana picked up a rosé, running her fingers along the label, and for the briefest moment, her thoughts drifted to Lind. He'd like this kind of small-town charm. A grin crossed her face but she pushed the thought away, focusing on the here and now, on the laughter around her as the group debated between a bold red and a crisp white.

Outside, their arms full of brown paper bags, they made their way to the chocolate shop. The rich aroma of cocoa wrapped around them as they stepped inside, the glass cases filled with decadent truffles and bark. Each woman picked out an assortment, sneaking a taste as they exited onto the sun-warmed sidewalk.

As they walked toward the car, Dana glanced at Brenda. "So, what's the plan for tonight? Do we cook, or are we just grazing on all this?"

"Grazing," Brenda answered with a grin. "There's no way I'm cooking. We've got wine, cheese, and chocolate. What else do we need?"

"Men?" Ann said, teasing. The group laughed as they piled into the car, their spirits light, the trunk packed with their finds. The short drive to the cabin was filled with easy chatter and music from the radio, anticipation humming in the air.

The sun was high, casting shadows through the trees as they pulled up. The cabin sat nestled in the woods, its wooden porch inviting, the scent of pine in the air.

"This is perfect," Becky said, setting down a bag of goodies. "I can already feel the stress melting away."

Dana looked around, the stillness of the forest wrapping around her like a comforting blanket. She exhaled slowly, letting the tension drain from her shoulders.

"Yeah," she murmured. "This is exactly what I needed."

As they unpacked and arranged their snacks and drinks, the conversation shifted to their plans for the evening—and, of course, the much-anticipated coffee run in the morning.

Shirley raised her coffee mug in a mock toast. "Here's to tonight. And here's to cinnamon lattes tomorrow."

Dana chuckled, the warmth of their easy camaraderie chasing away some of the uneasiness in her chest. Maybe, for this weekend at least, she could let herself breathe.

He's with her right now

The cabin porch creaked softly under Dana's chair as she swirled her wine, the deep red catching the last hues of the setting sun. A short distance away, the other women sat around the fire pit, their laughter weaving through the cool evening air, punctuated by the occasional crackle of burning wood. The scent of pine mixed with the smokiness of the fire, wrapping the night in a crisp stillness.

They could see at least three other cabins, people milling around, and the soft, inaudible sounds of other conversations.

Dana sat in a quiet bubble, lost in thought. Brenda sat beside her in a weathered wooden chair, her glass held loosely in one hand.

"You know," Dana murmured, staring at the rim of her glass, "on the way here, I almost... drove by his place."

Brenda paused mid-sip, her gaze flicking toward Dana. "Why?"

Dana let out a sharp breath, frustration laced in her voice. "To see if his truck was still there. To know if he'd already left."

Brenda studied her carefully before leaning back, exhaling slowly. "But you didn't."

Dana shook her head, gripping the stem of her glass tighter. "No. His place is in the opposite direction, and I knew it'd just... make me feel worse. So I fought it. But it was hard, Brenda. It was really hard."

Brenda nodded, her voice even. "That was the right call, Dana. Driving by wouldn't have changed anything—except making you spiral more. I know it's tough, but you've got to let this go. You're not going to find peace by chasing after answers that don't exist."

Dana snorted softly, though there was no humor in it. "Yeah, well, it doesn't feel like I'll find peace any other way, either."

Brenda set her glass on the small table between them, her expression shifting. "Dana, what are you really afraid of? That he's with Sam? Or that he's not thinking about you while he's with her?"

Dana stared into her wine, watching the liquid swirl. Her voice wavered. "Both, I guess. I know he cares about me. He tells me all the time. But when he's with her... and he's with her *right now*... I can't stop wondering if I'm enough. If I'll ever be enough."

Brenda's gaze softened. "Dana, you're enough. You've always been enough. This isn't about you being second best or some kind of backup plan. It's about Lind having room in his life for more than one connection."

Dana frowned, shaking her head. "I know that logically. And Lind has told me that several times. But it's hard to *feel* it sometimes. Especially when I think about how easy it is for him to switch between us."

Brenda's voice was gentle but firm. "You're giving him a lot of credit for being 'easy.' But relationships like this aren't simple for anyone. The fact that he's open with you, that he's showing you how much you mean to him—that says a lot."

Dana sighed, setting her glass beside Brenda's. "I just don't know if I'm built for this kind of relationship."

Brenda hesitated before choosing her words carefully. "You'd be surprised what you're capable of, Dana. And sometimes, the hardest part is learning to trust yourself—not just him."

Dana blinked, caught off guard. "That sounds... oddly specific."

Brenda laughed, her tone easy but knowing. "Maybe I've learned a thing or two over the years. Let's just say, if Lind's willing to put in the work, maybe you should give yourself a little credit too."

Dana leaned back in her chair, letting Brenda's words wash over her. The tight knot in her chest loosened—just a little.

"Thanks, Brenda. I mean it."

Brenda raised her glass. "Anytime. And for the record? You're doing great. Don't let that little green monster in your head tell you otherwise."

Dana chuckled, clinking her glass against Brenda's. "I'll try. No promises, though."

The fire crackled in the distance, their laughter weaving into the night. For the first time in a while, Dana let herself believe she might actually find her way through.

***

The little coffee shop sat on the corner of Main Street, its weathered brick facade and large windows catching the early morning sunlight. A cheerful bell jingled as Dana pushed open the door, stepping inside with the other four women. Their laughter blended with the quiet murmur of conversation, the warmth of the shop wrapping around them.

The scent of freshly ground coffee beans filled the air, laced with hints of cinnamon and vanilla. The place was lively but not overcrowded, the kind of cozy that made people linger over their drinks just a little longer. A large chalkboard menu stretched across the back wall, its colorful handwriting listing lattes, brews, and specialty drinks with playful names.

"This place is adorable," Brenda said, glancing around as they stepped into line. "Why don't we have anything like this back home?"

Dana grinned, nudging her with an elbow. "Because you don't go anywhere unless it has a drive-thru."

Brenda scoffed. "Drive-thru convenience is hard to beat, but this? Totally worth the detour."

Shirley grinned. "I still think we should move in. Just claim a corner and never leave."

When it was their turn to order, they chose a mix of drinks—lattes, americanos, and the signature cinnamon latte Brenda had insisted on trying. They added a tray of pastries to share: buttery croissants, flaky danishes, and warm, gooey cinnamon rolls.

Armed with their drinks and food, they grabbed a table near the window. Sunlight streamed through the glass, casting a golden glow over their little corner.

Becky stirred her cappuccino, watching the froth swirl. "So," she said, glancing around the table, "what's everyone's takeaway from this weekend? Did it live up to the hype?"

Dana held her latte with both hands, letting the spiced warmth seep into her fingers. "Absolutely. It was exactly what I needed—good company, good wine, and no distractions."

"You mean men?" Ann asked, "because I could've used that kind of distraction." She giggled.

"Yes, I mean men," Dana said, her brow tightened, her lips curled down.

"It could've been nice for us single girls." Ann said, ignoring Dana's look.

"I'm just saying this was about getting away and relieving stress," Dana retorted, "you know, the opposite of men."

Brenda jumped in, nodding. "I agree—less stress. This was a nice weekend, I feel human again. And this coffee? Definitely worth the trip back into town." She was watching Dana, and steering the conversation away from her thoughts of Lind.

Shirley leaned back, her mug cradled in both hands. "I agree, but if we do this again next year, we need to extend it. Overnight isn't long enough."

A murmur of agreement passed through the table. Brenda glanced Dana's way and offered a quiet, knowing smile.

They finished polishing off their pastries, their plates and cups emptying faster than they'd realized.

Outside, the morning sunlight had risen higher, warming the quiet streets.

The ache of missing Lind

After their coffee stop, the group made their way to the small gas station on the edge of town. Dana took the driver's seat, slipping behind the wheel as the others wandered inside to grab bottles of water and road trip snacks.

She let her head rest against the seat for a moment, staring out at the sleepy little town. The weekend *had* passed too quickly, but for the first time in a long while, she felt lighter—like she could finally breathe without the weight pressing so hard against her chest.

When the others returned and buckled in, Dana started the engine, pulling onto the main road. The town shrank in the rearview mirror, giving way to rolling fields and stretches of open highway. The road ahead blurred into green and gold as the trees flashed by, the miles carrying them back toward their everyday lives.

The conversation in the car drifted between the weekend's highlights, plans for the upcoming week, and the inevitable grind of returning to work. But the laughter continued, filling the space between them.

Dana listened, smiling at their easy chatter. The ache of missing Lind tugged at her, a quiet pulse beneath everything else, but it no longer felt like it would swallow her whole.

She had her friends.

She had her own strength.

And for the first time in weeks, she believed she could face whatever came next.

Chapter 47

I know he loves me

The store hummed with its usual Monday morning routine. The morning meeting was quick—just long enough for assignments to be handed out before everyone dispersed onto the floor. Dana and Lind hadn't even made eye contact, let alone spoken.

She wasn't sure if that was a good thing or a bad thing.

Near the entrance, she arranged a display of summer picnic supplies, aligning bright plasticware beside neatly folded tablecloths. The cheerful scene contrasted sharply with the quiet war in her chest. The weekend with the girls had helped. Brenda's words lingered, gentle reminders she was trying to hold onto.

I know he loves me. I am enough.

But waking up this morning had changed everything. The creeping unease, the doubt, the jealousy—it had all come flooding back, no longer dulled by the distractions of laughter and wine.

Lind's voice pulled her from her thoughts.

She heard him before she saw him, his easy laugh carrying across the floor as he greeted a coworker. The sound tightened something inside her.

Then, suddenly, he was there. His eyes lit up when they met hers, his smile warm, familiar.

"Morning," he said.

Dana forced a polite smile. "Morning."

Lind studied her face for a moment before asking, "How was your weekend?"

"It was fine," she replied lightly. "Had a good time with the girls."

"That's good." His smile deepened. "I'm glad you got away for a bit."

"Yeah. It was nice." Her voice was steady, but her thoughts weren't. *Did you have fun? What did you do with her? Did you think about me at all?*

Lind's brow furrowed. "You okay?"

Dana busied herself straightening a stack of paper plates, avoiding his gaze. "Yeah, just tired. Mondays, you know?"

He didn't press, but his voice softened. "Let me know if you want to talk."

She nodded quickly. "Sure. Thanks."

As he moved on, she exhaled slowly, her shoulders sagging. *He's acting so normal.* Like nothing had changed. Like he hadn't just spent the weekend with Sam.

***

The morning dragged. Dana moved from the picnic display to restocking sunscreen, her hands moving automatically while her mind raced. She could hear Lind occasionally—his voice, his laughter, the effortless way he chatted with their coworkers. Each time, her chest tightened.

How could he sound so... unaffected?

By lunchtime, she'd almost convinced herself to let it go. *Almost.*

She sat in the break room, pushing a few grapes around in her container when Lind walked in. His smile was instant, brightening at the sight of her, and that only made the ache in her chest sharper.

"Mind if I join you?" he asked, holding up his sandwich.

She hesitated but nodded. "Sure."

Lind sat across from her, unwrapping his food. "So," he started, his tone light, "any funny stories from your weekend with the girls?"

Dana forced a small smile. "Nothing wild. We explored the town Saturday, hung out at the cabin the rest of the time. Brenda kept us laughing, as usual."

Lind chuckled. "Sounds like a good time. I'm glad you had fun."

His easy warmth twisted something inside her. She wanted to ask about his weekend, but the words stuck in her throat.

Instead, she took a sip of water. "Yeah, it was nice to get away."

A beat of silence. Then, Lind's tone shifted slightly.

"So, about Wednesday. Want to hang out at my place this time? I'll cook something."

Dana's heart skipped. "Your place?"

He nodded, his expression open. "Yeah, if that's okay. Thought it might be nice to switch it up."

Her mind raced. *If I go to his place, I can leave whenever I want. If he comes to mine... he might... stay.* She knew Lind would do whatever she asked, but going to *his* place gave her control.

"Yeah, your place sounds good," she said finally, keeping her voice steady. "What time?"

"Five?" He smiled, hopeful.

She nodded. "Five works."

His grin widened. "Great. I'll text you later with the details."

"Details?" she asked, confused.

"You know, like what to bring," he said, smirking. "Bread, wine, work clothes."

"Oh." She forced a smile. "Right."

As he finished his lunch and got up, he reached out, squeezing her shoulder. "Can't wait," he murmured before heading out.

Dana managed a faint smile until he was out of sight. Then, the weight returned, pressing heavy against her ribs.

The rest of the day blurred—tasks completed on autopilot, half-hearted conversations, her mind circling the same thought:

He's acting so normal. Like nothing's changed. Like he didn't just spend the weekend with Sam. Like he didn't sleep with her, like they didn't... She had to stop thinking.

By the time her shift ended, the knot in her chest had tightened again.

Why is it always Sam

Wednesday was Lind's turn. The apartment smelled of garlic and fresh herbs as Dana stepped inside, the warmth of the space a welcome contrast to the crisp evening air.

The small dining table was set simply but thoughtfully—two plates, a bottle of wine, a flickering candle.

He greeted her with a soft smile and a quick kiss on the cheek.

"Dinner's almost ready," he said, nodding toward the kitchen. "We're doing pasta again, our favorite."

"Pasta sounds perfect," Dana replied, shrugging off her jacket and draping it over the back of a chair. "Garlic bread?" she asked.

"Of course," he said, stirring sauce, checking the pasta, the quiet sounds filling the space. Dana sat at the table, watching the smooth efficiency of his movements. Soon, he set two steaming bowls in front of them and poured their wine, and set out the bread.

"Bon appétit," he said with a small grin.

They ate in comfortable silence for a few minutes, the rich garlicky sauce easing some of Dana's tension.

Then Lind leaned back slightly, looking at her.

"So," he said, warmth in his voice, "tell me more about your weekend with the girls."

Dana sipped her wine, her mind flickering back to the cabin, the laughter, the fleeting moments of peace. "It was nice. We rented a cabin at a resort about an hour away. Spent Saturday poking around the little town, had wine by the fire that night, and Sunday morning we found this adorable coffee shop." She let out a soft breath. "It was... good. Relaxing."

Lind nodded, his expression thoughtful. "Sounds great. I'm glad you got a chance to unwind."

She hesitated. Then, carefully, "What about you? How was your weekend?"

The question was out before she could stop herself.

She wasn't sure she wanted to hear the answer.

Or if she'd like how it made her feel.

Lind's pause was brief but noticeable. "We stayed at a cabin, too," he said, setting his wine glass down. "It's a couple of hours out, backs up to public land, as I told you. We spent most of the time hiking, getting off the grid a bit. Stopped in town to try this little coffee shop that we spotted there. Quiet, tucked away."

Dana's fork paused mid-air. "Why don't we ever do that?"

Lind frowned slightly. "Do what?"

"Go to a cabin. Hike. Spend the weekend somewhere quiet." Her voice sharpened, unbidden. "Why is it always Sam?"

His posture remained relaxed, but his eyes studied her carefully. "It's not *always* Sam," he said evenly, though there was a quiet correction in his tone. "We've done hikes together before, but... I get why it feels that way."

Frustration swelled in Dana's chest. "Then explain it to me, Lind. Because from where I'm sitting, she gets the best parts of you. The quiet weekends, the hiking, the *off-the-grid* stuff. The things I'd love to do with you."

Lind sighed, his fingers tracing the base of his glass. "Dana... we do a *lot* together. More than you're remembering right now."

His words gave her pause, a quiet truth, a realization.

But the feeling still nagged at her, an ache that whispered Sam had something with Lind that she didn't.

Why can't I do that for you

Lind exhaled, running a hand through his hair. "It's not about her getting the best parts of me. It's about... balance. Sam is like a pressure valve for me."

Dana's stomach twisted. "What does that even mean?"

He leaned forward, resting his arms on the table. "It's like this—life, society, everything we're expected to be—it builds up. The conformity, the pressure, the noise. It's like—a prison. Most of the time, I deal with it. I function. But every so often, it gets to be too much, and I need a way to let it out. To clear my head. That's what my weekends with Sam are... a reset."

Dana blinked, confusion colliding with frustration, tinged with anger. "A reset from what?"

Lind's voice softened and his head tilted. "From *everything*." His words were measured, careful. "Sam has this way of helping me let go of all the garbage I carry. Her life, her presence, her touch—it strips all of that away. She *resets* me."

A sharp pang shot through Dana's chest. "Why can't *I* do that for you?"

"I believe someday you will. That's why I love you, it's one of the reasons I'm with you." He hesitated, his voice steady but low. "I think we're going to be exactly what each other needs... to balance out our lives, to be *happy*. But not until you recognize the prison you're in, too."

Dana's breath caught, a hollow ache expanding in her chest. "What prison?"

Lind sighed, his gaze steady. "The same one I'm trying to escape from. The expectations. The compromises. The roles we're all taught to play. You don't see it yet, but you're locked in there—just like me. Until you're free, you can't help me get free."

She shook her head, her voice low and strained. "I don't understand what you're saying. Any of it."

"I know," Lind admitted softly. "And I don't expect you to right now."

Dana gripped the stem of her wine glass, staring into its depths, trying to make sense of his words. She *wanted* to argue, to demand that he explain it in a way she could understand. But she didn't even know where to start.

Across the table, Lind watched her quietly, not pushing further. The candle flickered between them, the only steady thing in the room.

That is the prison, Dana

Lind took a slow breath, leaning back in his chair. The weight of Dana's confusion and frustration hung heavy between them, but not immovable. He reached for his wine, swirling the liquid thoughtfully.

"Dana," he said gently, meeting her eyes, "we're all told we're free. That we can be whoever we want. But only *within* a tiny, acceptable box. Step outside of it, and people look at you differently. They judge you. Pressure you back in."

Dana frowned, her irritation shifting into something closer to curiosity. "What does that have to do with... Sam? With *us*?"

Lind set his glass down. "Think of those cackling geese at work. The ones who judge everyone else's lives based on their narrow little worldviews."

Dana's lips twitched, despite everything. "You mean like last week, when they said any woman over thirty who isn't married must have 'baggage'?"

Lind chuckled. "Exactly. That's an extreme example, but it's the same idea. We're all expected to follow these unwritten rules—how to act, what to believe... who to love. And *you hate it*. I know you do. I see it every time you roll your eyes at their bullshit."

She tilted her head slightly, some of the tension in her shoulders easing. "Yeah, it's ridiculous. But what does that have to do with this 'prison' you're talking about?"

Lind's tone grew earnest. "That *is* the prison, Dana. The invisible walls. You don't see them until you start questioning the rules."

Dana leaned in, her unease still present but softened by curiosity. "So, Sam... she's outside the box?"

"She's not just outside of it," Lind said with a small smile. "She's never lived within it! She doesn't care what people think or what they expect. When I'm with her, it's like all that weight disappears. She reminds me of who I am *without* the rules."

Dana's gaze dropped to her glass, her fingers tracing the rim. "And you think I'm still stuck in there."

"I think *we're all* stuck in there," Lind said gently. "But you're already pushing against the bars. You see it, even if you don't fully understand it yet."

He looked at her thoughtfully. "Let me give you an example of why I think that."

"Okay," Dana said hesitantly. "Go ahead."

"You knew all about Sam in my life before we started... *this*," Lind pointed out, "and here we are making it work."

With the way Dana had been feeling lately, she wasn't sure she'd call it *making it work*.

"You are stepping outside the box," he said, "a foot, or maybe just a toe, but outside the box. Wondering what's out there."

She exhaled slowly, her expression softer now. "And you think I'll get out eventually?"

Lind's smile was small, but sure. "I believe you'll find your way out in your own time. And when you do, we'll figure out the rest together."

Dana let his words play over in her mind, their weight both comforting and unsettling. She wanted to believe him—to trust that whatever he was trying to explain would one day make sense.

But right now, it didn't.

Right now, she just knew that Sam had something with Lind that she didn't.

Still, she nodded, her voice quiet but steady. "Okay. I'm... really not sure I understand what you mean, but I'll try."

Lind reached across the table, his hand resting lightly over hers. "That's all I'm asking."

The tension between them eased, though the shadow of doubt remained.

As they finished their meal and drifted into their usual banter, Dana felt the weight in her chest lighten *just* a little.

Lind's words still swirled in her mind—pieces of a puzzle she couldn't quite put together.

But for now, it was enough to keep moving forward.

Whatever my Dana needs

Later, they sat on Lind's couch, the soft flicker of the television casting shadows along the walls. A classic sitcom played, filling the space with laughter, and Dana couldn't help but dissolve into it, her body tucked against Lind's side, his arm resting comfortably around her shoulders.

For the first time all evening, her mind felt still. No spiraling thoughts, no weight pressing down on her chest—just warmth, closeness, and the simple joy of laughter.

"See?" Lind said, nudging her gently. "Laughter's the best medicine."

Dana tilted her head, glancing up at him with a soft smile. "You're not wrong."

As the credits rolled, Lind grabbed the remote, muting the TV before stretching his arms behind his head. His voice was light, but his eyes held quiet curiosity as he turned to her.

"So," he said, "you didn't bring work clothes tonight. Planning an early escape?"

Dana sat up slightly, running her fingers through her hair. "No, I didn't." She hesitated, then admitted, "Honestly, I wasn't sure what to expect tonight. After everything you said at dinner... it didn't feel right to assume I'd stay over. Not with everything I've been feeling."

Lind's brow furrowed slightly, but he didn't interrupt.

Dana sighed, searching for the right words. "It just didn't feel right. Though..." She let out a quiet laugh, blushing slightly. "I'll admit, I'm tempted now."

"You know you're always welcome," Lind said gently, his hazel eyes steady on hers. "No expectations, no pressure."

"I know." Her voice softened, his patience both comforting and supportive. "But I think I should go home tonight. Give myself some space to rethink things. To process."

Lind nodded, his expression soft. "Okay, I understand. Whatever my Dana needs."

She liked the sound of that, *my Dana*.

But still, she stood, gathering her things, and paused before stepping away. "Do you have any ideas for the weekend? Something low-key?"

Lind leaned back against the couch, considering. "How about Friday night here? I'll cook, and you can stay over if you want. Then Saturday, we could take a day trip to the lake. It's been a while since I've been out there, and the weather's supposed to be nice."

Dana gave a small, knowing smile. "That sounds good."

"We'll come back to my place Saturday night," Lind continued, his tone casual, as if he weren't mapping out an entire weekend just for them. "You can stay over again if you'd like, and Sunday morning, I'll make breakfast. We could catch a movie afterward if you're up for it."

She tilted her head, her smile softening. "You've got it all planned out."

"I try," Lind said with a grin. "What do you think?"

"I think I like it," Dana replied. "It'll be nice to have a whole weekend together. Just us."

Lind stood and walked her to the door, pausing as she slipped on her jacket. He reached out and brushed his thumb along the bridge of her nose before leaning in to kiss her.

"Drive safe, okay?" His voice was quieter now, his eyes searching hers. "And text me when you get home."

"Don't I always?" Dana grinned, as she leaned in, pressing a light kiss to his lips. "Goodnight."

"Goodnight," Lind murmured, his smile lingering as she stepped out into the cool night air.

Thinking of you. Goodnight

The drive home was quiet, the streetlights casting rhythmic glows along the road. Dana gripped the steering wheel, her mind replaying the night—the easy laughter, the warmth of Lind's body beside hers, the softness in his voice when he told her to drive safe.

Had she made the right choice in leaving?

Her fingers tapped absently against the wheel. Space. That's what she needed, wasn't it? To think, to breathe, to figure out where she stood in all of this?

But even now, with the distance she'd asked for, she wanted him.

Dana exhaled, her fingers drumming lightly against the wheel as she pulled into her complex. She could still feel the weight of Lind's hand against her cheek, the warmth of his lips lingering on hers. She wanted to be strong, to take the space she knew she needed.

But damn, she also wanted him.

Maybe she'll tease him a little.

A slow wicked smile curled her lips as an idea took shape.

Lind's phone chimed just after he'd climbed into bed, the familiar notification tone catching his attention. He glanced at the time—she'd taken longer than usual to text. A flicker of concern crossed his mind as he unlocked the screen.

Then his breath caught.

It was a selfie—Dana, in bed, her face flushed, her bare skin glowing softly in the lamplight. The angle framed the curve of her breasts, the peak of her nipples, the slow arch of her body. And below, nestled between her thighs, the unmistakable presence of her vibrator in action.

Her message was simple: *Thinking of you. Goodnight. Sweet dreams.*

Lind blinked, then let out a low, stunned laugh. His fingers flexed against his phone, his entire body reacting before his brain caught up. Heat pinged between his legs, and he exhaled slowly, shaking his head at the audacity of it.

You don't play fair, woman, he typed back quickly, shaking his head as he smirked at the screen.

I'll be thinking about you all night. You know I can't sleep hard—see you tomorrow.

Setting the phone down, he exhaled, still grinning. The warmth of her kiss at the door, now layered with the image she had burned into his mind.

She might have needed space.

But she also needed him.

They needed each other.

Chapter 48

There you were, in all your glory

The apartment was warm and inviting, the rich aroma of spices filling the air as Lind moved around the kitchen. Dana sat on his couch, a soft blanket draped over her lap. She flipped through her phone, the familiar rhythm of their evening easing her tension.

"What's cooking tonight, Chef?" Dana called, her tone light and relaxed.

Lind turned, a wooden spoon in hand and a grin on his face. "Chicken curry. Think you can handle a little heat?"

"Bring it on," she challenged, sitting up straighter. "But don't forget—last time, you promised me something sweet if I survived."

"Fair enough," Lind said, stirring the pot. "Dessert is in the freezer—ice cream with your name on it."

Dana laughed softly, surprising even herself. "You always know how to bribe me."

"It's a skill," Lind replied, flashing her a playful wink before turning back to the stove.

As they ate at the small dining table, their conversation flowed easily. Dana recounted a funny encounter with a customer at work, and Lind shared a story about a childhood hiking trip gone hilariously wrong. The tension of the past week was tucked away for now, as neither wished to address it, choosing instead to focus on the comfort of the moment.

After dinner, they moved to the couch, a movie playing softly in the background. Dana leaned against Lind, his arm draped casually over her shoulders, his thumb gliding back and forth against her warm skin.

During a commercial break, Lind chuckled softly, breaking the comfortable silence.

"What's so funny?" Dana asked, glancing up at him.

He looked down at her, his eyes sparkling with amusement. "Just thinking about that text you sent me Wednesday night. You know, the one where you weren't playing fair."

Dana's cheeks flushed, a mischievous grin spreading across her lips. "Oh, that one?" she said innocently.

"Yes, that one," Lind replied, his voice warm with humor. "I was lying in bed, a little worried you hadn't text sooner, and then boom—there you were, in all your... glory."

Dana laughed, leaning into him. "I was just trying to make sure you got some sweet dreams."

"Oh, I got them," Lind said as he winked at her. "And I'm still recovering!"

They shared a laugh, the moment breaking through any lingering tension.

Later, as they lay in bed, they held each other close in their usual spooning position. Dana pressed herself tightly against Lind, feeling his excitement at having her there. His arm draped protectively over her, her hand cradling his. The earlier playfulness faded into quiet affection. Neither of them made any moves for more intimacy; instead, they were content to simply be.

"I love this," Dana murmured, her voice soft in the darkness.

"Me too," Lind replied, his lips against the back of her head.

They drifted off to sleep, wrapped in each other's arms.

I Really Miss Not Being Upset With You

They made a quick stop at his favorite coffee place, more crowded than usual on a Saturday morning. Dana had to admit they had the better sweet roll, worth standing in line for—with coffees in hand, they were off to the lake.

The drive was filled with music and light conversation. Dana stared out the window, watching the countryside blur into a patchwork of green and gold. Lind reached over to rest a hand on her knee, giving it a gentle squeeze. She took his hand in hers, holding it there for a while before bringing it up to her lips and pressing a soft kiss against his knuckles. Then she lowered their hands to rest on the console between them.

"You doing okay?" he asked, his tone gentle.

"Yeah," Dana replied, glancing at him with a small smile. "Thanks, this was a good idea."

They unpacked a picnic blanket and basket near the water under a big shade tree. They loved this spot. The first time they came here, they'd camped out overnight, fished in the early morning, and made coffee over a camp stove.

Every time they'd returned since—just a handful, really—they'd ended up right here, spreading out a blanket beneath this same tree. It had good shade, easy access to the water, and trails they both liked. It had quietly become *their* spot.

Dana kicked off her sandals and let the cool grass tickle her feet.

Lind handed her a sandwich and a bottle of water. "You know, you don't give yourself enough credit for being outdoorsy."

Dana raised an eyebrow, taking a bite of her sandwich. "I think I'm more 'outdoor chic.' I like nature, but I also like showers."

He laughed. "Yeah. But you always hold your own out here."

She smiled knowingly at him.

They spent the afternoon walking along the trails, their conversations drifting between light topics and comfortable silence. At one point, Lind stopped, shading his eyes as he pointed to a hawk circling overhead. Dana followed his gaze, but her attention soon shifted to him—the way his hazel eyes tracked the hawk's movement, the calm that seemed to radiate from him in the quiet of nature.

As he watched the hawk soar in slow, lazy circles, Dana let herself focus on the moment. Her thoughts grounded themselves in the present, away from doubts, from Sam, from expectations. She centered herself on how she felt about him right now. She stepped closer, gently reaching up to pull him down to her. Their lips met, soft and unhurried.

"I really miss... not being upset with you," she murmured against his mouth, her words tentative but honest.

Lind smiled faintly, his forehead resting lightly against hers. "If we stay in the present moment as much as possible, it makes it harder to be upset."

Dana gave a quiet laugh, her smile slowly forming. "Yep, that's why I'm saying it," she said, leaning into him, her voice softer now. "You make it easier to stay here."

Her words hung in the air as she kissed him again, this time with more intention, letting the warmth of their connection push away her doubts.

The rest of their walk continued in easy conversation, the comfort between them almost natural. By the time they reached the truck, Dana felt lighter. They stood there, her arms around his waist as he leaned against the truck, his arms wrapped securely around her.

Neither spoke as they stood there, the afternoon sun casting long shadows around them. Lind held her, not rushing, not moving, just being with her for as long as she needed. And for the first time in what felt like weeks, Dana allowed herself to simply be held, the weight of her worries lifting, if only for a while.

Today was nice

The savory aroma of chicken cordon bleu filled Lind's apartment, the scent of crispy breading, melted cheese, and smoky ham mingling with the warmth of the kitchen. Dana stood at the counter, whisking a rich, creamy Dijon sauce while Lind worked beside her, keeping an eye on the oven.

"You know," Dana said, tapping the whisk against the bowl, "for two people who spend so much time in a store, you'd think we'd have better cooking skills."

Lind huffed as he checked the timer. "Hey, I know exactly what I'm doing. You, on the other hand..." He glanced at the sauce with mock skepticism.

Dana scoffed. "Excuse you, this sauce is going to be *perfect*."

"We'll see," he said, nudging her with his hip as he reached for the roasted asparagus cooling on the stove top. "Worst case, we drown everything in wine and call it gourmet."

Dana laughed, shaking her head as she turned off the burner. "For the record, this is a step up from all the pasta we've been eating."

Lind chuckled. "I figured we needed variety. Next time, I was thinking steak and baked potatoes."

"Now you're talking my language."

By the time the food was plated, the counter was a mess of breadcrumbs, stray cheese shavings, and flour-dusted utensils, but neither of them seemed to care. They carried their plates to the small dining table, the glow of candlelight flickering between them.

Dana sliced into her chicken, watching the melted Swiss and ham ooze from the center. She took a bite and let out a satisfied hum. "Okay, I take it back. You *do* know what you're doing."

Lind looked up at her as he took his own bite. "Told you."

They stayed at the table long after the food was gone, sipping wine and drifting into quieter conversation. Dana swirled her wine, watching the liquid catch the light.

"Today was... nice," she murmured.

Lind nodded, his gaze steady on hers. "It was. I needed it too."

The comfortable quiet between them filled the space as Dana felt her tension begin to dissolve—not completely, but enough.

With a wicked little smirk

Later, as they settled into bed, Lind wrapped an arm around Dana, pulling her close. He pressed a soft kiss to her temple, his voice low and gentle. "Thanks for today."

Dana nestled against him, resting her palm lightly on his chest, feeling the steady rhythm of his heartbeat beneath her fingertips. She tilted her head, her lips playful against his neck in a quiet, tentative invitation.

Lind responded in kind, his hand gliding down her back, fingers tracing a slow familiar path that sent shivers through her skin.

Dana shifted herself up until his face was against her chest, cradling his head as his lips, tongue, and teeth played over her nipples. The soft sounds escaping her urged him on, her hands threading through his hair in silent approval.

His fingers found their way between her legs, touching, coaxing, drawing sharp breaths from her. She reached down, guiding him exactly where she needed him most. With a gentle push against his shoulder, she rolled him onto his back, climbing on top straddling him, her body pressed against his as she matched his touch with her own.

Sitting up, she gave him space to continue exploring her, her own hand wrapped around him, stroking him in return. She watched the way his face twisted with pleasure, the way his breath hitched as she tightened her grip. The sight alone made her ache. The need to feel him inside her became overwhelming.

She guided him into her, the sensation sending a simultaneous shudder through both of them as he entered her. Their mutual gasps filled the quiet room, the slow rhythm building naturally between them.

Lind rolled her onto her back, her legs wrapping around him, pulling him deeper. Their movements quickened, the tension between them mounting until it unraveled all at once—Dana's cry of pleasure muffled against his shoulder, her climax tightened around him, drawing his own release with a deep groan, pleasure bursting through him in raw, shuddering waves, rolling out to all parts of his body. As he collapsed against her.

After a moment, he shifted to the side, pulling her with him so they lay face to face. Soft kisses, lingering touches, their breathing gradually slowing.

Dana slipped out of bed, returning a few minutes later with a warm washcloth. She knelt beside him, cleaning him gently, her eyes tracing over him with quiet appreciation. Her fingers were playful as she dried him off, trailing lightly along his length, watching him flinch at the sensitivity.

With a wicked little smirk, she took him briefly into her mouth, flicking her tongue over his head—just to see him react.

He flinched. "Tease," he muttered, his voice stuttering.

Dana smiled, reaching up to kiss him softly before returning the cloth and towel to the bathroom.

When she got back under the covers, their bodies naturally entwining. Dana's fingers traced lazy patterns over his chest and stomach, occasionally drifting lower just to make him chuckle.

Her voice was a whisper in the dark. "Thank you."

Lind kissed the top of her head, his hand covering hers. "Anytime."

In the stillness Dana allowed herself to believe that they could find their way back to each other—one day at a time. And today had been one of those days.

Chapter 49

You're spoiling me

The rich scent of coffee pulled Dana from sleep. She threw on one of Lind's T-shirts and followed the scent into the kitchen, her bare legs chilled against the hardwood as she pulled the shirt down in front. She found him flipping pancakes, his hair a rumpled mess, his T-shirt and boxers slightly askew.

She smiled, leaning against the counter. "Good morning, sleepyhead," he said, glancing over at her.

"Morning." Her eyes flicked to the pancakes. "You're spoiling me."

"Always," Lind said with a grin. "Eat up. We've got a big day ahead."

Dana giggled, spinning back toward the bedroom. "I should put on more clothes if I'm sitting down to eat."

Lind didn't argue, only watched her disappear into the bedroom, unable to help but admire the view.

After breakfast, Dana joined him in the shower, their laughter echoing in the small space as they playfully fought over the hot water. Soap-slicked hands slid over skin, kisses pressed between bursts of laughter, touches lingered longer than needed... but less than they wanted. The intimacy was lighthearted and unhurried, a moment of normalcy that eased Dana's heart in ways she hadn't expected.

She allowed herself to hope

The scent of buttered popcorn filled the air as they walked into the theater, their fingers loosely laced together. Dana felt a quiet happiness, a rare moment where she wasn't overthinking, where she wasn't bracing for the ache of Sam's presence to creep back in.

"You know," she said, glancing at Lind as they found their seats, "we haven't done this in a while."

"We'll have to make it a regular thing," he replied, giving her hand a soft squeeze. "As long as you won't hog the popcorn."

She grinned at him, "no promises."

As the lights dimmed and the previews began, Dana exhaled, allowing herself to sink into the moment.

The shadow of Sam felt faint—still there, wandering in the corners of her mind, but vague enough that it didn't consume her.

She knew it wasn't gone; It would creep back in eventually.

But right now, in the quiet dark of the theater, with Lind's fingers warm in hers, she allowed herself to hope, to be.

Hope that they were finding their way back to each other, and staying in the moment.

Fridays, Saturdays and, Sundays

A steady familiar rhythm set in over the next two months, a welcome calm that Dana needed. While the shadow of Sam taunted her now and then, the time she spent with Lind softened its edges, making it easier to ignore.

Sundays became mini-adventures—small, shared moments that felt like their own kind of escape. One weekend, they rented kayaks at a nearby river, the late-morning sun glinting off the water as they paddled out into the current.

"You're going to eat my wake," Dana challenged, digging into the water with her paddle as she surged ahead.

Lind laughed, adjusting his strokes. "I didn't realize it was a race. Let me show you how it's done."

A playful splash sent water arcing toward her, Dana shrieking and laughing as she retaliated. By the time they reached shore, both were drenched, breathless, their faces flushed with laughter.

***

Friday nights, in contrast, were quiet and cozy. At Lind's apartment, Dana sat cross-legged on the couch, shuffling a deck of cards.

"You're going to lose this time," she said, her tone mock-serious.

"You've been saying that all night," Lind replied with a lopsided grin. "And yet, here I sit—only missing my shoes."

"Not for long," she said, down to just her panties, dealing the next hand with a determined glint in her eye.

Their banter carried them late into the night, punctuated by laughter, longing, and desire that occupied them long after the game ended.

***

At work, they maintained professional distance, but there were moments that carried a spark of risk.

In the stockroom one afternoon, Lind handed Dana a box of supplies, catching her eye as their fingers touched.

"Careful," she murmured, glancing around. "Someone might think you like me."

Lind leaned slightly closer, his eyes glinting with amusement. "What if I do?"

Dana's cheeks warmed as she turned back to the shelf. "You better."

Another time, during a team meeting, Lind stood behind her while Georgette handed out assignments, and spoke in a low voice, just for her.

"You look good today."

Dana shot him a quick glare, but her twitching lips betrayed her.

Brenda, ever watchful, just smiled—seeing everything.

***

Saturdays were filled with little adventures—hiking, craft fairs, farmers markets, walks on local park trails, trying new coffee shops—always returning to their own. Drives through the country and the occasional B&B.

But it wasn't just weekends. From the beginning, their Wednesdays were sacred too—midweek dinners, sometimes a hike or a late-night dessert run. Always a soft landing before finishing out the week.

Every now and then, Dana would test the boundaries.

"You know," she'd say lightly, trailing a finger along the rim of her wineglass, or up his arm, or down his chest, "if you stayed over on Thursdays too, we'd practically have the whole week together."

Lind would smile. "I know. But we agreed to take it slow, remember? Build this to last," he'd say, gesturing between them.

"I know," she'd sigh. "But I want you more than I'm getting you." Then she'd throw on a pouty face for emphasis.

"I know what you mean," he'd say quietly. Then smile, and tell her to quit looking at him like that. "You know that's the point of taking it slow."

"I know. But it's cruel," she'd mutter. No heat in it.

Just want.

That Thursday, while restocking end caps in the home goods section, Dana caught a few lyrics floating down from the overhead speakers—something catchy, something bold. Something that spoke to her.

She paused, tilted her head, then pulled out her phone and looked up the lyrics. A wicked little smile formed on her lips—one that would've made Lind nervous.

It came to her like an epiphany. A simple plan. One she was *sure* would work.

Thank you, Jessica Simpson.

That night, she sat on the couch wearing only one of his T-shirts and the white panties Lind loved to peel off her. Same smile. Same plan.

She dialed his number and waited for him to answer.

"Hey you. What's up?" he asked.

She didn't reply. Just put him on speaker, and held the phone up to the stereo, and hit play.

Leave your dishes in the sink, leave your laundry on the floor...

Just come on over... I need you now, I need you bad...

Just come on over...

She didn't say a word. Just mouthed the lyrics silently—and hung up when the song ended.

Across town, Lind stared at his phone, the song still echoing. A slow grin spread across his face as the same thought passed through him—the same quiet resignation he'd carried since the first time they were together.

Yeah. I've got no fucking chance against this woman.

He grabbed his truck keys, locked the door, and headed straight for Dana's.

When she answered the door, she was wearing his favorite outfit—their favorite outfit.

Without a word, she offered her hand. He stepped inside as he took it.

She closed the door behind them and led him upstairs.

They should have stayed home

The gravel parking lot crunched beneath the tires as Lind pulled the truck into a spot near the edge of the lot, easing around a tall hedge of small trees and thick bushes that lined the entrance. Sunlight filtered through the windshield as Dana stretched in the passenger seat, a playful grin on her lips.

As Lind turned off the engine, they took stock of the area. Not empty. A handful of vehicles scattered around suggested they weren't alone on the trail today.

Dana barely seemed to notice. She was still flirting, touching, playing—it hadn't stopped since they stepped out of the shower this morning. Lind was beginning to wonder if they should have just stayed home.

At this rate, the hike might have to wait.

They stepped out of the truck and wandered toward the trail head bulletin board, where Lind explained the route he had in mind. Or, at least, he tried to.

Dana nodded absently, her fingers slipping under the back of his shirt, tracing his spine, dipping lower.

Yep. *They should have stayed home.*

Lind cleared his throat, trying to stay focused on the map, but when Dana gave his ass a slow squeeze, he knew she hadn't heard a word he'd said.

They glanced around the lot—no one immediately in sight. Just as Lind was about to suggest heading back to the truck for an entirely different kind of warm-up, he had a better idea.

With a sudden move, he pinned Dana against the thick wooden post that held up one end of the bulletin board, pressing a deep, heated kiss to her lips. She responded instantly, her arms winding around his neck as her body molded against his.

She lifted one knee, bringing it slowly up the side of his leg to his hip, her breath warm against his lips.

Lind reached down, gripping her thighs, lifting her effortlessly as she wrapped her legs around his waist. His hands found her ass, pulling her tighter against him, her hips rolling against him instinctively.

But something was missing.

Dana stilled against him, her breath coming fast. "Where's my big guy?" she asked, frowning slightly.

Lind let out a low chuckle, shifting slightly. "Oh, he's there. Very there. Just pointed in the wrong direction, and it's... uncomfortable."

Dana's lips curved into a wicked grin. "Oh, my poor guy. Let me fix that."

She shifted just enough to slip her hand down, past his belt, into his pants, fingers pushing under his boxers until she found what she was looking for.

Hard. Very hard.

The heat of him, the smooth texture of his skin against her palm, sent another rush of desire flooding through her. Slowly, deliberately, she adjusted him to a better position, her fingers stroking him ever so slightly.

Lind groaned softly, his hands tightening around her thighs.

And just as they started scanning the area, looking for a more secluded spot to take things to the next level...

The crunch of tires over gravel.

Lind released Dana... back on her own two feet just as a new vehicle pulled into the lot.

But before they could fully recover, another sound caught their attention—car doors slamming shut nearby.

Turning their heads to the right, they spotted a pair of women stepping out of a car. As they reached into the back seat for their backpacks, Dana and Lind exchanged a look of realization.

They'd been there the whole time.

Probably saw... everything.

The two women walked past them toward the trail head, big grins on their faces, their expressions far too amused.

Dana and Lind just stared at each other for a beat—then burst out laughing.

Yep, they saw everything.

When they finally composed themselves, they turned back to the now much more innocent task of choosing their hiking route. As they headed up the trail, Lind's erection faded gradually, while Dana shifted uncomfortably, her panties uncomfortably damp from everything that almost happened.

Though they never let go

Hand in hand, they followed the winding path, the thick foliage closing in around them in a cocoon of green and gold light. Occasionally, one of them would take the lead, depending on the narrowness of the trail. But the best view was always the one directly in front of them.

Now and then, they caught glimpses of the two women ahead—always far enough ahead that they weren't within earshot, but close enough to be noticed.

And they were definitely holding hands when the trail allowed.

Dana and Lind exchanged a knowing look, raising matching eyebrows.

When they reached a scenic overlook, they spotted the women again—this time, arms wrapped around each other, sharing a deep, passionate kiss.

Dana and Lind slowed, not wanting to interrupt.

But the crunch of their boots gave them away.

The women glanced their way, breaking apart slightly—though they never let go.

As Dana and Lind passed, they exchanged the same sheepish grins from the parking lot.

Lind smiled. Dana bit her lip.

They continued up the trail, the moment shared between them.

Have you ever had a threesome

At the top of the overlook, Dana turned to Lind, curiosity in her voice. "Does Sam like women?"

Lind frowned slightly. "Where's that coming from?"

Dana exhaled, leaning against a rock. "I don't know. Just... watching those two back there got me wondering." She shifted, the simmering heat from their earlier encounter still buzzing in her body. "And honestly? I think I'm just as turned on from them as I was from what we did."

Lind raised an eyebrow, intrigued. "Yeah?"

Dana hesitated, then nodded. "Yeah."

Lind considered for a moment. "Sam has a bi-curious nature. She's never had a relationship with a woman, but she enjoys playing with them once in a while." His eyes flicked to Dana's. "Why do you ask?"

Dana chewed on her lip. "It's just... something I've thought about before." She glanced over. "You remember Wayne?"

Lind nodded. "The ex?"

She smirked. "Yeah. He once asked me for a threesome with another woman. I told him I'd be down if I could have a threesome with him and another man."

Lind chuckled. "I remember you telling me about that. I asked you if you'd have actually gone through with it if he said yes."

Dana tilted her head. "And I told you I *think* I would've."

A beat of silence stretched between them.

Dana finally asked, "Have you ever had a threesome with Sam and another woman?"

Lind shook his head. "No. That's not what our relationship is about." He paused. "I don't even know how I'd feel about the idea. My relationship with Sam has always been just us."

Dana was quiet for a moment before asking, "Do you think you'd be into it? A threesome with another woman... and me?"

Lind studied her carefully. "Would you be into it?"

Dana shrugged, her expression playful as a dozen images flashed through her mind—some curious, some wild. "I'll give you the same answer I gave Wayne—I might want to try it... if I could have a threesome with you and another man."

Lind nodded slowly. "Well... I'm not Wayne." His voice was even, thoughtful. "So that particular fantasy of yours could happen, if you really want it."

Dana hesitated before asking, "How do you feel about being with another man?"

Lind's expression didn't change. "I've never been with one. The only cock I've ever had in my hand is my own." He paused. "But I'm not opposed to being around another naked man if that's what you wanted."

"Hmm..." Dana said, a playful look on her face. "Both ideas sound—intriguing."

"This is a side of you I've not seen before," Lind said with a crooked smile.

Dana's mind was starting to race. "So... you'd be into two women playing together?"

"Most men would be." He shrugged. "From my perspective I think it's more natural, more passionate. The feminine being together... that's a different kind of energy."

Dana exhaled, looking out over the landscape, her mind turning over new possibilities.

Lind squeezed her hand. "It's something more to think about."
And Dana knew... she definitely would.

When they finally made it home about dinner time, well...
They ate dinner late.

***

Sundays became their favorite ritual—and this Sunday morning
was no different, a slow morning filled with pancakes, coffee, and
unhurried conversation at Dana's condo.

"I've been thinking about taking some art classes," Dana said,
swirling her coffee absentmindedly.

Lind raised an eyebrow. "I didn't know you liked art."

"I used to," she admitted, her voice softer. "It's been a while, but
I think it's time to get back to it."

Lind's smile was warm, encouraging. "You should. I bet you'd
be amazing."

They talked more about it. Lind learned Dana used to paint
and draw all the time growing up—sketchbooks stacked in her
bedroom, easels her dad had built just for her. Somewhere at her
parents' house, those supplies still waited.

She wasn't sure when she'd find the time again, but she wanted
to.

In the weeks that followed, they fell into an easy rhythm. Dana
started carving out more evenings with friends, mostly Brenda, and
returned with stories that made Lind laugh.

"And then Brenda tried to convince everyone she invented
karaoke," Dana said, shaking her head. "I thought the bartender
was going to lose it."

"She's a riot," Lind chuckled.

Now and then, Lind took a weekend for himself—hiking,
tinkering, just unwinding. Dana didn't mind the quiet. The space

helped her breathe. She even started to think that maybe, when Lind was with Sam, she wouldn't unravel so much.

But knowing he was with Sam wasn't the same as knowing he was just down the road.

One felt manageable. The other hurt.

The shadow of Sam was still there, softer. Quieter.

And for now, Dana let herself be here—grateful for the warmth they'd built, for the peace she'd managed to find.

This has been the best night

By the time they arrived at the July 4th festival, the next town over was alive with energy. The streets near the park had been closed off, making way for food trucks, carnival games, and live music. A local band played upbeat covers under a canopy of twinkling lights, casting a warm glow over the festivities.

"This is amazing," Dana said, taking in the sights and sounds—the laughter, the music—as they strolled through the crowd.

Lind grinned. "Told you it's worth the drive. They go all out here."

They wandered through the vendor stalls, stopping to share a basket of funnel cake dusted with powdered sugar. Dana laughed as she tried to take a bite without making a mess, a puff of sugar sticking to her nose.

"Hold still," Lind said, leaning in to wipe it off with his thumb, Dana felt a rush of warmth that had nothing to do with the summer evening.

The scent of kettle corn and grilled sausages filled the air, wrapping the entire evening in nostalgia.

As sunset deepened, they found a grassy hill overlooking the launch field, just far enough from the crowd to feel like their own little corner of the celebration.

The first firework shot into the sky with a crackling whistle, exploding into a burst of gold that shimmered against the dark backdrop. The crowd let out a collective "Ooh!" followed by scattered applause.

Dana tilted her head back, eyes wide with wonder. "I forgot how magical this feels," she whispered.

Lind looked at her for a moment, his eyes warm. "It's even better when you share it with someone."

The fireworks built in intensity, the booms and bursts filling the air, each explosion bigger and brighter than the last. Dana leaned into Lind's side, his arm wrapping around her instinctively.

Between bursts of color, they exchanged quiet, playful commentary.

"That one looked like a starfish," Lind mused, pointing at a golden burst that spiraled outward.

Dana smirked. "No way. Clearly a dandelion."

"You're impossible," Lind said, shaking his head.

She laughed, resting her head against his shoulder for a brief moment.

As the grand finale began, the entire park seemed to hold its breath. A cascade of golden willows, crackling stars, and vibrant comets erupted into the sky all at once, leaving the crowd in awe.

As the last firework fizzled out, Dana turned to Lind, her smile radiant. "This has been the best night."

"Agreed," Lind said, squeezing her hand. "You make everything better."

***

The drive back was quiet but content, the cool night air drifting in through the open windows, the hum of the truck quiet, comfortable, relaxing.

After a while, she glanced at Lind. "So," she began, "what's the plan for next weekend? Maybe another day trip, like the lake. Or—oh! We could check out that winery Brenda was raving about."

Lind smiled, his grip on the steering wheel relaxed. "The winery sounds great. Let's plan for that."

"Great," Dana said. "And the weekend after?" She turned excitedly to face Lind. "I have a few ideas for that too."

That's the music festival

Lind hesitated for a second. His eyes stayed fixed on the road.

"The weekend after..." he started, voice careful. "That's the music festival."

The words landed softly but carried weight. Dana blinked, her mind catching up.

"Oh," she said after a beat. "Right. The festival with Sam."

Lind nodded, glancing at her briefly. "I didn't mean to forget to mention it. It's just been a while since we talked about it."

"No, it's fine," Dana said quickly, forcing steadiness into her tone. "I remember. You told me about it months ago."

She turned back on her seat to face the road.

Lind reached over, his hand resting lightly on her knee. "You sure you're okay?"

Dana forced a smile, but inside, the dam cracked just a little.

She inhaled deeply. "So... when do you leave?"

"Friday morning," Lind said. "I'll be back Sunday night."

Dana nodded. "Okay."

The rest of the drive carried lighter conversation, but the thought of Sam never left her mind.

By the time they reached her condo, she was smiling again, kissing Lind goodnight with a warmth she didn't entirely feel.

As she closed the door behind her, leaning against it with a sigh, the crack in her dam widened.

She wasn't sure how much longer she could hold everything back.

Outside, Lind crossed the lot to his truck, but the usual ease in his step was gone. His fingers tapped idly against his keys, as he looked at Dana's closed door.

He could feel it. Something shifting, something breaking.

And he knew how to fix it.

If he gave up Sam, Dana wouldn't have to suffer like this.

But at what cost?

He clenched his jaw, exhaling sharply.

He could stop Dana's pain.

But not without causing his own.

Lind climbed into the driver's seat, gripping the wheel a little too tightly.

There might be no way out of this without hurting someone.

And tonight, he wasn't sure if there was anything he could do.

As he drove home, his mind spiraled.

His hand curled in his lap, the ache settling somewhere deeper than he could reach.

Chapter 50

Ready for some wine and countryside

Lind's truck idled in front of Dana's condo, its low rumble blending with the distant hum of a lawnmower down the street. Dana stepped outside, her sundress swaying gently in the morning breeze. The warmth of the sun kissed her bare shoulders as she climbed into the passenger seat, her cheeks already flushed from the heat of the day—or maybe from the anticipation of the trip.

She fastened her seat belt, determined to stay in the moment. This weekend was about the winery, about Lind. About them.

Lind leaned over, brushing a light kiss against her cheek. "Hey."

"Hey," she echoed, returning his smile.

"Ready for some wine and countryside?"

"Absolutely," Dana sighed, sinking into the seat. "This is exactly what I needed this weekend."

Lind pulled away from the curb, the drive unfolding in an easy rhythm. The windows were rolled down, letting in the scent of fresh-cut grass and wildflowers as they passed rolling fields and farm stands with handwritten signs advertising fresh peaches and local honey. Dana tapped her fingers idly against her knee, matching the soft beat of the music drifting from the radio.

She turned to Lind. "So, what's the plan once we're there?"

"Wine tasting, definitely," he said, flashing a grin. "Maybe a tour if they have one. And Brenda mentioned they've got some kind of cheese and charcuterie setup, so that's a must."

Dana laughed. "Mmm... cheese."

***

419

Perched on a gentle slope, the winery stretched out before them, its vineyards sprawling in neat, endless rows. The afternoon sun cast long shadows across the landscape, turning the leaves a vivid green.

Dana inhaled deeply, the air thick with the scent of ripening grapes and freshly turned soil.

"This place is gorgeous," she murmured as they walked toward the main building, its rustic stone walls blending beautifully with the surroundings.

Inside, they joined a small group for a tasting session. Dana cradled her first glass, swirling the crisp white before taking a sip. Lind, ever curious, leaned forward, asking the sommelier questions about the winemaking process. Dana, on the other hand, had her own method of evaluating the wines.

She took another sip and held up the glass. "This one is officially the 'Friday night on the couch' wine."

Lind chuckled, swirling his own deep red. "And this Cabernet is definitely the 'impress your friends at dinner' wine."

They worked their way through the tasting, pausing to debate their favorites before sitting down under the shade of a pergola. A platter of cheeses and cured meats sat between them, the salty tang of prosciutto pairing perfectly with their wine selections. Conversation flowed as smoothly as the drinks, laughter threading between easy silences.

Dana let herself sink into the moment. The last few weeks had been heavy—questions she wasn't ready to answer, feelings she hadn't fully untangled. But here, in the warm afternoon sunlight, with Lind beside her, everything felt simple again.

Sam would've loved this place

By the time they wandered back toward the truck, the sun had begun its slow descent, bathing the vineyard in a warm amber glow.

Dana leaned against the passenger door, watching as Lind loaded their purchases into the back seat.

"This was such a good idea," she said, her voice soft with contentment.

"I'm glad you enjoyed it." Lind shut the back door with a solid thud, a satisfied smile on his face. "You know, Sam would've loved this place. She's always going on about how wine is an experience, not just a drink."

The words were effortless, spoken without a second thought. Lind didn't see it, didn't feel the way Dana's entire body stilled for a second.

The warmth of the day faltered, the easy glow dimming just slightly. She recovered quickly, pasting on a polite smile.

But she replayed the words, again and again. *Sam would've loved this place.*

It shouldn't matter. Of course, Sam had come to mind. Lind shared his life with her too.

But even knowing that, the moment fractured just a little. A crack, barely visible, but there all the same.

"That sounds like her," Dana said lightly, as she got into the truck.

Lind hesitated for a beat, the door still open beside him. His smile faltered just slightly.

Too easy, he realized. The way Sam's name had rolled off his tongue—effortless, natural—maybe too natural.

He closed her door and got in beside her.

If Dana noticed the change in his demeanor, she didn't mention it.

He started the truck, the engine humming beneath them as he turned toward home.

***

The drive was quieter. Lind hummed along to the music, his hand resting casually on the console between them, his fingers drumming against the leather in time with the song.

Dana stared out the window, her reflection faint in the glass. *Sam would've loved this place.* The words looped in her mind, insistent and unshakable.

It probably didn't mean anything. It shouldn't.

So why was it still sitting in her chest like a weight?

The vineyards blurred into rolling fields, the hills stretching endlessly toward the horizon. She took a slow breath, willing the tension from her shoulders. They had shared a beautiful day.

She didn't want to let doubt ruin it.

***

As they neared the city, Dana's thoughts churned.

I know he cares about me. He says all the right things. He does all the right things. He always has. So why were these feelings creeping back in?

She glanced at Lind, his profile seemed calm, content. Unbothered.

Her fingers tightened in her lap. *Maybe letting it go was the only way forward. But deep down, she knew it wasn't that simple.*

This moment, this shadow—it wasn't just about today.

It wasn't just about the winery.

And it wasn't over yet.

The purple Buddha out front

The drive back to Dana's condo was quiet, reflective. It wasn't uncomfortable, just... subdued. Lind tapped the steering wheel lightly in time with the music, occasionally glancing over at Dana, who had her legs tucked up on the seat, staring out the window.

As they neared her neighborhood, he cleared his throat. "Feel like grabbing dinner before we get back?"

Dana hummed in consideration, then glanced over. "Chinese?"

Lind grinned. "I was hoping you'd say that."

They pulled into the parking lot of the small, unassuming restaurant with the purple Buddha out front, the one they'd come to love for its crispy egg rolls and perfectly spiced Mongolian beef. The neon sign flickered in the dusk, casting a soft glow over the entrance. Lind went inside while Dana waited in the truck, watching the last of the sunset streak the sky in shades of orange and pink.

When he returned, the cab of the truck filled with the rich scent of garlic, ginger, and soy sauce. Dana sighed happily. Something about Chinese takeout in cartons felt like comfort.

Are we ready for bed

Back at Dana's, they spread the containers across the coffee table, digging in with chopsticks as an old movie played in the background. Lind stole bites of her General Tao's; Dana retaliated by swiping pieces of his sesame chicken. The easy banter and familiar flavors slowly unraveled the last of the tension coiling in her chest.

After dinner, Lind stretched out on the couch, patting the space next to him. Dana curled against his side, tucking her feet beneath her as he draped an arm around her shoulders. The rise and fall of his breathing, the steady warmth of his body—it should have been grounding. But even as she nestled closer, her thoughts drifted.

Lind absently ran his fingers through her hair, and she sighed, tilting her head slightly into his touch. She wanted to be here, in this moment, fully. But she wasn't.

Eventually, Lind flicked off the TV and stood, stretching. "Are we ready for bed?"

Dana nodded, following him upstairs. Lind headed into the bathroom first to wash up.

When it was her turn, Dana stepped into the bathroom and paused. The small hand towel still lay on the counter—along with the toy she'd left out to dry. She folded the towel around the toy and calmly slipped them into the top vanity drawer.

Then she washed up, moving slowly, methodically, her thoughts drifting.

He must've seen it. Definitely had. But he never said a word.

That quiet grace, that honest acceptance—it always caught her off guard.

And tonight, she needed that.

She stripped down to her panties and pulled on an oversized pajama top before climbing into bed. A silent signal—one she knew he'd recognize.

Lind pressed close in behind her, fitting their bodies together in their usual spooning position. He kissed the back of her shoulder, soft and sure, but didn't push for more.

She exhaled slowly, relieved.

"Goodnight, baby," Lind murmured, even as he was wondering what was going through her mind now, knowing his comment about Sam had contributed to it.

Dana covered his hand with hers. "Goodnight."

Shower? Together? Absolutely

The morning sun filtered through the curtains, casting long golden streaks across the sheets. Lind stirred, stretching before rolling over, reaching for Dana. His arm wrapped around her waist—except there was no fabric beneath his palm.

His eyes flickered open, adjusting to the dim light. Pajama top—gone. Panties—gone.

A slow smile crept across his face as he shifted closer, his fingers tracing the bare curve of her hip. Dana stirred, a soft sound escaping her lips before she turned toward him, eyes half-open, warm and inviting.

"Morning," Lind murmured, gently kissing her shoulder.

Dana hummed in response, pressing against him. Her body was soft and warm, melting into his touch.

His hands moved slowly, gliding over familiar lines and shapes he knew so well. Dana responded, tilting her head back, inviting more. It was slow, unhurried—not the desperate heat of Friday night, but something deeper.

Her fingers tracing down his chest, his stomach—and down further. The feel of him in her hand had her wanting more.

She pulled him on top of her, grinding against him, shifting her hips to guide him in.

As he moved inside her, Dana's fingers dug into his back, her breath catching in the stillness of the room. This was Lind. Steady. Patient. Always there.

God, I love this man.

So why couldn't I stop thinking about all this shit?

The thought flickered, unwelcome and bitter, but she shoved it aside, focusing instead on the way Lind looked at her—the way he always looked at her.

She pulled him close, kissing, wanting, feeling every thrust, lost in the growing tension...

Afterward, she stayed wrapped in his arms for a long moment before nudging his shoulder. "Shower?"

"Together?"

Dana rolled her eyes but grinned. "Absolutely."

***

Steam rising into the air as the warm water cascaded over their skin. Dana sighed, tilting her head back under the water, eyes fluttering shut.

Lind's hands glided down her back, fingers ghosting over wet skin. "You okay?"

She cracked an eye open, offering a small smile. "Yeah."

He didn't push, just leaned in and kissed the corner of her mouth, slow and deliberate. Touch was his language, and right now, he was saying: I'm here.

Dana ran her hands over his chest, palms gliding over damp skin before dragging him closer. This was intimacy—not just in the kisses, but in the way they touched, the way they laughed when Lind nearly knocked over the bottle of shampoo. It wasn't about sex. It was about them.

By the time they emerged, wrapped in towels, the tension that had sat in Dana's chest the night before had loosened—not gone, but manageable.

You just like taking care of me

Downstairs, Lind moved around the kitchen with the ease of familiarity. He scrambled eggs while toast browned in the toaster, his movements unhurried, comfortable. Dana leaned against the counter, watching as he plated everything.

"This is nice," she murmured, stealing a piece of toast before he could set it down.

Lind swatted at her hand, grinning. "I slave over a hot stove, and this is the thanks I get?"

"I never asked you to slave." Her expression mischievous. "You just like taking care of me."

"Maybe," he winked.

They ate quietly, the kind of silence that wasn't awkward, just easy.

***

Dana wrapped her hands around her coffee mug, letting the warmth seep into her palms as she carefully measured her next words. "So... this music festival. It's three days long?"

Lind nodded, a small smile tugging at his lips. "Yep. Three days of bands, sunshine, and a whole lot of great energy."

She hesitated, her grip tightening slightly around the ceramic. "Where do you stay when you go?"

"Sam always books one of the cabins at the resort," Lind explained. "If you wait too long, they get snatched up fast."

Dana forced a chuckle, though something inside her twisted. "Sounds like there'll be a lot of people there. Naked people, right? You said it was a nudist resort."

Lind let out a laugh, lifting his hands in an easy shrug. "I'd guess a few hundred at least. And yeah, it's a nudist resort, so most of them will be."

Her lips pressed together briefly before she forced her tone to remain light. "You and Sam among them?" she asked, turning her coffee cup in her hands.

"Yes," Lind admitted without hesitation, his gaze steady on hers.

Dana exhaled slowly. "It sounds... uninhibited."

Lind's expression softened as he leaned in slightly. "It's not as wild as you're picturing. It's just about being comfortable in your own skin. No pressure, no judgment. It's actually really relaxing. And the music? Worth it."

Dana nodded, but her voice came quieter now. "It's... more than I imagined. A lot to take in."

Lind reached out, his fingers resting lightly over her hand. "I know it's not easy. But you're doing amazing, Dana. I hope you know that."

She managed a faint smile, but her thoughts were already spiraling.

***

Later that night, long after the lights were off, Dana lay staring at the ceiling. Lind's arm was draped over her, his breathing slow and steady, the warmth of his body pressed against her back. It should have been comforting. It should have been enough.

But the conversation replayed in her mind. She couldn't silence it.

I know he's with me. I know he cares about me.

But the thought of them together, so uninhibited, so exposed to each other... It felt like a door she couldn't walk through, no matter how much she wanted to.

The ache in her chest deepened. If this is how it feels now, what happens when he comes back? Would she always be left wondering where she stood?

How do I help us out of a prison I don't even know exists?

What does that even mean?

The ceiling offered no answers. The quiet hum of the fan was the only sound in the room, but inside, her thoughts churned, restless and heavy.

Part 11

Dana and I are playing the right song—
  but we're never quite in tune.
  A little flat. A little off rhythm.
  Sometimes we're there, sometimes we're not.
  With Sam, the harmony comes easy.
  She doesn't need sheet music.
  She just hears it, feels it—
  pulls me into her rhythm like we've always known the beat.

Chapter 51

One step at a time

Dana stepped into the store, forcing herself to focus on the routine of the day.

Breathe. Ground yourself. One step at a time.

The weekend at the winery had been good—a brief reprieve, a reminder of how much she loved Lind. But no matter how much she tried to hold on to that feeling, the weight of the upcoming trip loomed.

Near the front of the store, Lind stood talking to a coworker. When he caught her eye, his smile was warm, genuine. Dana returned it, but even as she did, she knew—it wasn't as genuine as she would have liked.

As she walked past, she felt his gaze on her, a flicker of concern tightening the space between them.

***

At Break, Lind sat down in the seat beside Dana, setting his coffee on the table between them. "Morning," he said softly.

"Morning," she replied, her voice quieter than usual.

He studied her for a moment, turning his mug in his hands. "You're in your head again, aren't you?"

Dana huffed out a small breath, a faint smile tugging at her lips. "You know me too well," she said as she glanced around to see if anyone else might be listening.

Lind caught her eye. "If there's anything you want to talk about, I'm here."

Dana's faint smile grew a little fainter. There was plenty to talk about. But where would she even start?

"I know," she said instead, voice steady but distant. "I'll be okay."

Lind nodded, though his expression remained thoughtful. "Just don't forget that, okay?"

"I won't," she promised, though the knot in her chest told a different story.

There's nothing to measure

Dana stared down into the swirling liquid of her coffee mug as if the answer to all her questions lay somewhere at the bottom.

"I wasn't going to bring this up," she admitted, lifting her gaze to Brenda's. "But this weekend... it just feels bigger than the others. Like I can't ignore what it means."

Brenda leaned back, nodding slowly. "And what does it mean, Dana? To you?"

Dana hesitated. "It means... they'll be spending three days together. Naked. Doing things I can't even begin to imagine, or don't want to." She exhaled sharply. "And I know it's not the first time. But somehow, it feels more real now."

Brenda studied her, considering her words. "I get it. It's in your face this time, and you can't just pretend it's not happening. But, Dana, you've made it this far. You've built something solid with Lind. Don't let fear tear that down."

Dana's fingers tightened around the ceramic. "It's not just fear. It's this constant feeling that I'm not enough. That I'll never be what she is to him."

Brenda leaned forward, her tone firm but gentle. "You're not supposed to be. There is nothing to compare. This isn't a competition. What Lind has with Sam is its own thing. What he has with you is something completely different. And if he didn't think you were enough, he wouldn't be with you."

The words were a thin layer of comfort to Dana—not deep enough to fully sink in, but familiar enough to hold onto.

"I just... I don't know if I'll ever get used to it."

Brenda softened. "You don't have to get used to it overnight," she said. Then, after a long moment, she caught Dana's eye. "But you do have to decide if it's worth trying."

Dana's gaze lowered back down to her coffee as she nodded.

Their conversation shifted to lighter topics even though Dana couldn't stop her thoughts from circling back again and again.

And suddenly she needed more

Dana moved through the kitchen, plating the grilled salmon and roasted potatoes with quiet precision. She'd spent all day pushing thoughts of the weekend aside, focusing instead on this—tonight. She needed tonight to be hers—a memory to hold onto before the storm hit.

Lind arrived on time, bringing his usual warmth with him. Dinner was easy, conversation flowing in that effortless way she loved, safe and familiar.

He teased her about her obsession with cheesy rom-coms, made her laugh with a story of yet another stockroom mishap, and for a while, everything felt normal.

Afterward, they cuddled on the couch, the flickering candlelight softening the edges of the room. Lind's fingers moved through Dana's hair, slow and grounding, as if he could tether her here, now, and nowhere else.

"You've been quiet tonight," he murmured.

Dana sighed, resting her head against his chest. "I'm just... processing."

"About the trip?"

She nodded. "I know it's something you've done for years. I'm trying to understand what she does for you, and I know it doesn't change how you feel about me. But... it's still hard."

Lind pressed a kiss to the top of her head. "I understand, Dana. And I don't expect it to be easy. But I want you to know that I'm here for you. Always."

His words should have soothed her, but they didn't quite quiet the ache in her chest.

And suddenly, she needed more.

She needed to feel him, all of him. To drown in him, in them, to remind herself why she was here, why she stayed. To feel Lind as part of her, something no doubt, no shadow, no name could take away.

Dana shifted, lifting her head to look at him. Lind met her gaze, searching, sensing the shift before she even spoke.

She didn't give him time to ask. Instead, she surged forward, crashing her lips against his, hungry, desperate and unrelenting.

Lind responded instantly, his hands tightening around her waist as he pulled her against him, letting her take what she needed. Their mouths moved in sync—hot, messy, full of want. She pushed at his shirt, needing it off, needing skin against skin without space between them.

They barely made it upstairs, shedding clothes as they went, urgency making them clumsy. Lind caught her, his grip firm, steady even as she was unraveling.

The need in her was fierce, raw.

She clung to him as he moved above her, their bodies meeting in frantic rhythm, in unspoken desperation. Harder. Closer. She whispered his name, pleaded without words—trying to fuse them together and make everything else disappear.

Lind groaned, burying his face in her neck, his own restraint slipping as he followed her over the edge.

When it was over, he didn't move right away, still catching his breath, still tangled with her in the sheets. Dana held onto him longer than usual, arms wrapped tight, unwilling to let go just yet.

Lind shifted after a moment, pressing a kiss to her temple before easing off the bed.

He returned a moment later, warm cloth in hand, and cleaned her with the same quiet care as he always did—thoughtful, patient, gentle.

Every time he did, it anchored her to him in ways nothing else could.

When he finished, he tossed the cloth aside and got back into bed.

She pulled him close again, pressing her forehead to his shoulder, holding on like life itself depended on it.

She wasn't ready to go, to let the moment fade.

Lind stroked her back, pressing another kiss to her hair. He didn't say anything—he didn't need to.

Eventually, she sighed, forcing herself to loosen her grip.

"Sleep," Lind murmured, pulling the blankets around them.

Dana nestled against him, listening to the steady beat of his heart.

But sleep didn't come easy.

Not how I remember it

Lind's alarm blared, far too early for either of them. The shrill sound felt cruel in the quiet room. He groaned, rolling onto his back, rubbing a hand over his face. Dana grumbled in protest, tightening her grip on the blankets, not remotely ready to move.

Lind chuckled, voice rough with sleep. "We should have gone to sleep earlier."

Dana peeked one eye open. "That was your fault."

Lind smirked, leaning over to kiss her. "Not how I remember it."

She groaned but didn't argue.

Lind sighed, stretching before dragging himself out of bed. He was leaving for work straight from Dana's, both of them dragging from not getting enough sleep. But neither of them regretted it.

Dana watched him pull his clothes on, knowing this was the last morning they'd have together before the weekend.

Before the distance set in.

She exhaled, rolling onto her side, determined to hold onto this warmth for as long as she could.

I'll miss you this weekend

Dana buried herself in work, determined to keep her mind occupied. But as the day wore on, the weight of the weekend pressed heavier.

There wasn't a moment alone with Lind—too many tasks, too much movement. It wasn't until that evening, when her phone buzzed, that she finally heard his voice again.

"I've got everything packed and ready," Lind said, his tone warm, familiar. Comforting, if she let it be. "I'll be leaving early tomorrow, but I'll text you when I'm on the road."

"Okay," Dana said quietly. "Drive safe."

"I will." A pause. Then, softer, "Dana, I'll miss you this weekend."

Her throat tightened. "I'll miss you too."

She ended the call and set the phone down slowly, staring at it in her lap.

Lind and I spent weekends apart before, but I wasn't looking forward to the deafening silence of this weekend without him. Especially because of the reason he's not here.

She turned the phone over in her hands.

I want to be okay with this. I want to trust him. So why does it feel like I'm standing on the edge of a cliff?

Hey, where's Lind

The store felt quieter without him. Dana couldn't decide if that was a relief or a curse.

She threw herself into work, but the hum of coworkers' conversations kept pulling her back into reality.

"Hey, where's Lind today?" one of them asked. "Thought he never missed work."

Dana forced a casual tone. "Just a quick trip to see a friend. He'll be back Monday."

"A friend?" another coworker mused. "And he's taking a 3 day weekend?"

Before Dana could respond, Brenda smoothly stepped in. "Yeah, he mentioned it to me. Someone he hasn't seen in a while. Sounds like a quick catch-up thing."

Interest faded, and the conversation shifted elsewhere. Dana exhaled, casting Brenda a grateful glance.

"Thanks for that," Dana said softly when they were alone.

Brenda shrugged. "No problem. You holding up okay?"

Dana hesitated. Then, after a long pause, she nodded. "Yeah. I'm fine."

***

The knock at Dana's door came just as she sank into the couch, beer in hand, trying to lose herself in something mindless. She wasn't surprised when she opened it to find Brenda standing there, a bottle of wine in one hand, determination in her eyes.

"Figured you could use some company," Brenda announced, stepping inside without waiting for an invitation.

Dana let out a quiet breath, closing the door behind her. "I appreciate it."

For the next two hours, Brenda worked her magic—steering the conversation away from Lind and Sam, keeping things light, distracting. She even tried to convince her to go out, but Dana shook her head, sinking deeper into the couch.

"I just need a quiet night," she admitted.

Brenda studied her for a beat, then nodded, pulling her into a quick hug before heading for the door. "Call me if you change your mind. Or if you just need to vent."

When she was gone, the silence crept back in, thick and oppressive.

Dana curled up on the couch, wrapping her arms around her knees. She fought the burn behind her eyes, whispering into the empty room, "Get through this. Like a big girl."

***

The sun streamed through the blinds, too bright for how heavy Dana felt.

She made coffee, standing at the window, staring without really seeing. The thought was immediate, impossible to ignore.

Is he having breakfast with her right now? Laughing with her?

Her grip tightened around the mug. She shook her head, trying to chase the thought away.

She needed to stay busy. Anything to keep from thinking.

She scrubbed the counters, reorganized her closet—even sorted through old mail she had ignored for weeks. But no matter how much she moved, the weight in her chest stayed.

Brenda texted: *"Lunch?"*

Dana hesitated before typing back: *"Thanks, but I'm okay. Just keeping busy."*

Lying. But what else was she supposed to say?

***

The walls of her condo felt too small, too suffocating. She grabbed a light jacket, easier than putting on a bra, and headed outside, hoping the fresh air would help.

Her steps were aimless, slow. The quiet of the neighborhood should have been calming, but it only made the noise in her head louder.

She replayed Lind's words from Thursday night. *I'll miss you this weekend.*

She knew he meant it. She believed it.

But belief didn't erase the image of him with Sam, the moments she could only imagine and couldn't stop picturing.

By the time she got back, her legs ached, but her thoughts hadn't quieted.

She collapsed onto the couch, scrolling through her phone. Her thumb hovered over Lind's name.

Should she call?

No.

He's probably busy. I don't want to interrupt.

She dropped the phone onto the cushion beside her, turning on the TV instead. Anything to drown out the undercurrent of anxiety and longing.

***

The phone buzzed again. For a split second, her heart jumped.

She grabbed it. Not Lind.

Brenda: *"Hope you're holding up okay. Call me if you need to vent. Or wine. Or both."*

Dana smiled faintly, thumbs tapping out a quick reply: *"Thanks, Brenda. I might take you up on that soon."*

She set the phone down and flipped through TV channels, finally stopping on a sitcom she didn't care about.

The laugh track rang hollow.

But it was better than silence.

Then she could breathe again

Dana stood at the stove, staring at the mess she had made of her scrambled eggs.

Lind would've laughed.

"They're still edible," he'd say, grinning as he drowned them in hot sauce.

She exhaled softly, a small, fleeting smile touching her lips. But when she sat down to eat, her appetite was gone.

She poked at the food, pushing it around her plate.

He'll be back this afternoon.

He said he'd text.

She forced herself to take a deep breath, stood, and started cleaning the kitchen.

One more day. She just had to get through one more day. And then—maybe—she could breathe again.

Chapter 52

Want to grab brunch

Her phone buzzed on the counter.

Brenda: *"Morning, sunshine. How you holding up? Want to grab brunch?"*

This time, Dana didn't hesitate.

Dana: *"Brunch sounds good. Usual place?"*

Brenda: *"Perfect. See you in 30."*

She tossed the eggs in the trash and headed to her room. Sweatpants off, jeans on. She grabbed her bra... hesitated and threw it back down again in favor of an oversized sweatshirt.

A little concealer under her eye. Not much. Just enough to feel like herself again.

You could use a mimosa

The café hummed with the comforting noise of a weekend morning. Clinking mugs, quiet laughter, the smell of coffee thick in the air.

Brenda waved from a small table by the window, her presence comforting as ever.

"You look like you could use a mimosa," she grinned as Dana took her seat.

Dana let out a small breath of a laugh. "That obvious, huh?"

Brenda grinned, flagging down the server. "Two mimosas and... avocado toast, fruit bowl. Sound good?"

Dana nodded, grateful not to have to decide.

When the server left, Brenda leaned in, resting her chin on her hand. "Alright. Talk to me. How are you holding up?"

Dana traced the rim of her mug. "I don't know. I thought I could handle this better than I am."

Brenda tilted her head, watching her carefully. "It's a big adjustment. No one figures this out overnight."

"It's not just that." Dana swallowed. "I keep wondering if I'm enough for him. Knowing he's with her—spending time, connecting, resetting—it feels like I'll always come second."

Brenda reached across the table, squeezing her hand. "You're not second, Dana. Relationships don't work like that. Lind wouldn't be with you if he wasn't fully in it. I know I keep saying that but..."

Dana frowned, her voice quieter. "What if I'm just... not built for this? What if I'm fooling myself into thinking I can handle it?"

Brenda leaned back, considering her words. "It's okay to feel that way. It doesn't mean you're failing—it just means you're figuring things out. That takes time."

Dana sighed. "I hate feeling like this. Like I'm not strong enough."

Brenda smiled gently. "You're stronger than you think. And you're not alone in this."

***

The server arrived with their food, and Brenda smoothly shifted the conversation—work gossip, funny coworker stories, a new show she was obsessed with.

Little by little, Dana felt herself relax.

As they finished, Brenda gave her a knowing smile. "You're doing better than you think. And whenever you ever need a sounding board, you know where to find me."

Dana's smile this time felt real. "Thanks, Brenda. I really needed this."

"Anytime," she said, "and hey—don't spend the rest of the day overthinking, okay? Do something that makes you happy."

Dana laughed softly, nodding. "I'll try."

As she walked back to her car, the weight in her chest wasn't gone—but it was lighter.

Brenda's words echoed in her mind.

You're stronger than you think.

Just got home. I'll call you soon

Dana buried herself in a book, forcing her mind to focus on the characters instead of the thoughts threatening to creep in. Escape. That's all she needed right now.

Every few pages, her gaze flickered to her phone. She wouldn't check it. She wouldn't obsess.

He'll call when he's ready.

The day dragged, emotions swinging between frustration and reluctant acceptance. When her phone finally buzzed, she snatched it up without hesitation.

Lind: *Just got home. I'll call you soon.*

She stared at the message for a long moment, then typed back: *Okay.*

The knot in her chest loosened—just slightly. The ache remained, but at least now, there was an endpoint.

We'll talk soon. And maybe we'll get through this after all.

***

The book lay open on Dana's chest, her eyes scanning the same sentence for the fourth time. She wasn't really reading.

Late afternoon sunlight stretched across the walls, the stillness of her condo too heavy, too loud.

Her phone vibrated on the coffee table.

Lind: *Can I call you now?*

Dana inhaled sharply, typing back: *Yes, of course.*

The phone rang almost immediately. She answered on the first ring.

"Hey, Dana." Lind's voice was warm but tired.

"Hey."

A pause. Comfortable for him. Heavy for her.

"I'm back," he said. "Got in about an hour ago."

"How was your drive?"

"Long," Lind admitted. "But it wasn't too bad. Traffic was light for a Sunday."

Dana nodded, even though he couldn't see her. "That's good."

Another brief pause. Lind filled it quickly, his tone light.

"I've been thinking about that stir-fry we made last week. I swear, I've been craving it all weekend. Yours was better than the restaurant."

Dana managed a faint smile. *He was trying.*

"You're biased," she murmured. "But I'll take the compliment."

"Always." His voice softened. "What about you? How was your weekend?"

She chose her words carefully. "It was fine. Just stayed in mostly. Caught up on some reading and cleaned the condo."

"Ah, the productive route." Lind hesitated for half a beat, then added, "Meanwhile, I went full raccoon mode—ate my way through one food truck after another."

Dana gave a soft laugh. "Food trucks? That sounds... fun."

He knew. Maybe not everything, but enough to sense this weekend hadn't been easy for her.

"Yeah." He exhaled. "They had a bunch at the festival. Tried some stuff I hadn't had before. One stand had this spicy Thai fusion—I think you'd love it."

A dull pang twisted in her chest. She had asked—he wasn't rubbing it in. But still...

"Maybe," she said, voice quieter than she intended.

Lind caught the shift. He always did.

He was trying. She knew that

"What are you reading?" he asked, redirecting smoothly. "Anything I'd know?"

"Probably not. Just a mystery novel. It's... okay."

"Well, you've always got good recommendations." A smile crept into his voice. "Let me know if it gets better."

He was trying. She knew that.

And yet...

***

The conversation wound down after a few more minutes of light chatter.

"It's good to hear you," Lind said softly. "I've missed you."

Dana swallowed, then answered honestly. "Missed you too."

"I'll let you get back to your book. But I'll see you tomorrow."

"Yeah. Tomorrow."

"Sleep well, Dana. I love you."

She hesitated for just a fraction of a second. "Love you too."

Dana's Reflection

As the call ended, Dana set the phone down and leaned back against the couch. Relief. Frustration. Both tangled in her chest.

He called. He sounded happy. *That should be enough... shouldn't it?*

She shook her head and pushed the thought away.

It's just one weekend. Tomorrow, things will be back to normal. We'll be okay.

But as she climbed into bed, alone, the ache remained.

DANA SAMANTHA LINDSEY

Chapter 53

I'm driving this year

The sun filtered through the trees as Lind pulled into the driveway of Sam's apartment complex. She was already outside, leaning against the railing, her duffel bag at her feet.

Lind's gaze flickered to her empty parking space.

She waved him forward as he stepped out of the truck. "Go ahead and park in my spot. I'm driving this year."

Lind raised an eyebrow. "I'd be happy to drive again. You know I don't mind."

Sam grinned, mischief lighting her eyes. "I know, but you drove last year. It's only fair we share this part of our weekend, too."

Lind chuckled, shaking his head as he grabbed his bag from the truck. "Fair enough. But don't say I didn't offer."

Sam popped the trunk, tossing her bag in before getting behind the wheel. "Buckle up. You know how much I love the open road."

Lind grimaced as he sat in the passenger seat, seat belt in hand. "That's why I drive."

With a laugh, Sam peeled out of the driveway, their annual escape officially underway.

You're in cabin 6

The gravel road curved gently through the woods, the canopy above filtering sunlight into a shifting pattern of gold and shadow across the windshield. The scent of pine and campfire filled the car, mingling with the faint hum of anticipation as Sam and Lind approached the familiar gatehouse.

The rustic building stood at the entrance, adorned with colorful banners announcing the festival's return. Everything about it was familiar—welcoming, relaxed, effortless.

Sam rolled down her window as they pulled up, her smile widening as the gatehouse attendant, Michelle, stepped forward.

"Sam and Lind!" Michelle greeted, eyes twinkling with recognition. "Back for the festival, as always. Wouldn't be the same without you."

Sam leaned out, resting her arm against the door. "Wouldn't miss it, Michelle. You know us—always up for a good time."

Lind nodded from the passenger seat, his tone friendly. "Good to see you again. How's the turnout this year?"

"Packed," Michelle said, handing over their wristbands and a detailed map of the resort. "Record numbers this year. You're in Cabin 6—great spot near the lake and not far from the stage."

"Perfect, as always." Sam flashed a grateful smile.

Michelle waved them through, and as they drove onto the grounds, the festival's familiar energy wrapped around them like a second skin.

People strolled leisurely in various states of undress, some chatting beneath shade umbrellas, others already gathered near the pool. The soft strumming of a guitar floated through the air, blending seamlessly with laughter and the rustle of leaves in the warm breeze.

The second I walk in here

Nestled among tall pines, their cabin was a quiet retreat—just a stone's throw from the lake, its wooden porch offering a perfect view of the shimmering water. The air smelled fresh, tinged with the distant scent of sunscreen and barbecue smoke.

Lind carried their bags inside while Sam immediately pulled open the curtains, letting in the late morning sunlight.

"It's like clockwork," she sighed, stretching. "The second I walk in here, I feel ten pounds lighter."

Setting his bag down, Lind gave her a once over. "Figuratively, right? Because I don't see how you could be any lighter."

She shot him a dry look, but gratitude flickered in her eyes. "You're a charmer, you know that."

The cabin was simple but familiar. A queen-sized bed against the far wall, a small dresser and kitchenette rounding out the space. Through the large windows, the lake glistened, the curtains billowing slightly in the soft breeze.

In the distance, the murmur of the festival was already building.

Now get naked so we can get going

They made quick work of organizing—towels thrown over chairs, sunscreen lined up on the dresser, sandals kicked off by the door.

Sam, already shifting into festival mode, peeled off her tank top. "Time to lose these for the weekend," she said matter-of-factly.

Lind watched, shaking his head as he unzipped his bag. "This has gotta be about my favorite time of being here, watching you transform into... well *you*."

She tossed her clothes into a drawer. Grabbing her towel, she shot him a look. "You coming, or are you just going to stand there admiring the view... as always?"

Lind let his gaze take her in. Long legs, lean frame, effortless confidence. She looked just as vibrant as the first time they met.

"I could, you know, it's been 3 months since I've seen you."

Sam's laughter filled the room. "And I'm so glad we're together now," she said, enjoyment in her eyes, her smile warm. "Now get naked so we can get going."

Lind chuckled. "Yes, ma'am."

Moments later, as Sam was the one admiring the view, she tossed him a towel—they slung them casually over their shoulders, laughing.

Outside, the weekend waited.

***

The path leading into the main festival area widened, and the familiar buzz of the event drew them in. Laughter, clinking glasses, the occasional cheer from a volleyball game.

People milled about, completely at ease in their bare skin, stopping to chat or lounging beneath the shade of colorful umbrellas. The scent of grilled food and fresh-cut grass carried on the breeze, mingling with the rhythmic strumming of a band warming up on stage.

Lind inhaled deeply, letting the atmosphere sink in.

"This is it," Sam mused beside him, a lazy grin on her face. "Every damn year, it's like stepping into another world."

"Yeah," Lind agreed. "The kind where nothing really matters except the next song and the woman beside me."

Sam nudged him playfully, heat rising in her cheeks. "And tacos. Don't forget the tacos."

***

They followed the scent of sizzling meat and warm spices, weaving through the growing crowd toward a row of vibrant food trucks lining the central lawn.

The options were endless—tacos, burgers, wood-fired pizza, smoothies, and even a vegan comfort food stand.

Lind asked, scanning the menus. "So, tacos or burgers?"

Sam barely had to think. "Tacos."

Lind said, "Fine, but that smoothie stand is calling my name."

"Priorities," Sam said, taking him by the hand, leading the way to the taco truck.

As they waited in line, Lind glanced around, taking in the easy camaraderie of the festival goers. A man with a guitar slung across his back chatted animatedly with a woman in a wide-brimmed hat, while a nearby group shared plates of food, their laughter carrying on the breeze.

By the time they had their tacos, it felt like they had fully arrived.

After eating, they wandered toward a row of tents displaying handcrafted goods—beaded jewelry, tie-dyed sarongs, hand-carved leather, and locally made soaps and candles.

The rich scent of patchouli and lavender filled the air as Sam lifted a polished stone necklace, holding it up to her collarbone. "What do you think?"

Lind studied it. "Suits you. Colorful, just like you."

She laughed, adding it onto a growing list of things to buy before the weekend ended.

Lind scanned the table of wooden figurines, fingers trailing over the smooth craftsmanship. "Amazing what people can do with a simple piece of wood," he murmured.

"Talent everywhere," Sam agreed, running her fingers over a silk scarf.

They moved slowly, taking in the festival at their own pace. The sun had passed its zenith and was beginning its slow descent, bathing the grounds in warm golden light.

The weekend had only just begun, and already, it felt like everything outside this place had faded away.

I'm very bendy, you know

Near the shopping tents, a large chalkboard stood propped on an easel, listing the weekend's scheduled events in colorful, looping handwriting. Sam grabbed Lind's arm, practically bouncing with excitement.

"Look! They're doing yoga on the beach tomorrow morning. And there's a pickleball tournament later today."

Lind scanned the board, nodding. "Volleyball at one, live painting by the pool at two... looks like there's plenty to keep us busy."

Sam's eyes gleamed. "We should definitely do pickleball. And maybe the painting—it sounds fun."

Lind glanced over the board. "Dana would love the painting."

Sam glanced over at him. "Yeah? You said she might be getting back into her art."

"She's been talking about it more," Lind said, a faint smile tugging at his lips. "She hasn't painted in a while, but I think she's feeling the pull again."

"That's great," Sam said sincerely. "Maybe this live painting thing will give you some inspiration to bring back to her."

Lind chuckled. "Maybe. Or maybe I'll just watch and pretend I know what I'm looking at."

Sam nudged him playfully. "Hey, supporting the arts is important, even if you're just there for moral support."

"Agreed," Lind said. "Though I might skip the yoga. Watching *you* attempt a headstand while I drink my coffee might be entertainment enough."

Sam swatted his arm. "Don't mock my yoga prowess. I'm very bendy, you know."

Lind gave her a suggestive tap on the butt. "Yes, I know."

She turned toward him, stepping closer, her hands resting flat against his chest. A mischievous grin played on her lips. "You're not bad yourself, mister."

Lind smiled knowingly, his hazel eyes warm. "Alright, you talked me into it—pickleball it is."

Sam giggled, stealing a quick kiss before quipping, "Go ahead, change the subject, I'll let you."

Lind chuckled, kissing her back before wrapping an arm around her shoulders. "Fine, let's check out the pool before I get myself into more trouble."

This place is magic, isn't it

Drying off after water volleyball, they made their way back to the cabin to hang up their wet towels and grab fresh ones.

They wandered toward the main stage, as afternoon approached, their arms wrapped comfortably around each other as they walked. The first band of the day was in full swing, the lead singer's voice carrying over the crowd.

Attendees lounged on blankets or chairs or swayed to the rhythm—the energy effortless and free.

Sam leaned into Lind, her expression content. "This place is magic, isn't it?"

Lind nodded, taking in the sight. The sense of freedom here was unlike anything outside these gates. No expectations, no pressure—just music, warmth, and the ease of being.

"It really is," he admitted. "Every year, it feels like the perfect reset."

"Agreed." Sam's eyes scanned the crowd, a soft smile on her lips. "And it's nice to share it with you, as always."

Lind returned the smile, leaning in to kiss her.

For now, the music, the sun, and the simple joy of being here together were all that mattered.

She means a lot to you

By early afternoon, the festival had hit its stride—music filling the air, the smell of food trucks weaving through the chatter of festival goers.

Lind and Sam drifted through the crowd, catching up with familiar faces, exchanging hugs and easy laughter with old friends.

They draped towels over their chairs near the main stage, Sam glanced sideways at Lind. "I really hope Dana's okay with all of this. I mean... this can't be easy for her."

Lind hesitated before exhaling. "She's trying. It's been an adjustment for her, but she's doing her best."

Sam nodded thoughtfully. "That's all anyone can ask for. She means a lot to you, I know."

"She does," Lind said, a small smile on his lips.

Sam grinned. "Well, then she's a lucky woman. And you're a lucky man. I have to say, after Sharon, I really didn't think you would take this kind of chance again."

Lind let out a short chuckle, but the comment made him reflective.

"It wasn't an easy decision," he admitted. "A year in the making, really. But I think she's worth the risk."

Sam studied him for a moment before nodding in approval.

Lind leaned back, gazing up at the blue sky as the music played. He hoped Dana knew how much she meant to him.

Chapter 54

This time is for us

After a long first day, Lind and Sam sat outside their cabin, a fire pit crackling between them. The flames cast a soft glow over the porch, the scent of burning wood mixing with the faint aroma of wine.

Their conversation had been light—reminiscing, laughter woven between sips of red. But occasionally, Lind's thoughts drifted elsewhere.

"You're quiet tonight," Sam observed, tilting her head.

Lind exhaled. "Just thinking."

"About her?"

"Yeah," he admitted. "I know this isn't easy for her, and I hate that I can't be there to reassure her right now."

Sam reached across, placing a hand on his arm. "She'll be okay, Lind. She's strong. And she has you. That's enough."

"I hope so," he murmured, watching the flames flicker.

Sam swirled her wine, her expression shifting. "This time is for us," she reminded him. "We only get a few times a year to reconnect, to take care of each other. I'll talk about Dana all you want—I hope it works out, truly. But this weekend is ours. Will you spend it with me? At least, mostly?"

She leaned forward, shimmying playfully, her grin mischievous.

Lind chuckled, raising an eyebrow in mock amusement. As his eyes found their way back up to hers, his laughter faded, his expression softening.

"You're right," he said with quiet conviction. "I'm sorry. This isn't fair to you either."

Sam squeezed his arm. "Lind, we've been friends for over a decade. I love you, and I want the best for you. And honestly? I think Dana might be the one to make that happen."

"I believe she will," he admitted. "She's worth the effort."

He exhaled, shaking his head slightly. "But you're right. Dana has dominated most of our conversation, and that isn't fair." He sighed slightly. "Alright, your turn—what's going on in your love life? How are your guys?

Sam's grin returned, mischief sparking in her eyes. "Oh, you want the details?"

Lind leaned forward, resting his elbows on his knees. "Absolutely. Spill."

Sam swirled her wine dramatically. "Well, Brian's still Brian. Dependable, steady, the kind of guy who makes sure my tires are rotated and my coffee machine is descaled."

"The practical boyfriend." Lind raised an eyebrow. "Does he schedule your dentist appointments too?"

"He would if I let him." Sam grinned. "But I need to keep *some* independence."

Lind chuckled. "And Jake? Still around?"

"Oh, very much so." She waggled her eyebrows. "He's my *take me to fun places* guy. We hit a new rooftop bar last week, and Lind—you wouldn't believe it. Cocktails served in tiny plant pots. He was over the moon."

Lind shook his head, laughing. "Classic Jake."

"And," she added conspiratorially, "he's still great in bed, so that's a win."

Lind groaned, raising his glass. "Good to know your priorities are in order."

"Hey, it's important." She winked.

"Alright," he said, "now the big reveal—anyone new?"

Sam's grin turned sly. "Ah, I *knew* you'd ask. Yes, actually. Mateo. From California. Just moved here."

Lind leaned back, intrigued. "Serious, or just a test drive?"

She tapped a finger against her glass. "Not sure yet. Laid-back but not lazy, super attentive, great cook—oh, and bonus? He's *not* intimidated by the rest of the lineup."

Lind laughed. "He's not running for the hills knowing you've got a Brian *and* a Jake?"

"And *you.*" She smirked, reaching for his hand. "No, not even a little. If anything, he finds it fascinating."

"Well," Lind said, raising his glass, "here's to Mateo. May he pass the test of passion and patience."

Sam clinked her glass against his, grinning. "Cheers to that."

I keep coming back here with you

Sam tilted her head back, eyes tracing the constellations scattered across the sky. The hum of distant music and laughter softened, blending into the night like an afterthought. She stretched lazily, the firelight casting warm, flickering tones across her skin.

"You know," she mused, voice light but thoughtful, "I always forget how much I miss this until I'm here. No noise, no stress, just... people being people."

Lind nodded, tossing another small log into the fire. "It's a reset. I think that's why we keep coming back. I know that's why I keep coming back here—*with you.*"

Sam smiled, leaning toward him. "And maybe the fact that you look great naked."

Lind chuckled, shaking his head. "If that's all it took, we could just have wine nights at your place."

"True," Sam said, flashing a grin. "But then we wouldn't get to enjoy all this." She gestured at the darkened woods, the glow of the fire, the way everything here felt just a little easier. "There's something freeing about the whole package."

Lind exhaled, his gaze flickering over the embers. "Yeah. There is."

For a while, neither of them spoke. The silence between them wasn't empty—it was the kind of quiet only old friends could share.

Sam shifted, propping her chin on her hand. "So, I don't think I've asked—how's work been? Still navigating Georgette's... particular leadership style?"

Lind chuckled, rubbing the back of his neck. "Yeah, she's still got spreadsheets for her spreadsheets. Super organized, super detailed—but I'll give her credit, she catches things no one else does. Just wish she didn't enjoy it *quite* so much."

Sam laughed, the sound bubbling up naturally. "Poor you. Tell me you're at least staying out of the drama in the break room?"

"For the most part." He grinned. "But you know how it is—put enough people in one place, and someone's bound to stir the pot. And I've got to call out the phonies with the facts."

Sam laughed. "What do you call them..the ducks or geese or something?"

Lind chuckled a little. "You mean the cackling geese?" he retorted.

"Those are the ones. They still at it?" she asked.

"They try, but haven't gotten under my skin yet." He said, rolling his eyes.

Sam nodded knowingly. "That's why I stick to freelance work. My biggest coworker complaint is when the cat walks across my keyboard."

Lind let out a low chuckle. "That does sound nice. But then I wouldn't get front row seats to the *Geese vs. The Lunchroom* saga."

Sam grinned, stretching her arms over her head before letting out a yawn. "Okay, I think I'm officially fire-roasted and wine-soaked. Ready to call it a night?"

Lind stood, offering her a hand to pull her up. "Yeah, let's head in."

Always prepared

The cool night air gave way to the warmth of their cabin, the scent of wood and faint traces of sunscreen lingering in the space. Sam grabbed a bottle of water from the kitchenette while Lind secured the door behind them.

In the bedroom, they moved easily around each other, falling into a rhythm as familiar as breathing. Lind reached into his overnight bag, pulling out the small box they always kept on hand. He passed Sam a condom, a practiced exchange that needed no words.

"Always prepared," Sam said with a wink.

"Always," Lind echoed, his voice low, warm.

"That's good, then we won't need mine."

There was no rush between them—no urgency, just the ease of knowing.

Sam's fingers trailed along his jaw, her smile lazy and knowing as she pulled him closer.

Lind kissed her deeply, slow at first, then sinking into the rhythm they had refined over years. Their laughter mixed with quiet sighs, their bodies moving with familiarity and trust.

Somewhere between breath and touch, Sam murmured his name, her voice full of something deeper than just want.

Lind responded in kind, his grip firm yet gentle. Not claiming, not taking—just being.

This was Sam's time

Later, when the warmth between them had settled into something softer, steadier, Lind got out of bed.

He returned moments later with a warm cloth, cleaning her with the same quiet care he often did.

Sam watched him, eyes heavy with sleep, a lazy smile playing at her lips. "You always know how to take care of a girl."

"That's what friends are for," he said with a sly grin, punctuating the words with one last playful lick.

She giggled softly, eyes fluttering shut. "Lucky me."

He rinsed the cloth and hung it up. He joined her under the covers and wrapped her up in his arms.

She hummed in response, already drifting off, her breath slowing against his chest.

Lind stayed awake for a few moments longer, his mind flickering—just briefly—to Dana.

He exhaled through his nose, gently redirecting his thoughts. *Not now. Not here.*

This was Sam's time.

So instead of chasing the thought, he focused on the now—the steady rise and fall of her breath, the warmth of her against him, the quiet of the cabin, and the rare, unfiltered ease of the moment.

Tomorrow, they'd wake to sunlight through the windows, coffee at the resort cafe, and another full day ahead.

For now, this was enough.

Consider this your preview

The soft glow of dawn filtered through the thin curtains, casting warm streaks of light across the cabin's interior. Sam stirred first, stretching lazily before rolling toward Lind. Her hand found his chest, her fingers tracing lightly over his skin.

"Morning," she murmured, her voice low and flirty.

Lind's eyes fluttered open, a sleepy smile tugging at his lips. "Morning," he replied, his voice still thick with sleep.

Sam's fingers wandered lower, her touch light but deliberate. Lind chuckled, his body reacting instinctively.

"Starting the day like this, huh?"

She grinned, leaning in to whisper in his ear. "Just waking you up the fun way."

Lind's hand found her hip, pulling her closer as he kissed her neck, their movements slow and caressing—never rushed. Sam shifted, her lips trailing lower, her touch growing bolder.

"You're trouble," Lind murmured, his tone caught between amusement and desire.

"Good trouble," she quipped, her voice muffled against his skin. But just as the tension built, she pulled back with a mischievous smile. "We'll save the rest for later. Consider this your preview."

Lind groaned in mock protest, running a hand through his hair. "You're cruel."

Sam laughed, tossing the covers aside as she stretched. "Shower time. Then food. Let's move."

Lind glanced down at himself and arched an eyebrow. "Really? You want me to go outside like this?"

"What's wrong with that? You've done it before."

Lind shook his head, grinning. "Yeah, as I recall, the last time this happened..."

Sam quirked a brow. "Mm-hmm, and as *I* recall, you didn't mind that time either."

Lind exhaled, defeated but amused. "No... I really didn't."

Grabbing their towels—hers draped over her shoulder, his slung in front of him as a temporary cover—they stepped outside.

461

The short walk to the showers felt longer this morning, thanks to the effect of Sam's playfulness. Fortunately, their cabin was set a little farther back, giving Lind some time for his body to relax.

Look, it was almost gone

A couple occupied the far end of the row of open-air showers, so Sam and Lind moved to the opposite side. The cool tiles and warm spray of water felt refreshing as they stepped under neighboring shower heads, letting the steam rise around them.

Lind kept his back to the other couple, waiting out the last traces of their... morning.

Sam, already lathered up, turned to him. "Want to wash my back?"

Lind took the soap from her, his tone light. "You've already washed everywhere else you can reach."

She handed it over without argument, turning slightly to give him access.

Lind's touch was slow and knowing, gliding over the wet smoothness of her back as he had a hundred times, then lower to skim lightly between her cheeks.

Sam let out a slow breath, arching slightly.

Lind's other hand followed, fingers trailing along the curve of her hips before gliding up, knuckles lightly over the dip of her spine.

He reached around her side, his forearm lifting just beneath her breast, soap held out in his open hand, waiting.

Sam looked down, pausing, feeling the solid press of his arm supporting her.

After a beat, she took the soap.

Lind withdrew his hand slowly, his arm brushing the underside of her breast as he stepped back.

"My turn," he murmured, voice low, at the base of her neck.

Sam swallowed, grinning as she met his eyes. "Fair's fair."

Lind turned as she started with his shoulders. She took her time, mirroring his movements, exploring his body with the same mix of care and playfulness. Her fingers traced down from his shoulders to the dip of his spine, the strength in his lower back.

By the time her hand slid lower, lightly teasing him the way he had teased her, Lind exhaled sharply.

Sam glanced over her shoulder—the other couple had left.

She took her time. Her fingers trailed over his firm ass, between his legs, then forward—grazing his balls and stroking his cock with soapy fingers. It responded instantly. Smiling, she retreated again.

Lind groaned, turning to face her, his expression caught between amusement and exasperation.

"Great. It was almost gone—and now it's back," he muttered, motioning downward. "Thanks to you."

Sam burst into laughter, delighted at how easily she could stir him up.

By the time they dried off, the evidence of their playful morning had nearly vanished—again.

Chapter 55

Karen! Steve!

Freshly showered, fresh towels draped over their shoulders, Sam and Lind strolled toward the resort's open-air café. The scent of coffee, sizzling bacon, and fresh pastries filled the air.

As they found a table with a big red shade umbrella, a voice called out.

"Sam!"

Turning, they spotted a familiar couple approaching—a tanned, fit man with salt-and-pepper hair and a petite woman with sun-streaked curls.

Sam's face lit up. "Karen! Steve!"

She stood, throwing her arms around each of them. "I was hoping you'd be here this weekend!"

Steve grinned. "We never miss the festival. And seeing you is icing on the cake."

Karen nodded enthusiastically. "We were hoping we'd run into you. Last year was... unforgettable."

Lind remained seated, offering a polite smile, hands wrapped around his coffee cup.

As the conversation drifted, Karen leaned in with a knowing smile. "Any chance we can reconnect later? Maybe after dinner?"

Sam smiled. "I'd love to."

Karen's eyes flicked to Lind, her smile deepening. "Will Lind be joining us?"

Lind returned the look with a small, easy smile and a shake of his head.

Before he could answer, Sam stepped in gently. "Lind won't be joining us."

Karen's smile faltered slightly. "Oh? Why not?"

Sam's tone softened. "It's... complicated. But don't worry—it'll be just like last year."

Steve nodded, sensing the shift. "Well, we're looking forward to it. Let us know what works for you."

As the couple moved to grab their food, Lind arched an eyebrow at Sam.

"Complicated?"

Sam shrugged, offering a small smile. "It is. But we don't need to get into all that. Let's just enjoy the day.

***

The sun hung high, warm but not oppressive, as Sam and Lind lounged by the pool. Nearby, festival goers swam lazily or gathered in shaded spots, the murmur of conversation and music blending into the easy rhythm of the morning.

Sam nudged Lind with her elbow. "Volleyball? We're signing up."

Lind sighed dramatically. "You *know* I'm terrible at volleyball."

"Exactly why we're signing up. Come on, it'll be fun, especially when I win... again."

Before he could protest, Sam grabbed his arm, dragging him toward the pool.

They joined a group of players, the game quickly turning into a mix of friendly competition and playful chaos. Lind managed a few decent serves, earning exaggerated applause from Sam.

"See? You're a natural."

"Thanks, but you know I'm not," he shot back.

***

After volleyball left them flushed and laughing, Sam tugged Lind toward the pickleball courts with renewed energy where Lind's

465

coordination fared much better. They played a few casual rounds with another couple, exchanging jokes, light competition, and easy banter.

It didn't take long for the men to claim that the game was *unfair*—the women's constant movements proving to be a distraction. But fairness went both ways. The men's own... movements turned out to be just as distracting for their opponents, leading to just as many missed plays and poorly aimed shots.

In the end, everyone had a good laugh about the "natural obstacles" of nudist sports, and the game remained *a fun, albeit occasionally unfocused, match for all.*

This is the life

The afternoon brought a shift in energy as live music filled the air, weaving through the resort like an unspoken invitation to relax. Sam and Lind found a spot near the main stage. They unfolded their chairs under the shade of their umbrella, draping their towels over them. Sam reclined with a cold drink in hand, her foot tapping lazily to the rhythm.

"This is the life," she sighed, stretching out in her chair.

Lind nodded, scanning the crowd. "You can't beat it. Good music, good company..."

Sam raised her glass in a mock toast. "And good vibes."

As the band played on, Sam began pointing out familiar faces, offering Lind snippets of their stories—who was dating whom, who had *just* broken up, who had switched partners since last year.

Every now and then, they got up and danced near the front, caught in the pulsing energy of the crowd. When the sun began its slow descent, they returned to their chairs, pulling fresh drinks from the small cooler and letting the music carry them into an easy stillness.

Fundamentally different

The music played softly in the background, but Lind's mind was elsewhere.

Sam, beside him, leaned back in her chair, face tilted toward the sky, eyes closed, completely at ease. The way she swayed, the way she let the rhythm move through her—it was so effortlessly natural, so unlike the tension he'd felt growing in Dana lately.

It hit him all at once, like a bolt of lightning—how fundamentally different these two women were. Not just in how they viewed love, but how they approached everything.

Dana's Worldview

Dana's life had always followed the traditional script. One boyfriend at a time, each relationship progressing step by step toward something more serious—until it didn't. She viewed love as a commitment that was linear and exclusive, a foundation built on belonging *to* someone and having them belong *only* to her.

He thought back to something she'd said once—an offhand remark at the time. *"I can't imagine sharing someone I love."* It had seemed innocent then. Now, it explained everything.

To Dana, love had always been a zero-sum game. If Lind loved Sam, what did that take away from *her*? If Lind had a full, meaningful relationship elsewhere, how could that not mean she was getting less? The rules she had built her relationships around didn't allow for what he was asking her to accept.

No wonder she was struggling.

Sam's Worldview

And then there was Sam.

If Dana's love had always been about singular devotion, Sam's was the exact opposite—fluid, open, unbound by limits.

From the moment Lind met her over a decade ago, Sam had been clear about who she was.

Her heart had room for more.

She didn't measure love in exclusivity but in connection, variety, and freedom.

For Sam, love wasn't something to be guarded or protected. It wasn't something that could be *taken*—it could only be given, it could only grow.

And because of that, she had never seen Dana as a threat. If anything, she was invested in Lind's relationship with her, genuinely hoping it would work.

For Sam, this world was easy.

For Dana, this world was foreign.

Lind's Realization

Lind leaned back in his chair, his mind racing.

Now, he finally understood why Dana's weight grew heavier with each passing weekend.

This wasn't just about her sharing him with Sam.

It wasn't just about jealousy.

It was about Dana trying to exist in a world that wasn't made for her.

A world where the rules she had always relied on—the ones that made her feel *safe, secure, loved*—no longer applied.

And Sam?

Sam navigated that world effortlessly.

With a confidence Lind had never fully appreciated until now.

The differences between them weren't about who was better or stronger.

They were about who they were at their core.

They were about the lives they had lived, the choices they had made, and the beliefs that had shaped them.

Dana's world was part of the prison Lind had spent his life trying to escape *from*.

Sam's world was the type of freedom he had spent half his life trying to escape *to.*

I'm just now really getting it

"You're listening to the music," Sam murmured, eyes still closed, "but your mind's somewhere else."

Lind blinked, pulled from his thoughts. "I'm sorry."

"Thinking about Dana?"

He sighed, nodding. "Yeah."

She turned toward him slightly, waiting.

"I think I'm just now *really* getting it," Lind admitted. "Why this is so hard for her. Why it feels so *easy* for you."

Sam tilted her head, intrigued. "Oh?"

"It's who you both *are*," he said quietly. "You've always lived this way. Multiple relationships, openness—it's your normal. For Dana, this is completely uncharted territory. She's always had one partner at a time. That's what she *knows*. And now I'm asking her to accept something that goes against everything she's ever believed about love and relationships."

Sam nodded thoughtfully. "It's like speaking two different languages."

Lind exhaled, rubbing a hand over his face. "She's *trying*. She really is. But I don't know if it's fair to ask her to keep trying when it's *this* hard for her."

Sam reached over, squeezing his hand. "It's not about what's fair, Lind. It's about what *she* wants."

Lind frowned slightly.

"If she's still here, still working through it," Sam continued, "then she sees *something* worth fighting for. Trust her to figure out her own limits."

Lind nodded, her words lending him encouragement.

"I just hope I'm not pushing her too far," he murmured.

Sam smiled softly. "You're not. You're giving her the chance to grow, to find out what she's capable of. And that's not a bad thing."

The music swelled around them, the air warm, the weight in Lind's chest heavier than before.

This wasn't just about whether Dana *wanted* to fit into his world.

It was about whether she even could.

For now, he let the moment go. But the questions wouldn't disappear.

They never did.

There you are

The warm buzz of music filled the air, blending with the hum of laughter and conversation. Lind and Sam sat close, their fingers intertwined, her head resting lightly on his shoulder.

The weight of Lind's thoughts from earlier still present, but the warmth of Sam's presence soothed him. No matter what questions circled in his mind, this—being here with her, feeling the easy rhythm of their connection—was something steady.

They let the music wash over them, the weight of the day slipping away. This was their weekend. Their time. And right now, he needed to relax back into that, into them.

Then—

"There you are!"

Sam and Lind turned toward the familiar voices. Steve and Karen were weaving their way through the crowd, their faces bright, their energy infectious.

"We were wondering where you might be camped out," Karen said as they reached them.

Sam grinned, standing to give Karen a warm hug and Steve a quick squeeze. "We've just been sitting here enjoying the music. But I'm glad you found us."

Lind stood as well, shaking Steve's hand with an easy familiarity. "Good to see you again," he said, the words genuine. He didn't know Steve and Karen well, but Sam did—and that was enough. They appeared to be good people. Easy. *Safe*.

Steve's grin widened. "We were hoping to catch up again before it got too late."

Karen's glance at Sam wasn't exactly subtle. "And maybe steal you away for a little while," she added, her voice light but layered with meaning.

Sam's eyes flicked to Lind. She didn't need to explain; he already understood. They'd talked about this possibility earlier.

He held her gaze for a second, giving her a small nod, quiet and steady. "Go have fun," he said, his tone warm.

Her shoulders eased, and the grateful smile she gave him said all it needed to. "I won't be gone long. Meet me back here later?"

"I'll be here, take as long as you want."

Sam pressed a kiss to Lind's lips. "Thanks," she murmured, then grabbed Karen's hand as they made their way through the crowd.

Lind watched them go for a moment, then sat back down, stretching out his legs as he placed his hand on Sam's empty chair...

As the music rolled on he let his breath ease out slowly.

"God, that woman is adventurous. Love her for that."

Would Dana ever fit here

The music swelled around him, a slow rhythm building into something lively and irresistible. He closed his eyes, letting the melody fill him. For a while, he just listened. Let the warmth of the festival pull him back into the moment.

But soon, the music became background noise.

And the thoughts he'd been pushing aside all day surfaced again.

Dana's face appeared first—the way her green eyes softened when she was happy, the faint crinkle in her nose when she laughed. He pictured her smile, not just the one she gave so freely, but the one she reserved for quieter, more vulnerable moments.

His chest tightened as he remembered their last night together.

The feel of her hands on him, hesitant yet intentional, like she was trying to hold on and let go at the same time.

Lind exhaled, the ache of her absence almost painful.

He knew this wasn't just hard for Dana. It was excruciating.

She'd spent months trying to reconcile her feelings, wrestling with doubts and fears he couldn't quiet—no matter how much he tried.

Yet, despite everything, she stayed.

She fought.

She loved him.

And he loved her.

Lind's gaze drifted toward the stage. The band's tempo shifted to something upbeat, and the crowd responded with cheers, swaying and twirling in easy harmony.

His thoughts turned to a question he hadn't dared voice before:

Would Dana ever fit here?

He pictured her standing beside him, her hand in his, her body swaying to the music.

But just as quickly, the image wavered—replaced by the tension he'd seen in her so many times before.

The tightness in her jaw.

The flicker of unease in her eyes.

Would this place—this part of his life with Sam—push her further away?

The empty chair beside him seemed to amplify the contrast.

Dana wasn't here. And she might never be.

Sam, on the other hand, thrived in this world.

She was at home here, unencumbered by the questions and conflicts that weighed on Dana's heart.

Lind rubbed a hand over his face, leaning forward slightly.

He didn't have answers.

Only the certainty of his feelings for both women.

And the stark, undeniable reality of their differences.

As the song shifted into a slow, soulful ballad, he let himself wonder, not for the first time, if the love he and Dana shared could survive the storm this life had brought into hers.

Three naked bodies

The trio moved through the softly lit paths of the resort, the distant hum of music and laughter fading into the background. Steve and Karen led Sam, making their way toward the cabin, a cozy space nestled near the edge of the grounds. Warm light spilled through the open door as Steve stepped inside.

As the women stepped in, Karen was still holding Sam's hand, her touch light and familiar. "It's really good to see you again," she murmured before leaning in, pressing a kiss to Sam's lips—soft at first...

Sam sighed into it, smiling as they parted. "You got yourselves a cabin this year?" she noted, glancing around.

"Yep. After talking with you last year, we booked it before we even left," Karen admitted with a mischievous grin. "We were really hoping we'd see you again."

Sam laughed. "Smart thinking. I'm glad you two made it back. This is going to be fun." Her smile turned playful, full of promise.

Steve quietly shut the door behind them and chuckled. "We've been looking forward to this too."

They moved easily into each other's space—Steve's arm draped over Sam's shoulder, Karen's hand tracing circles along her back. Sam turned toward Karen first, kissing her again, deeper this time, before pulling back just enough to do the same to Steve. Karen laughed against Sam's lips, while Steve exhaled a contented sigh.

Sam smirked. "Well, you certainly know how to make a girl feel wanted."

"Always," Steve murmured, pressing a slow kiss just beneath her ear.

Karen studied Sam for a moment, her eyes warm and appreciative. "You look amazing."

"So do you," Sam said, shifting toward her. "Both of you." She turned back to Steve, capturing his lips briefly before returning her attention to Karen.

Steve chuckled. "You have this energy, Sam. It's infectious."

Sam grinned, her laughter soft but genuine. "I guess I do."

She tangled her fingers into Karen's hair, pulling her closer. The kiss that followed was slow, exploratory, a rediscovery of the easy familiarity they shared last year.

Steve's hands skimmed along Sam's waist, down over her ass, and back up to her shoulders, his touch both intimate and inviting.

With one hand trailing down to grip Steve and the other gliding along Karen's jaw, Sam let herself sink into the moment—into them.

They moved together easily, touch turning to desire, desire turning to heat. And just like that, the space between them vanished—lips meeting skin, hands exploring, laughter giving way to soft sighs as three naked bodies tangled into each other.

You're a good man

An hour later, a familiar hand landed on Lind's shoulder.

He looked up to find Sam standing over him, cheeks flushed, eyes bright with contentment.

"Hey," she said, sinking down beside him and stretching her legs out. "Miss me?"

Lind handed her the bottle of water he'd been saving. "You know I did."

She took a long sip, exhaling as she leaned back. "They're just as much fun as I remembered. Maybe even more."

Lind chuckled, his voice easy. "Good." There was no judgment, no tension—just the simple acknowledgment that this was who they were. "I'm glad you enjoyed yourself."

Sam studied him for a moment, her expression softening. "You're a good man, Lind. I don't say it enough, but I really appreciate you. Not just for making space for my fun, but for being here. For being you."

He met her gaze, his smile faint but genuine. "It's not about 'letting' you have fun, Sam. This is your life. Our life. We've always known how to balance it."

Sam tilted her head, considering him. Then, with a small, knowing smile, she leaned her head against his shoulder. "Still. It means a lot."

Lind wrapped an arm loosely around her, resting his chin lightly against her hair.

"So," she murmured, "what did you do while I was gone?"

Lind huffed a soft laugh. "Listened to music. Thought about life. The usual."

"And Dana?"

He didn't even hesitate. "Always."

Sam reached for his hand, threading her fingers through his. "She's lucky to have you, you know."

475

Lind exhaled, his gaze fixed on the stage. "I'm lucky to have her." His voice was quieter now. "I'm lucky to have both of you."

Sam squeezed his hand in silent understanding.

They sat like that for a while—shoulder to shoulder, hand in hand, the night wrapping around them as the music played on.

Chapter 56

But this? This is special

The festival's energy mellowed as the night deepened. The music shifted to slower, soulful rhythms, and the crowd began to thin—some drifting toward their cabins, others gathering at communal fire pits. Lanterns cast a warm glow, flickering across the relaxed faces of Sam and Lind as they sat in their chairs, soaking in the atmosphere.

As the band announced the final songs of the night, inviting couples to come up near the stage to dance, Sam turned to Lind with a playful smile. Without a word, she held out her hand. He took it, his own smile soft and knowing, and together they joined the others swaying beneath the canopy of stars.

The music wrapped around them, slow and intimate. Lind pulled her close—she rested her head against his shoulder, her hands idly tracing his back and waist. Occasionally, her fingers dipped lower, giving his butt a playful squeeze. Each playful touch earned a quiet chuckle, their laughter shared between them like a private joke.

Lind leaned down, his face buried in her hair as he murmured, "I really don't know what I'd do without you, Sam."

She tilted her head up, her eyes warm as they met his. "I love you too, Lind," she whispered. "Being here with you... it's my favorite. We've had a lot of good times, but this? This is special."

His hold tightened. "Yeah," he said softly. "It really is."

For a little while, they let the world fade away, moving in sync with the music. It wasn't about the festival anymore—it was about them, two people who knew each other so well that even silence between them felt full.

When the last song ended, Sam wrapped her arms around Lind's neck, studying him with a small, contented smile. "Ready to head back?"

Lind nodded. "I think we've danced the music out of them for tonight."

They headed back to their chairs to gather their things, catching sight of Karen and Steve leaving the dance area. They exchanged easy waves and smiles.

As Sam turned back to Lind, she pressed a quick kiss to his cheek. "Thank you."

"For what?" he asked.

"For you," she said simply, resting her head against his shoulder, content in their quiet little corner of reality.

Eventually, they gathered their things—folded their chairs, slung towels over their shoulders, and picked up their trash bag before strolling hand in hand toward the cabin.

The cool night air carried the faint scent of pine and the smoky remnants of bonfires. The sounds of the festival faded into the background, replaced by the rhythmic crunch of gravel beneath their feet. Sam hummed softly, her mood light and reflective, as they made their way through the dark.

Sure you don't want anything

Lind closed the door behind them, shutting out the faint echoes of the resort. The cabin was warm and inviting, the glow of the bedside lamp casting golden light across the rustic walls.

Sam turned to him with a mischievous smile, stepping closer as she trailed her fingers lightly over his chest. "Anything I can do for you before bed?"

Her voice was playful, but beneath it was something more—a quiet sincerity. Her gaze locked on his, her fingertips skimmed just below his collarbone.

478

Lind chuckled softly, shaking his head. "I'm good, really. I'm just glad you got to spend some time with Steve and Karen. You look like you had fun."

Her smile widened, eyes sparkling with amusement. "They're always a good time." Then, her expression turned coy. "But are you sure you don't want anything? I wouldn't mind."

Her touch drifted lower, the back of her hand skimming over his growing erection—light, familiar, knowing.

Lind exhaled, reaching out to rest his hands on her shoulders, steadying her. "I'll wait till morning," he said, his grin matching hers. "I know you'll be ready for more by then."

Sam laughed softly, the sound warm and knowing. She leaned in, pressing a light kiss to his lips. She held it just long enough to feel the connection between them—more affectionate than seductive.

"You do know me too well," she murmured, stepping back with a grin.

Lind let his hands drift down her arms, his fingers grazing the sides of her breasts as he smiled. "I think we've had enough for one night. You'll get your energy back, and tomorrow's going to be a full day."

Her laughter came easily, her expression full of warmth. "You always know how to read me, don't you?"

"You're not as much of a mystery as you think."

Sam rolled her eyes, playfully dramatic, as she moved toward the bed, pulling back the covers. "I'll take that as a compliment."

"You should," Lind called over his shoulder. "It's one of my rare talents."

As he disappeared into the bathroom, Sam climbed into bed, pulling up the covers with a contented sigh. The day had been full but satisfying, and the quiet of the cabin felt like the perfect ending. She rested her head on the pillow, staring at the wooden ceiling, her body fully relaxed.

***

When Lind returned, Sam's gaze followed him. She patted the space beside her, a soft smile on her lips.

"You coming?" she asked, her voice low and inviting but free of pressure.

He nodded as he sank into bed beside her. The quiet intimacy between them comfortable, familiar.

Sam turned onto her side, facing him, her fingers tracing light patterns on his arm. "Thanks for being here with me," she said softly. "I know this isn't always easy."

Lind met her gaze, steady and sincere. "It's not about easy. It's about being true to what we've built. You've been there for me, and I'm here for you. That doesn't change."

Her fingers drifted down to his, intertwining with his as she smiled faintly. "You always know what to say."

Lind reached over and briefly tangled his fingers in her hair before leaning in to kiss her. "Goodnight, Sam."

She turned onto her other side, her back pressing into his chest. "Goodnight, Lind."

Lind draped his arm over her, and she took his hand, holding it to her breast as a contented sigh left her lips.

As they lay there, the sounds of the festival fading into the night, both felt the ease of shared history and trust—a connection, an understanding.

Let Me Take Care Of You

The soft light of dawn filtered through the cabin's curtains, casting a glow over the tangled sheets and warm bodies beneath them.

The air was still, save for the faint rustle of leaves outside and the rhythmic breathing of Sam and Lind, their limbs comfortably entwined.

Lind stirred first, his eyes adjusting to the hazy morning light. When he turned his head, he found Sam already awake, her gaze soft and steady as she studied him.

"Morning," he murmured, his voice thick with sleep.

"Morning," she replied. Her fingers traced a lazy line down the side of his face. "You look well-rested."

Lind exhaled, shifting closer, his hand finding her hip beneath the sheet. His touch was warm, firm but unhurried. "I feel it. I'm glad we didn't overdo it last night."

Sam chuckled, the sound a low, intimate hum. "You planning on making up for it now?"

His answering smile was lazy, knowing. He leaned in, his lips meeting hers as an invitation, and she responded in kind, her fingers tangling in his hair. The kiss deepened, their movements slow but deliberate, each touch a reaffirmation of the connection they shared.

Sam's hand traveled downward over his chest, her touch light and promising. Lind let out a quiet sigh of anticipation. She pulled back just enough to whisper against his skin, her breath warm and inviting.

"Let me take care of you this morning," she murmured, her voice laced with playful affection.

Lind tilted his head back slightly, surrendering to the moment as her lips moved to his neck. His breathing hitched as her hands explored him, their pace unhurried. She moved lower, each kiss, each flick of her tongue sending slow waves of pleasure through him.

Retrieving a condom from the nightstand, Sam rolled it onto him with practiced ease, her fingers confident yet filled with care.

Then she straddled him, her movements steady and sure. Lind's hands found her waist, guiding her as they moved together, their rhythm as natural as breathing.

His hands trailed up her back, his mouth playing on the warmth of her skin. The rise and fall of her breasts, the look of want in her eyes, the way she bit her lip when she knew she was driving him crazy—it was intoxicating.

Their pace was unhurried, savoring every sensation. Sam arched slightly, her breath catching as she shifted her hips, deepening the connection. Lind tightened his hold, pulling her flush against him, burying his face in her chest as the tension built between them.

"Oh, God, Sam..."

"Yes, Lind..."

Their pleasure peaked in tandem, bodies trembling, breath mingling. And when it was over, Sam collapsed onto his chest, her breathing heavy, her heartbeat syncing with his.

Even after all this time

They lay in the stillness, their bodies cooling in the soft morning air. Sam fingers on his chest, her touch light.

"Thank you," she whispered.

Lind frowned slightly. "For what?"

Her hand moved to cup his face. "For always making me feel seen, even after all this time."

For a second, Lind found himself speechless. After all these years, Sam could still surprise him. He'd thought they'd said everything they needed, but here she was, reminding him that the simplest things mattered most.

Lind leaned into her touch, his voice low but steady. "It goes both ways, Sam. You've been there for me in ways no one else ever has. I hope you know how much I appreciate you."

Her lips curved in a small, knowing smile. "I do." She pressed a warm kiss to his forehead before pulling back, their eyes meeting in the quiet understanding they had always shared.

For all the complexities of their lives, in that moment, there was only this—the simplicity of being fully present with someone who understood, accepted, and loved them exactly as they were.

Shower first, then food

Eventually, the warmth of the rising sun coaxed them from bed, the sounds of the resort waking up filtering through the open window—the distant hum of music, the chatter of people heading to breakfast, the occasional burst of laughter from those already starting their day.

Lind stretched, his movements languid and relaxed. "Shower first, then food?" he asked, watching as Sam stood by the window, her bare skin glowing in the morning light.

She turned, grabbing her towel with a playful smile. "Sounds like a plan."

They shared the shower in easy silence, the water cascading over them as they rinsed away the last of sleep. Sam lathered his hair with a mischievous grin, her breasts brushing against his chest more than once. Lind returned the favor, washing her hair from behind, making sure to nudge against her ass a few times in playful retaliation.

Their laughter mingled with the sound of the spray, the moment light and teasing, their comfort with each other effortless.

"I'm ready for breakfast," Sam said, stepping back with a wink.

"Let's go," Lind replied, grinning. "This shower is a little too public for where this is headed."

Once dry, they returned to the cabin to hang up their wet towels and grab fresh ones before heading toward the outdoor cafe, greeting familiar faces along the way. The resort was alive with energy, the scent of fresh coffee and sizzling bacon drifting through the air.

Breakfast was a mix of fresh fruit, scrambled eggs, and warm pastries. They sipped their coffee, the conversation flowing as naturally as ever, punctuated with laughter and the occasional side comment about the night before.

As they finished eating, Sam stretched with a satisfied sigh. "So, same plan as last year?"

Lind nodded. "Stay for the first band, then pack up and hit the road."

Sam grinned. "Perfect. One last dose of music, then back to the *real* world."

Taking the last sip of his coffee, Lind said, "If we have to get back to it, at least we can ease into it."

Sam chuckled. "Exactly."

Later, they claimed a spot on the grass, sitting down on a blanket, leaning against each other as the first band took the stage. The music rolled out easy and familiar—nothing flashy, just good tunes and a crowd that swayed along. Sam's fingers tapped absently against Lind's knee, and he rested his chin lightly on her head. They didn't talk much. They didn't need to. They just listened.

When the last song ended, they shared a quiet look and a smile, then stood to pack up their things. Folding towels, shaking out blankets, stowing chairs. It was a well-practiced routine, neither rushed nor reluctant, well... maybe a little reluctant.

Heading back later today

After grudgingly putting clothes on for the first time in over 48 hours, Sam and Lind loaded their bags into the truck.

Lind pulled out his phone, tapping out a quick message to Dana.

Lind: *Heading back later today. I've missed you. Can't wait to see you tomorrow.*

Sam, tossing her towel into the backseat, gave him a playful nudge. "You're going to be texting her the whole drive home, aren't you?"

Lind laughed, shaking his head as he slipped his phone into his pocket. "I might. I want her to know I'm thinking about her."

Sam grabbed his shirt and pulled him in for a kiss, looking up at him. "If nothing else, Lind, you are a romantic."

He grinned against her mouth. "That's one of the things you like about me."

She pulled back, her eyes gleaming with warmth. "Yes, it is," she said, squeezing his hand. "Yes, it is."

As Lind pulled out of the resort, he glanced once in the rearview mirror—the open meadow now quiet behind them—and then turned his gaze forward. His thoughts drifted to Dana—what she'd say, how she'd feel, and how he could remind her, once again, how much she meant to him.

Part 12

<u>Holding On While Letting Go</u>

He kissed like we had time.
    Touched me like we had a future.
    But...
    This wasn't about making love.
    It was about remembering.
    Creating something to keep.
    I didn't tell him.
    I couldn't.

Chapter 57

Pretending it's a normal Monday

The store bustled with its usual Monday morning activity. Dana stood in the break room, stirring a sugar packet into her coffee, her back to the door. The faint hum of coworkers chatting around her was drowned out by the pounding of her heart.

She tried not to look at him during the morning meeting—but every time she risked a glance, he wasn't looking back.

Then, as she was fixing her coffee, his voice—casual, warm—filtered in from just outside the break room door.

Her stomach clenched.

She braced herself, hands trembling slightly, eyes fixed on the swirling coffee as he walked through the door.

"Dana."

Lind stood in the doorway, his eyes searching for hers.

She turned slowly, keeping her expression neutral. "Morning."

He stepped closer, a small smile tugging at his lips. "Morning."

A silence stretched between them—not awkward for him, but suffocating for her. Unspoken questions pressed against the back of her throat.

Lind tilted his head slightly. "You okay?"

"I'm fine," she said too quickly, turning back to her coffee. "Just... pretending it's a normal Monday morning."

His brow furrowed, but he didn't press. "Let me know if you want to talk later." His voice was soft, patient.

Dana forced a small smile he couldn't see. "Sure. Thanks."

As he left, she exhaled shakily, fingers tightening around the cup.

He's acting so normal.
Like nothing happened.

Like the weekend didn't even matter.

***

Dana left the break room, but the weight of the morning stayed with her. Clipboard in hand, she moved through the store, trying to shake the knot in her chest.

She hadn't expected Lind to act differently... but his calm demeanor still stung.

How can he be so unbothered, when I feel like I'm barely holding it together?

A few aisles away, Lind stood near the registers, caught up in conversation with a small group of coworkers. His voice carried lightly over the morning hum.

"So, Lind, you disappeared this weekend! What were you up to?" one of the coworkers asked.

"Yeah," another added with a grin, "must've been some trip to keep you away for three days. Spill it!"

Lind chuckled, scratching the back of his neck. "Just caught up with an old friend. Relaxed a bit. Nothing wild."

"An old friend, huh?" a third coworker grinned. "That's all you're giving us? Sounds suspiciously like a girlfriend to me."

Lind laughed lightly. "Trust me, not as exciting as you're making it sound."

The group chuckled, their curiosity piqued. One of them leaned in conspiratorially, just as Brenda appeared. She stepped into the circle, her knowing smile light but deliberate.

"Oh, come on, give Lind a break," she said, tone breezy. "He mentioned the trip to me last week—some old friend he hadn't seen in forever, right, Lind?"

Lind blinked, his gaze meeting Brenda's briefly before he nodded. "Yeah. Exactly. Nothing more than that."

Brenda remained casual but firm, smoothly redirecting the group. "Now, unless you're all planning to share your weekend escapades, maybe let the guy get back to work?"

Laughter rippled through the group, and the conversation moved on. Lind shot Brenda a small, grateful smile.

"Thanks for that," he said quietly once they were alone.

Brenda shrugged. "You'd do the same for me. Besides, you're not exactly subtle. People were bound to ask."

Lind's eyes narrowed slightly as he studied her. "You seem to know a lot about my weekend."

Her smile didn't falter. "You don't have to worry about me, Lind. I'm just here to keep things... uncomplicated."

He nodded slowly, but as she walked away, a flicker of uncertainty crossed his mind.

How much does she actually know?

***

A short distance away, Dana caught the exchange from the corner of her eye. She appreciated Brenda's quick thinking...

But a bitter thought surfaced: Even he needed saving from this. From me.

She turned toward the stockroom, willing herself to push past the pang of jealousy and doubt. But one thought persisted, sharp and unshakable.

How long can we keep pretending this is normal?

You're not going to give her up

Dana's condo felt smaller than usual as she set the table.

Lind arrived with a bottle of wine, his easy smile filling the doorway. He kissed her cheek as he stepped inside.

The pasta sat waiting, but the tension in the room was unmistakable.

"Want me to pour you a glass?" he asked, holding up the bottle.

Dana lifted her beer in response. "Already covered."

Then, without missing a beat: "You want one?"

He nodded. "Sure."

"Good," she said, grabbing one from the fridge. "Because it's beer time again."

Lind glanced toward the table, then back at her. "Dana," he said gently, "what's going on?"

The calm feeling he'd carried from the weekend had already started to unravel in just three days. She was hurting, and he was powerless to fix it.

She hesitated, then sighed. "I don't know. I just..." Her voice trailed off before she found it again. "I'm still... working through the weekend."

Lind leaned a shoulder against the counter, his expression open, patient. "I figured. Talk to me."

Her voice was quieter now. "It's hard to explain. I know we talked about it, and I know you're honest with me, but... knowing you spent the whole weekend with her? It's different from just hearing about it in theory."

Lind nodded. "I get that. And I don't expect you to adjust overnight. But Dana... it means a lot that you're trying."

Dana looked down at the bottle in her hands. "I am trying. But sometimes, it feels like I'm not enough. Like no matter what I do, she'll always be this... part of your life that I can't compete with."

Lind reached out, gently touching her wrist. His voice was steady, filled with warmth.

"Dana, this isn't a competition. What I share with Sam doesn't take away from what I have with you. You mean so much to me—that's never going to change."

She nodded, but her chest still felt tight. "It's just... hard sometimes—all the time."

"I know," Lind said, giving her wrist a soft squeeze. "And I'm here, Dana. You don't have to carry this by yourself."

She let out a hollow chuckle. "That's the thing, Lind. You are the thing I need to figure out. So how are you supposed to help me?"

Lind hesitated—just for a second, caught off guard. Then, softly, "I love you, Dana. I'll do whatever I can to make this easier."

Dana thought, *There's only one way to make this easier... and you're not going to give her up.*

And I'm not ready to walk away... yet.

I'm not ready for that

After dinner, they moved to the couch. Lind pulled Dana close, wrapping an arm around her as she leaned against him.

"I've missed this," he murmured.

She closed her eyes, exhaling slowly. "Me too."

After a long pause, Lind glanced at her. "I packed a bag, by the way. It's in the truck. Just in case..."

Her hand clenched around the bottle, knuckles whitening. "I'm not ready for that... not yet."

Lind didn't hesitate. His nod was calm, understanding. "That's okay. I just wanted you to know the option was there."

She exhaled, tension softening. "Thanks."

The evening ended with a quiet kiss at the door.

As Lind walked to his truck, Dana stood in the doorway, arms crossed, watching him go. The weight in her chest hadn't lifted. If anything, it felt heavier.

Dana leaned against the frame, her emotions tangled in a mix of relief and longing.

Chapter 58

Stop it! That's Ridiculous

Dana sat at her kitchen table on Thursday afternoon, a beer growing warm in front of her. Lind had shared a few vague details about the weekend—how great the music was, how Sam had a knack for picking the best food trucks—but nothing too personal. Nothing about *them.*

Her fingers tightened around the bottle as her mind drifted. She pictured them lying on a blanket under the stars, the hum of a guitar floating through the air. Lind's head rested on Sam's chest, nestled between her bare breasts, his arm draped lazily across her stomach and down between her legs. Sam's fingers moved slowly through his hair, her gaze soft and content. The world around them faded, leaving only the two of them, completely at ease in their own bubble.

The image burned in Dana's mind, vivid and relentless. Her chest tightened, her stomach flipped.

Stop it. That's ridiculous, she told herself, trying to push the image away.

She leaned back in her chair, forcing herself to take a deep breath. There were hundreds of people there. The festival was about *Social nudism,* not a *sexual orgy.* She knew that. And besides, they always brought chairs, not blankets. Lind had even joked about how hard it was to lug them across the festival grounds.

She shook her head sharply, as if to dislodge the thought. "Get a grip, Dana," she muttered.

Still, the image was stubborn as a weed. She hated how easily her mind conjured it, how real it felt. She *trusted* him. She did. But trusting Lind didn't make the jealousy any easier to swallow.

Her phone sat beside her on the table. She picked it up and scrolled through her messages, searching for some reassurance. His last text was there, light and sweet: *Missing you already. Let's plan our weekend soon?*

Dana sighed, fingers hovering over the keyboard. She wanted to believe him. She wanted to stop imagining things that weren't true. But her own insecurities clung to her like a shadow, refusing to let go.

The silence didn't help. The stillness in the condo felt dense, like a fog enveloping her. She reached for her phone, opened her music app, and hit shuffle—anything to drown the silence.

She closed her eyes to let the music take hold of her. She sipped her beer as she let one song after another try and calm her, to take her somewhere else, anywhere but here.

Then a soft piano note drifted in. Familiar. Slow.

Her body stiffened. She paused. She opened her eyes, her thumb hovering over the screen.

Gravity.

Of course it would be this song.

God, do I let it play? I don't know if I can.

She didn't move. She just sat there, staring at nothing as the first lines played.

... always brings me back to you

... never takes too long

No matter what I do...

The sting in her eyes grew with every word...

You hold me without touch... you keep me without chains...

Dana's throat tightened. It wasn't the lyrics themselves—it was the truth in them. That quiet ache of being tethered to someone without trying. Of being pulled back to him every time.

And maybe that was the part she hated most. Not Lind. Not even Sam. Just this feeling—like no matter how hard she tried to protect herself, her heart kept circling back to him. Kept falling toward him. Like gravity.

She closed her eyes.

I can't rise above this. God damn it Lind, I love you so much I hate you sometimes.

The song played on. She let it. Let it wrap around her like a weight, pulling her under.

When it ended, Dana blinked slowly, wiped her cheeks and then her mouth. She set her phone down on the table. She didn't even hear the next song. Her thoughts too loud to hear anything else.

She's not sure how long she sat like that.

***

Dana's phone buzzed again, breaking the silence. Lind's name lit up the screen.

Hope you're alright. If you need or want anything, just let me know. I was thinking we could revisit Coffee Brews & Muse and walk around a bit if you'd like?

She stared at the screen for a long moment. She didn't have the energy to answer right away—her chest still ached, her emotions raw.

She loved that he was always like this. Thoughtful. Gentle. Never pushing too hard, just leaving space for her to come back.

And she hated how much that mattered—how much it hurt, knowing she always did.

Dana took a slow, deep breath. Got up. Walked to the sink and rinsed her face with cold water.

She didn't feel better. But she felt clearer.

She came back to the table. Read the message again.

Her lips pressed into a thin line. Then, finally, she typed:

That sounds nice. Let's do Saturday morning.

His reply came quickly: *Great. Would you like to come over tomorrow night for dinner? I'll cook.*

Dana stared at the message, her chest tightening. She didn't want to go over Friday night, didn't feel up to it. But how could she explain that without sounding cold? She'd already cut their usual Wednesday date night short and barely spoke to him at work. She typed back carefully.

Thanks, but I'll pass on tomorrow. Looking forward to Saturday though—pick me up at 8:30?

Lind set his phone down, rereading Dana's message. She'd passed on dinner but agreed to Saturday morning. A sense of uneasiness began to sink in. She hadn't been herself lately—quieter, distant.

His mind drifted to their last few interactions. How she avoided meeting his eyes at work. How her usual teasing remarks had been replaced by polite smiles. Even her message tonight felt... restrained.

Am I pushing too hard? Maybe she just needs space. But what if space was the last thing they needed right now?

After a moment, he replied: *You got it. Looking forward to seeing you.*

Dana set her phone down and let out a slow breath. Saturday morning felt manageable. She could put on her happy face for a few hours, sip coffee, and pretend everything was fine.

Lind exhaled, reminding himself to be patient. *Just give her time.*

No one does this kind of thing

Lind's truck pulled up outside Dana's condo promptly at 8:30. She had to smile at his reliability, even if the knot in her stomach hadn't loosened since she got out of bed.

She greeted him with her usual playful banter.

"Right on time. Should I be impressed or suspicious?" she grinned.

"Always impressed," Lind shot back with a grin, though he couldn't ignore the absence of her usual affection.

They drove to her coffee shop keeping the conversation light, but Dana felt like she was walking a tightrope. His hand rested on the console between them, where they always shared space. Not today. Instead, she filled the silence with a story from work.

When they arrived they each ordered their usual brews.

She sipped her coffee slowly, letting Lind steer the conversation. *Stop avoiding it,* he thought. *Can't believe you're nervous to talk with her.* He took a breath. *Open your mouth and talk to her.*

"So," he began, leaning back in his chair. "How are you? I mean, really."

She hesitated—just a fraction of a second, but he caught it. "I'm trying," she said finally, her voice quieter than she intended. "This whole... arrangement is just... odd. Difficult."

Her words hit him like a small, sharp weight. *I figured as much, but hearing her say it...*

Lind nodded, his expression thoughtful. "I figured. I know it's not easy. I just—I want us to keep talking about it, you know? To figure it out together."

"I don't know anyone else who has to go through this, Lind. No one does this kind of thing," she said, exasperated.

"Dana," he said gently, steady and calm, "this might sound self-serving but... there are lots of people that do." he paused, catching her eye. "Can I give you... some... perspective?"

"What do you mean?" she asked, her voice tense and weary.

"Can I share some facts? Statistics, really." Another pause. "Maybe it'll help. Maybe it won't, but I think you'll be surprised."

She folded her arms as she leaned back in her chair. Her eyes never leaving his. "Fine. I'm listening," she said, her tone tinged with disbelief.

He began slowly. "How many people work at our store?"

"I don't know," she said flatly, wondering what that had to do with anything.

"About 165—full and part-time—according to Georgette," he said. "I'll bet you're wondering what that has to do with anything."

Dana raised her brows and tilted her head in response.

"Well, here's the thing. Around 6% of people in this country are in arrangements like ours—though often more equal. About 20% have been at some point, and 16% *want* to be."

Dana frowned, trying to follow where this was going. "And?"

"That means, statistically, about 10 people in *our* store are *currently* in a relationship just like ours."

Dana held up her hand. "Wait, 10 other people we work with?"

"Yes—or work around," he said. "Store side associates or night crew or whoever. Yes."

"I've never heard anyone say anything about being in a relationship like this," she stated flatly.

"Do we talk openly about ours?" He challenged.

She broke eye contact with him, looking down at her coffee without seeing it, processing. But didn't say anything.

"It also means that thirty to thirty-five people we work with have been in this kind of relationship. And another twenty-six *want* to be." He paused to let Dana catch up to the implications of that.

Dana frowned, trying to follow his words. The numbers buzzed in her head, sounding almost too impossible to be true.

He moved his hand towards hers but stopped just short of touching her. "So, when you say no one does this kind of thing... that's not exactly true."

Dana blinked, catching up. "You think other people in the store—?"

"Statistically, yeah," Lind said with a small smile. "It's more common than you think."

"I've been working at the store for years now Lind and NO ONE has ever talked about it," she countered.

"I'm sure they haven't," he conceded. "But people don't talk about who they're cheating with either, do they? Doesn't mean it's not happening..."

"Ya, I guess." Dana had to admit. "So?"

"So... just because people don't talk about it," Lind pointed out, "doesn't mean it isn't going on right under our noses all the time."

He paused, watching her face. "If you look for it Dana, you just might see the signs," he stated.

Dana wondered if that might be true.

"Love isn't as limited as we've been taught." he said softly as he inched his hand a little closer to hers, an invitation he was hoping she'd accept, "most believe love is finite—jealous, small, possessive... imprisoning." He said slowly, his eyes locked on to hers, his voice unwavering. "But love isn't any of those things. It's bigger than we can imagine..."

His hand reached hers rubbing his fingers lightly over her knuckles. "And I *love* you. I don't want to lose you."

A lump rose in her throat. "I love you too, Lind. I really do. But... this is so hard to *live*. It sounded okay in the beginning, but living it? That's something else."

"I know, Dana. I really do." He took her hand lightly in his . "And I'm here. Whatever you need."

Dana's fingers tightened around his, her thumb brushing lightly over his skin. The smile she gave him—tired but sincere—was the first he'd seen in days.

It was enough to give him hope—enough to lift his heart.

Dana nodded. "Thanks. I'll keep trying." *God, I need to stop saying that.*

I cannot say no to this man

The morning's conversation left Dana feeling raw, her mind swirling with Lind's words. As they strolled through town, his statistics kept circling in her head.

Ten people in the store in relationships like ours? Thirty-five who've done it before? Twenty-six who want to?

She shook her head, a wry smile on her lips. Some of the people she pictured made her laugh. *No way. Not Sheila in accounting.* She paused. *Or... actually, maybe.*

The mental exercise gave her a surprising sense of relief. Maybe she wasn't as alone in this as she thought. Maybe it wasn't so crazy. Maybe she wasn't the only one trying to fit into a world she didn't understand.

Lind glanced over, catching a smile beginning at the edge of her lips. Her shoulders had loosened, the tension in her jaw softened. She looked more like herself again—at least for now.

Their hands swung close as they walked, brushing once... but she didn't take his.

They meandered through their favorite shops, browsing shelves of handmade trinkets and quirky gifts. He picked up a small ceramic cat—rounded, cozy-looking, with soft colors and just a hint of mischief in its painted eyes. He turned it in his hand, smiling.

"This one reminds me of you."

Dana gave him a sideways look. "Oh yeah?"

He held it gently, admiring it. "Sweet and warm. The kind of girl who curls up next to you and makes everything better just by being there." He tapped the tiny ceramic paw. "But anyone who doesn't know better might forget about the claws. Until they earn them."

Dana's smile softened, touched more than she let on. "You're not wrong."

She looked down at the little cat, her smile softening with a quiet affection... that she didn't try to hide.

She nudged his shoulder with her forehead, letting out a playful laugh.

They wandered a little more, still smiling, the mood light between them.

They picked up a soft pretzel from a nearby stand to share, and soon found themselves flipping through pages at a cozy bookstore—novels, cookbooks, quiet conversation—a break from the tension that had been sitting between them.

Lind watched her as she thumbed through an art book, her expression relaxed for the first time... in a while. *Look at that smile, that happy face. Welcome back, my love.*

As the afternoon sun began to dip, they headed back to his truck.

"So, can I make you dinner tonight?" Lind asked, holding his breath.

Dana nodded. "Yeah, sounds good." *I cannot say no to this man.* Then, a whisper of doubt. *Yes, you can. You have several times this week already.*

Maybe. But not tonight.

Lind started the engine, sneaking a glance at her as she sat beside him. *Maybe she'll stay over. God, I miss her when she's not sleeping beside me.*

As they pulled onto the main road, Dana exhaled slowly. Then the thought hit her—she hadn't brought anything for the night.

Her stomach flipped. *I'm probably staying over... Of course I'm staying over.* She resigned. The certainty came out of nowhere, and it rattled her.

But as Lind hummed softly beside her, one hand loose on the wheel, she let herself accept the idea. *It's who we are.*

The realization came with a mix of emotions—comfort, unease. She hadn't planned for this. Hadn't even considered it. But now, the idea felt... natural.

She glanced at Lind as he drove, humming absently, hands loose on the wheel.

For all my doubts, I still want to be here. To feel close to him. That has to mean something... doesn't it?

More and more like beer time

Dana sat up on the couch, watching Lind move through the kitchen. When she'd asked if he needed help, he waved her off.

"No, just relax. Want some wine?" he asked, already reaching for a bottle.

"No thanks," she said.

"Oh. Okay." He hesitated. "Can I get you anything else?"

"You got a beer?"

Lind paused, raising an eyebrow. "A beer?"

"It's been feeling more and more like it's 'beer time' in my life lately."

That unsettled him. "Sure. Bottle or can?"

"Oh, bottle for sure."

He popped the top and handed it to her, watching as she took two long sips, staring blankly at the dark screen of the TV.

Beer time? That's twice now. What does that mean? Something inside him didn't like the feel of that.

"I'm going to fry up some chicken fingers, mashed potatoes with white gravy, and green beans with bacon. A little comfort food tonight."

"Sounds delicious," she murmured absently.

Lind prepped the chicken, glancing at her every so often. *What is she thinking about? Am I the reason she's so far away? Of course, I am. Am I enough? Am I too much? Am I asking for more than she can give?* The questions wouldn't stop.

"Want to watch something?" he asked. "We could pick up that series we started."

"No, I'm good."

She still hadn't looked away from the blank screen. Her mind swirled. *What did he mean by 'arrangements' like ours but more equal? Does he think I should have someone else too? Would he even be okay with that?*

The idea felt alien. Like trying to imagine herself as someone else entirely.

Does Sam really have multiple boyfriends? Lind says they all know about each other. How does that even work? Would I ever be able to live in that kind of relationship?

Then, a sharp realization struck her.

I am living in that kind of relationship. And I don't think I like it.

Lind peeled potatoes, lost in his own thoughts. *How do I get this woman to accept me, all of me? To understand how much she means to me?*

Dana exhaled, pushing away the storm in her head. "Are you sure I can't help?"

"Actually, I thought we'd have biscuits too. Want to handle that?"

"Sure."

She got up, beer in hand, and grabbed the tube of biscuit dough. Bumping it against the counter, she peeled it open, placing each one on a baking sheet. *Easy. Simple. Unlike my thoughts—twisting, turning, looping back on themselves.*

"The oven's already set," Lind said, smiling as she worked. *Thank God she's stopped overthinking, at least for now.*

He wanted to reach for her. To pull her into a hug. But would she let him?

He didn't want to risk the answer.

Yes, she matters—but so do you

When they sat down to eat, it looked like a feast. Crispy golden chicken strips, mashed potatoes smothered in rich white gravy, green beans with smoky bacon.

Dana's appetite hadn't been normal lately, but the smell of home-cooked food helped quiet her thoughts. She dipped a chicken strip into the gravy, savoring the way it melted in her mouth.

Damn, the man can cook, she thought.

"This is really good," she said aloud, smiling. "The Colonel is probably rolling over in his grave."

Lind chuckled, returning from the fridge with another cold beer. He held it out to her as she handed him her empty bottle, her fingers brushing against his, light, hesitant.

"Thank you," she said softly.

Lind sat down, reaching for a biscuit. "What's going on in that head of yours?" He tried to keep the tone light, but there was an edge of worry in his voice.

Dana blinked, startled by the question. "Everything and nothing. Just... tired, I guess."

"You've been pretty quiet all evening." He hesitated. "You don't have to talk, but... I'm here. If you want to."

Her fork clattered softly against the plate as she set it down. She wanted to tell him everything—the jealousy, the fear that she wasn't enough. But the words wouldn't come.

Instead, she met his gaze and said, "I'm trying, Lind. I'm really trying."

Oh, fuck. There I go again with the trying.

He reached across the table, his hand covering hers. "I know you are," he said. "And I appreciate it more than you know. I just wish I knew what to say to help."

Dana nodded, her throat tight. She pulled her hand back. Picked up her beer, and took a long sip, hoping it would calm her thoughts.

How do I tell him? What do I say? Why can't I just say it?

Lind watched her carefully. *I thought she was back. I hoped she was back. I don't want to drive her away—she's too important.*

Just then a quiet voice deep inside him whispered:

Yes, she matters—but so do you!

Later, as they cleaned up the dishes, Dana's mind wandered. She watched Lind rinse the plates, his focus steady and unhurried.

Does he ever doubt this? Does he ever wonder if it's worth it?

She didn't know how to ask, didn't even know if she wanted to hear the answer.

Her thoughts turned inward. *Am I really trying? Or am I just pretending to try?* She hated the doubt, the way it made her feel like she was failing at something she hadn't even chosen.

Chosen? Her breath caught. *I did choose this. I just didn't understand what this was.*

Then she looked at Lind—standing beside her, present and steady.

Something about his presence in that moment calmed her. Not because he had answers. Just because he was there.

Maybe that was enough.

Maybe *he* was enough.

Maybe *right now* was enough.

For all my doubts

When the last dish was put away, Lind wiped his hands on a towel and glanced at Dana. She looked tired, her shoulders slightly slumped, but the tightness in her expression had eased.

"You wanna watch something?" he asked, tilting his head toward the living room.

She hesitated, then nodded. "Sure."

Dana tucked herself into the far corner of the couch as Lind grabbed the remote. He flicked on the TV, landing on something neither of them cared much about. Tossing the remote onto the coffee table, he stretched his arm along the back of the couch.

Dana hesitated, then shifted closer, pressing her side against him. His arm slid naturally around her shoulders, pulling her in just enough to feel his warmth.

She let out a breath, long and slow, resting her head on his chest.

Lind felt the knot in his chest loosen slightly. *She's here. She's with me. Let's count that as enough for now.*

He rested his cheek against the top of her head, his fingers lightly gliding over her arm.

Dana closed her eyes. *For all my doubts, I still want to be here. Right here.*

"You okay?" Lind asked, his voice warm and low.

"Mm-hmm," she murmured. Speaking would pull her out of the moment, and right now, she just wanted to stop thinking.

Her fingers wandered down his arm, then to his thigh. She moved in slow circles, careful to avoid going too high. She'd done it before—let her touch become an invitation—but tonight, she didn't want that.

Lind noticed. The way her touch stayed soft and distant.

Not tonight.

His disappointment was mixed with understanding. He tightened his arm around her, pulling her just a little closer. *Whatever she needs, I'm here.*

Dana felt the shift, the subtle reassurance. She sighed into him, her body relaxing further.

For once, the relentless storm in her head seemed to quiet.

Dana's hand rested on his thigh, as if anchoring herself to him.

"Thank you," she whispered.

Lind glanced down at her, his fingers stilling on her arm. "For what?"

"For... just this." Her voice was thick with emotion.

Lind pressed a kiss to the top of her head, his hold on her unwavering. "Always."

And for that moment, the world felt a little smaller. A little quieter. A little more manageable.

***

The steady hum of the TV lulled them into a haze, their breathing synced, their bodies warm against each other.

It wasn't clear who drifted off first, but when Dana stirred, the room was dim, the only light coming from the soft flicker of the screen.

Lind's voice came low and gravelly, thick with sleep. "Hey. You ready to go to bed?"

Dana blinked slowly, lifting her head. His expression unguarded in a way that made her chest ache.

She nodded. "Yeah. I think so."

Lind stood, stretching. "I'll meet you there," he said, pausing before heading toward the bedroom.

Dana made her way to the bathroom, flipping on the light and squinting as her eyes adjusted.

The spare toothbrush he'd bought her sat in its usual spot, nestled next to his.

Something about the sight of it steadied her.

She brushed her teeth in silence, her thoughts, for once, still.

After rinsing, she caught her reflection in the mirror and sighed. Slowly, she undid the buttons of her blouse, letting it fall from her shoulders before pulling her V-neck over her head. Her bra followed, discarded onto the counter. She slipped the soft, loose V-neck back on, hesitating for a moment before taking off her jeans as well.

For a moment, the vulnerability of sharing a bed with Lind—of being *close* to him while feeling so unsteady inside—made her stomach flutter.

But then she thought of his arm around her earlier. The way he'd held her like she was something precious.

And that was enough.

***

When Dana stepped into the bedroom, the bedside lamp cast a soft glow across the room. Lind sat on the edge of the bed, barefoot and relaxed, scrolling through his phone. At the sound of her footsteps, he glanced up, a quiet smile on his lips.

Oh, God, he thought.

"Everything okay?" he asked.

She nodded, setting her folded blouse and jeans on a nearby chair. "Yeah."

For a moment, she took in the space—the warm light, the faint scent of his detergent, the quiet hum of the apartment. It felt safe. Familiar. *His.*

Lind stood, passing her on his way to the bathroom. In the dim light, he caught a glimpse of her—the soft V-neck clinging to her curves, the smooth lines of her body beneath it. Beautiful. Sexy. His breath hitched. Of course, her nipples were showing.

Dana climbed into bed, tugging the covers over herself. She usually wore less when sleeping beside him, but tonight, the soft fabric of her shirt and panties felt like a shield—a small piece of herself she could hold back while still being close to him.

By the time Lind returned, the lights were dimmed, and Dana lay on her side, facing the wall. He paused in the doorway, his gaze lingering on her before he crossed the room.

He stripped down to his boxers with easy familiarity, completely at home. The bed dipped as he got under the covers, his warmth instantly filling the space beside her.

Goodnight, beautiful

Lind shifted closer, his arm draping gently over her waist as he pulled her into him. The heat of his chest pressed against her back, his presence solid and familiar.

"You feel good," he murmured, his voice low and soft.

Dana sighed, her hand resting lightly on his forearm. "So do you," she whispered.

She let herself sink into the feeling—his breath warm against her shoulder, their legs tangling slightly beneath the sheets. The steady rhythm of his breathing soothed her, lulling her toward sleep.

For Lind, the moment felt like a fragile kind of perfection. The tension that had hovered between them all day was still there, but quieter now. *This is what I want,* he thought. *Her, like this. Us, like this.*

Dana slowly ran her fingers up and down Lind's arm, her touch light and soothing. She wanted to say something—something about how much she appreciated this, how much she loved him—but the words felt too heavy for the quiet space between them.

Instead, she leaned further into him, pulling his arm tighter around her. Maybe he was enough. And maybe, just maybe, that's what she needed to believe. To trust in him, in them... again.

Lind pressed a slow kiss to the back of her head.

"Goodnight, beautiful," he whispered.

"Goodnight," she murmured, her voice soft but steady.

The room fell silent, save for the rustle of sheets and their synchronized breathing. Wrapped up in each other, the questions and doubts that had plagued them earlier seemed to fade—at least for now.

Chapter 59

She didn't rush

Lind stirred awake, stretching before slipping out of bed to use the bathroom. The early light filtered through the curtains, casting a soft glow over Dana's form.

When he returned he laid down behind her molding his body against hers.

Dana stirred, reaching for his hand, patting it gently before slipping out from under him. She rolled away, swinging her legs over the side of the bed as she made her way to the bathroom as well.

Lind stayed where he was, only half-awake, waiting.

When Dana returned, he hadn't moved. Eyes closed, facing the same direction, breathing slow and steady.

She slipped back under the covers and pressed herself against his warmth. His arm automatically draped over her, their bodies syncing in the quiet, easy way that felt like home.

For a while, they just lay there, quiet, relaxed, together.

Then Dana began to move.

Her fingers traced slow, feather-light patterns on his arm, exploring. The sensation sent a pleasant hum through Lind's skin, his muscles flexing slightly under her touch.

She reached back, her fingers dancing over his stomach, circling his belly button before moving lower.

Lind exhaled, relaxing into her touch.

Her hand found the waistband of his boxers, slipping inside, touching, playing. She ran her fingers through the soft hair beneath, tugging gently before moving lower still.

When she brushed against his cock, he twitched, his breath catching in his throat.

He reached under her shirt, cupping her breast in his palm, the weight of it familiar. He grazed her nipple, then rolled it softly, coaxing a quiet moan from her lips as it sent that familiar sensation down between her legs.

Dana moaned softly, her grip tightening around his cock, stroking lightly as he grew harder beneath her touch.

Lind let out a quiet groan as her fingers explored him fully—trailing along his length, testing his reactions, listening to the subtle shifts in his breathing. She felt the way he pulsed under her fingers, the heat of him, the way he twitched with each teasing stroke.

She didn't rush.

Lind reached down, wanting her, but when his fingers reached between her legs, he found her thighs pressed together—closed.

But... no panties.

The realization sent a fresh wave of arousal through him, but still, she didn't open for him.

He hesitated—then adjusted, letting his hand glide up over her hip instead, his fingers dipping lower, searching from behind.

The feather light touch sent another pulse of sensation through her, anticipation and deliberation colliding as she breathed in deeply, her body already slick and wanting.

His fingers explored between the wet, swollen lips—nothing demanding, nothing insistent. Just slow exploration and light pinches, letting her decide how far this would go.

Dana sighed softly, gripping his erection and shifting her hips closer to him, adjusting so she could use him to play against herself.

Lind caught on immediately, moving his hand away to give her access. He pushed his boxers off as the sensation of her rubbing his length between her lips caused him to shudder, her wetness made each pass more intense, sweeter—his desire building with every stroke.

The newness of it—from someone he knew so well—caught him off guard, changing the rules, undoing him. But he wouldn't chase it. Not yet. Not before her.

And Dana was in no hurry, taking her time, dragging out every movement—pushing his restraint to its limits.

Then she stilled, holding him at her entrance, letting the head of his cock rest just inside her lips without pushing in.

Lind waited. She didn't open her legs.

Instead, she coaxed him inside a little more, just a little.

She pulled him out, then slid him back in, slowly, maximizing her pleasure and driving him crazy.

Caught between that wonderful ache and curiosity, Lind exhaled a shaky breath.

What is she doing?

He liked it—God, he liked it—but it felt... different. She wasn't her usual self. She was definitely someone else this morning.

Lind reached for her breast again, squeezing lightly, playing with her nipple, but she caught his hand, slowing him down.

She didn't *stop* him. She *showed* him. Through touch, through pressure, she guided him—Showing him the pace she wanted.

She wanted the control

She stroked him a few more times before releasing him, reaching back to grip his hip. She guided him deeper, letting him fill her completely, moaning softly as she adjusted to the sensation.

Her grip on his hip set the rhythm, directing how fast and how deep she wanted him.

Lind's instinct was to push harder, to chase the build-up, but she was setting the pace. He would wait for her.

Her rhythm was slow, at times she stopped his movements entirely, keeping him buried inside her, holding him there, pressing her body closer to his, as if she were trying to *merge* with him.

She placed her hand over his on her breast, stopping it, holding it there.

Lind stilled, *feeling* the moment—not chasing it.

And that's when it hit him.

This isn't about sex.

Not entirely. It's about *connection*. It's about Dana creating something more.

The realization struck deep, pulling him further into the experience—for herself, for him, for *them*.

At one point, she stopped entirely, keeping him inside her for so long that his erection started to soften.

Dana felt it too.

She started again—short strokes, keeping him deep. Within moments, he hardened inside her again.

This wasn't just about pleasure between them. It was about control—something in her needed this, needed to take him back, to feel that power between them again. She needed to claim what was hers.

She nudged his hip, signaling him to pull out.

She rolled him onto his back, climbing on top of him, straddling his hips.

Lind reached for himself, wanting to guide himself back into her, but she stopped him, moving his hand away.

She wanted the control.

She rubbed him along her folds, circling her clit, chasing her own pleasure.

Then, finally, she guided him back inside, sinking onto him at her own pace.

Lind let out a low groan, his hands finding her hips, his natural reaction to push up against her.

She didn't let him. She sat down fully, pressing her weight into him, stopping his movements.

The look in her eyes told him everything. *Let me lead.*

Lind surrendered, letting her take him exactly how she wanted. Her rhythm started again, slow, controlled.

Her eyes fluttered closed, head tilting back as the pleasure took over. Then she opened them again, locking onto him, making him *see* her, making him *feel* her.

Her hands roamed over his chest, his face, his hair.

When he reached for her shirt, she stopped him. Instead, she took his hands, guiding them—one to her hip, the other to her ass—placing them exactly where she wanted them.

Then she pressed against him, her body flush against his, tucking her head beneath his chin. Her hips kept moving, rolling, deepening the sensation. Every deliberate grind sent another pulse of pleasure between her legs, her clit rubbing against his body as she lowered herself onto him completely, again and again.

Lind groaned, his hands roaming over her back when they weren't gripping her ass, pulling her tighter against him.

Dana's moans were muffled against his neck, her hot breath sending shivers through him.

Then she lifted back up, locking eyes with him once more.

The love.

The want.

The *need.*

She pulled her V-neck off, tossing it to the floor.

Her rhythm shifted.

More... Faster.

Lind groaned, his fingers digging into her hips, matching her frantic pace. The pleasure built fast, tightening in his core, surging through him with devastating force. There was no more holding back. His release tore through him, raw and consuming, his body stiffening as a deep, primal groan escaped his lips. The moment he lost control, Dana saw it—the sharp edge of pleasure and pain flickering across his face, completely unguarded.

The sight of it, the feel of him pulsing inside her, sent a shiver straight through her, that thrill she'd come to love. The guttural sound he made—somewhere between a groan and her name—triggered something deep inside her, tipping her over the edge right after him.

Her orgasm surged through her in waves, tightening every muscle, igniting every nerve. Her thighs trembled around his hips as the pleasure pulsed through her, relentless and consuming. Her breath hitched—short, desperate gasps—before dissolving into a long, shaky sigh.

The final waves of pleasure washed over her as she exhaled soft and breathless, pressing herself down against him fully, locking him inside her for just a little longer.

Their bodies pulsed together in the quiet aftermath, every nerve humming, their hearts pounding.

Neither of them spoke.

Neither of them moved.

Neither of them wanted to.

Dana closed her eyes, savoring the warmth, the way his skin felt beneath her, his steady breathing. Lind shifted slightly, wrapping his arms fully around her, keeping her close as his own breathing steadied.

A few minutes passed, wrapped in that stillness, before Lind pressed a kiss to the top of her head.

"Damn," he murmured, his voice low, rough with satisfaction.

Dana smiled against his skin, her fingers grazing lazily over his chest. "Yeah."

She wasn't ready to move. Wasn't ready to let the moment slip away.

So they stayed—tangled together in the dim morning light, their bodies still connected, holding on to the warmth.

Eventually, Lind rolled her off him and onto her back, pressing a soft kiss to her shoulder before slipping out of bed. Dana exhaled a slow breath, her body still warm and tingling, listening to the quiet sounds of him moving through the bathroom.

When he returned, he held a warm washcloth and towel, his expression tender as he kneeled beside her. She watched him, savoring every little sensation as he ran the cloth gently over her, the warmth soothing against her skin.

She sighed softly as he dried her, the careful way he handled her only made her feel more cherished. When he finished, he set the towel and washcloth off to the side before leaning down to kiss between her thighs, his breath warm, ghosting over her.

His lips teased against her, licking, tasting. Her hips lifted instinctively, a moan slipping from her lips, her hand reaching for his hair.

Lind took his time, his tongue tracing familiar patterns, slipping into a rhythm he knew well. He read her every movement—the way her breath hitched, the way her fingers twisted in the sheets. The way her legs tensed and relaxed with each flick, each aching stroke over her clit.

Her pleasure built fast, a current that swept through her in waves, but he wasn't in a hurry. He savored the way she reacted beneath him, pushing her higher, then easing her back, drawing it out just enough to make her squirm.

It wasn't long before her breath turned shaky, her moans turning desperate . Her body tensed, her thighs trembling as her hips lifted off the bed, chasing the pleasure he was giving.

And then, she came.

Her orgasm rolled through her in thick, pulsing waves, her back arching, a cry slipping from her lips as he stayed with her, drawing it out. He worked her through the high, using every little trick—the slow flick of his tongue, the way he pressed just right as the tension broke, the way he held her hips steady as she writhed beneath him.

Dana whimpered, her body trembling, caught between the deliciousness of it and the overwhelming sensitivity creeping in. She reached down with a shaky hand, fingers threading through his hair, pushing him away—*no more.*

Lind pressed one last kiss against her before pulling back.

Dana let out a breathless, satisfied laugh, her chest rising and falling in uneven waves.

"That was... a lot," she murmured.

Lind smiled, licking his lips as he crawled up beside her. "Good?"

She turned her head to look at him, a ragged smile on her lips as she tried to catch her breath. "Always."

Lind reached over to where he had left the towel and washcloth. By now, the washcloth had cooled.

"Want me to warm it back up?" he asked softly.

Dana shook her head. "No, it's fine."

He pressed the cool cloth between her legs, but before he could move to clean her, she reached down and took it from him. The coolness was refreshing against her oversensitive skin, offering as much relief as it did cleansing. She took her time, breathing slowly, letting herself relax.

When she was done, she handed the washcloth back to Lind. He took it without a word, pressing a kiss to her shoulder before handing her the towel and slipping out of bed.

As he disappeared into the bathroom, Dana gently dried herself before folding the towel and tucking it between her legs.

The room was quiet except for the familiar sound of running water coming from the bathroom. She sighed softly, rolling onto her side, falling into her usual position.

When Lind returned she felt the bed dip as he wrapped his arm around her waist, pulling her into him, their bodies falling into the well-worn shape of comfort and familiarity.

Dana took his hand and brought it up between her breasts, tucking it under her chin, the way she so often did.

She pressed herself back against him, as close as she could, wrapped herself in him.

"I love you, Lind."

His arms tightened around her, and he kissed the back of her head. "I love you too, Dana."

They held each other in silence, wrapped in the same warmth, the same moment.

Their breathing slowed. Their bodies softened. Sleep began to claim them.

His last thought was hope.

Hers was doubt.

Chapter 60

Mornings like this, I could do forever

The soft light of the morning sun filtered through the bedroom curtains.

Lind blinked a few times, glancing at the clock before turning his attention to Dana. She was curled up on her side, her hair spilling over the pillow, her breathing slow and steady.

Not wanting to wake her, he slipped lightly out of bed and made his way to the bathroom. When he returned, she hadn't moved. A small smile tugged at his lips as he climbed back under the covers, putting his arm gently around her waist.

Dana stirred at his touch, her fingers tangling in his before she mumbled, "Bathroom," lifting his hand away as she rolled out of bed.

Lind stayed where he was, propping his head up on one arm as he watched her shuffle toward the bathroom, her naked frame disappearing behind the door. He smiled to himself. *God, I love mornings like this.*

The sound of running water filled the apartment for several minutes before it stopped. Lind closed his eyes, listening, waiting for her to return.

Then her voice called out, "Hey, do I have any more panty liners here?"

"Bottom right-hand drawer under the sink," he answered without hesitation.

A pause. Then, "Got it, thanks."

When she emerged a few minutes later, she was dressed in her jeans and the loose V-neck shirt from last night. Her button-up blouse was draped over her arm, and it was obvious she wasn't wearing a bra.

Lind watched her cross the room, the way the shirt moved over her body—unintentional, but impossible not to notice. As he sat up and reached for his boxers and a T-shirt, Dana caught his gaze, hesitated for a beat, then turned and walked out of the bedroom, heading for the kitchen.

Her eyes fell on the bookshelf near the window. The half-disassembled piece she'd noticed on her last visit was gone—replaced by something new. A small brass clock, polished and whole, sat neatly on the top shelf like it had always belonged there.

She hadn't heard him mention it. But clearly, he'd been tinkering again.

She smiled to herself.

This man.

Just then, Lind strolled out of the bedroom. She turned to face him.

"So, are you cooking breakfast, or are we going out? If we're going out, I should probably finish getting dressed."

Lind followed behind her as he pulled his T-shirt down, enjoying the way she moved so effortlessly through his space.

"I'm cooking," he said with a grin. "No question."

"Good choice." Dana leaned against the counter, crossing her arms. "But first, coffee."

"You know where everything is," he said, pulling out a cutting board. "I'll let you be in charge of that."

Dana gave him a look but got to work.

Lind grabbed ingredients from the fridge. He snuck glances at her between slicing peppers and onions, the way her breasts moved under her shirt, the shifting of her hips, the way she stood barefoot in his kitchen like she belonged there.

Oh my God, I could never get enough of this.

Breakfast was simple—scrambled eggs with vegetables, crispy bacon, and toast—but the atmosphere between them felt lighter than it had in weeks. They sat across from each other, eating in shared silence until Dana finally spoke.

"Thanks for cooking," she said, her voice softer than usual

Lind met her eyes. "Always. I like taking care of you."

Dana held his gaze for a beat before taking another sip of her coffee. "Do you have any plans for us today?"

Lind picked up his mug, pretending to think. "Hmm, let's see. I thought I'd surprise you by making breakfast.".

"Great plan," Dana replied dryly, though the hint of a smile played at her lips.

He chuckled, leaning forward. "Actually, I saw a flyer at work for that arts and crafts fair over by the community center. Thought maybe we could check it out? Walk around, see the fall decorations, eat something pumpkin-flavored."

Dana tilted her head, considering. "I haven't been to one of those in a long time."

"You have mentioned more than once that you might want to get back into painting and sketching," Lind said, his tone light but hopeful. "Might give you some inspiration."

She raised an eyebrow. "You've been paying attention."

Lind smiled. "Always."

She hesitated, then nodded. "Okay. Let's go. But I'm blaming you if I come home with a trunk full of art supplies I don't need."

Lind laughed, grabbing their empty plates and headed to the sink. "Deal. Just don't drag me into one of those DIY candle-making booths."

"No promises," Dana said, heading into the bedroom.

Lind wandered into the bedroom right behind her, leaning against the door frame as she slipped her arms out of her V-neck, leaving it around her neck, reaching for her bra.

Even though all he could see was the bare expanse of her back, and a hint of breast, the sight made him reconsider their plans.

Maybe we should just stay in instead.

He smiled to himself, watching as she fastened her bra and pulled her V-neck back into place. When she turned, catching him staring, she shot him a crooked smile.

"Do you like what you see?"

Lind shot right back. "Are you seriously asking me that?"

Dana just shook her head, amused, as she slipped her button-up blouse over her shirt. "You ready to go?"

"Yep, just need my jacket—oh, and maybe some pants," he said as she walked past him.

She laughed, and grabbed his ass briefly as she headed toward the living room.

"And socks," he called after her. "Maybe shoes would be helpful too."

"Well, hurry up, or I'll leave you behind," she called back.

Lind grinned as he grabbed his jeans. "Yes, ma'am!"

I like seeing you like this

The fair was alive with energy. Autumn was in the air, carrying the rich scents of caramel apples, cinnamon-roasted nuts, and hot cider. Booths lined the square, each one a display of handcrafted goods—knitted scarves in warm hues, ceramic mugs with hand-painted designs, vibrant paintings, and rustic wooden ornaments shaped like leaves and pumpkins.

Dana walked slowly, taking it all in. The hum of conversation and the occasional bursts of laughter filled the air, but her focus was on the artwork displayed at a couple of the booths. The colors of the paintings caught her first—bold, abstract strokes capturing the essence of nature in a way that felt both chaotic and intentional.

She paused in front of a piece depicting a golden forest, the trees stretching upward in warm, earthy tones.

"This one reminds me of the hiking trail we did last spring," she said, tilting her head slightly.

Lind stepped closer, looking over her shoulder. "You're right. That's gorgeous."

Dana ran her fingers down the edge of the canvas, her thoughts drifting back to that day—the scent of pine in the air, the sound of Lind's laughter, the easy rhythm of their steps on the dirt path.

"I miss that," she admitted, her voice quieter now.

"The trail?"

She shook her head, smiling faintly. "No, painting. Creating."

Her mind drifted to their first camping trip to the lake—the towering tree where they'd pitched their tent, its branches stretching over the edge of the lake. She could still picture the way the water reflected the early morning light, the quiet stillness before their first cast. The memory came steady and warm. That would make a beautiful painting.

They wandered deeper into the fair, stopping at booths that piqued their interest. Dana admired a set of hand-carved wooden trays, running her fingers over the smooth, polished surfaces, while Lind got caught up watching a pottery demonstration.

"Are you going to sign up for a class?" Dana arched a brow, crossing her arms as she leaned against a nearby post.

"Don't tempt me," Lind replied, grinning. "I'd make a killer coffee mug."

Dana chuckled. "I have no doubt."

The morning ended at a food stand, where they shared a slice of warm pumpkin pie with fresh whipped cream. When they finished, Dana leaned into Lind's side, savoring both the comfort of the moment and the steady warmth of his arm draped over her shoulders.

"This was nice," she murmured, almost as if she were speaking to herself.

"Yeah," Lind agreed, pressing a kiss to her temple. "I like seeing you like this."

Dana didn't ask what he meant. She didn't need to. The words landed warm, comforting—something she hadn't felt in a while.

***

The ride back to Dana's condo was quiet but comfortable, the weight of the morning still resting between them. Once, this would have been everything she needed—quiet moments, easy conversation, Lind's steady presence beside her. She wished it still felt that simple.

When Lind pulled up in front of her building, Dana unbuckled her seatbelt but hesitated before reaching for the door handle.

"Want to come in for lunch?" she asked, her voice casual but inviting.

Lind grinned, turning off the truck. "I'd love to."

Inside, Dana moved easily through the kitchen, pulling out bread, deli meat, and chips while Lind leaned against the counter, watching her with a soft smile.

"You're not going to help?" she hinted, glancing over her shoulder.

"Just enjoying the view," he replied, flashing her a crooked grin.

Dana rolled her eyes but didn't hide her smile as she handed him a plate. "Flatterer."

They sat at her small table, eating and exchanging lighthearted stories about work—laughing over Brenda's latest sarcastic remark, rolling their eyes at Marcy's lunchroom gossip, and trading complaints about customers with no sense of personal space.

As the conversation drifted, Dana set her sandwich down, leaning back slightly.

"I was thinking about the trail we hiked a while back," she said, brushing a crumb from her finger. "The one that painting reminded me of. Think we could do that again?"

Lind looked up, pleased. "Sure. Any weekend you'd like."

Dana smiled, the idea of making plans again felt calming and hopeful.

Lind took another sip of his drink, considering. "And how about that frozen waterfall we hiked to last winter? I'd love to see it in warm weather, without the risk of losing a toe to frostbite."

"Let's put that on our to-do list, then," she said, amused.

They continued planning, tossing out ideas for day trips, places to visit before the weather turned cold. Nothing overnight—just simple outings, something closer to the easy rhythm they used to have.

It felt good.

For both of them, it was a quiet step back toward normalcy.

Forgetting—for just a little while—the weight of the past few months.

Chapter 61

Playful glances

By Monday, Dana and Lind had found their rhythm again though there was still a slight hesitancy beneath the surface—like a song they both knew by heart—but were still figuring out how to harmonize again.

During the morning meeting, they exchanged their quick nod and playful glances—subtle enough that no one noticed, not even Brenda.

In the break room, Dana stood by the coffee maker, the steam rising softly from her cup as she stirred in a splash of creamer.

Lind walked in, the sound of his boots echoing lightly against the tile floor. Their eyes met as she gave her cup one last stir.

"Morning," he said, offering a small smile.

"Morning," Dana replied, her tone light, warm even. There was a softness in her gaze that made his shoulders relax.

Lind reached for his own mug, pouring himself a cup, the silence between them easy, familiar. Dana hesitated a moment, as if waiting for something, before finally heading back to the floor.

It wasn't perfect—but it was familiar enough to make both of them feel like things were okay, at least for now.

***

The store was unusually calm for a Monday morning—only a handful of customers drifting through the aisles, making the whole place feel quieter than normal.

Dana stood in the seasonal section, rearranging a display of small decorative pumpkins when Lind passed behind her, carrying a box of stock.

"Hey," he murmured low enough that no one else could hear.

She turned her head slightly, catching the faintest hint of his smile.

"Hey," she replied, her voice just as quiet.

As he moved past her, his hand ghosted lightly against the small of her back—a touch so subtle it might have gone unnoticed by anyone else. But Dana felt it, the warmth of his touch, even after he had walked away.

Lind glanced back over his shoulder, watching her for just a moment before disappearing into the stockroom.

Still here, Dana thought, a small, content smile touching her lips. *Still us.*

***

A few hours later, Dana was kneeling in the seasonal aisle, carefully arranging a row of ceramic turkeys when Lind crouched down beside her, with a boyish grin.

"You missed one," he said, holding up a turkey with a slightly crooked beak.

Dana glanced up, unimpressed. "That's not even from this display."

"Maybe not," he admitted, turning it over in his hands. "But look at this thing—it's got personality. A little flawed, a little off-kilter. Kind of like someone I know."

She shot him a dry look. "Are you seriously comparing me to a lopsided ceramic turkey?"

"I'm just saying it's got personality. One of a kind. Just like you."

Dana exhaled through her nose, shaking her head as she turned back to her work. "You're treading on thin ice, mister."

"Oh ya? And yet, here you are, talking to me anyway—with a smile," he said, setting the turkey down with exaggerated care before standing. "I'll leave you to find her a home here," he said grinning.

Dana didn't look up, but she could feel the playfulness in his voice as he walked away. She tried hard to bite back her smile—nope.

You're shameless

The lunchroom was unusually busy, coworkers scattered across the tables in groups. Dana sat alone at one end, scrolling through her phone, while Lind sat in the opposite corner, engaged in conversation with another associate.

Her phone buzzed.

Lind: *I can see you from here. Your sandwich looks suspiciously small. Do I need to rescue you with some snacks?*

Dana glanced up, meeting his gaze across the room. He was watching her, his lips twitching in amusement.

Dana: *Don't judge my sandwich. It's small but mighty.*

She looked up in time to see him type back, his smirk deepening as he read her reply.

Lind: *I'm not judging. Just offering my heroic snack-saving services. For a price.*

Dana: *Oh? And what's the price?*

Lind lifted his head, locking eyes with her, and mouthed the word: *Kiss.*

Dana felt warmth rise to her cheeks. She quickly glanced around to make sure no one had noticed before typing back.

Dana: *You're shameless.*

Lind: *Yes I am.*

Her smile lingered long after the conversation ended, her mood lighter as she finished her lunch and headed back onto the floor.

Just Lind being Lind

By early-afternoon, Dana was back in the seasonal section, rearranging a display of ceramic pumpkins to make the colors blend more naturally. She was so focused she didn't notice Zach approaching until he stopped a few feet away.

"Hey, Dana," he greeted casually.

She looked up, brushing a stray hair behind her ear. "Oh, hey, Zach. What's up?"

"Not much," he said with a small shrug. "Just noticed you over here being all productive."

Dana gave him a dry smile. "Trying to make these things look like they weren't just tossed in a pile."

He chuckled, glancing at the display. "Well, you're making them look good. Not that they didn't already, but, you know... you've got a touch for this stuff."

She tilted her head slightly, her smile softening. "Thanks. That's nice to hear."

Zach chuckled, then let his gaze linger on her a second longer. "You've got a good energy today."

Dana looked at him, a little surprised.

He shrugged, still casual. "You just seem... I don't know. Like you're in a better place lately. Happier. It's nice to see."

She blinked, caught off guard by his sincerity—but something about the way he said it made her chest loosen.

"Thanks," she said, her tone lighter now. "I guess I'm just... trying to keep my head above water, one day at a time."

Zach smiled, easy and warm. "That's the best way to do it—isn't it?"

She laughed, shaking her head as he walked off. "Thanks for noticing," she called after him, a playful edge in her voice.

Zach turned briefly, giving her a quick wave before disappearing down the aisle.

As she returned to the display, Dana couldn't help but think about his comment. *Happier?*

She wasn't sure if that was true. But she appreciated that someone had noticed her effort to stay positive.

A few seconds later, she felt a presence nearby.

She glanced up just as Lind passed from the opposite direction, carrying a stack of folded inventory boxes.

Their eyes met briefly, and just before disappearing around the corner, Lind gave her a quick wink, the kind that was barely perceptible but made her smile despite herself.

Then, as he passed, he muttered under his breath, just loud enough for her to hear—

"Nice melons."

Dana froze, turning toward him just in time to see the grin he barely concealed as he disappeared around the aisle.

She let out a slow breath, shaking her head, biting her lower lip to keep from laughing.

Just Lind being Lind.

The heat in her cheeks lasted long after he was gone.

But she was here, with him

Over the next several weekends, Dana and Lind found themselves slipping into something that resembled their old rhythm—one small adventure at a time.

The first Saturday after their conversation, they revisited the trail Dana had mentioned, winding their way through the woods as the late-summer sun filtered through the trees. The air was crisp but not yet cold, a reminder that fall was creeping in. Dana led the way, her pace steady, her energy lighter than it had been in weeks. Lind walked just behind her, watching as she reached out now and then to run her fingers over the rough bark of a tree.

They paused at a clearing to take in the view of the lake—and the tall tree near the shoreline where they'd camped the first time. The one that shaded their picnics.

Dana watched how it cast its reflection on the water, framed by the blue sky. "It does look like a painting," she murmured.

Lind stepped up beside her, close enough that their arms touched. "Maybe you should paint it," he said.

Dana glanced at him, then back at the water. "Maybe I will."

The following weekend, they drove out to see the frozen waterfall Lind had been eager to revisit, only this time, instead of a treacherous, ice-covered path, they found a lush, green gorge, the water cascading down in shimmering ribbons. The sound of it filled the air, powerful and constant, and Dana leaned against the wooden railing of the overlook, letting the mist cool her skin.

"You were right," she admitted, glancing at Lind. "This is better without the risk of frostbite."

Lind chuckled, stepping behind her on the empty overlook. "Glad we finally made it out here."

Lind reached around her as he rested his chin on her shoulder. She felt his fingers drift higher, purposeful in their aim. Dana grabbed his hands before they reached her breasts.

A playful smile formed on her face. She glanced over her shoulder—no one around.

Her pulse raced anyway as she guided his hands higher, holding them to her breasts. He gave them a playful squeeze before she giggled and moved his hands away. It was the kind of reckless thrill they used to share sparking in her chest. *Just like before. Just like us.*

They spent the rest of the afternoon exploring the trails around the falls, stopping to read trail markers, snapping pictures, and enjoying each other. It was easy in a way that things hadn't been for so long. Dana was holding back a little—Lind could feel it—but she was *here*, with him, present in the moment, making memories instead of making excuses.

One weekend, they visited the farmers' market. Dana wandered slowly between stalls, pausing to smell a loaf of cinnamon bread before tucking it into her basket. Lind stood at an apple stand, holding up two different kinds, debating with the vendor about texture like it was a wine tasting.

Another afternoon was spent at a small-town fall festival, where Lind somehow convinced Dana to go on the Ferris wheel with him, despite her initial protests. She grumbled as they climbed into the seat, muttering something about death traps. With every creak of the old structure, she glanced around nervously. Lind just grinned as they settled in, Dana's arm locked tightly around his, practically cutting off the blood supply. Her other hand clutched the safety bar.

When they reached the top, Dana went quiet. Her eyes stayed wide, fixed on the view.

It was beautiful—orange and gold treetops stretched endlessly in every direction—but Lind barely looked at it. His attention stayed on her.

His hand had been resting gently over hers from the start—steady and comforting.

She didn't speak for a long time. Then finally—softly, without turning—she said, "It *is* kind of pretty."

Lind nudged her shoulder, playful. "Worth it?"

She let out a breath. "Yeah. Maybe," she said, her voice a little shaky.

He didn't push. He just kept his hand over hers, letting the moment settle between them as the ride carried them slowly back down.

For a while, things felt good. Not perfect—Dana was still guarded, and Lind was still hoping—but the heaviness between them had eased—not gone, but no longer pressing against every thought.

They were laughing more. Her hand found his thigh beneath the table more often now, his fingers drifting over the back of her neck in quiet moments. They were planning things again.

And for a while, Lind let himself believe that maybe—just maybe—Dana was coming back to him.

He could feel her trying.

And sometimes, that was enough to keep the doubt at bay.

But only sometimes.

Chapter 62

What am I doing wrong

As their weekends filled with plans, something beneath the surface had shifted...

Some nights, Dana curled into him on the couch like nothing had changed—her body warm and seeking, her mouth insistent on his, her limbs tangled with his like she couldn't get close enough.

Other nights, she shifted away with a quiet, *"I'm just tired,"* and fell asleep wishing she hadn't said that.

The swing between the two left Lind reeling. One moment, she wanted him with a kind of urgency that took his breath. The next, she felt miles away.

It wasn't just distance—it was unpredictability. Like she couldn't decide whether to pull away or pull him under.

He didn't know what to do. So he held her close whenever she'd let him—held her like it might keep her from drifting.

But the ache, the uncertainty inside him was growing—quiet, but constant.

What am I doing wrong?

Dana felt his tension. She knew she was causing it, but didn't know how to stop. She often lay awake long after he fell asleep, staring at the ceiling—trapped between what she wanted and what she couldn't live with.

I love him too much to make him choose. But I can't live like this either.

She tried to understand. *Really tried.*

But Lind's description of Sam as someone who "reset" him played in her mind like a broken record.

Reset you? How?

She didn't want to ask—not yet. Didn't want to force a conversation she wasn't ready for. Didn't want to back him into a corner with a question that had only one answer—*her or me.*

But *not* asking didn't make it go away.

If he *did* choose her, she knew that shadow would always be there. The *what if*, the unanswered possibility.

How do I live with that?

***

Lind felt the difference in her. The inconsistency in her actions. The spaces between their plans. The way she left his bed more often than she stayed.

He wanted to ask, wanted to break through the growing distance, but every time he tried, the words stuck in his throat.

If I push, will I just drive her further away?

So he held on.

Held on to the good moments, the soft laughter that still slipped out of her sometimes, the way she reached for his hand without thinking, the familiar comfort of her falling asleep in his arms.

If he just kept showing her how much she meant to him, maybe—

Maybe she'd come back to me.

Maybe she *wanted* to.

Maybe.

***

The late September sun hung low in a pale blue sky, casting golden light over the countryside as Lind's truck rumbled along the narrow road. Fields stretched endlessly on either side, green and brown with hints of fall creeping into the treeline. The window was cracked open, carrying the scent of dry leaves and late-season hay, and Dana closed her eyes, letting herself take in all of it—the smells, the breeze, the quiet, the calm.

"This is nice," she murmured, tilting her head against the glass.

Lind glanced over, his hand resting loosely on the steering wheel. "Yeah," he said softly. "It feels like us again."

Dana turned slightly, giving him a smile—bittersweet but real. *If only it could stay this way.*

I was right back where I started

The orchard was alive with the hum of families and couples, kids laughing as they climbed onto hay wagons for rides through the property. The air smelled of warm cider and fried donuts, sweet and comforting.

"Where to first?" Lind asked, holding the door open as Dana stepped out of the truck.

"Let's get cider and donuts," she said, slipping her sunglasses on. "That feels like the right place to start."

They walked side by side, the tension between them had faded—if just for the moment. At the small stand by the entrance, Lind handed her a paper bag of cinnamon-sugar donuts and a cup of hot cider.

"These smell amazing," Dana said, tearing off a piece and popping it into her mouth.

Lind took a bite of his own, sighing in exaggerated pleasure. "If they don't serve these in heaven, I'm not going."

Dana laughed softly, shaking her head. "Funny man."

They strolled leisurely, stopping to admire the flower gardens, their vibrant colors fading with the season but still beautiful. The air was crisp but warm, the perfect kind of autumn afternoon meant for lingering.

"I bet this place will be gorgeous in a month," Dana mused, glancing around. "We should come back. The leaves will be changing, and we could pick apples too."

Lind nodded absently, hands tucked into his pockets. "Yeah, Sam and I planned a similar trip last year out past her place. That big orchard way up north."

Dana paused for a split second before keeping her tone light. "Oh yeah?" She raised an eyebrow as they walked. "Did you go?"

"No," Lind said, kicking a small stone along the gravel path. "I bailed on her a few days before the weekend."

Dana took a slow sip of her cider, curious but careful. "Why's that?" she asked, watching his face. "Did she go anyway?"

Lind shrugged. "When her guys found out... she had two of them volunteering, so I knew she wouldn't miss out. I don't know which one ended up going."

Dana snorted lightly. "Maybe both? She does like to keep busy."

Lind chuckled but shook his head. "No, not likely. Sam has this thing with her guys—when she's with one of them, it's just the two of them. No distractions, no third wheels."

Dana tilted her head, giving a crooked smile. "That's... kind of sweet. In a weird way."

Lind grinned, appreciating her humor. "Yeah, I guess it is."

But Dana's mind turned over what he'd just said. Her curiosity got the better of her. "So... why'd you bail on her at the last minute?"

Lind stopped walking for a moment, shoving his hands deeper into his pockets. "That was the weekend after you were sick last year."

Dana frowned, caught off guard. "What?"

Lind looked at her, his voice steady but quiet. "I wanted to be there. To take care of you."

Her brows pulled together. "You couldn't have known I'd let you back into my condo."

Lind gave a small shrug. "True. It was a risk. But... I had decided you were worth it." His lips twitched. "I was terrified, though. I thought for sure you'd slam the door in my face after we talked that morning. You hit me with all your 'what ifs' and your stubbornness..."

Dana felt something tighten in her chest. "And yet you stayed."

"Yeah," Lind said softly. "And when you closed the door and led me back upstairs... well, it was worth it. It gave us this, right?"

Dana stared at him, her heart doing an unsteady flip. *He gave up a weekend with Sam for me.*

She couldn't help herself—she needed to hear it again, just to make sure. "So... you canceled on Sam for me?"

Lind nodded. "Yeah. Sam said I should go for it. That maybe you *were* the one."

Dana's breath caught, the words hitting her harder than she expected. *She said to go for it? Lind picked me over her.*

But just as warmth began to bloom inside her, Lind's next words shattered it.

"That made it six months before I saw Sam again," he admitted, his voice quieter. "I was just about fucking crazy. I didn't realize how much I needed her reset until I didn't have it. I felt like I was going to start biting people's heads off."

The cider turned sour in Dana's stomach. She swallowed hard, her grip tightening around the paper cup.

And just like that... I was right back where I started.

As though he realized what he'd just said, Lind hesitated, shifting uncomfortably. He exhaled, running a hand through his hair.

"This October..." he started to say, not really sure he should, "we're doing that trip we missed last year. Same orchard, same fall drive."

Dana kept her tone measured. "That sounds fun. How long are you going for?"

Lind hesitated, choosing his words. "Friday and Saturday night. I'll be back Sunday afternoon. I could call, or come over if you'd like."

Dana smiled faintly, though it didn't reach her eyes. "That would be nice. Give me a text when you're back, and we'll see."

Inside, her mind churned. *Why? Why would I want to see you so soon after you've been with her?*

She turned, looking out at the endless stretch of fields, the beauty of the day suddenly feeling hollow. "When's the trip?"

"Two weeks," Lind said, his voice low and questioning.

Dana nodded slowly, her voice distant. "Okay. Let's see how you like *that* orchard first before deciding if you want to go to another with *me*."

Lind's eyes darted to her, searching her face. "We could do something else. Anything else, as long as I get to spend time with you." His voice rose in pitch slightly.

He meant it—she could hear the hope. It made her heart ache, because she couldn't give him the future he was asking for.

But Dana ignored his offer, keeping her expression neutral. "The week after... that's our anniversary."

Lind blinked, caught off guard. "Wow. You're right. We need to plan something special."

Dana gave him a small smile, nodding. "Yeah."

But the words felt heavy.

Plan something special... for what?

Chapter 63

Spending the whole weekend together

Dana caught sight of Lind at his locker just as they were about to clock out. She hesitated for a fraction of a second, then stepped closer, keeping her voice even. *Just make it feel natural.*

"Hey," she said, tucking her hair behind her ear. "What do you think about spending the whole weekend together? Friday to Sunday."

Lind paused mid-motion, his fingers still on the combination lock. He turned to her, surprise flickering across his face before his expression melted into a slow, warm smile. "A full weekend?"

"Yeah," Dana nodded, forcing a small laugh. "I was thinking you could come over Friday night. I'll pick up whatever ingredients you need to cook—if you're up for it."

Lind grinned. "You know I'll cook. What are we thinking—fancy, or comfort food?"

"Let's plan it all," she said, shifting slightly on her feet. "Sides, bread, everything. Oh, and wine. Do we need wine?"

"Definitely," Lind said, already pulling out his phone. "I'll bring it."

Dana tucked her hands into her pockets. "I'll grab stuff for breakfast, if you'll make that too?"

Lind chuckled. "Deal. And Saturday?"

She hesitated, then shrugged lightly. "We should plan something... Maybe dinner at your place? I'll pack a bag for Saturday night."

His smile softened, something unreadable flickering behind his eyes. "Sounds perfect."

For a brief moment, Dana thought he might ask why she was suddenly making all these plans—why she wanted an entire weekend after weeks of pulling back. But Lind just shut his locker and reached for her hand, giving it a quick squeeze before letting go.

"Looking forward to it," he said, his voice easy.

Dana swallowed against the lump in her throat and smiled back. "Me too."

Lind hesitated for a second, then tilted his head. "Did you want to do something tonight? Go over the plans for the weekend, get our ducks in a row? I could make some hamburgers and homemade fries."

"Homemade fries? Now who isn't playing fair?"

"5:30 okay?" he asked hopefully.

Dana hesitated so long he thought she'd back out—again, but finally, she nodded. "Sure, 5:30 sounds perfect. See you then."

She reached out, trailing her fingers along his arm before turning toward the time clock.

***

Lind had everything prepped when Dana arrived—potatoes soaking in cold water, burger patties seasoned and waiting for the grill pan. The moment she stepped inside, the scent of garlic and herbs filled the air, wrapping around her in something warm, something comfortable.

For the first time in weeks, their evening together felt effortless.

They talked as he cooked, laughter slipping into their conversation as naturally as it always had. Dana sat on the counter, stealing fries straight from the pan while Lind shook his head, pretending to scold her. They threw out more ideas for the weekend, debating meal choices and movie preferences.

"Okay, but you have to admit," Dana argued, popping another fry into her mouth, "that maple syrup would make an amazing glaze for the pork."

Lind eyed her skeptically. "I feel like you just want an excuse to drown your chops in syrup."

Dana grinned. "No comment."

It was *easy*—the back-and-forth, the shared moments, the little touches that reminded them of what they had. Lind felt it in the way Dana leaned into him while she sipped her wine, in the way her laughter curled around the edges of his heart.

And Dana felt it, too. The comfort of their space, the undeniable pull toward him—even as the reality of what she was planning gnawed at the edges of her mind.

She wanted this. Wanted him

Later, after the dishes were done and the wine was nearly gone, Dana stretched, rolling her shoulders. "I should probably head home soon."

Lind, sitting back on the couch, tilted his head at her. "Already?"

Dana hesitated just long enough for Lind to see it.

She didn't want to leave.

And that moment—her pause, her eyes flicking to his—was all the invitation he needed.

She didn't protest when he reached for her, pulling her down onto the couch with him. She didn't stop him when his lips met hers, slow and searching, pulling her closer.

And she didn't stop herself when she responded.

She *wanted* this. *Wanted* him.

It had been weeks since she felt truly present in their intimacy, and now, wrapped in his warmth, with his breath ghosting over her skin, something inside her *needed* this connection.

Their clothes peeled away in quiet urgency, fingers tracing familiar territory, relearning, remembering.

She pushed him onto the bed, sinking down onto him, setting the pace, losing herself in the heat of it, in the heat of *him*.

And Lind—he didn't question it, didn't overthink it. He just held her, kissed her, moved with her, let himself believe—for just a little while—that things between them were okay.

***

After, Dana stretched beside him, catching her breath. She felt the tension leave her body, but something in her chest still ached. She kissed his shoulder before sitting up.

Lind wrapped his arm around her waist, trying to keep her there. "Stay," he murmured, his voice thick with sleep.

She hesitated but shook her head. "Not tonight."

Lind sighed, fingers trailing lazily over her thigh before pulling back. He didn't argue, but there was something unspoken in the way he looked at her. A quiet disappointment.

Dana smiled, running her fingers through his hair. "We have all weekend," she reminded him.

Lind nodded slowly, watching as she got dressed, as she slipped back into the woman he couldn't quite hold onto.

"We do," he agreed, but as she kissed him one last time before heading out, something inside him whispered that this moment—this night—felt like it was a memory already.

Chapter 64

This is what I'll remember

The smell of garlic and rosemary filled Dana's kitchen as Lind worked at the stove, flipping thick cuts of chicken breast in the skillet. Dana leaned against the counter, a glass of wine in her hand, watching him with a small smile.

"You make it look so easy," she mused, taking a sip.

Lind glanced over his shoulder, grinning. "Thanks, and we'll just skip over the part where I forgot the bread earlier."

She laughed softly, sipping her wine. The candlelight flickered on the table, adding to the warmth of the night. It felt... different. Not in a bad way—just heavier.

Dinner was slow, filled with light conversation—stories from work, light banter, memories of past trips, their best meals together, and all the little moments that made them *them*.

Afterward, Dana insisted on doing the dishes while Lind poured the last of the wine. They settled onto the couch, Dana tucked into his side, her fingers softly tracing over his arm... lost in thought.

"You're quiet tonight," Lind murmured, pressing a kiss to the top of her head.

"I'm just enjoying this," Dana said softly, her voice almost too quiet. "You, me, here, like this."

Later, as they fell into bed, their lovemaking was unhurried—each touch deliberate, every kiss soft. Dana clung to him, her hands mapping his body like she was memorizing him. She wanted to hold onto this, wanted to bottle this feeling—every sigh, every whispered name, every slow, aching moment.

This is what I'll remember, she thought as she drifted to sleep, Lind's arm wrapped tightly around her.

DANA'S LOVES

***

Dana packed her bag with careful precision Saturday morning, folding each item neatly as Lind sat on the edge of her bed.

"Are you packing for more than one night?"

"Just being prepared," Dana replied as she zipped it shut and tossed it at him.

They drove to Lind's place after a quick breakfast, the easygoing energy between them still lingering.

"I thought we could check out that art gallery downtown," Lind suggested as she unpacked. "You've been talking about getting back into painting for months now. Thought this might give you some ideas."

Dana blinked, surprised. "An art gallery, not just a craft fair?"

"Yes, it'll be fun," Lind said simply, smiling.

"That's a great idea," she said, her voice a little higher, "thank you."

The look on her face was all the thanks he needed.

***

She was surprised at the anticipation she felt as Lind drove. She hadn't been to an actual art gallery in years.

The gallery was quiet, filled with the hushed voices of art lovers moving through the space. Dana paused in front of a large painting—swirls of deep blue and warm gold, blending seamlessly into one another. It was striking yet soft, chaotic yet soothing.

"I love this one," she murmured, tilting her head as she studied it.

Lind stood beside her, hands in his pockets. "It looks like you."

Dana turned to him, raising an eyebrow. "Like me?"

He shrugged, his gaze still on the canvas. "It's calm on the surface, but if you look closer, there's so much more happening. Layers."

Dana blinked, caught off guard. She looked sideways at Lind. "Layers, huh?" she said, nudging his arm. "Sounds like a polite way of saying I'm complicated."

"'Complicated' can be such a complicated word," he said as he nudged her. "Let's just say you can be an *intricately tangled knot of bewildering perplexity*..." He almost said it with a straight face.

Dana stared at him, trying not to smile. Then she smacked his shoulder and lost it, laughter bubbling up as she shook her head. "I am *not!*" she insisted, feigning shock.

"Okay, okay," he said, backing off with a grin. "You're not *any* of those things." He leaned in to kiss her lightly.

She pretended to resist—just for a beat—but then cupped his face, kissing him back.

As she pulled away, she couldn't help thinking...

Our relationship is every one of those things lately. Intricate, tangled, beautiful and bewildering—and almost over.

Her smile faded into something quieter as the thought circled in her mind. When she glanced at Lind again, the shift in his expression brought a realization of her own.

Her eyes drifted back to the painting in front of them—swirls of golds and greens and deep blues, movement layered into color, emotion hiding in the brushstrokes. It stirred something inside her.

"It really does look like me, doesn't it?" she said, her voice distant. "I really do want to get back into creating my own..." her thoughts trailed off.

"Then you should." Lind's voice pulled her back.

Dana wanted to. She *really* did.

Lind slipped his hand into hers, giving it a small squeeze. She squeezed back, but something inside her felt hollow.

Because this was perfect. It *should* be enough.

And yet, she already knew—deep down—this was the last time they'd ever have a weekend like this.

Promise me you will

The gallery left a quiet calm over them as they stepped outside into the late afternoon sun. The hum of the city had softened, the midday rush giving way to something slower, more peaceful.

"That place was incredible," Dana murmured, tucking her hands into her jacket pockets. "I'd forgotten how much I missed seeing real art."

Lind walked close enough to put his hand lightly on the small of her back, his gaze flickering toward her. "Then you really should start creating it again."

Dana looked up at him, a small smile curving her lips. "I think I will."

Lind stopped mid-step, turning fully to face her. "Promise me you will?"

Dana hesitated, caught off guard by the quiet intensity in his voice. He wasn't teasing, wasn't saying it in passing—he genuinely wanted this for her.

She tilted her head, searching his face. "Okay," she said softly. "I promise."

His expression brightened with a pleased nod before they continued toward his truck. The fading sunlight stretched long across the pavement, the warmth of the day slowly slipping away.

"Hungry?" Lind asked as they climbed into the cab.

"A little," Dana admitted. "But... we could just grab something simple. I don't feel like a big dinner."

Lind smiled faintly, glancing over at her. "How about we just pick up some snacks and hang out? We can do a real dinner tomorrow."

The corners of her lips relaxed into a smile. "Snacks and hanging out sounds perfect."

***

The small market near Lind's apartment was nearly empty, making their slow wander through the aisles feel even more easygoing.

"You and your chips," Dana said, arching an eyebrow as Lind grabbed a bag of salt and vinegar.

"And you and your dark chocolate," Lind shot back, tossing a bar into her basket. "We all have our weaknesses."

Dana smirked, reaching for his hand and pulling him toward the small deli counter. "Let's get a sandwich and a bowl of soup to share."

Lind chuckled, liking the way her fingers felt wrapped around his. "Sounds perfect."

He nudged her with his shoulder as they walked toward the checkout. "Chips to go with the sandwich, chocolate for dessert, and beer at home to wash it all down. This is why we work."

Dana gave a small, amused hum, the words hit something deep in her. *Yes,* she thought with a bittersweet familiarity, *That's true. Almost always.*

I'm just enjoying this

They kicked off their shoes as they stepped inside, setting the grocery bags on the counter. Lind grabbed two beers from the fridge while Dana unpacked their haul, arranging the sandwiches, chips, chocolate, and strawberries on the coffee table as she put the soup in the microwave.

"This," Lind said, cracking open a beer, "is dinner."

Dana grinned, pulling out the warmed soup before sinking onto the couch. She patted the cushion beside her. "Only the finest."

Lind joined her, handing over a beer before flipping on the TV. Some random cooking show filled the room with the murmur of background noise. For a while, they ate, joked, and debated which chef's dish looked the best, the quiet comfort between them as natural as breathing.

At some point, Dana leaned into Lind, resting her head on his shoulder. His arm looped around her easily, pulling her close, and he pressed a slow kiss to the side of her head.

"You're quiet again," he murmured, his voice warm, familiar.

Dana tilted her head slightly, looking up at him. "I'm just enjoying this," she said, and for once, she meant it without reservation.

She held his gaze—on the softness in his hazel eyes, the way he looked at her like she was something irreplaceable. Her throat tightened, emotion pressing in, but she pushed it aside.

Instead, she leaned up, her lips against his in a kiss that started light but deepened quickly, melting away everything else.

Lind smiled against her mouth, pulling her fully into his lap. "So... this is where we're headed?"

Her fingers traced along his jaw. "Yes! Yes, it is."

Lind didn't need any more encouragement. He lifted her easily, standing with her in his arms as she let out a soft laugh. Their bodies stayed tangled together as he carried her to the bedroom, their laughter trailing behind them, blending into the quiet hum of the night.

Chapter 65

Oh, God, Lind

Lind sat her down on the bed, his gaze trailing over her as if seeing her for the first time. Gorgeous. Sexy. Smart. Loving. He couldn't decide which one defined her best.

He leaned in, capturing her lips in a deep kiss. Dana's hands shot up to his face, pulling him in, her fingers pressing against his jaw as she kissed him fiercely. Lips and tongues tangled, speaking everything they felt.

When he pulled back, breathless, he didn't break eye contact as his fingers moved to the button of her jeans. He unfastened them slowly, then dragged them down her legs, as she lifted herself up a little to help, her panties slipping halfway off with them. Before she even had the chance to kick them the rest of the way off, Lind was between her legs, his mouth on her.

Her sharp inhale filled the room. Hands buried in his hair, she pulled him tighter against her, her hips rising to meet him. The heat of his mouth, the pressure of his tongue—it sent jolts of pleasure through her, arching her back as moans spilled from her lips.

Lind groaned against her, feeling the way she responded, the way she let go completely. He could spend forever like this. But not tonight—tonight was different.

He pulled back, standing to strip off his T-shirt, kicking off his pants and boxers in one smooth motion. Dana was already discarding her own shirt, unclasping her bra in one swift movement. She flung it at him playfully, and Lind caught it one-handed, bringing it to his nose for a deep inhale before letting it drop to the floor.

Dana scooted back on the bed, waiting for him. He climbed over to her, settling between her legs, feeling the heat of her against him as she wrapped her legs around his waist, pulling him in. Her hips tilted just right, guiding him as he pushed into her, and the sensation shot through her like fire and electricity.

Her head snapped back, eyes rolling closed as she let the pleasure take over, gripping his back, needing him closer. Every thrust sent another pulse radiating outward, lighting her up from the inside.

Dana pushed against his shoulders, rolling them over so she was on top. Sitting up on her knees, she rode him, her rhythm slow, deliberate. She reached for his hands, guiding them to her breasts, and then—surprising him—she moved his fingers just how she wanted them. Press, squeeze, pull. Showing him exactly what she craved.

Lind groaned, loving this side of her—wild, unfiltered. *Where was this coming from?* He had never seen her this free, this uninhibited.

Still, he couldn't resist taking back control, flipping her onto her back again, burying himself deep inside her. But just as he found his rhythm, Dana pushed at his chest, urging him off of her.

Confusion flickered across his face for only a second before she rolled onto her stomach, reaching back to guide him where she wanted him.

His breath hitched. *Oh.*

Straddling her, he entered her from behind, and the moment he did, he felt the way her body clenched around him. This was the position where his cock rubbed her just right, stroking that sweet spot with every thrust. She was close—he could feel it.

"Oh, God, Lind," she moaned, her voice raw, her body trembling. "Fuck me. Oh, God. Yes."

His hands gripped her hips tighter. *She never says things like that.* The way her voice broke, the way her entire body surrendered—it sent a rush of heat straight to his gut.

Her orgasm hit suddenly, violently. Her arms pulled in close, her head pressing into the bed, her back arching forward as the waves crashed over her. The tremors ran through her in long, pulsing waves, rolling one after the other, unstoppable.

Lind was mesmerized, feeling every shudder, every pulse against him as she came.

Slowly, her hand reached back, pressing against his hip, wordlessly telling him to slow down. To stop. But she didn't let him pull out—not just yet—her fingers stayed on his skin, holding him in place as the last aftershocks rippled through her.

Finally, she nudged him back, turning onto her back. Without hesitation, she took his face in her hands, pulling him to her lips.

Lind barely had time to react before she pushed his head down, guiding him lower—her collarbone, her nipples, her stomach, lower still, until he was between her legs again.

Her fingers curled into his hair as his mouth worked her, making her thighs tremble. She was already so sensitive, her sounds coming faster, breathless, almost desperate.

Lind let instinct take over. He pushed two fingers inside her—not deep, just enough to stroke the spot that sent her hips shifting in rhythm. His free hand trailed lower, his thumb brushing the tight ring of muscle of her ass, slick with all the wetness between them.

Dana gasped, her body reacting instantly, a fresh wave of pleasure rolling through her.

"Oh—fuck—" Her body seized up, her thighs tightening, her hips grinding against his face. This orgasm more violent than the first.

Lind groaned against her, feeling every ripple, every clench of her body against his fingers, his mouth, his touch.

He knew when to pull back, when to slow down—first easing away from her ass, then slipping his fingers out of her, finally letting his tongue soften against her until she was the one gripping his hair, holding him still.

Her body quivered beneath him, every nerve lit up, but instead of pushing him away like she always did, she tugged at him—pulling him up to her.

He barely had a second to think before she was kissing him. Hot, hungry, not caring that she could taste herself on his lips.

Lind groaned into her mouth, his body already responding again as she wrapped her legs around him. She reached between them, guiding him back inside her, the sounds of pleasure escaping his lips as he filled her again.

This time, she kept control. Pushing at his shoulders, she had him sit back on his knees as she lay beneath him, tilting her hips just enough to watch. She lifted her head, her gaze fixed on the place where their bodies joined, mesmerized by the slow, deep thrusts.

She let her head fall back, pleasure surging through her, before lifting again—watching, needing to memorize it, as if she was committing the entire moment to memory.

Lind groaned, gripping her hips, his rhythm speeding up.

Faster. Harder.

His climax building, rushing toward what felt like an explosion.

"Oh—God—Dana." Her name falling from his lips over and over.

She clung to him, soaking in everything—the look on his face, the sound of him coming apart, the way his body shook, the way his fingers tightened on her skin as he lost himself completely inside her.

She held on as long as she could, as long as he let her, before his body stilled, trembling, his head dipping forward.

Lind remained kneeling over her, chest heaving, staring down at her with something unreadable in his eyes.

Dana just smiled. Slowly, she reached up, dragging her fingertips down his chest, tracing every muscle, every ridge of his stomach. She closed her eyes, memorizing the feel of him beneath her touch.

Every hair. Every curve. Every inch of him. Because this is the last time.

But she wouldn't tell him that.

Not yet.

Who was this woman tonight

"Dana..." Lind started to say, his voice quiet, full of something unspoken.

"Shhh..." she murmured, pressing a finger to his lips. Her gaze was warm, steady, full of emotion he couldn't quite decipher.

For a few long moments, they remained like that—his body still nestled inside hers, the heat between them still tangible, still pulsing in the aftermath of everything they'd just shared. Then, with a slow roll of her hips, Dana signaled for him to slip out of her.

Lind did as she silently asked, laying back beside her, watching her.

He opened his mouth to speak again, but she shook her head, placing a single finger against his lips once more. There was something different in her eyes—soft, loving, but also... something else. Something deeper.

Before he could question it, Dana slid out of bed, making her way to the bathroom.

Lind watched her go, his gaze trailing over her body as she moved, her hips swaying ever so slightly. The bedside lamp cast gentle shadows over her, illuminating the sheen of sweat still clinging to her skin.

She disappeared into the bathroom, and Lind let his head sink back into the pillow. His body was spent, but his mind was racing.

Who was this woman tonight?

It was perfect

Dana turned on the faucet, running a clean washcloth under the hot water, the warmth spreading through the fabric as she pressed it between her legs.

She was so tender, so sensitive. Every nerve was still thrumming, her body still humming with the echoes of pleasure. She held the cloth against herself, lifting one foot onto the toilet for better access.

And yet... she hesitated.

The whole scene replayed in her mind. It was everything she had planned. Everything she wanted.

She exhaled, a slow, shuddering breath, before rinsing the cloth out again. Then, instead of using it immediately, she slipped her hand between her legs, her fingers sliding inside her, gathering some remnants of Lind.

Bringing her fingers to her lips, she closed her eyes, feeling the slick warmth of them, tasting the mixture of him and her. A quiet moan vibrated in her throat as she let herself sink into the memory of his face when he came. The way his body tensed, the way he gasped her name, the raw intensity of the moment.

It was perfect.

She exhaled softly, washing herself once more before rinsing the cloth thoroughly. With a final pass over her skin, she dried herself with a hand towel and stepped back into the bedroom with both in hand.

Mesmerized by her every movement

Lind was still lying in bed, he propped himself up on one elbow, watching her as she returned. The concern in his eyes was subtle, but present.

"Is everything okay?" he asked, his voice quiet, careful.

Dana nodded, sitting down on the edge of the bed beside him. She reached out, resting her hand on his chest, feeling the slow, steady rise and fall of his breath.

"I just..." Lind started again, but she silenced him once more, pressing her finger gently to his lips.

She pushed him back onto the bed, her touch deliberate, but tender.

She reached for his cock, feeling its warmth, its softness in the aftermath. She moved her hand slowly, tilting him, examining him in the dim light, taking in every inch of him like she was studying a piece of art.

Her grip was gentle but firm, reverent in a way she had never done before. Lind watched her, entranced by the way she handled him, by the silent fascination in her eyes.

Then, without a word, she leaned down, taking him into her mouth—to taste him, to *feel* him in this moment—raw, still coming down from everything they had shared. She sucked lightly at the tip, drawing out the last remnants of his release, swirling her tongue around him.

He let out a slow exhale, his hands resting loosely on the bed, surrendering to whatever she wanted to do.

When she pulled back, she reached for the warm washcloth, moving carefully, methodically, as she cleaned him. Every touch was slow, intentional—his cock, his balls, even down to his ass, a place she had rarely touched before.

Lind shivered slightly at the sensation, not from discomfort but from the sheer unexpectedness of it. Another first. Another thing she's never done before.

He let her do it, let her take care of him, fascinated by her every movement.

When she finished, she grabbed the towel and dried him off just as carefully, her eyes never leaving his body.

Lind didn't move. He just watched—the way her breasts swayed ever so slightly as she leaned over him, the way her nipples hardened in the cool air, the way her body was still flushed from earlier. She was beautiful, sexy, loving, affectionate... and tonight, something more.

Something raw. Something savage.

His fingers skimmed over her hip, the swell of her ass, tracing absent patterns on her skin, lost in the moment.

When she finished, she took the towel and cloth back to the bathroom, rinsing them out and hanging them on the rack.

Lind was still watching when she returned, standing near the light switch for a moment.

She knew he was taking her in—the shape of her, the small swell of her belly, the little patch of hair he said he liked. He drank her in, his eyes slowly roaming back up to meet hers.

She smiled softly, flicked off the light, and made her way back to bed.

Goodnight, Lind. I love you

Beneath the blankets, Dana turned onto her side so they were face to face.

Lind exhaled, reaching out to tuck a strand of hair behind her ear. "Now can I say something?" he murmured, his tone soft and warm.

Dana didn't answer right away. Instead, she leaned in, pressing her lips to his.

It was long, slow—not a kiss of passion, but a kiss of *love*. Of *appreciation*. Of *connection*.

When she finally pulled away, she whispered, "Goodnight, Lind. I love you."

Then she turned her back to him, pressing herself close, molding against him in their familiar spooning position.

Lind sighed, wrapping his arm around her waist. She reached back, taking his hand and pulling it between her breasts, tucking it under her chin, holding it there.

He pressed a kiss to the back of her head. "I love you too, Dana. Goodnight."

Within moments, sleep overtook them both, wrapped in warmth, in silence, in something that felt *perfect*.

For Lind, this was everything.

For Dana, this was goodbye.

Chapter 66

If you don't put some clothes on

Dana woke to the faint sizzle of bacon and the warm scent of pancakes filling Lind's small apartment. A slow, lazy smile spread across her face as she stretched beneath the covers, savoring the lingering warmth of the bed before making her way to the bathroom.

As she moved from the bedroom, she passed through the open space of the apartment, fully aware that Lind had a perfect view of her naked body.

"Good morning," she said, flashing him a knowing smile as she disappeared into the bathroom.

Lind barely managed to flip the bacon. His gaze stayed frozen on the empty doorway where she had been just seconds ago. *Oh my God... what is she trying to do to me?*

A few minutes later, she reappeared, leaning casually against the bathroom doorway. "Is there anything I can help with?" she asked, her voice teasing, her smile downright sinful.

Lind turned, taking her in—still bare, still radiant, her damp hair hanging on her shoulders. He exhaled slowly, eyes flickering with heat. "If you don't put some clothes on, we won't be having breakfast."

Dana giggled and disappeared back into the bedroom, returning in her usual white panties and one of Lind's T-shirts. The fabric was just loose enough to drape over her curves, the hem brushing the tops of her thighs, the faint outline of her nipples visible through the thin cotton. She wore this look often, but today...

"You look—nice," Lind said, trying not to stare.

She picked up the steaming coffee he had already poured for her and took a slow sip, watching him over the rim of the cup.

"What's for breakfast?" she asked, her voice carrying a mischievous tone.

Lind forced himself to focus on the food. "Pancakes, scrambled eggs, and bacon—crispy, the way we like it."

Dana hummed approvingly. "Stiff bacon—love it," she said, still grinning as she leaned against the counter.

Her arms were tucked up as she held the coffee to her lips—hiding the beautiful shape of her breasts from his view, playing with him without even trying.

Taking in a deep breath, Lind forced himself to look up at her eyes.

She held his gaze. "Is this your plan? Seduction by breakfast?"

"Just making up for all those skipped Wednesdays," Lind shot back.

She just smiled, sipping her coffee again, watching him as he finished cooking. His growing distraction was becoming increasingly evident beneath his boxers, and from the knowing gleam in her eyes, she had noticed.

"All done," Lind finally announced, setting the plates down. "Ready to eat?"

Dana grinned. "You're good to me."

They ate at a leisurely pace, enjoying the warmth between them, their connection, the ease of it.

After breakfast, a shared shower led to playful touches and stolen kisses, before they got dressed and headed to the theater.

It was certainly a night to remember

Lind had let Dana pick the movie—a romantic comedy that he barely tolerated. When the previews started, he leaned closer.

"You owe me for this," he said, elbowing her lightly.

Dana turned to him, shaking her head. "No. You suggested this chick flick, remember?"

Lind chuckled, sinking back into his seat. "I'm a man of contradictions."

She just nodded. Amusement flickered in her eyes.

She knew he had picked the movie for her—but still.

After the movie, they sat across from each other at Brews & Muse, coffees in hand. The air between them felt lighter than it had in months.

Lind leaned in slightly, lowering his voice so no one else would hear. "What was last night about?"

Dana met his gaze, taking a slow sip before replying. "What do you mean?"

Lind tilted his head, studying her. "I mean... you were... different. More..." He searched for the right word. "Intense."

A sly, knowing smile formed. "You didn't like it?" she asked.

Lind scoffed. "That's not the problem." His voice dipped lower, his expression unreadable. "You were just... different."

Dana traced the rim of her cup with her finger. "It was certainly a night to remember, wasn't it?"

Lind exhaled, shaking his head with a soft chuckle. "Yeah, that it was."

But something about her answer felt... incomplete.

You know I love you, right

Back at Lind's apartment, they curled up on the couch, the TV playing in the background, but neither of them really watching it. Dana lay with her head in Lind's lap, his fingers threading absently through her hair.

They didn't speak much, just existing in the quiet comfort of each other's presence.

"I don't want this weekend to end," Lind murmured after a while.

Dana's throat tightened, but she forced a small smile. "Me neither."

She didn't add the rest: *But it has to.*

As the afternoon faded into evening, Dana finally stood, stretching slightly.

"I should get going," she said softly.

Lind sighed, reluctantly pushing himself off the couch. He followed her to the door, neither of them in any rush to part ways.

Standing there, Dana reached for his hand, lacing her fingers through his. With her other hand, she tucked her fingers into his hair, her thumb tracing slow circles against his cheek.

Looking deep into his eyes, she whispered, "You know I love you, right?"

Lind frowned slightly, sensing something in her tone—something heavy, something final.

"Of course I do, Dana," he said gently.

She gave a small nod, as if reassuring herself. "Good."

Then she leaned in, pressing her lips to his in a long, loving kiss—saying everything she couldn't.

As she reached for the doorknob behind her, she kept kissing him, prolonging it, soaking in the warmth of him, the taste of him, the feel of him.

When she finally pulled away, she rested her forehead against his chest for just a second, memorizing his scent, the way his arms felt around her.

"See you at work tomorrow," she murmured, before stepping through the doorway—not letting Lind see the tears in her eyes. She didn't look back. She couldn't. If she did, she wasn't sure she'd be able to leave at all.

Lind stood frozen, watching her walk away, a nagging feeling twisting in his stomach.

Something was *wrong*.

Something was *shifting*.

He didn't know what—but he didn't like it.

Picking up Sam after work

Dana sat at her kitchen table, flipping absently through a grocery store flier when her phone buzzed.

Lind.

She took a deep breath before answering. "Hey."

"Hey yourself," Lind replied. She could hear the faint hum of his truck in the background. "How was the rest of your day? After that god-awful project Georgette put you and Brenda on, I was hoping it got better."

Dana let out a small laugh. "It wasn't that bad."

"You?"

"Same old, same old. Just heading home from the store." A brief pause. "So... I wanted to check in about this weekend."

Dana's stomach tightened slightly. *Here it is.*

"Oh, right," she said, keeping her tone even. "You're leaving tomorrow, right?"

"Yeah," Lind confirmed. His voice was soft, careful. "Picking up Sam after work, but I'll be back Sunday afternoon."

"That sounds like a nice trip," Dana said, forcing a lightness she didn't feel. "Hope the weather holds out for you."

"Yeah, me too. It's been warm, but you never know." Another pause. "We'll have to do something when I get back. It's our anniversary next weekend, right?"

Dana's fingers clenched slightly around the flier. "Yes, it is."

Lind's voice softened. "We'll plan something special when I get back. Dana, I... I love you."

Dana closed her eyes for a brief second, willing herself to stay composed. "Love you too, Lind," she murmured. "We'll talk tomorrow at work before you leave."

"OK, beautiful. I really missed seeing you last night," he said with a little hitch in his voice.

"I know, me too." She lied, though it really didn't feel like it. "I was just too tired to be good company."

"Well we'll get together next week, right?"

"Yes, I'm sure we will," she said.

"See you tomorrow Dana, I appreciate you."

"Goodnight, Lind."

She wouldn't cry now

Dana set her phone face down on the table, staring blankly at the bright grocery flyer beneath it. Her chest felt tight, like an invisible cord had wrapped around her ribs and was slowly pulling.

"We'll have to plan something special when I get back."

Why?

She picked up her mug of tea, though it had gone cold. He appreciates me, he'd said.

What does that even mean?

Appreciates what? That I don't argue? That I stay quiet? That I don't complain when he talks about her? That I'm still here, even when I hate this part of his life?

Her eyes dropped to the table, focusing on the edge of the flyer as her thoughts looped in endless circles. She wasn't mad—not really. That was the worst part. The numbness had taken over, she could feel it in her bones like a quiet resignation.

I said I'd try to understand this... and I did.

But this weekend—this Sam weekend—was different. More final. Like something inside her had already decided, even if she hadn't spoken the words yet.

What would she even do while he was gone? Stay busy? Paint? Sit in the quiet, telling herself it doesn't matter anymore. Wondering if that's true.

Then a bitter smile tugged at her lips.

Maybe I'll pick up some apple cider and donuts for myself. Just to see if they taste better when I'm alone.

She closed her eyes and leaned back in the chair, her fingers dancing over the edge of the phone.

He appreciates me.

But does he see me? Really see me? Or am I just the space he comes back to after resetting with her?

The thought landed like a sharp needle pressing into her chest.

And yet—guilt twisted inside her.

No, that's not fair.

She knew Lind loved her. He had shown her over and over again this past year. The way he looked at her. The way he showed up for her. The way he made her feel like the center of his world—when they were together.

But when they weren't...

Her throat tightened, but no tears came.

Not yet.

She wouldn't cry now.

There would be plenty of time for that.

Taking a deep breath, Dana stood and walked toward the kitchen sink.

The day's coming soon.

I'll tell him.

This has to end.

I've tried, but I can't do this anymore.

She turned the faucet on, letting the sound of running water drown out the silence.

Part 13

<u>Still, I Let Myself Believe</u>

She was softer.
Sweeter.
Harder.
Fiercer.
Dana wasn't herself.
She held my hand longer.
Laughed a little easier.
Touched me like she already knew—
and hoped I wouldn't ask.
And Sam—
She knew.
But didn't press.
Didn't try to fix it.
She just opened her arms—
and made room

Chapter 67

Something's wrong with Dana

The drive north had been smooth, the sun dipping low behind the hills as Lind's truck rumbled along the winding road. Crisp autumn air drifted through the cracked window, carrying the scent of wet leaves and cedar. The sky stretched in hues of amber and violet, casting long shadows over the rolling landscape.

When they pulled into the driveway of the cozy B&B, gravel crunched beneath the tires, and Sam let out a contented sigh as she unbuckled her seat belt.

"This place looks amazing," she said, her eyes scanning the rustic wooden facade, ivy creeping along the edges. "You've been holding out on me, Lind."

Lind chuckled, though his smile barely reached his eyes. "I thought you'd like it."

He grabbed their bags while Sam walked ahead, her confidence as effortless as always. The B&B was clothing-optional—one of the things she loved about it. She had already teased him at check-in, remarking that she was "overdressed for comfort" and hinting at how long that would last.

Later that evening, after dinner and a glass of wine by the outdoor fire pit, they settled into the communal lounge, sinking into a large couch covered in their soft towels. The fire crackled beside them, its golden light flickering against the wooden beams, warming the space.

Lind leaned back, wine glass in hand, staring into the flames. A quiet tension pressed against his chest.

Sam shifted beside him, studying him for a moment before speaking. "You're quiet tonight." Her voice was light but laced with perceptiveness. "What's up?"

Lind hesitated, fingers fiddling with his wine glass. He let the silence stretch between them before finally exhaling.

"Something's wrong with Dana."

Sam folded her legs under her, resting her chin on her hand. "Wrong how?"

He sighed, eyes still on the fire. "She's... different. The last few months, she's been pulling away. Turning down date nights, staying in more. Even when we're together, it's like she's somewhere else."

Sam didn't interrupt. She just listened.

"And I haven't asked her about it," Lind admitted, his voice lower now. "I don't want to push her, but... it's not the same. She's not the same."

Sam tilted her head, her expression thoughtful. "Describe it to me. What's different?"

Lind's grip on his glass tightened. "The way she touches me, the way she talks to me. It's subtle, but I feel it. She doesn't lean into me like she used to. She doesn't kiss me quite the same. Even when she smiles, it doesn't always reach her eyes."

He paused, shaking his head. "Then this last weekend, everything changed. It was like she flipped a switch—loving, attentive, fully present. We spent the whole weekend together. She planned it out, made sure it was perfect. It was so different, I had to ask her about it."

Sam raised an eyebrow. "And?"

"She told me it was 'a weekend to remember.'"

A beat of silence hung between them, the fire crackling softly in the background.

Sam exhaled slowly. "Wow. That really sounds like she's pulling away. In fact... it sounds like she's done."

Lind's throat tightened. "I was afraid you were going to say that."

Sam reached over, squeezing his arm gently. "Lind... from what you're describing, it sounds like she's already planned her exit."

The words landed like a heavy weight in his chest, even though he'd been bracing for them. "I was hoping I was just reading too much into it."

Sam shook her head. "You're not. Women don't just start acting differently for no reason. If she's been pulling back this much, and then suddenly gave you this... perfect weekend? It's because she's already letting go."

Lind dragged a hand down his face, frustration bleeding into his voice. "Is there anything I can do to stop it?"

Sam hesitated, her tone careful. "If you go monogamist, she might not leave."

Lind's head snapped toward her, his expression unreadable as silence stretched between them. Sam didn't flinch. She just met his gaze, calm and steady.

She wasn't making a suggestion. She was stating a fact.

I really had high hopes for you two

Lind exhaled slowly, his fingers gripping the wine glass as he stared into the fire.

"I don't want to lose her," he admitted finally, his voice raw, just barely holding together. "But if I go that route, I'll lose me. That's not who I am, and it's not what I believe. And if I did change... it'd only push her away down the road anyway."

Sam nodded, her expression softening. "Then you already know what's going to happen." She leaned back slightly, resting her arms on the couch. "You can't change someone's wiring, Lind. And Dana... doesn't sound like she's built for this." She paused. "I really had high hopes for you two."

Lind let out a humorless laugh, shaking his head. "So did I." He rubbed his jaw absently, his thoughts tangled in the same loop they'd been stuck in for weeks. "I really thought she'd see what I was trying to show her. She knew about you and me before we even started dating. I thought..."

"You thought she'd adapt," Sam finished gently.

Lind nodded slowly, "I hoped she would adapt." The words caught in his throat.

Sam studied him for a moment before speaking. "And she tried, Lind. You keep telling me, 'She's trying, she's trying.' But sometimes... trying isn't enough."

Lind swallowed hard, staring into the flames. *She tried. And I'm still losing her.*

That night, he told himself not to think of Dana. But the weight of her absence was affecting him in ways he didn't expect. Holding Sam a little tighter, pressing his face into her warmth, loving her a little softer—it was more than what he usually let himself take from her.

But Sam understood.

She didn't ask for words, didn't question the way his hands lingered or why he wrapped himself around her like he was trying to anchor himself. She just let him. Because she loved him, and because she knew him. And that, more than anything, was the comfort Lind needed.

***

Determined not to let the heaviness of the night before follow them, Lind focused on making the most of their weekend—to stay present.

The crisp autumn air swept through the open truck windows as they drove through winding country roads, the trees ablaze with deep reds, golden yellows, and fiery oranges. The whole world looked like it had been dipped in warmth.

Sam leaned out of the window slightly, grinning as the wind tossed her hair. "Okay," she announced, turning back to Lind. "This is officially better than last year's orchard trip. You're forgiven for bailing on me."

Lind smirked, though the comment struck a nerve he tried to ignore. "I'll take it."

The orchard was alive with the energy of fall—families picking apples, kids darting through the pumpkin patch, the scent of cinnamon and cider thick in the air. They wandered the rows of trees. The weight of yesterday fading into the easy comfort of now.

Sam had a way of pulling Lind out of his own head, of making him laugh when he wasn't sure he had it in him. She stole bites of his donut, teasing him when he protested, and raced him through the corn maze like they were kids.

It was simple. It was them.

"You're being extra sweet today," Sam noted at one point, bumping her hip against his playfully.

Lind smiled faintly, his arm draping around her shoulders. "Just reminding you how much I appreciate you."

Sam rolled her eyes at him. "I already know, Lind."

Lind exhaled softly. "Every so often, I forget to just stay in the moment," he admitted. "And you... you're really good at helping me do that. That's why I love you, Sam."

Her expression softened, and she reached up, pulling him down into a kiss that lasted just a little bit longer than usual.

Pulling back, she looked into his eyes, "I love you too," she murmured, resting her forehead against his for a brief moment before pulling away.

***

Back at the B&B, the fire in their private room cast a soft glow across the bed as Lind lay beside Sam, his arm wrapped around her, fingers trailing absentmindedly over her skin.

She sighed in contentment, running her fingers through his hair as his head rested against her chest. Their breathing had slowed, their bodies relaxed—but Lind wasn't quite ready to fall asleep.

His hand drifted lower, tracing along the curve of her breast, toying with her nipple between his fingers. He wasn't trying to start something again, not really. He just needed to feel connected to someone who wasn't slipping away.

Sam let him, but after a few moments, she laid her hand over his and stilled his movements, lacing her fingers with his.

She didn't ask what was wrong. Didn't need to.

Instead, she just held him there—pressed against her, safe in her warmth—until his breathing evened out and sleep finally pulled him under.

I'm a woman. I know things

The morning came too soon. Lind lay in bed, one hand stroking Sam's hair as she rested comfortably on top of him. The warmth of her body, the slow rise and fall of her breathing—it should have been grounding, but his thoughts drifted elsewhere. *Tomorrow. Work. Dana.* He wasn't looking forward to any of it.

"What are you thinking about?" Sam's voice was muffled against his chest, but her knowing tone was unmistakable.

"How do you know I'm thinking anything?" Lind countered.

Sam shifted slightly, the soft press of her smile against his skin. "Twelve years of being with you—and I'm a woman. I know things."

Lind exhaled through his nose, his fingers still idly tracing patterns through her hair. "Just overthinking."

She waited. He knew she would.

"When I get back to the 'real' world," he admitted, "what happens then? And when?"

Sam propped herself up on his chest, meeting his gaze. "You're right, you *are* overthinking. And overthinking won't make it better. Or easier." She cupped his cheek. "Just stay here. In this moment. Be with me while we have this. And when it's over—when you're back with Dana—stay in *that* moment, too. Whatever it brings, whenever it comes."

Lind held her gaze. "You make it sound so simple."

"It is." Sam smiled softly. "It's the *worrying* that complicates it."

He let out a slow breath. "I know... you're right. I've tried, and she's tried. Whatever happens now, happens, I guess." He frowned. "I don't like it, but—" He sighed, pushing the thoughts aside. "Okay... I'm back."

Sam's smile brightened, playfulness slipping back into her voice. "Good, because I still have time left with you—and I intend to use it."

Lind chuckled, his easy grin returning. "Shower and breakfast?"

"Yep." Sam slipped off of him, stretching as she stepped onto the floor. She reached one hand toward him while using the other to remove the condom, tossing it into the small trash can as she led him toward the bathroom.

They simply existed in the moment

A cool mist rose up and swirled through the air as Lind started the shower, the warm spray hitting against the tiles. Sam sat on the toilet, finishing her morning routine, giving him a crooked smile. "You always rush the water. Let it warm up."

Lind rolled his eyes but grinned. "I like a challenge."

Their banter continued as they stepped under the water together, hands automatically moving to wash each other's backs. The feel of soupy fingers gliding across wet skin had a sensation all its own.

Sam lathered shampoo through his hair, fingers scratching gently at his scalp.

"You know," she mused, "I've almost come to think of this as foreplay." She giggled.

Chuckling, Lind rinsed out his hair. "Yeah? You might be onto something. My turn to wash yours."

Sam groaned. "Oh, God, please be gentle. You always rush through this too."

He winked. "Just trying to get to the best part."

She swatted his arm, but the playfulness softened into quiet contentment as she leaned back against him, letting the warm water cascade over them. His soapy hands found her breasts, cradling them as they simply existed in the moment, no words needed.

**

After drying off, they made their way downstairs to breakfast, towels draped over their shoulders. One of the other couples lounged at the table, nursing their coffee as they chatted idly about weekday plans.

Sam and Lind arranged their towels and sat in seats nearby, exchanging an easy smile with them.

"Headed out today?" the man asked.

"Soon," Sam replied, reaching for the carafe to fill Lind's cup. "But not before breakfast and another hour of pretending we don't have to go home."

The woman laughed. "That's the right attitude."

Lind chuckled softly, his hand brushing Sam's knee under the table. "We're good at that."

A little while later, after the couple left with a wave, Sam leaned in. "See? We're practically domestic."

Lind raised an eyebrow. "Scary thought."

Sam leaned into Lind's side and stole a bite of his toast.

"So predictable," he laughed, nudging her shoulder with his.

She grinned. "I only steal the *best* bites."

Conversation was easy, the shadow of last night's discussion momentarily forgotten in the simplicity of breakfast, shared space and laughter.

Chapter 68

Well, his other girlfriend

With their bags packed, Lind and Sam made one last stop at the orchard before heading home. The scent of warm cider and freshly fried donuts drifted in the crisp morning air.

"I don't know if Dana will even want these," Lind admitted as he grabbed a small bag of donuts. "But I'm bringing some anyway."

"It can't hurt," Sam said, her expression unreadable. "Brian, on the other hand, is going to *inhale* these."

Lind chuckled. "Just Brian?"

"Yeah. He's off work all week, so we're playing house for a bit." Sam smirked.

Lind raised a brow. "And the other two? Still around?"

He realized, with a twinge of guilt, that he hadn't asked about *her* life all weekend. So wrapped up in his own unraveling relationship, he hadn't checked in on hers. The realization left him feeling a little ashamed. *Selfish.*

Sam didn't seem to mind. "I still have all my guys," she said easily. "Mateo's coming over Friday and Saturday. Then Jake's taking me to a house party on Sunday. They do this huge bonfire—used to be even bigger, he said, until the cops cracked down a few years ago."

"Sounds wild." He grinned.

"Oh, definitely." Sam grinned.

"Wait—" Lind paused, frowning. "I thought you said Brian was staying the *whole* week?"

"No, I said Brian has the week *off*, and we're playing house," she corrected, laughing. "But only until Thursday. Then he's off for a long weekend with his... well, his *other* girlfriend."

She winked, clearly amused at Lind's expression.

He shook his head with a chuckle. "It's funny," he admitted. "As much as I understand this lifestyle, I still catch myself thinking you have your four guys and that's *it*. But..."

"But that's not how it works," Sam finished for him. "Right. That's because I rarely bring up what *they* do with *their* other girlfriends. I don't get involved in their outside relationships."

Lind nodded. It made sense. Sam had always been clear about her boundaries—her guys were her guys, but she didn't entangle herself in their other commitments.

Still, he gave her a pointed look. "You do with me."

Sam sighed, shaking her head with a small smile. "Yeah, but *you're* different, Lind. You're special." She hesitated before admitting, "If I were the monogamous type... I'd probably pick you."

Lind's breath caught for just a second, but Sam laughed it off before the moment could turn heavy. "But I'm *not*—so I love you, leave you, and then love you again later. That's how I like it."

She pulled him into a tight hug, and Lind wrapped his arms around her, exhaling.

"Me too, Sam," he murmured. "Me too."

You two haven't met, have you

The drive back to Sam's was easy, filled with comfortable conversation and light laughter. The fall scenery blurred past in streaks of gold and rust, but Lind barely noticed. His mind was clearer than it had been the night before, though a quiet heaviness still sat in his chest.

When they pulled into the parking lot, across from Sam's apartment, he let the truck idle as she grabbed her bag from the back seat. Lind stepped out with her, meeting on the passenger side for a proper goodbye. She set her bag down to give him a hug.

Brian strolled over from the apartment, his posture relaxed, a casual smile on his face. "Hey," he greeted, scooping up Sam's bag effortlessly, giving her a one armed hug.

Sam turned toward Lind. "You two haven't met, have you?"

"Nope," Brian said, letting go of Sam and shifting the bag onto his shoulder. He held out a hand. "Good to finally meet you."

Lind shook it firmly. "Same here."

Brian's expression softened. "Thanks for keeping an eye on her this weekend."

Lind chuckled. "She was definitely the one keeping an eye on me."

Sam rolled her eyes but didn't argue.

Lind turned to her, hands settling on her waist. His goodbye hug, tighter than usual, a silent *thank you* woven into the embrace. "I love you, Sam," he murmured. "Thanks for putting up with me this weekend."

She squeezed him back just as tightly, her voice steady. "I love you too. Call me if you need anything."

A quick kiss, then a pause—he leaned his forehead against hers, and she let him. He pulled back, looking at Sam and then turned and nodded to Brian as he walked back around his truck.

As he climbed in he glanced in the rear view mirror, watching as Sam and Brian walked toward the apartment, arms draped comfortably around each other. The ease of it—their world—was impossible to ignore.

I love them both

As Lind pulled onto the highway, the image of Sam and Brian replaying in his mind. The way she had said *I love you* so easily, the way Brian hadn't flinched—no hesitation, no insecurity. Just an acceptance of what was.

This was what reset him—being with someone who didn't need anything from him but who welcomed everything he was. This was why being with Sam brought balance to everything again. It made him feel whole in a way nothing else could.

Stepping into her world—a world without jealousy, without conditions, where love wasn't singular or boxed in—felt like stepping into sunlight after a long, dark winter.

Sam wasn't just a person. She was a space. A space where he could breathe, where he never had to defend who he was.

His grip on the wheel tightened. *Why couldn't Dana see that?*

He'd spent the last year trying to show her. Trying to make her understand that this wasn't about *less* love for her, but *more* love in general. That being with Sam didn't take anything away from what he felt for Dana. That these two worlds didn't have to collide—they could coexist.

But Dana didn't see the ease. She didn't see the freedom.

All Dana saw was the pain—the waiting, the worrying, the wondering. All she felt was the absence. She couldn't feel the balance it gave him.

And the thought of that—of her sitting alone in her apartment, wrestling with emotions she didn't deserve—tore at him.

His jaw tightened. *I love her more than I can put into words, but what do I do if she just... can't do this?*

The road stretched out ahead of him, winding through hills dotted with autumn's fiery colors. But Lind barely saw any of it through the clouds in his eyes.

He thought of Sam's laughter, of the way she made everything seem so *simple*. And then he thought of Dana, alone in her apartment, her mind cycling through emotions she hadn't asked for, hadn't wanted.

I love them both. His fingers flexed around the steering wheel. *But love, it seems, isn't always enough.*

Chapter 69

But calm wasn't peace

Dana sat on the couch, legs tucked beneath her, barely paying attention to the movie playing on the TV. The images flickered shadows across the living room. The glass of wine on the coffee table remained untouched.

Her phone buzzed.

Brenda's name lit up the screen.

Dana hesitated before answering, forcing a lightness into her voice. "Hey, Bren."

"Hey yourself," Brenda replied, her usual warmth shining through. "Just thought I'd check in. How's your Friday night going?"

Dana glanced at the wineglass. "Quiet," she admitted. "Just relaxing at home."

Brenda paused, her tone shifting. "You okay? You don't sound like yourself."

Dana forced a small smile, though Brenda couldn't see it. "I'm fine. Just a quiet night in."

"You want company?" Brenda offered. "I can swing by with a bottle of wine and some snacks. We can watch something awful and talk shit about life."

The offer was tempting. But Dana shook her head, even though Brenda couldn't see that either. "Not tonight, Bren. I just... need a night to myself."

Brenda was quiet for a moment before pressing gently, "You sure? Because I don't believe for a second you're loving this self-imposed isolation."

A small chuckle escaped Dana. "You know me too well."

"I *do*," Brenda said warmly. "And you know where to find me if you change your mind."

"Thanks, Bren," Dana said, her voice softening. "I mean it. I'll talk to you soon."

After they hung up, Dana leaned back against the couch, phone still in hand.

She was keeping up appearances well enough—at least for now. She'd already made up her mind about the breakup. *That* decision gave her an odd sense of calm.

But calm wasn't peace. And as the hours stretched out before her, the weight of it all settled heavier on her chest.

Stop it. Just stop

Dana lay sprawled across her bed, the covers tangled and forgotten, her breath still uneven as she stared at the ceiling. The condo was silent except for the faint hum of the ceiling fan, but inside her head, the noise was relentless.

She turned toward the clock on her nightstand. *9:03 a.m.*

He's probably having breakfast right now.

The thought landed with a dull thud in her chest, triggering a flood of questions she couldn't stop. *What does the B&B look like? What are they serving? What is Sam eating?*

Her jaw tightened as the spiral deepened. *Is she one of those 'eats like a bird to stay effortlessly sexy' types? Or is she the cool, carefree kind who devours pancakes with syrup dripping down her fingers?*

What does her body look like? Is her hair softer than mine? Are her legs longer?

Does she do things for him that I don't?

The jealousy in her thoughts was sharp, ugly, but she didn't try to shove it down. She let it burn through her, fueling the ache.

What if she's better at sex than I am?

Her fingers curled into the sheets, gripping them tight. The ache in her chest twisted into something darker.

Is that how she 'resets' him?

The thought made her want to scream.

Dana squeezed her eyes shut. *Stop it. Just stop.* But it didn't stop. It never stopped.

She had spent months convincing herself that she was okay. That she *could* be okay. That she trusted Lind. That she believed him when he said he loved her.

But trust wasn't the problem. The problem was that no matter how much she loved him, she *wasn't enough.*

That voice had been whispering to her for months. Soft at first, easy to ignore. But now it was screaming.

She took a slow, shaky breath. *I have to stop this. Right now. Right fucking now.*

Pushing herself upright, Dana swung her legs over the edge of the bed. She grabbed the toy from where it lay beside her, carried it to the bathroom, then set it on the sink. Everything she did was mechanical—going to the toilet, washing the toy, laying it out to dry.

When she stepped into the shower, she let the hot water scald her skin, hoping—*praying*—that it would wash the thoughts away.

But they followed her—relentlessly.

***

By midday, Dana felt suffocated by the quiet. The walls of her place felt smaller than usual, pressing in on her. She paced for a while, trying to distract herself, but nothing worked.

Her phone sat on the counter, silent.

She grabbed it and scrolled to Brenda's name.

Dana hesitated for only a moment before pressing *call.*

Brenda answered on the second ring. "Dana? Didn't expect to hear from you this early. Everything okay?"

Dana sighed. "No. Not really." She rubbed a hand over her face. "I need to get out of my head for a while. Can we just go somewhere? Anywhere. I don't care."

"Of course," Brenda said immediately. "Bar? Something else?"

Dana closed her eyes, the tension in her chest easing just slightly. "Bar's fine."

She's not the problem

The low hum of music and quiet conversations surrounded them, the bar comfortably busy but not overwhelming. Dana sat across from Brenda in their usual corner booth, fingers wrapped around her glass.

Brenda took a slow sip of her margarita, watching Dana carefully before leaning in. "So... are we gonna talk about it, or keep pretending nothing's wrong?"

Dana let out a humorless laugh, swirling the amber liquid in her glass. "What gave me away?"

Brenda let out a chuckle, but her eyes were kind. "You're drinking whiskey and chasing it with a beer. And you don't drink whiskey unless something's eating at you."

Dana exhaled, her shoulders sinking as she swirled the amber liquid. "It's about Lind."

Brenda nodded, setting her glass down. "Yeah... and?"

"It's just... everything, Bren," Dana admitted, her voice low, almost drowned out by the music. "His lifestyle. What he shares with Sam. It's too much."

Brenda frowned slightly, stirring her straw in her drink. "You don't think Sam's a threat, though. Right?"

Dana shook her head immediately. "No. It's not *her*. She's not the problem." She paused, her fingers tightening around her glass. "It's... the whole *thing*."

Brenda's brow furrowed. "What do you mean?"

Dana sighed, her gaze distant. "How *easy* it is for her. How *comfortable* she is with knowing that Lind loves me too."

Brenda was quiet for a moment before nodding slowly. "And you *can't* be like that."

Dana's throat tightened. "No," she admitted, her voice cracking slightly before she steadied it. "I can't. I *thought* I could. I thought I could try. And I *did* try, Bren. I've tried for a year now."

Brenda reached across the table, covering Dana's hand with hers. "I know."

Dana swallowed hard, blinking against the sting behind her eyes.

Brenda didn't push. She just held Dana's gaze, waiting.

And for the first time, Dana let herself say it out loud.

"I think I have to let him go."

The words sat heavy between them, final and inevitable. She didn't even flinch. She'd already said it a hundred times in her head.

Brenda squeezed her hand. "Then I'll be here when you do."

Dana nodded, pressing her lips together. She wasn't ready yet. But soon.

Because love wasn't enough. Not for this. Not for her.

And she was done pretending it could be.

Brenda sat back, saying nothing, giving Dana the space to feel the truth she finally said out loud.

She traced the condensation on her beer, her voice barely above a whisper. "I'm not built for it. I'll never be okay with it. And the worst part is... I love him."

Brenda's chest ached at the rawness in her friend's voice. She reached across the table again, giving Dana's wrist a gentle squeeze. "I know you do."

Dana offered a faint smile, but it didn't reach her eyes. "I just... I need something else to hold on to. Something that's mine. Something that makes me feel... whole."

Brenda studied her for a moment, then smiled. "Then let's find it."

Dana looked up, brow furrowing slightly. "What do you mean?"

Taking another sip of her drink, Brenda said, "you mentioned that art gallery a couple of weeks ago. You keep saying you miss painting. Maybe it's time you picked up a brush again. Let's hit the art supply store after this—my treat for something... small."

Dana blinked, a flicker of surprise crossing her face. "Brenda, you don't have to—"

"No arguments," Brenda said firmly, grinning. "You need this, and I'm gonna help you get started. Besides..." She twirled her straw between her fingers. "If you're gonna drown me in sad Dana vibes, the least I can do is get you some paint to work it out."

That earned a small laugh from Dana—real, if only for a moment. "You're... Thank you."

"I'm your friend," Brenda stated. "And when you're ready to talk more—really talk—I'm here."

Dana's grip tightened slightly around her glass, her expression softening. "Thanks, Bren. You have no idea how much I needed this today."

Brenda raised her margarita. "To new beginnings, one brushstroke at a time."

Dana lifted her glass, clinking it gently against Brenda's. The sound was small, but grounding.

***

An hour later they stepped through the door of the local art store. The scent of paper, paint, and fresh wood greeted them as they stepped inside. Shelves stretched toward the ceiling, packed with sketchbooks, canvases, and tubes of color arranged like an artist's dream.

Dana stood at the entrance, taking it all in.

Brenda nudged her playfully. "Don't just stand there, artist. Go explore."

Dana wandered toward the paint aisle, her fingers ghosting over the neat rows of color. Brenda followed, her voice light. "So, what's your style? Landscapes? Portraits? Abstract?"

"Mostly abstract, but I've tried all of them," Dana murmured, picking up a tube of cobalt blue. "It's less about what it looks like and more about what it feels like, you know?"

Brenda nodded. "Sounds like exactly what you need right now."

Dana smiled, adding the blue to a small basket. She selected a few more colors—warm ochres, deep reds, a rich forest green. A sketchpad and a set of brushes followed.

Brenda stopped beside a display of canvases, lifting a medium-sized one. "Start with something manageable. Not too big, not too small."

Dana chuckled, taking it from her. "You're more excited about this than I am."

"Of course I am!" Brenda grinned. "This is the start of something good, Dana. I can feel it."

At the register, Brenda waved off Dana's protest and bought the brushes. "Consider it my contribution to the Dana Renaissance."

As they walked back to the car, Dana clutched the bag to her chest, a quiet anticipation stirring inside her.

"Thanks for pushing me to do this, Brenda."

Brenda gave her a sidelong glance, smiling. "Anytime. Just promise you'll invite me over when you're ready to show off your masterpieces."

Dana laughed, the tension in her shoulders easing just slightly. "Deal."

Hey, I'm back home

Lind's fingers hovered over his phone, his thumb hesitating before he finally typed out the message. He had made it home and was now parked outside his apartment, the truck engine ticking softly as it cooled.

Hey, I'm back home. How was your weekend?

He typed the message, then stared at it for a few seconds.

It felt too casual. Too small for the ache in his chest. But he sent it anyway.

A few minutes later, Dana's reply came.

It was okay. Hope you had a good time.

Lind exhaled slowly, running a hand through his hair. The words on the screen felt distant, hollow.

He stared at them for a long moment before finally dialing her number.

Chapter 70

We need to talk

Dana answered on the third ring, her voice quieter than usual. "Hey."

"Hey," Lind replied, his tone soft, careful. "I just wanted to check in. How are you?"

"I'm fine," she said, though the words felt thin, tired. "It's been a long weekend."

Lind leaned back against his seat, closing his eyes for a moment. "I'm sorry if it was hard. I—" He hesitated, exhaling slowly. "I don't want you to hurt, Dana."

"I know," she said simply. "But it's not something you can fix, Lind. Not really."

Silence stretched between them, heavy and unspoken.

Lind finally spoke again, voice softer. "Do you want me to come over? We don't have to talk about anything heavy. I can just be there. Oh, oh, I brought you some donuts and cider, maybe I could drop them off to you?"

Dana's response came too quickly. "Thank you, but no, not tonight. I'm going to bed early. It's just... been a rough weekend." Her voice softened just a little. "Thanks for thinking of me. The donuts and cider, that was sweet."

Lind's stomach twisted, but he didn't push. "You're welcome. Okay. I'll see you at work tomorrow, then."

"Yeah," Dana replied, hesitating for a beat. "Oh, one more thing."

"Yeah?"

"I'd like to come over to your place on Wednesday," Dana said, her tone steady—too steady. "Would that be okay?"

Lind's heart skipped, but he kept his tone even. "Of course. What would you like me to cook for us?"

"Nothing," she said, pausing just long enough for him to notice.

"We need to talk."

Lind's breath caught, and though he already knew—knew deep down what he didn't want to admit—he still said, "Alright. Whatever you need, Dana."

"Thanks," she said softly. "Goodnight, Lind."

"Goodnight, beautiful. I love you."

There was a pause. Then, quietly, she said, "I know, Lind."

The line clicked, and Lind sat there, staring at the darkened screen.

The ache in his chest had become something familiar now—something he was beginning to understand.

This is the world Dana lives in.

And it hurts me as much as mine hurts her.

He sat in silence, eyes beginning to glisten, the weight of it all settling into him like fog.

Subtle nods

Dana and Lind exchanged subtle nods across the meeting room as Georgette handed out assignments. It was one more thing they had done from the early days of their relationship—a silent way of acknowledging each other without drawing attention. They had abandoned it when Brenda started to notice—but now it didn't matter.

They had used it to keep their relationship hidden. Dana never imagined she'd be using it now to keep their breakup hidden.

Later, she stepped into the break room, pausing when she spotted Lind at the coffee machine, his back to her, chatting with another coworker.

For a moment, she considered walking away. Skipping coffee this morning. But her body moved before she could talk herself out of it.

Lind turned as if sensing her presence. "Morning," he said softly, his voice warm but searching.

"Morning," Dana replied, keeping her tone light, offering a polite smile as she poured her coffee. Her hand remained steady, though her chest ached.

The break room filled with chatter, but Lind didn't press. He just let her go.

***

By Tuesday, the space between them was obvious. Dana found ways to keep her distance—staggering her breaks, not spending time in shared spaces. But working in the same store made avoiding him completely impossible.

"Dana," Lind called from across the store, holding up a pricing sheet. "Can you double-check this with me?"

Her stomach twisted, but she nodded, walking over. "What's up?"

They worked in near silence, the tension thick between them. Lind's brow furrowed as he stole a glance at her, as if searching for something unspoken.

Dana found the error and pointed it out. "Great. Easy fix," he said, offering her a small, hopeful smile.

She forced one in return. "You're welcome." Then, before her resolve could crack, she turned and walked away.

I'm going to tell him

Lately, the silent nod they exchanged in the morning meeting had become their primary form of communication at work. Lind didn't like it—it told him too much about how Dana was feeling, and he didn't like that either.

The weight of the coming conversation pressed heavily on Dana's chest. She spent the morning avoiding his gaze, throwing herself into tasks with single-minded focus. But by lunch, the strain was impossible to hide.

Brenda caught her in the supply room, shutting the door behind her with a knowing look. "Alright, spill. What's going on?"

Dana let out a slow breath, leaning against the metal shelf, exhaustion written across her face. "I'm going to tell him," she admitted. "I'm ending it tonight."

Brenda's expression softened, but concern flickered in her eyes. "You sure?"

Dana nodded, swallowing hard. "I've tried, Bren. I've tried so damn hard. But I can't... I can't live like this anymore. It hurts too much."

Brenda stepped closer, her voice careful. "Does Lind know? Does he have any idea?"

Dana shrugged helplessly. "He knows something's wrong. But I haven't told him outright. I'm doing it at his place tonight. That way, I can control when I get there... and when I leave."

Brenda's gaze held steady, then she reached out, squeezing Dana's shoulder. "You're strong, you know that? And if you need me tonight, you call me. I mean it."

Dana managed a faint smile, though it didn't quite reach her eyes. "Thanks, Bren. I just... I hope I'm doing the right thing."

Brenda's voice was gentle but firm. "You're doing what's right for you. That's all that matters."

As Dana stepped back onto the sales floor, the conversation steadied her.

Tonight was going to be one of the hardest nights of her life. But she knew—it was time.

Am I really doing this

Dana sat at the kitchen table, elbows braced on either side of a notepad she hadn't touched in twenty minutes. Her eyes traced the same four words she'd scribbled at the top of the page.

We need to talk, Lind.

She sighed, folding her arms over her chest. The silence in the condo felt thick again—dense and watching. She reached for her phone, not to text, not to check the time, just... something.

The playlist opened automatically.

She blinked at the title. **Us.**

Right. The one Lind had made her a few months ago. A strange, sweet blend of their worlds—her easy classic rock tangled with his smooth country and acoustic twang. She had rolled her eyes when he sent it but saved it anyway. Letting him build a bridge between their tastes had felt oddly intimate.

Without thinking, she tapped play. Just background noise. Something to fill the space. Some little bit of him, maybe.

She paced to the sink, grabbed a glass of water. Muted a practice line or two aloud, testing her voice against the quiet.

Then the song changed.

Dana froze.

The chords weren't familiar, but the voice was—nasal, aching, grounded. She glanced at the screen.

Rascal Flatts. One of Lind's favorites.

Put on your best face... fake another smile and just pretend.

The words spilled out like truth she didn't want—but needed.

You're just putting off the pain... nothing's going to change.

Her breath caught. She lowered herself into the nearest chair, water forgotten on the counter.

Let it knock you down to your knees... it isn't what you want—but it's what you need.

She closed her eyes.

593

She didn't understand country, not really. But she understood this. The rawness. The surrender. The way the song didn't try to fix the pain—just named it, and gave it room to live.

Sometimes the only way around it is to let love do its work...

Her chest tightened.

Let it go, let it leave... let it do what it's gotta do.

She wasn't sure she was ready.

All she knew was—it was time.

Let it hurt, let it bleed...

***

Lind sat on the couch, his eyes flicking to the door at every muffled sound from outside. Anticipation twisted in his stomach, a cold weight of dread pressing against the faint hope that whatever was coming could somehow be salvaged. He exhaled slowly, running a hand down his face just as a soft knock echoed through the quiet apartment.

His breath caught.

Crossing the room quickly, he opened the door to find Dana standing there, posture tense, expression unreadable. Her eyes flicked past him into the apartment before looking back at him. Her lips parted, but no words came.

"Come in," Lind said softly, stepping aside.

Dana nodded and stepped inside, her heart pounding so hard she thought it might shake her resolve. *Am I really doing this?* she thought. *I have to. The longer I stay, the more it hurts.*

As Lind shut the door, he turned to her with cautious patience. "Do you want to sit on the couch, or—?"

"The table," Dana interrupted quickly. "I think the table would be better."

Lind's brow furrowed slightly, but he didn't question it. "Alright."

They sat across from each other, the small wooden table between them feeling like an impossible distance. Dana clasped her hands in her lap, her gaze fixed on the smooth surface in front of her. She didn't know where to begin—but she knew that once she opened her mouth, the words would come.

Lind leaned forward slightly, his voice steady but gentle. "Dana... what's going on? Just tell me."

She looked up, meeting his gaze finally. And for a moment, her resolve wavered. But then, she took a deep breath and spoke.

"I've tried, Lind," she said, her voice trembling despite her efforts to control it. "I've tried so hard to make this work. I told myself I could handle it, that I could adjust to this... *this lifestyle*. But I can't. I've been lying to myself... it's killing me."

Lind's jaw tightened, his fingers slowly closing into fists—trying to hold on to her. "Dana, I love you. You know that. This isn't about choosing her over you. It never has been."

"I know," Dana said, her voice rising slightly. "I *know* it's not about her. It's about me. I can't live with this constant ache, Lind. Knowing that you're with her, sharing things with her, while I'm here—waiting, pretending it doesn't hurt. It's *too much*."

Lind shook his head, his voice thick with emotion. "I don't want to lose you. I don't *want* this to end. Tell me what to do, Dana. *Please*."

Tears burned in her eyes, but she blinked them back. "I can't ask you to change who you are. That wouldn't be fair to you, and it wouldn't work. You've built a life that fits you, that makes you happy. And I *can't*—" Her voice cracked. "I *can't* be a part of it without losing myself."

The silence between them was suffocating. Lind stared at her, his heart splintering at the pain in her expression. He reached across the table for her hand that wasn't there, desperate for a connection, but she leaned back, shaking her head.

"For my sanity, Lind," she whispered, barely able to get the words out. "I have to let go."

His throat was too tight to speak. He swallowed hard, his voice barely above a whisper. After a long moment of resignation, he said, "Can I have one more hug?"

Dana hesitated, but the look in his eyes broke something in her. Slowly, she stood and opened her arms.

Lind crossed the space between them in an instant, wrapping her in a tight embrace. Dana buried her face in his shoulder, inhaling his scent one last time, memorizing the feel of his arms around her.

Neither of them wanted to be the one to let go.

Eventually, Dana pulled back, her fingers lingering on his chest for a moment before she stepped away.

Turning toward the door, she felt the tears finally spill over, hot against her cheeks. Without looking back, she opened it and stepped outside, the sound of the door clicking shut behind her echoing in her ears.

As she walked away, her chest ached with every step.

I love him, she thought, the pain sharp and unforgiving. *But it isn't enough.*

It's done

Dana sat curled on her couch, knees pulled to her chest, exhaustion beginning to overtake her. The weight of the evening pressed down on her, making it hard to breathe.

Her phone sat on the coffee table. After a long moment of hesitation, she reached for it and dialed.

Brenda answered on the second ring. "Hey, how'd it go?" Her voice was cautious, gentle.

Dana exhaled shakily. "It's done," she murmured. "I told him. I ended it."

A beat of silence stretched between them. Then Brenda spoke, steady but soft. "How are you holding up?"

Dana swallowed against the tightness in her throat. "I don't know. I feel... empty, I guess. Like I left a part of myself there."

Brenda sighed, her heart aching for her friend. "I'm sorry, Dana. I know how much you love him."

"I do," Dana admitted, her voice breaking slightly. "But I *can't* do this anymore, Bren. I can't keep tearing myself apart."

"You did what you had to do," Brenda said firmly. "And that takes strength. It's going to hurt for a while, but you're going to get through this. You know you will."

Dana closed her eyes, pressing her forehead to her knees. "Thanks for being there for me. I just... I needed to tell someone."

"Always," Brenda replied. "And if you need anything—*anything*—you call me, okay?"

"Okay," Dana whispered. "Goodnight, Bren."

"Goodnight, Dana. Hang in there."

As Dana hung up, the silence of her apartment was deafening.

She had done the hardest thing she'd ever had to do.

But that didn't mean it hurt any less.

She's gone

After watching Dana walk out the door and close it behind her, Lind couldn't move. Her final words clung to him, anchoring his feet to the floor. The feel of her arms around him—still. Then the tears came—quiet, but insistent.

He didn't know how long he had stood there.

Eventually, he made his way back to his chair. It felt farther than it should have, like his body had to cross some great emotional divide just to sit down. He sank into it, exhaling as the full weight of it landed.

She's gone.

The words echoed in his chest, hollow, painful.

If Dana feels even a fraction of this pain, it's a wonder it took her so long.

The tears came harder then—not because he didn't understand, but because, on some level, he did.

Chapter 71

It's about Dana and Lind

Brenda hovered just outside the office for a moment, debating whether this was a good idea. Dana hadn't asked for this. Hell, Dana might not even want it.

But Brenda had seen the look on her friend's face after the breakup, and she wasn't about to leave her stranded in close quarters with Lind day after day.

She rapped lightly on the door frame. "Got a minute?"

Georgette glanced up, setting her pen aside. "For you? Always. What's up?"

Brenda hesitated, choosing her words carefully. "I wanted to talk to you about something... it's about Dana and Lind."

That got Georgette's full attention. She leaned back in her chair, arms crossing over her chest. "Is there an issue?"

Brenda exhaled, stepping closer. "Sort of. They were... seeing each other casually, but it ended."

A flicker of surprise crossed Georgette's face before she masked it with her usual neutrality. "I see. And?"Brenda licked her lips, feeling the weight of what she was about to ask. "Dana's having a hard time with it. Casual or not, she lost something important to her. They both did. I was wondering if—without making a big deal out of it—you could keep them on separate tasks as much as possible... just until things settle."

Georgette frowned slightly. "Brenda, you know I can't always do that. This is a team, and we have to work together."

"I know," Brenda said quickly. "And I'm not asking for a permanent arrangement, just a little... breathing room. I think it would help them."

Georgette studied her for a moment before nodding slowly. "You said it was casual, right? Nothing too serious?"

Brenda forced herself to nod. "Yeah, casual. Not much drama, but Dana's a bit sensitive about it."

Georgette's gaze sharpened. "If it was *casual*, why's she so upset?"

Brenda hesitated, realizing too late how flimsy her words sounded. She covered quickly. "Because it still meant something to her, even if it wasn't... you know, a full-blown relationship."

Georgette exhaled, her expression softening. "I get it. These things can get messy, no matter what labels you put on them." She drummed her fingers against the desk. "How's Lind handling it?"

Brenda was caught off guard by the question. "He's... Lind. Quiet. He's not the type to talk, but I think he's feeling it too."

Georgette sighed, nodding. "Yeah, he's always been steady, but that doesn't mean he's not hurting."

Brenda gave a small, relieved smile, grateful that Georgette was taking this seriously. "Exactly. So, if there's any way to give them a little space, it'd really help."

Georgette was quiet for a moment before finally nodding. "Alright. No promises, but I'll do what I can."

"Thank you," Brenda said sincerely. "I appreciate it."

As she left the office, her little white lie was poking at her. She'd told herself that downplaying Dana and Lind's relationship was for the best—that keeping things light would make it easier for them both.

But it still felt like a betrayal.

Because the truth is, Dana's in love with Lind. And Lind... well, Brenda wasn't sure Lind even knew the depth of what he'd lost yet.

Maybe... This space would give them both time to heal.

Part 14
Epilogue

The Farmhouse

Dana – age 80 – family matriarch

The living room smells like jasmine tea and old wood. One of the candles burned too long and bent sideways like it couldn't hold itself upright anymore. Outside, the sky's still gray from this morning's drizzle, but inside, the farmhouse hums with a soft kind of quiet—the kind that settles after a long day of remembering.

They've all gone still—my grand-kids and great-nieces and borrowed daughters and sons. Some sit cross-legged on the carpet, some curled on the armchairs. A plate of half-eaten lemon cookies rests on the piano bench. I'm in Lind's old recliner, wrapped in the blue shawl he always hated—said it smelled like lavender and guilt. He wasn't wrong.

Clara, home from college with a nose ring and two new partners, tilts her head. "So... Aunt Sam broke you two up? I can't imagine a time when you two weren't practically sisters."

There's a quiet in the room. Not the reverent kind. The kind that waits to be corrected.

I glance toward the hallway—Sam's not in here, but she's close. For the last 40 years, she's been close.

I smile. "I didn't know Sam back then, Clara. I only knew *of* her. And I couldn't accept the sharing. I couldn't do it. I thought love had to be divided. Lind tried to show me it could be multiplied." I paused here, with so many memories flooding back. "I wasn't ready to believe him."

Clara leans forward, eyes wide, like she's stumbled on a secret. "Oh my God, Grandma D—you were such a monogamist."

I laugh. Not loud. Just the soft kind that knows better now.

"Yes, darling," I say, tucking my hand around my mug, "I really didn't know there was another way. Your grandpa Lind was trying to show me, but I couldn't see it at the time."

She looks at me like I must've been blind. Maybe I was.

"That must've been brutal," Liz says, tone soft but knowing. She's not really mine, but she's called me Mom for forty years. That counts for more.

"Trying to go solo after everything you two had... I don't know if I could do it."

"Yes," I admit, and this time I don't laugh. "It tore me up."

I pause, let my thoughts drift a little. "I wasn't sure I was doing the right thing. I just knew I needed the hurt to stop."

And I did. I needed it to end—the longing, the split attention, the ache that came every time Lind mentioned her name. I needed something clean. Something I could name without choking on it.

"Wait," Shawna jumps in, wide-eyed and already grinning, "didn't you and Grandpa still work together through all of that?"

She always has a soft spot for emotional chaos.

"Yes, we did," I say, smiling like it's a memory I've forgiven. I let the silence stretch until someone breaks it. That used to drive Lind crazy.

"And you didn't strangle each other?" Miles asks. He's Liz's oldest. Been calling me Grandma D since before he could walk, raises an eyebrow from his perch on the windowsill. "Impressive."

He says it lightly, but I know he's filed this away for the next time one of his partners forgets a dinner date.

"How did that even work?" Clara asks, genuinely curious. "I mean, going from all that heat to cold space. How'd you hold the line?"

I give her the kind of smile you earn with age. The kind that says: *You'll find out someday.*

"In the beginning," I say, "it was the worst."

Then I glance up and meet her eyes. "In the end... It was the best."

A pause stretches through the room. I can feel them thinking it over.

I can feel Lind in the room. Not haunting. Just... lingering, like the warmth left on a pillow.

"What do you mean, 'in the end,' Grandma?" Wendy asks, her voice caught somewhere between challenge and awe.

"It obviously means they got back together," Liz mutters.

"Yes, I know, Mom." Wendy rolls her eyes. "But how did that happen, Grandma D? After all that?"

She's not asking out of disbelief. She's asking because she wants to *believe.*

That's the moment. The air shifts. Everyone leans in.

I cradle my mug a little tighter. I take a slow breath.

"Well, dear..." I say, my voice quieter now. "Let me tell you..."

Acknowledgments

To the late-night whispers and the early morning doubts—

to every blank page that dared me to fill it—

I see you.

To the only teammate I had on this journey:

Thank you for your honesty, your grace, and your relentless commitment to this story.

You made sure I never felt alone.

And to the readers—wherever you are, whoever you love—

Thank you for letting Dana and Lind into your hearts.

This story is for all of us who still believe in messy, complicated, extraordinary love.

And like all extraordinary love stories—

it's never over.

Dana's Loves

Book 2: Zach

Inside her car, Dana gripped the steering wheel, her thoughts racing as she stared at the windshield. The conversations with Lind and Zach played in her head, each carrying its own weight.

One was a door she was trying to close—

and the other... a door she wasn't quite sure she was ready to open.

***

Visit **DanaSamanthaLindsey.com**[1] to learn more about Dana's world.

***

Visit **DanasLoves.com** to learn more about *Book 2: Zach*.
(Scan the QR code below to go directly to the site.)

---

1. http://danasamanthalindsey.com/